first
was
the
and
with
their gambling. It was not until Madame clapped her hands peremptorily to attract attention that everyone looked towards the orchestra and saw the girl in green with her face masked.

Nonna began to sing, and as she did so she closed everything out. The actress which had always lurked in her came bubbling out as she moved around the little stage, swaggering a little as she sang the cheeky words of the latest song. She smiled, flirted and teased as she sang, flicking her skirts playfully.

From the side of the room, Madame watched, her fan tapping slowly. She glanced round and saw that, apart from a hard core of gambling men at their usual corner table, Nonna had claimed full attention and interest. Madame smiled to herself; the Masked Lady was a success.

Also by Sandra Heath
in Hamlyn Paperbacks

THE WHISPERING ROCKS
GREEN GIRL
LILY OF THE SUN

THE OPERA DANCER

Sandra Heath

Hamlyn Paperbacks

THE OPERA DANCER

ISBN 0 600 20239 9

First published in Great Britain 1982
by Hamlyn Paperbacks

Hamlyn Paperbacks are published by
The Hamlyn Publishing Group Ltd,
Astronaut House,
Feltham,
Middlesex, England

(Paperback Division: Hamlyn Paperbacks,
Banda House, Cambridge Grove,
Hammersmith, London W6 0LE)

Reproduced, printed and bound in Great Britain by
Hazell Watson & Viney Ltd, Aylesbury, Bucks

1

'You are dismissed, madam! With*out* reference!'

'But it wasn't my fault, it. . . .'

'Dismissed! Your behaviour this morning has left much to be desired, too much for a respectable establishment like Ackermann's Repository of Fine Arts!' Mr Dimchurch nodded at his assistant who brought Nonna's pelisse, bonnet and reticule.

Without another word Nonna took them, stepped over the shattered pieces of the once-exquisite Wedgwood vase, and went out into the cold, crisp air of the Strand.

The gentleman who had been the cause of her dismissal was inevitably waiting outside, but she looked through him, walking away and ignoring his affected voice as he called her. He hurried to catch her up, seizing her arm and making her turn.

'I say,' he drawled, 'this ain't the thing, you know.'

'Leave me alone, sir, for you've caused me enough trouble today already!'

'Come now, a pretty bit of muslin like you should be more friendly to a gentleman. . . .'

'Gentleman? I see no *gentleman*, I see a prinked, painted, toad-faced, vulgar oaf who thinks himself bang up to the mark but who is in fact the beginning and end in arrogance!'

His face changed then, and he released her abruptly, walking away towards his waiting landau. She watched him climb inside, taking note of the excellence of his coat, the fullness of his intricate cravat and the tightness of the trousers which revealed his fine legs so well. A gentleman. A *gentleman*!

The team of bays pulled the fashionable carriage into the crush of the busy London street, and with a heavy sigh Nonna put on her pelisse and bonnet, shivering a little in the cold. Dismissed. And for what? For dropping the vase she had been carrying when pinched from behind by that so-called gentleman in the landau.

He had denied doing it, of course, and as he was aristocratic and fashionable, his word was accepted without question. Without a reference she would find it virtually impossible to find suitable employment anywhere.

Sunk in the misery of her position, she walked west along the Strand. What could she do now? In her reticule she had a few shillings, not even enough to pay for her lodgings at Mother Carter's, and it was winter – what if she was thrown out into the streets? She paused by the bow windows of an apothecary's shop. Her broken reflection shone in the many uneven panes. She was slender and red-headed, her skin pale and clear and without the freckles which so often went with her colouring. Her eyes were large and green, their lashes thick and dark. The dark red woollen pelisse she wore had been a fashionable garment once with its black silk lining and fur trimmings; but now it was shabby and worn. The same could be said of her Leghorn straw bonnet – its brown ribbon was the fifth she had bought for it. Beneath the pelisse, visible only because of its frilled, white collar, she wore the drab grey dress necessary for working at Ackermann's. The toggery was completed by her brown kid gloves and reticule, and buttoned boots. Oh, she had been so proud of her clothes once, she had felt so fashionable and eyecatching, stepping out of her father's carriage in Bond Street, or inspecting the ribbons and laces at Christian's in Wigmore Street. But that was all over now, and had been for nearly five long, long years.

She walked on quickly, holding her head high. She mustn't give in to the misery, she mustn't! Ignoring the glances of two gentlemen who turned in admiration, she crossed the thoroughfare, slipping between the drays and carriages and down an alleyway.

How long she walked she didn't know. There was so much to think about, so many problems to be overcome. She must find work, but what kind of work was open to her without a good reference? No one would want even a kitchen maid unless a previous employer spoke well of her. There was always the possibility of walking the streets, of course. She stopped. The enormity of what she had thought swept sickeningly over her. Walk the streets? Be like the whores she had seen at Seven Dials? Paint her face, accost any likely gentleman, do his bidding no matter what and then take money for her services? *James Lambert's* daughter a common prostitute?

She must have walked for over an hour, worrying and becoming more frightened with each passing minute, but she was roused sharply from her thoughts by the angry shouting of a waggoner as she nearly stepped under the hooves of his team. The waggon rumbled on past and she looked around. Where was she?

To her right she saw Hyde Park. She was in Park Lane, and it was nearly mid-day. The grass in the park was white with frost, for the sun had not penetrated the winter mist which hung over London. She crossed the road to the park, watching a herdsman driving milch cows over the grass. The cows' breath was sweet-smelling, drifting over her as she sat down on a bench to think. The sounds of the city went on all around her, but she felt alone and insular – had she been on a tiny island in the middle of a vast ocean her situation could not have been worse. She was nineteen and beautiful, and her life should have been so good now, but instead it was poorer than she had ever dreamed possible.

She had been born into an important theatrical family; her Italian mother had been a well-known opera singer, and her father, James Lambert, *the* choreographer, *the* dancing master. Everyone had sought his services, his name had been a byword before family tragedies left his will and his career in shreds. The Lamberts had lived in a fashionable house and enjoyed a high standard of living, and when Nonna's elder sister Melisande had gone on the stage of the New Opera House as a ballerina, she had been praised for her beauty and brilliance. But now it was as if it had never been, as if Nonna had dreamed it once. They were all gone – her mother wasting with consumption, Melisande taking her life because of an unhappy love affair, and James Lambert dying of a broken heart. It was now January 1816, and Nonna was the sole surviving member of that once illustrious family.

She stared across the cold park, looking through the carriages as they bowled past. Hyde Park was where the *monde* displayed itself each day, driving or riding simply to be seen by peers – or betters. The women ignored the girl on the bench, but the gentlemen all noticed her, doffing their hats and smiling. She pretended not to see them, but she had. She knew the expression which would be in their eyes, assessing her, wondering if a price would purchase her. Yes, there would always be the possibility of the oldest profession awaiting a girl of Nonna's outstanding beauty. But she was James Lambert's daughter, proud of her name and birth, determined that prostitution was the last course she would take. The very last.

A gentleman on a prancing chestnut horse rode towards her, reining in by the bench and smiling down at her. It was an obvious and unspoken advance, but she looked icily at him and his encouraging smile faded as he rode on. Nonna watched him as a little further on he reined in again, this time leaning down to speak to another girl who was walking alone. The girl paused, looking up at him, and then she slapped her lozenge-shaped reticule against his horse's rump sending it dashing forward and almost unseating the rider. The girl's loud laughter floated to Nonna, who watched with interest as the girl sauntered on towards her.

She was a pretty, dark-haired girl of about twenty-one, with her curly hair cut *à la victime*. She wore a ridiculously light white muslin gown, far too thin and flimsy for the winter weather, and Nonna couldn't help noticing how its undergown had been dampened to cling to her legs as she walked. Her figure was full and curved in all the right places, helped by the exceedingly tight stays which pulled her already small waist in further and pushed her breasts up into the *décolletage* of her gown. The only concession she made to the weather and to convention was a light blue spencer with white fur collar and cuffs, but even that remained unbuttoned to reveal the low neckline of the gown. Her gipsy bonnet of white straw was decorated with immense floppy feathers dyed to match the spencer, and she twirled her Chinese parasol gaily as she stopped by Nonna.

'That showed him, eh?'

'Yes.'

'Think they own the world, some of them. Because they've got blue blood they reckon they're buck enough to appeal to any woman. Sir Daniel Carstairs is one of the worst too.' She sat down, putting her parasol, reticule and a brown paper parcel down beside her. 'You know Sir Daniel?'

'Me? No.'

'I think he'd *like* to know you – he saw me coming, but he stopped at you first.'

Nonna smiled, but it was a poor effort. She looked at the girl again. Close to, the over-abundance of rouge on her lips and cheeks spoiled her prettiness, and there were far too many gold chains around her neck, chains for lockets, chains for scent cases and crosses, chains for everything under the sun. And she wore glittering pendant earrings which would have been more suited to a grand ball than a stroll in Hyde Park on a winter morning. There was even a hint of blue on her eyelids, Nonna noticed with surprise.

The girl grinned. 'Reckon you're not what Sir Daniel thought, eh?'

'What?'

'A *demi-mondaine* – for want of a better way of saying it.'

'No, I'm not.'

'I am,' said the girl with disarming frankness, holding out

her gloved hand. 'Josie du Bois – well, it's Josie Woods really, but the other sounds better.'

Nonna smiled then and shook hands with her. 'I'm Nonna – Park.' Something made her give the false name.

'So, you're sitting on a notorious bench in Hyde Park, all alone, and yet you're not a loose woman.' Josie rolled her eyes as she said the last two words.

Notorious bench? Nonna glanced nervously around. 'I – I'm out of work, I was given the way to the proverbial door because I dropped one of Ackermann's prize Wedgwood vases.'

'Dropped it or threw it at the wall?'

'Dropped,' said Nonna, smiling at the girl's irrepressible humour, 'because a certain part of my anatomy was pinched. I was so startled that I dropped the horrible thing, and Ackermann's could not see me depart quickly enough. Without a reference of course.'

'Lord, that's not good for someone like you, is it? I mean, there's no one will employ you now, no one respectable that is.'

'I know.'

'Well, you've got the looks to do what I do.'

Nonna looked quickly at her. 'Which is?'

'Oh, come on – look at me. Tarted up like an altar piece, that's me. Josie du Bois of Madame Siffre's. You've heard of Madame Siffre's? In Jacob Street?'

'No.'

'You *are* green, aren't you?'

'Is that a bad thing?'

'It is if you've got to fend for yourself. Madame Siffre is a *madame*, and I'm one of her girls. We don't walk the street, we live well, have fine clothes, meet the gentlemen, and get well recompensed for our trouble. If you can call it trouble.' Josie winked. 'Sometimes it's a positive pleasure, I can tell you. Some of our clients are *so* handsome and *so* rich. It's not a bad life.'

'It sounds all right, I suppose.'

'But not for you, eh?'

'No.'

'Well, I can't blame you – if I was sweet and virginal again, maybe I'd try hanging on to it too. So, you were working at Ackermann's. What as? An assistant?'

'Yes.'

'What else can you do?'

'Nothing, I suppose – unless you count being able to sing and dance a little. I – I was taught as a child, my mother was an opera singer.' Nonna didn't elaborate.

Josie looked at her. 'Sing and dance, eh? That's interesting.'

'Handsome rich gentlemen aren't going to pay merely to watch me dance and trill a note or two!'

'Maybe not, but – oh, I don't know. Listen, I was going to take this back to the drapers in Grafton House – you know, in New Bond Street. English poplin at four and three a yard, and it's flawed! I'm going to make a solomon in there, I can tell you.' Josie smiled then. 'I only go there on a Thursday, when the manager isn't in, so that I can cause a stir. The snooty ladies look down their noses and step away from me, and the young man behind the counter is thrown into a positive vapour when I lean forward and reveal more than a decent young woman should. He's quite good-looking, and it does my vanity no end of good to fluster him so. Come on, we'll have a little laugh at his expense and you can cheer up a bit, eh?'

Nonna wasn't sure she really wanted to be seen walking with someone like Josie, but the girl's company was pleasing somehow, and her laughter and gaiety *was* heartening after the morning's disaster. 'All right.'

'We'll take a yellow bounder.'

'I haven't enough money.'

'I have. I only walk when I want to, Nonna. I told you, it's a good life.'

'While it lasts.'

'Ah, then it's every girl's ambition to either snare a rich husband, or to go on and become a *madame* herself. If one of the Wilson sisters can marry into the peerage, I don't see why I can't – I'm better looking anyway. You've heard of the Wilson sisters – Harriette you *must* have heard of! A family of stocking-menders – but they're doing well enough for harlots, eh?'

'Yes.'

'So, I live in hope. Oh, there's a chaise now!' Josie waved her parasol busily as the black post-chaise rattled up Park Lane towards Oxford Street. The yellow-jacketed post-boy turned the lead horse towards the two women, grinning as he looked at Josie.

'Carlton House, is it?'

She poked him with her parasol. '*Grafton* House, you cheeky ferret-faced nothing, you. And steadily, I have no wish to taste last night's dinner again!'

They climbed into the scruffy chaise and Nonna grabbed the leather grip as the tired team were urged into a break-neck canter back down Park Lane towards Curzon Street.

'Tell me about yourself then, Nonna. How old are you?'

'Nineteen.'

'And your mother was an opera singer? Italian, was she?'

'Yes.'

'Have to be to get on in London, eh?'

'Yes.'

'And she taught you to sing and dance?'

'Yes. She died when I was fourteen.'

'And you've been fending for yourself since then?'

'No, I was sent to my mother's sister in Colchester. She died last autumn and my cousins swiftly threw me out on the streets. I made my way to London with what I had been left in my aunt's will, and I took a room at Mother Carter's in Hebel Street.'

'A dump – a *Puritan* dump!'

'It's all I could afford. I found employment at Ackermann's – they approved of my looks and my speech and manner. I was doing quite well really, but for that awful man this morning. Thought himself such a dandy too.'

'They're the worst ones – they have little or no consideration for anyone else at all. Loud-mouthed strutting peacocks. I've met a few at Madame's, aye, and had trouble with one or two too. They are the ones we try to avoid, and so Madame gets angry and makes threats if we try to duck out. But we still grizzle.'

'And you still have – to go with these men, even when you loathe them?'

'Yes. That's what we're there for. It's not all that bad, you know, unless you get a strange one. There are a few of those about too, I can tell you. There's one who can't do anything unless he wears a gauze shift. Another one who has to be whipped first. Aye, and quite a number who like to do the whipping!' Josie grinned. 'Makes up for a few things, eh?'

'I suppose so.'

'I'm shocking you, aren't I?'

'A bit. I don't know much about it.'

'Too pure, that's you.'

'Maybe.'

'You live and learn, Nonna. We had Lord Byron come one night – yes, *the* Lord Byron. He actually took a fancy to me, and I was on top of the world – he's *so* handsome and romantic to look at, and everyone who's anyone knows about him. But he has some very odd ways – *very* odd. I didn't rush to catch his eye next time he came – far from it. And anyway, you've only got to listen to the rumours going round about him now. . . .'

'Rumours?'

'About him and his sister. I thought everyone knew – but maybe I do only because we get so many of the *monde* at Madame's. Yes, Lord B's bedding with his sister, and his wife's about to leave him over it. So they say. It'll be the scandal of the year when it happens – if it happens. The salons will rattle for months. And it's such a shame really, he's quite the most beautiful creature I've ever set eyes upon, and he can curl your toes with his voice. It's when he's got you in the bedchamber that the illusion shatters somewhat. Not the sweetest of gentlemen then by a long chalk.'

'Who *is* the sweetest of gentlemen then?'

Josie smiled then. 'William Lamb, Lord Melbourne's son. Now *there's* a man. And when I think that his wife – Caro Lamb they call her – actually left him to pursue Lord B. and caused all that kerfuffle a year or so ago. You heard it all, surely?'

'Lady Caroline Lamb and Lord Byron? Yes, I heard.'

'Well, her husband is William Lamb and the sweetest angel I ever knew. I'd die for him, truly I would. He's dark and handsome, and more manly than Lord B. But he doesn't come to Madame's much any more, which leaves me with a devastated heart and hollow life.'

'Not for long, I should imagine.'

Josie smiled. 'Life's too short to dwell, that's what I say. But I *could* dwell on William Lamb. So could quite a few I know. There'd be a veritable queue to pleasure him if he wanted.'

'Lady Caroline must be as mad as they say then.'

'She is – Lord B. says so. Can't get rid of her now, she writes constantly and badgers until he's driven hairless by it all. Am I boring you?'

'No, I find it all very interesting. I've never known anyone who knew all these people before.'

'They're the same as us really – only richer, and that makes the difference, eh? Nonna, I've been thinking. I could take you to meet Madame – no listen, not to become another of her girls. Listen, she's been toying with a notion for a while now, she thinks a girl to entertain the gentlemen as they play the gaming tables might be a good idea. Madame runs a gaming house too, you see, in the same house – that's why it's respectable for the *Monde*. If you can sing and dance, maybe you could fit the bill.'

'Oh, I don't know.'

'Afraid for your reputation?'

'Yes – to be frank.'

'Be frank then. You can always be disguised – a turban hat and a mask would see to that. And it would add a little something of interest, eh? Well? Would you like to come to see her with me? No strings or anything like that. But I like you and I'd like to help you if I can. Madame wouldn't want a reference.' Josie laughed at that. 'Though she'd like to get her hands on a genuine virgin like you. Oh, don't look so rabbit-eyed, there's no danger! Madame protects her girls, and if you were employed to sing and dance and *only* to sing and dance, then she'd stand by that. She's a tough old bird, but she's genuine and we all owe her a great deal. We stick by her too. What do you say? Shall you come with me?'

'I. . . .'

'Go on – you might see the magnificent William Lamb,' teased Josie.

'Seeing a paragon like that might prove too much for my innocent little heart!'

Josie threw her head back and laughed. 'You're all right, Nonna Park, you're all right! Say you'll come.'

Nonna nodded then. 'I'll come with you. But Josie, you promise it will be as you say?'

'I promise. Anyway, Madame doesn't want trouble and all her girls are there because they want to be. There'll be no funny business, honest and cross my heart. I'll just go and cause a stir in Grafton House and then we'll go.'

'Do you like causing stirs?'

'Yes. I like putting my tongue out at some high-born ladies who almost put pomanders to their noses when they see me – because *I* know I've bedded their husbands once or twice. Sometimes more than twice.' Josie smiled at her. 'And I know which bed those fine gentlemen find more entertaining.'

Madame Siffre's establishment in Jacob Street was innocuous enough to look at from the outside, thought Nonna as she climbed down from the chaise. She stood in the narrow street and looked up at the front of the tall building. It stood between two larger houses, each with marble and stone porches and many grand steps up to the front doors. The windows were tall and there were many of them. There was no way of telling from the outside what went on behind its walls.

Inside she followed Josie across the large green-tiled hall and up the golden staircase which swept to the columned first landing. There were paintings on the walls of naked gods and goddesses, and the air was warm and smelled of candlewax. On the carpeted luxurious landing with its hot-house plants and roaring fires, two little negro pages in green and gold livery hurried to throw open the great white and gold doors they guarded.

Nonna and Josie walked past the gaming tables, which were quiet now. Josie nodded at the green baize surfaces with the green-shaded lamps. 'It gets busy here in the evenings, and then goes on all through the nights mostly. Madame's cooks serve up enormous breakfasts and the gaming goes on. Faro, baccarat, backgammon – anything you care to mention. I can hardly stay awake sometimes, but Madame will not let us go to our beds – unless we are with someone of course.'

'Of course.'

Josie looked at her. 'There's still time to say no, Nonna.'

'I would like to see Madame Siffre and find out if there is a place for me here.'

'Like a fish out of water, aren't you?'

'Yes.'

'How've you managed to stay green for so long? Six months alone in London and still you're like something from a convent!'

Nonna looked around the gaming tables again and then up at the shimmering chandeliers high above. There was a hint of cigar smoke in the air, but the prevailing perfume was that of flowers from the large opened *Pot-Pourri* jars by the fire. It was a green room, from the floors to the moulded plaster ceilings high above, an elegant room – which surprised her. She already had an impression of Madame Siffre in her mind, and that impression did not coincide with the taste and grace of this large room.

Josie glanced at her. 'Nice, eh – not vulgar.'

'I was thinking how beautiful it was.'

'It's the Duke of Hannerson's house really – Madame leases it from him. And yes, before you ask, he *does* know all about what sort of establishment it now is. The Duchess was a prude and she created a terrible scene when she discovered it, but he wouldn't budge. Said it was his house to dispose of as he pleased and she could either accept or do the other thing. She did the other thing and left him. He comes here a lot – a funny old man, but not unpleasant. He likes Belle, claims her each time he's here, much to her chagrin. Belle likes one or two of the younger bucks, you see. Come on, the pages have gone to tell Madame we're here.'

Madame Siffre's rooms were closed and perfumed. The walls were of maroon, gold and white striped silk, and hung with voluptuous paintings of nude women. There were thick, rose-pink Axminster carpets on the floor, and huge vases of chenille and silk roses in the corners. More *pot-pourri* jars stood by the fireplaces, releasing the smell of rose petals into the stifling warmth of the rooms. Three or four white toy dogs lay curled up together in a basket before the fire and they hardly bothered to look up as the two women came in. Nonna glanced at her reflection in an ornate, gold-edged cheval mirror. How dull and drab she looked beside Josie. Some heavy, red velvet drapes moved, their golden tassels shivering, and Madame was there.

She was exactly as Nonna had pictured her, a short, fat woman with hennaed hair and a heavily rouged face. She was in her fifties, and so obese that it was impossible to tell if she had once had any claim to beauty. Her ample person was laced into a dainty white gown which was flounced and frilled like a young girl's, and her hair was almost hidden by a high, lace-lined bonnet. The light from the window caught huge diamond earrings which wobbled as she walked.

'Josie?'

'Madame.'

'What's this then? A new recruit?'

'Not exactly, Madame.'

'Well?' The voice was surprisingly light and sweet.

'Her name is Nonna Park, Madame, and she can dance and sing. I was thinking. . . .'

Madame held up a lace handkerchief and flicked it irritably at Josie. 'I know what you were thinking, missy, I know it well enough. So, Miss Nonna Park, you claim to be able to dance and sing, eh? Take off your bonnet and let's take a closer look at your face and hair.'

Hesitantly Nonna obeyed and Madame came closer, reaching up to take out the restraining pins so that the cloud of dark red hair fell warmly around Nonna's shoulders. 'Genuine, eh – not henna like mine.' Madame laughed. 'And very lovely. Such skin, so clear and white. By all the saints, you'd be a prize, Nonna. You'd be made if you came here as one of my girls.'

'No! No, Madame.'

Madame studied her face for a moment and then looked at Josie. 'You've heard her perform somewhere?'

'No, Madame, I just thought you'd like to meet her – to see if she. . . .'

'If she's any good? Very well, we'll see. Nonna, I want this to be a high-class performance – not something more suited to a burlesque show, do you understand?'

'Yes, Madame.'

'Not Opera House though – my gentlemen must not be overwhelmed, but merely entertained and enchanted by your daintiness, beauty and, above all, your *class*. Now then, what shall we try you on? Ah, yes.' Madame went across to the piano which stood against one wall, seating herself carefully and slowly, and then leafing through the sheets of music on the top of the piano.

She began to play, and to Nonna's relief it was a Mozart song she knew well and she sang it without needing the music for the words. Madame nodded as she finished and then leafed through the music sheets again, taking out a newer paper. When she played this time, it was a popular song, jaunty and pleasant, and Nonna read the words as she sang.

Madame turned to her as she finished. 'If I play something, will you dance to it? Are you classically trained, Miss Park?'

'Yes.'

Without another word Madame launched into some fiery Spanish music, and Nonna danced as well as she could in her cumbersome winter clothes. Afterwards Madame beamed. 'Excellent, Miss Park – no, I will call you Nonna! I am quite taken with your cleverness, Nonna, quite taken indeed, and I know that my gentlemen will more than love you.'

Josie glanced at Nonna and then spoke to Madame. 'She – well she would prefer not to be recognised.'

Madame looked closely at Nonna. 'Why?'

'Personal preference,' said Nonna, hoping that the answer would be enough.

'Lofty words for concealing the fact that you have a specific reason not to wish to be known here? Very well, Nonna, how would you suggest we disguise your red hair and green eyes, eh?'

'A turban would conceal my hair. The eyes do not matter.'

'A turban? Very well. And a small mask, to add piquancy to the situation. Gentlemen are always intrigued by such things, eh, Josie? A mysterious, beautiful lady who sings and dances exquisitely, and performs here at such an establishment and yet is beyond their reach! Excellent! I do perceive that this will prove a fortunate day for us all, Nonna. And with Princess Charlotte returned to London and rumoured to be about to become engaged *everyone* will be in Town again. Business, as they say, will be brisk.' Madame got up and went to a padded pink brocade chair by the fire, bending to scoop one of the sleeping dogs on to her lap. 'I shall pay you well for your services, Nonna. You could be paid a very great deal, you know, if you would consider. . . .'

'No.'

Josie looked her. 'Nonna, they'd pay handsomely for being the first.'

'No. Look, I am prepared to dance and sing – to entertain them like that, but I will not become a –a —'

'A harlot, Nonna?' asked Madame, smiling. 'If that is your wish, foolish chit, then I shall respect it. But maybe you will find it impossible to stand by such a condition once you are here. I do not know who you are or the society in which you have hitherto mixed, but I'll warrant it don't come anywhere near the type of man you'll encounter here. The gentlemen who come here are from the highest families in the land, and they come to indulge themselves in pleasure of one sort or another. Gentlemen bent upon pleasure can be so charming, Nonna. There are some who will never have an ounce of charm in their being, it's true, but there are others – young, handsome, wealthy, accomplished. And talented in the art of seduction. There will be one, there always is – eh, Josie?'

Josie flushed immediately.

Madame laughed. 'Yes, even someone as sensible as Josie can have her fool head turned by someone as handsome and appealing as William Lamb – with his unfortunate, unhappy marriage, unbalanced wife and sickly son, and those huge sad eyes which he knows well enough how to use. Josie is a sitting target for a man like that. And if Josie is, Nonna, you most certainly will be too. We all are in the end, eh. It's our lot in life. But, we shall see. The moment they know you are untouchable, they will be laying bets upon who will succeed – so I warn you, be prepared for an onslaught. But, for the moment, we must concern ourselves with your costume, and with the music you will want the orchestra to play when you perform. So, Nonna, if you will come here early tomorrow afternoon, then we can attend to everything in readiness for tomorrow evening. There's a gala at the Opera House, I believe, and I know we will have a large party of gentlemen come here afterwards, for the girls have been forewarned. I will send a chaise to your lodgings, Nonna – where do you live?'

'Mother Carter's lodging house in Hebel Street,' said Nonna reluctantly.

Madame raised an eyebrow. 'Indeed? A somewhat low address for a young lady as well-spoken and accomplished as you. Tell me, are you concerned to be anonymous here because you fear someone among the clients may recognise you?'

'In a way.' *They'd know me for I look so like Melisande.*

'I trust there is no scandal which may cause me embarrassment, because, if so, I wish nothing more to do with you.'

'There is no scandal, Madame, I merely wish no one to realise that I am now forced to earn my livelihood in this way. It is family pride and nothing more. I am not of noble birth, I have no furious husband, no lover, no row of starving children, no guilty secret – nothing. I just do not want my father's name to be dragged down because of my actions.'

'And who is or was your father, Nonna?' asked Madame softly.

'I would prefer not to tell you, Madame.'

The old woman nodded. 'Very well, but woe betide you, missy, if I find you to have been lying to me in any way. I am a benevolent mistress, wise and protective to those who serve me well – but God alone can protect those who displease or embarrass me. Is that clear?'

'Yes, Madame.'

'My chaise will come for you tomorrow afternoon at half past two then. Good day, Nonna.'

'Good day, Madame.'

Outside in the green room, Josie took Nonna's hands. 'I'm glad you're coming here. Oh, don't be afraid of Madame – if you're honest with her, she'll do well by you, I promise you. But I must go now, I have to bath and wash my hair for this evening. Until tomorrow, Nonna.' Josie kissed Nonna's cheek and then was gone.

Nonna stood alone looking around the empty gaming room. The tables and carpets muffled the sound of the fires' crackling, their heat moving the fronds of palm leaves lining the dais where the orchestra would sit. The instruments lay on the chairs, the boxes open and the music tossed idly on a table. The huge clock on the wall struck two, and Nonna walked from the room and down the stairs. Tomorrow she would come here properly. What would it be like?

At the outer doors she glanced back at the hallway and the golden staircase. Her breath was frozen in the ice cold January air as she went down into the quiet street, but it wasn't just the cold which made her shiver.

2

'There's a chaise come for you.'

Nonna got up from the stool by the smouldering fire and looked at the black-clad figure in the doorway. 'I'm coming, Mother Carter.'

The landlady glanced around the sparsely furnished room with its cracked windowpanes and solitary bed. The dull winter light made the room more unwelcoming than usual, and the smoke from the fire billowed out in the draught from the passageway. Mother Carter was tall and thin, with a face as cold as her lodging-house; there was no softness, no warmth in her and she kept her strict house with no bending of the rules at all. If they wanted respectable lodgings, then they must all pay a good and firm price for the privilege.

Nonna put on her pelisse, buttoning it slowly. Now that the chaise had come, the misgivings she'd endured the previous day came swinging back over her like a great pendulum. 'I – I do not know when I shall be back tonight, I may be very late.'

'Oh, yes?'

Nonna glanced at her, catching the sarcasm. 'Yes.'

Mother Carter stepped aside for the girl to go out into the passageway. 'Remember the rules of this house, missy,' she said warningly.

'I will.'

The landlady's keys jingled heavily as she followed Nonna down the steps and out into the grey coldness of the afternoon. She watched the girl climb into the chaise and smiled coldly. Given in, eh? Well, it was inevitable – a girl like that. Just let there be one slip though, just one, and out she'd go, bag and baggage.

Nonna clasped her reticule tightly as she looked out at the passing streets. The chaise swayed and bumped over the cobbles and ruts, rattling towards Jacob Street. She listened to the clatter of the hooves and the crunching of the iron-rimmed wheels. There was still time to escape, still time to keep her father's name honourable. Indecision clouded her thoughts, confusing her so that she slid from pride to desperation. But it *would* be all right, surely it would? No one would know who she really was, and she was only going to dance and sing, there was no harm in that, no real harm. Her fingers twined in the strings of the reticule and she bit her lip, staring out at the busy thoroughfare. No one would know.

The house in Jacob Street was still quiet as she went up the steps to knock on the door, but the door opened before she reached it and the negro pages led her up to Madame's rooms.

'Ah, Nonna, so you came after all.' Madame put down the toy dogs.

'Yes, Madame.'

'I did not somehow think you would, not when you had had time to contemplate. But then, you need the money the position will bring, don't you?'

'I have to live.'

'As we all do.' Madame snapped her fingers and the negro boys came in again. 'Show Nonna to Josie's room.'

They bowed low and Nonna followed them again.

Josie was lounging on a sofa with a ladies' journal on her lap. She wore a flimsy, almost transparent robe and her short hair was wet from being washed again. 'Nonna! Oh, Nonna, I'm glad you came!' She got up and hugged Nonna. 'And you're to have the room next to me too.'

'Room?' said Nonna quickly.

'Why yes – to change in. It's only a *dressing* room!' Josie laughed.

'Oh.'

'Well, you can't sing in those clothes, can you? You have to wear the gown Madame has selected. Come on, I'll show you. *I* stitched it – I do a lot of dress-making.'

The dressing room was small, containing only a wardrobe, a dressing-table and stool. It had no window and Josie had to light the oil lamp standing on the polished surface of the dressing table.

Josie took the gown from its hook in the wardrobe and held it against herself. '*Mousseline de soie*, the very finest. What do you think?'

Nonna stared at it. It was of the palest green gauze, and open mesh which hid nothing. Its tiny puffed sleeves were covered in silver spangles, and the same spangles decorated the hem, but it was the *décolletage* which caught Nonna's instant and horrified attention. 'I can't wear that!'

'You have to – Madame has decided. Anyway, what's wrong with it?'

'It – it's vulgar to say the least!'

'Thc prude in you is showing again, Nonna.' Josie draped the gown over the stool. 'Besides, it isn't vulgar, it's the height of fashion. Good fashion too. All the society women wear gowns like this, or hadn't you noticed? Perhaps not in the winter; you'd only see them in spencers or pelisses, I suppose. But for evening wear, this is *de rigueur*. Try it on, maybe you won't feel so bad about it then.'

'But Josie. . . .'

'Look Nonna, you can't dress up like a nun in a place like this, you won't last one evening if you do, I promise you.

The gentlemen come here to see beautiful women and enjoy their company and enjoy more besides. If they can only look at you without touching, at least they want to see a fair bit of you. Well?'

Nonna nodded, unbuttoning the old pelisse. Josie helped her undress. 'Madame says no stays under this gown, either.'

'Why don't I just stand naked in the room – the effect will be the same!'

'The gown won't show half as much as you seem to think. There, I'll just do the hooks and eyes at the back. Now then, what do you think?'

Nonna looked at her reflection in the mirror. The gown was so light she could hardly feel it, and the spangles winked and flashed in the lamp light. Josie busied herself with the accessories which lay in a drawer of the dressing-table. A softly swathed pale green turban draped with dainty strings of pearls, a white ostrich feather fan, green-ribboned ballet shoes, white silk stockings, white leather elbow length gloves and a confusion of glittering bracelets. Finally she took out a small mask. Dutifully Nonna put them all on. She did not recognise herself, she looked like a courtesan, a Cyprian of the first order; and if that's how the society women chose to look, then it said everything about their morals, she decided firmly.

Josie smiled. 'No one would know who you were, eh? The turban hides your hair and the mask makes it difficult to see your face – but then it's the rest of you they'll be interested in. The underskirt is to be dampened, to show your thighs.'

'Oh, Josie, I feel most uncomfortable about all this.'

'Pretend you're someone else then.'

'I shall have to.' She stared at the reflection again. Even those she could remember from her childhood among the people of the theatre world could not compete with the licentiousness of that green gown. If she moved slightly she could plainly see her nipples, and the gauze fabric clung as she moved. She took a long breath and then smiled at Josie.

'I suppose I shall do.'

'Of course you'll *do*! You've got a lovely figure, you know: I wish I were as elegant.'

'You are.'

'No, I'm not – I'm too full-blown to be elegant. Plenty of meat on me.' Josie grinned. 'The gentlemen like it though. Do you want to see my gown?'

'Yes.'

'Come on then.'

Still wearing the green *mousseline de soie*, Nonna went back into Josie's room. As Josie disappeared into her dressing room, Nonna glanced around at the richly hung chamber. It was furnished in gold and white after the French style, and the walls were of pink brocade. The dressing room was separated by rich dusky pink velvet drapes, and the immense bed had the same drapes. The bedhead was a tortuous carving of lovebirds and cupids, twining improbably around each other like fat serpents. The carpet was so thick that she felt as if her feet were sinking in it. It was a welcoming, warm room which closed softly over you – which, she supposed, was the intention.

Josie reappeared. She wore a white tunic gown with no underskirt so that as she moved the skirt parted occasionally revealing an alarming amount of leg. A band of the same white velvet crossed her forehead, and a curling ostrich feather was attached to it. Long, fingerless silk gloves adorned her arms, and a mother-of-pearl fan dangled from her wrist. 'I designed it myself – Madame gave me an absolutely free rein for the first time – a special favour because I'm one of her best girls.'

'It's very beautiful – you're very clever, Josie. One of her best girls, eh?' Nonna smiled. 'And does the Hon. William Lamb think so too?'

'Would that he did. No, if he comes here now it's for the gaming tables and I yearn for him from a distance, living on a few sweet memories of the few times I *did* have my evil way with him.'

'By the look in your eyes I'd say those memories were

very sweet indeed.'

'They are, he was the most gentle, considerate lover I have ever known. Madame's right, you know, there's always one who reaches you. The trick is learning to live with it, which is what I do. There'll be someone you fall for, Nonna – maybe even the same man I've fallen for, who knows? But there *will* be someone.'

'I'm equally determined that there won't be anyone. Not here. Anyway, I just have to sing and dance and then go. . . .'

'Oh, no – Madame won't let you do that! You'll have to mix, move among them and be entertaining and good company. But now you have to see the musicians and decide what you're going to do. Come on, I'll lend you a wrap to save you getting in and out of that awful grey thing you call a gown!'

When darkness fell, the house was ablaze with lights. The chandeliers glittered and flashed in the rising heat from the fires, and the air was heavy with the perfume from the *pot-pourri* jars which had been newly opened. Footmen in green and gold livery talked quietly among themselves, and Madame, resplendent in white satin and diamonds, moved silently around the rooms inspecting everything.

Nonna had met the other girls now, and some of them she liked – although none so much as Josie. Some of them were hard and without feeling for anything, but maybe the life they led made them like that in the end.

It was Madame's plan to conceal Nonna until the very moment she was to sing, and so when the first carriage arrived in the street outside, Nonna was hidden away in a secret room behind the orchestra. From there she could watch the main room through a small peep-hole. The gentlemen began to arrive, some of them making for the gaming tables, but some of them obviously there for the company of the girls. Nonna watched how Josie sat on the arm of a chair, her arm around one man's shoulder, stroking his cheek as she laughed and chattered with him, flattering and flirting all the time. Nonna recognised him, his name was Sir Piers Alvney and he was an exquisite who had occasionally come to Ackermann's with his wife. He'd been so superior then, looking down his powdered nose at everyone, not deigning to speak unless forced to. And now look at him. How could Josie bear to be so close to a man like that?

One man was enjoying the attentions of two girls, an arm around each. He was a true dandy, wearing a tight dark blue coat and white cossacks. His voice carried to Nonna, a lazy drawl as affected as the man who'd been the cause of her dismissal from Ackermann's. His fingers must have been heavy with the weight of the rings he wore, and a ridiculously large bunch of seals hung from his fob. He was corseted and padded until he resembled a chicken, and his collar was so high he could hardly move his head from side to side to speak to his companions.

The hours went by and the gaming tables filled up as more and more carriages arrived in Jacob Street. Smoke hung in the warm air and the drone of male conversation was everywhere. The orchestra played softly in the background and Nonna waited in mounting anxiety. She felt sick and nervous, and glanced at the three empty glasses of cognac she'd consumed to bolster her fading nerve. Now that the moment was almost there she wished she had never met Josie.

Madame came into the secret room. 'Ah, Nonna, I think the time is come to launch the Masked Lady upon them. Smile, my dear, you look fit to faint away at any moment.'

'I *feel* like fainting away.'

'Nonsense, no one can possibly tell who you are. Tomorrow you must put on more rouge, you are too pale. Do you like the gown?'

'Yes.' Of all the gowns Nonna had seen here tonight, it was the one she *dis*liked the least.

Madame's sharp eyes noticed the empty glasses. 'I trust, my dear, that the 'fortification' does not have an adverse effect!'

Nonna smiled nervously. 'If I had not drunk those cognacs, Madame, then I *would* have fainted away by now.'

'Very well, if you are ready?'

'Yes.' *As ready as I'll ever be.*

'Some of the songs you've chosen are popular songs, are they not?'

'Yes, they are the rage.'

'And yet can die hopelessly if sung poorly.'

'I shall do them justice, Madame, I promise you. I was trained by the very best in the land, the very best. You'll have no reason to regret employing me.'

Madame studied her face for a moment and then smiled. 'Come then, my dear. And good luck.'

Nonna took a long, steadying breath. She was James Lambert's daughter, and she was about to give the performance of a lifetime!

Somehow she had expected her first entrance to cause a stir, but she was disappointed. The gentlemen with the girls carried on with their flirting and those playing cards continued with their gambling. It was not until Madame clapped her hands peremptorily to attract attention that everyone looked towards the orchestra and saw the girl in green with her face masked.

Nonna began to sing, and as she did so she stared at a potted palm at the far end of the room. She closed everything else out, imagining that she was singing for her father and that if she did badly he would scold her. The actress which had always lurked in her came bubbling out as she moved around the little stage, swaggering a little as she sang the cheeky words of the latest song. One young man in particular seemed interested, leaving his card game, his cards in his hands still, as he leaned against a column watching her, his dark blue eyes moving appreciatively over her. The words she sang were those of a young girl flirting with a stranger, and Nonna turned her attention from the potted palm to the fair-haired young man with the playing cards. She smiled, flirted and teased as she sang, flicking her skirts playfully, and he smiled at her.

He was about twenty-four years old, well-built and elegant, with his hair fashionably tousled. He wore a corbeau-coloured coat, white marcella waistcoat and cream kerseymere trousers, and there was a sensuousness about his good-looking face with its full lips and wide eyes.

From the side of the room, Madame watched, her fan tapping slowly. She glanced around and saw that, apart from a hard core of gambling men at their usual corner table, Nonna had claimed full attention and interest. Madame smiled to herself; the Masked Lady was a success – and with Lord Justin Farnsworth in particular, it would seem.

Nonna finished singing and the applause broke out. As she came down from the dais, Justin Farnsworth stood before her. He smiled again, bowing low. 'Your name, oh vision of loveliness?' he murmured, grinning then at using the grandiose words.

'My name is Nonna, sir, Nonna Park.'

' 'Pon me honna, Nonna!'

She smiled as he took her hand. 'And yours, sir?'

'Farnsworth. Lord Justin Farnsworth.'

At that moment Sir Piers Alvney joined them. 'Ah, Farnsworth, you fancy your chances tonight, eh?'

'Alvney.' Justin was cool

The dandy's eyebrows rose witheringly, and he turned to Nonna, offering her his arm. 'Madam?'

Her dislike, born at Ackermann's, returned instantly and she shook her head. 'No, thank you, sir, I was speaking with Lord Justin.'

Alvney was taken aback, and Justin grinned delightedly. 'That's you in your kennel, Alvney.' Taking her hand from the dandy, he walked past as if Sir Piers had ceased to exist. For Nonna it was a sweet moment of revenge for the supercilious contempt shown to her when she had been a mere assistant at Ackermann's.

Justin took two glasses of champagne from a footman's

tray and gave one to her. 'So, you take great delight in snubbing *beaux* like Alvney, eh? Which house were you in before coming here?'

'I beg your pardon?'

'Which house? You aren't new to this sort of thing are you?'

Her smile faded. 'I sing and dance, my lord, I am *not* a. . . .'

'Come now, am I to believe that? The way you moved around that dais just now leads me to think you. . . .'

She pushed her glass into his hand then. 'Think what you will, sirrah, you are wrong! I am not playing the coquette – I will speak with you and enjoy your conversation, but that is *all*!'

'What's this, a kennel for me too?'

'Yes.' She turned and left him to stare after her. From the outset she intended impressing upon the gentlemen that she was not one of Madame's girls, she was there to entertain them with her singing and dancing only.

Someone turned from the gaming table which had ignored her earlier. He was a plump man with soft, damp hands, and he caught her wrist as she passed. 'Farnsworth too much of a boy for you then, m'dear?' His voice was slow and boyish although he must have been somewhere in his fifties.

'Release me, sir,' she began, pulling her arm.

'Come on, sweetheart. . . .'

One of the other men stood then. 'Let her go, Henry,' he said quietly, running some playing cards through his fingers as he waited to be obeyed. He was slender, almost too slender, of medium height with unruly dark hair and a thin face. His eyes were dark brown and long-lashed, and his eyebrows were low. There was an air of authority about him, and although he was only in his early thirties, the older man obeyed him.

'All right, Hastings, all right – she's too scrawny for my taste anyway. Shall we play on?'

'No, I think not.' The dark brown eyes swept over Nonna

for a moment, and then he inclined his head slightly before turning and leaving the table.

She watched him go, a slight figure in a coat of dove grey velvet. There had been something about him, about his light, lazy voice, the knowing look in his eyes and the quiet confidence.

Justin was at her side again. 'My cousin makes a habit of rescuing damsels in distress. But Nonna, if I promise faithfully not to tread on your toes again, will you forgive me?' He smiled at her, raising her hand to his lips. 'Forgive me?'

She could not remain angry with him when he smiled so charmingly, and she returned the smile. 'But you must know, sir, that I am *not* playing the coquette when I refuse you.'

'Then I must try to win you, eh?'

She could not tell if he had decided she was playing a game and that he liked the rules, or if he truly accepted what she said, but with Madame's eye upon her, she felt disinclined to take the point any further for the time being. And Justin proved good company, deserting his favourite backgammon to seize her company and attention for the rest of the evening.

At midnight someone called for Nonna to sing again, and the call was taken up by many more until she found herself almost borne to the dais. It was a heady experience, the more so because of the champagne she had consumed after the earlier cognac, but the headiness was inspiring and she knew that she was singing well. It was like standing outside herself and watching with an objective eye, seeing the mistakes and correcting them. She had her audience in the palm of her hand and it felt good to be so powerful suddenly. They liked her and wanted her to go on singing, but Madame put an end to the proceedings.

'No, gentlemen, Nonna must sing again tomorrow and the day after, so we must not tax her now.'

'I'd like to tax her,' said someone, and a ripple of laughter went around the room.

'What's the price then, Madame?' asked one gentleman, tossing his cards on the table and leaning back, drawing on a cigar. His eyes were half-closed as he looked at Nonna. 'Or is guessing the order of the day?'

'My lord, Nonna is a singer and a dancer – no more than that.'

'Sounds a challenge no gentleman can ignore, eh?' he remarked, grinning around his companions at the table. 'What odds, my laddos?'

Nonna felt her face reddening as she watched them laying bets as to who would succeed with her, and Madame was laughing and encouraging them. But no one would succeed, *no one*!

Madame took her to her rooms afterwards, and poured a last glass of iced champagne. 'So, Nonna, your first night is a glorious success, eh?'

'I hope so.'

'It *was* so – you were exquisite, brilliant, possessed – call it what you will. And word will travel swiftly of my Masked Lady, of that you may be sure. The betting upon your chastity is proof enough of that. Lord Ryan can be relied upon to lay odds on anything under the sun.'

'You – you're pleased with me then?'

'Yes, what else could I be on tonight's performance? You have great talent, Nonna. Where did you learn to sing and dance so cleverly?'

'I. . . .'

'You won't say. Well, it does not matter, the point is that you are a success. Your health, my dear.'

'If I drink much more I shall have to be carried home.'

'You will not need the drink tomorrow, my dear. The first night is surely bound to be the biggest hurdle, after that, the world's yours, Nonna. But, a word of warning: beware of Lord Justin Farnsworth, he can be troublesome. I know, because I've had experience of him before. Over Josie. He thinks that because he will one day be Duke of Aldane then his wishes have to be obeyed in all things.'

'I will be careful.'

'Be assured that I will have my guards watching over your safety; the thought of you losing your chaste appeal does not please me.'

'Who – who was the gentleman who rescued me tonight?'

Madame smiled. 'The Corinthian in grey velvet?'

'Yes.'

'Lord Justin's cousin, Sir Philip Hastings. He interests you?'

'No, I just wondered who he was, that's all.'

Madame's smile deepened knowingly. 'A handsome buck, one of the most handsome, even to my jaundiced old eye. But he comes merely for the gaming tables, much to the chagrin of several of my girls who would dearly like to capture him. However, I must send you home now, Nonna. The chaise will collect you again tomorrow.' Madame pushed a small pouch of coins across the table to Nonna. 'I promise that the more attention and custom you attract, my dear, the more you will find jingling in your purse each night.'

'Each night?' Nonna looked at the coins; it was more than she earned in a week at Ackermann's.

'Yes, my dear. Each night.'

When she lay in her cold, hard bed that night, Nonna was wide awake, her mind turning over the things which she had seen during the evening. Josie and Madame had warned her that there would always be one man who stood out from the rest. Was that man Sir Philip Hastings? She remembered the cool smile, the slight nod of his head, the casual way he left the table. His sharp word had meant instant obedience from the man who had caught her wrist, and no one had commented at his leaving the game unfinished. A man to be respected? Certainly not a man to cross, that much was for sure. Nonna stared up at the dark ceiling where shadows thrown by the shaking lantern outside wove across the old plaster. Would he be there tomorrow night? Would the impression he had made tonight be reinforced then, or would it be destroyed?

3

Josie slipped into the secret room behind the dais. 'Nervous?'

'Not as much as I expected to be.'

'You've drawn a great crowd, eh?'

'There do seem to be a lot.'

'Any new rage draws them like pins to a magnet.'

'Am I a new rage then?'

'You're all set to be. You were really very good yesterday, you know – I was quite taken aback by your performance.'

'I don't know whether to be flattered at your praise, or annoyed at your surprise,' smiled Nonna, peeping through the little eye-hole again. 'I see Lord Justin Farnsworth is here again.'

'He's *always* here.'

Nonna looked at her. 'Don't you like him?'

'He's a selfish lover.'

'You know him that well, then?'

'Yes.' Josie smiled. 'He comes here to see me or to see Madeleine. But I think you've usurped us both in his thoughts, for he's already asked Madame about you at least twice tonight.'

'Oh.'

'His cousin's here.'

Nonna turned again. 'Who?'

'You don't fool me, Nonna Park, you know who I mean. I watched you yesterday, your great big eyes almost ate him as he walked away from that table. Sir Philip Hastings – the Great Untouchable.'

'You make him sound a little odd.'

'Oh, he's not *that* – he's what might be termed a dissolute rake from all accounts. But one thing's certain, he only comes *here* for the gambling. If you wish to capture his momentary interest, then you will need to know something about a subject like falconry.'

'Falconry?'

'He's a member of the High Ash Club. He's got quite a – mews I think the word is – at his big house in Dorset. A very exclusive club, the High Ash. Anyway, that's all I know of him.'

'Why is he supposed to be a dissolute rake?'

'Rumour hath it and all that. But strictly with those of his own class, he doesn't bother with the likes of us – we're beneath contempt. Well, perhaps that's a little unkind of me, he's not that bad. He's just beyond reach, that's the gall of it. I wouldn't mind a few hours alone with him, I can tell you.'

Nonna grinned at her. 'Shame on you, Josie Wood.'

'Shame – what's that?' Josie peeped through the hole. 'Madame's on the move; I think she's coming for you. I'd better make myself scarce or she'll accuse me of lazing.'

Josie's skirts rustled as she left, and in a moment Madame came in. 'Nonna? It's time for you to go on now.'

'Yes, Madame.'

'No cognac tonight?'

'No, Madame, none at all.'

'You see? The biggest hurdle is behind you now. But Nonna, have a care of Justin Farnsworth, he's already consumed two bottles of champagne and the Lord knows what before that and he came here with one thing on his mind – you. If someone else claims your attention, go with them. Try to avoid him tonight, he's unpleasant when he's in his cups.'

'Yes, Madame.'

'I'll not let harm come to you, I promise you that. Go on then, and charm them all over again.'

Cheers greeted Nonna's appearance, and the excitement and enjoyment of the previous night returned immediately. It was stimulating, and the hidden actress shone in Nonna's eyes as she began to sing. She saw Justin immediately, for this time he was close to the dais again, and as she passed close to him he reached out and touched the spangled hem of her gown. His fingers drifted over the green gauze for a moment and then dropped away, but he had achieved his aim and made her look down at him. She moved away, continuing to sing, and searching the sea of faces.

Philip sat at the far gaming table again, his back towards her, and even when the burst of applause rang out he did not glance around. She so wanted him to look at her that she could not turn her attention away from him throughout her performance, willing him to turn towards her just once. But to no avail, he merely carried on with his game of *vingt-et-un*, leaning back occasionally with an air of lazy disinterest in everything around him.

When she had finished, she went down from the dais, and immediately Justin moved towards her, but she turned to smile at a nearby gentleman in dark blue. He bowed sweepingly and took her hand, raising it to his lips.

'*Enchanté, mademoiselle, enchanté.*'

'*Monsieur.*'

He smiled, drawing her hand through his arm. 'So, a lady of education as well as artistic brilliance.'

'You flatter me.'

'I doubt it. Charles Webster, your servant.' He inclined his head, smiling. He was in his thirties, with sandy hair which defied control, and luxuriant sidewhiskers. There was a bright sharpness in his eyes and in the clipped tone he employed. 'Your name is Nonna, I believe?'

'Yes. Nonna Park.'

'An unusual name, Nonna. I've seldom heard it.'

'Yes, it – it is unusual.'

Charles turned suddenly, for someone had seized his arm. It was Justin. 'I say, Webster, the lady's mine, don't you know!'

'Remove your hand, Farnsworth, or it will be the worse for you!' snapped Charles, his bright eyes sharpening still more, with a new edge in his voice.

A third man appeared suddenly, stepping between the two and easing Nonna's hand from Charles. 'The argument is purely academic,' said Philip Hastings quietly, 'for the lady has already promised me her company for this part of the evening. Have you not?' he said, looking at Nonna.

'Yes, yes I have. Forgive me, sirs.' She nodded at the other two and allowed Philip to lead her away across the room.

He smiled faintly. 'You seem set to cause a solomon, one way or another, madam.'

'I do not *set out* to do anything of the sort, Sir Philip.'

'You know who I am?'

'Yes.'

'Which is more than I can say about you.'

'My name is Nonna Park.'

'Forgive my ignorance, but the name still means nothing. However, I must confess to disinterest in the inmates of this establishment, no matter how fair.'

She flushed slightly at the flippant tone. 'Disinterest? Or is it plain ill manners, Sir Philip?'

He paused, looking down into her green eyes. 'A vision with a sharp tongue? God above.'

'Well, I think we have exhausted polite conversation, don't you?'

'Maybe we have, but if I have blabbed about claiming your company then perhaps so sudden a breaking of our *tête-à-tête* might look odd. Champagne, Miss Park?'

She nodded. 'Thank you.'

'I am afraid that you might find my company thrust upon you from time to time if Justin becomes difficult. It is my lot in life to keep my cousin in check, I fear.' He turned suddenly as another man bowed before them. 'Ah, Cradleigh, another failure at backgammon?'

'I fear so, and another wad lost. Still, the luck of the night, eh?' Cradleigh inclined his head at Nonna. 'You must possess an enchanted leash, jess and bells to capture Hastings, madam.'

Before she could answer, Philip spoke. 'You know precious little about the skilled mystery of hawking, Cradleigh – it's the damned hawk you leash, not the handler.'

'That presumes you to be the handler then. So, madam, *you* are the hawk. Surely a goshawk at the very least,' said Cradleigh, grinning at her.

Philip raised his eyebrows. 'Goshawk? God above, Cradleigh, I like my women small and dainty – not big, powerful, savage and *fast*! If you wish to quiz me on falconry and so on then at least do me the honour of knowing your facts first. And now, your presence is superfluous.'

Cradleigh smiled, bowing with exaggeration. 'The floor's yours, Hastings, pray do continue with your pursuit.'

Philip watched him go away. 'A ramshackle fellow, Cradleigh.'

She said nothing, sipping her champagne as she watched his profile. He was handsome, but almost in a cold way, and his manner towards her was condescending. What Josie said was probably true: he considered her beneath him in station and was irritated at having to speak with her. But what if he chose to use his charm instead of his sarcasm? How would it be to have him pay court? Nonna knew she was not likely to find out. Determined to be the first to end the meeting, she suddenly pushed her glass into his hand. 'I think, sir, that the *tête-à-tête* can be satisfactorily ended now, don't you? Good evening, sir.' She turned and walked away.

For the remainder of the evening she moved among the gentlemen, talking and laughing, but all the time watching to see if Philip paid any attention to her. But he did not; he returned to his eternal card games and did not once turn around again, not even when at two in the morning he took his leave of the house.

Of Justin Farnsworth there seemed no sign, until a little later when he almost pounced upon her as she stood alone for a moment. 'Ah, Nonna, your company at last.' His voice was slurred and he almost leaned on her arm as he drew it through his elbow.

'My lord?'

'Name's Justin.'

'Justin.'

'I'm tipsy, you must forgive me.' He smiled.

'Shall I have Madame send for a carriage for you?' she asked quickly.

'God, no! I ain't done with yet. But maybe a supper would do some good, eh? Will you dine with me, Nonna?'

'Dine?'

'Eat.'

She smiled, but shook her head. 'No, Justin. Thank you.'

'Can't tempt you to Périgord pie? Truffles? Caviare?'

'No, thank you – I'm not hungry.'

'Then come to be company for me.'

'No.'

His dark blue eyes held her gaze. 'I *want* you to come, Nonna.'

'And *I* don't want to.'

'Damn it . . . !'

His voice broke off as Madame slid up beside them both. 'My lord, is something wrong?' she enquired smoothly.

'She won't dine with me!'

'Nonna has to go now, my lord, but I'm sure that Josie would be more than pleased to accompany you wherever you desire. Josie? Lord Justin needs your company.'

Josie smiled sweetly, slipping her hand on to his arm and leaning a little. 'My lord?' she said softly.

He smiled back. 'Josie, sweet Josie,' he murmured thickly, putting his arm around her shoulder. Josie moved closer, her arm around his waist, and Madame took Nonna's hand.

'Come, Nonna, his attention is diverted.'

'I'm sorry, Madame, there was nothing I could do.'

'There's no harm done, he'll be content with Josie for tonight.'

'And tomorrow?'

'Is another day, another bridge to cross when reached. He's very persistent, unfortunately – *and* a good customer, so he must not be antagonised. I will instruct the girls to watch him carefully and ensure that someone is to be with him constantly from the moment he arrives until the moment he leaves.'

Nonna followed Madame to her rooms. Inside, Madame sat by the fire where the toy dogs were curled up again, and indicated to Nonna that she should take the chair opposite. Nonna knew instinctively that this was an honour not extended to many, especially when Madame then leaned forward to stir the small saucepan wedged on the fire. A delicious spiced smell spread through the room from the bubbling liquid inside. 'Some caudel before you leave, Nonna? I warn you, I've laced it with brandy, not sherry as is suitable for women. But sherry can be a poor mouthwash at times. Here you are.'

'Thank you.'

'I'm very pleased with you, Nonna, you've drawn a great number here tonight, and the girls are more than occupied. If this continues I shall need more to cope – and so I shall not grumble, eh?' She chuckled wheezily. 'A satisfied Madame must be tantamount to a fairground curiosity! And it is because of you that I am so well pleased with life at the moment, Nonna.'

'Have I really drawn that many tonight?'

'Yes. You are set to be their darling, their favourite. The *monde* is fickle, and your success may vanish overnight, so we must make the most of it.' Madame sipped the caudel thoughtfully. 'I noticed that you actually succeeded in removing Philip Hastings from the gaming table tonight.'

'Only because it seemed there would be an altercation between Justin Farnsworth and Charles Webster. He deems himself to be Justin's guardian angel.'

'Yes, indeed. He *has* interceded from time to time when his cousin becomes too difficult. Oh, dear – if it weren't for the money Justin Farnsworth pours forth here, I'd ban him from the door. But it's very difficult, one has to be so careful, don't you know? My establishment is popular and fashionable among the gentlemen at the moment, but an incident of any kind can mean an abrupt and final end to everything I've worked for.'

'I'll be as careful as I can be, Madame.' Nonna lowered her glass, 'But I won't give in to him – or to anyone else.'

Madame nodded faintly. 'You have my word still, Nonna – your charm and attraction lie mostly in your unavailability. Mostly – not entirely of course, for your beauty is eloquent, the sort of beauty which crosses barriers of class and anything else you care to mention. There is beauty like that, both male and female. Lord Byron has such a beauty, a mystery and depth which reaches out to the beholder. Unfortunately for him, the depth comes from an inner torture, from all accounts.' Madame looked at her. 'Have you an inner torture, Nonna?'

'Not the sort of torture which besets Lord Byron,' smiled Nonna.

'I trust not – many a sin is glossed over by the *haut ton*, but incest cannot be endured, eh?' She chuckled. 'But you *are* unhappy, aren't you?'

Nonna looked away.

Madame looked at her. 'Whatever it is, men will find it appealing in the extreme to see it in your eyes. They flatter themselves that they can bring joy to the saddest of hearts. Conceited creatures, men – but what would we do without them?'

'The world would be an uninteresting place, Madame.'

'It would indeed. But now, you must return to your beauty sleep.' Madame got up and went to the table, picking up the jingling purse again. 'Your recompense, Nonna.'

Nonnna took the purse, and noticed that it was slightly heavier than the day before.

'Nonna, rumour is abroad that Princess Charlotte is soon to marry Prince Leopold of Orange. That will mean great social activity, and an influx of anyone who's anyone in the realm. I intend a great celebration here on the day of the wedding. These songs here are known to be favourites of the Princess's, can you make sure you know them? You can sing them that evening. It will go down well, I fancy. I don't think the straight-faced Slender Billy she's attaching herself to *has* any favourite songs. A handsome face, but no sense of humour, Prince Leopold. No damned fortune either – but Protestant and available, and that's what counts, eh? You'll learn the songs?' She held out a sheaf of music sheets.

'Yes, Madame.'

'*Au revoir, ma chère.*'

'Good night, Madame.'

Nonna undressed in her little room, and from Josie's room next door she could hear low voices and the occasional laugh. As she was tying on her old bonnet, she noticed that it was quiet now. She bent to pick up her reticule and knocked a hairbrush from the dressing-table, and a moment later she heard Josie's door open.

Josie looked in. She was wearing a very light, loose wrap, and nothing else. 'I thought I could hear you in here,' she whispered.

'Is he. . . .?'

'Out for the count, as they say. I plied him with more champagne and he suddenly went to sleep. I'll tell Madame and she'll have him taken home.'

'And you won't have to endure his attentions then.'

'No.' Josie leaned against the door jamb. 'And how was the handsome Sir Philip on second glance?'

'Insufferable.'

'That means you like him still.'

'I didn't say I liked him in the first place.'

Josie poked out her tongue and grinned. 'I'd not have plied *him* with too much champagne, I can tell you – I'd be too intrigued and eager. He could grace my bed any time he chose – well, maybe not if my Lamb was there first. Ah, the romance of romancing, eh? It does a girl good to fondly imagine such a situation.'

Nonna smiled at her. 'To change the subject – I was invited to sit and take some caudel with Madame tonight.'

'Honour indeed! She must find you a lucrative proposition.'

'She does, at least she says she does.'

'She wouldn't say it if it wasn't true. Madame doesn't mince her words. Oh, Nonna, I wish you were here all the time.'

'In a way, so do I. But at least Mother Carter serves to remind me how awful life can be if I don't succeed here. I might get complacent if I lived in luxury all the time.'

'Mother Carter – a *hair shirt*?'

'Yes, in a way. She looks like one too. Anyway, Josie, I must go now or I'll never be able to get up tomorrow.'

'Good night, Nonna. I'll go now and tell Madame about my sleeping dukeling in there.'

Nonna kissed her friend's cheek and left.

Mother Carter was waiting as the chaise drew up outside the lodging house. She watched Nonna climb down. The landlady prided herself on the quality of her house. She made a point of never asking her guests their names – asking the name was most definitely the first step in showing disapproval though, and maybe tonight was the occasion for bringing Miss Redhead up with a jerk.

The figure in black moved into the light from a lantern as Nonna went to the door, and Nonna gasped, startled.

'I do not think, missy,' said Mother Carter coldly, 'that this is a reasonable hour for you to return to a respectable house. There are many young ladies who seek accommodation such as I can offer. Many. God-fearing young ladies of stout character. Your name, Miss.'

Nonna stared at her. 'Park. Nonna Park,' she said automatically. 'But, I *will* endeavour to be a little earlier,

Mother Carter, and I assure you that I am doing nothing to bring disgrace upon your lodging house. Please believe me.'

The landlady studied the pretty face in the lamplight. There was something in those large green eyes with their innocent openness which made her want to believe her, but such unusual hours needed watching. 'Very well, Miss Park, but I warn you, one small whisper of anything untoward and out you'll go. I brook no indecent or Godless ways in my house.'

'I understand, Mother Carter.' Nonna went past into the chilly hall. She wasn't doing anything bad, but if Mother Carter should find out *where* she wasn't doing it! It *was* possible to remain innocent in a bawdy house, but Mother Carter would never believe it even if were carved on tablets of rock and brought down from the mountain.

A little later she lay shivering in her narrow, hard bed. The blankets were so cold they felt damp, and she curled up into a tight ball to keep warm. The hum of the city went on beyond the walls of the house, and closer she could hear the scratching of mice in the walls. Moisture dripped from the iron catch on the window, collecting in a pool on the window sill. She closed her eyes, making herself imagine the warmth and colour of Madame's. If her success went on as well as this she could buy new clothes, find herself rooms somewhere else – in an hotel maybe. Oh, *please* let it go on.

4

Word of the Masked Lady at Madame's spread like wildfire, and within a few weeks Madame found herself having to turn customers away. Carriages crowded outside the house in Jacob Street, and as Madame herself had predicted, Nonna was soon the latest rage. Wagers on who might be her conqueror were growing to huge sums, with Justin Farnsworth's name inevitably heading the list.

Justin's infatuation continued unabated, and although Madame had given strict instructions to the girls to make sure he was never left unattended at any time, he still managed constantly to badger Nonna. He seemed smitten beyond any other previous passion, begging her to be kind to him, flattering her, giving her presents and laying siege in the most persistent and vociferous way. His growing frustration at his inability to progress with her was beginning to become awkward, and its only merit in Nonna's eyes was that from time to time it forced Philip Hastings to intervene – the only occasions when Philip took any notice of Nonna at all. Otherwise, he took his place at the far gaming table and sat with his back to the rest of the room throughout the evenings. Perhaps, she thought wryly, it was a comment on his opinion of most of the clientele at Madame's.

January drifted into February, but it was not as cold as the year when the Thames froze over and there was a fair on the ice. Nonna had been in Colchester with her aunt at the time, but she listened enthralled to Josie's tales of the Frost Fair. This year there wasn't even any snow, and it was hard to imagine the bitter cold of that other winter.

Mother Carter's disapproval was becoming burdensome, her grumblings more and more unbearable, and so one morning, in brilliant February sunshine, Nonna set off to look for somewhere more suitable to live. She drove in a chaise, and wore the new toggery she had purchased in a fashionable dressmaker's in Wigmore Street.

Her winter dress was of oyster merino, and her new pelisse was white with rust-coloured fur trimmings. There were epaulettes on her shoulders to compliment the military style of her brown beaver hat with its tassels and braiding. Her hair was dressed *à la Egyptienne*, and as she looked at her reflection in the misty window of the chaise, she thought how her life had changed in these last few weeks. She had money in her purse now, and some new clothes – and here she was, sallying forth to seek accommodation in an hotel where there would be so much more comfort than at Mother Carter's.

She paid the post-boy in Bond Street, outside the Black Horse hostelry, for she had decided already that this was probably where she would like to stay. The mail coaches in the road outside and in the yard made it a noisy, bustling place, with jostling grooms, street traders, passengers, horses and harness all combining to make a general clatter. The landlord was only too pleased to welcome Nonna, casting his expert eyes over her clothing and concluding that she was a lady of some means. He showed her up to the first floor and a well-furnished room overlooking the street. From there she could look down at the stream of fashionable carriages and the endless parade of gentlemen coming and going to the tailors and clubs and shops for which Bond Street was famous.

The landlord waited by the door. 'Does it suit, madam?'

'Yes. I will take it.'

He nodded, glancing around. 'A fine room.'

'Yes. I'll have my things brought around before this evening.' She went out again, through the busy courtyard and into the street beyond.

She sauntered down towards Bond Street Straits, pausing to look in the windows of the jewellers. It was then that she saw Philip Hastings, his image quite clear in the polished glass.

He wore a dark blue coat, full white cravat and white breeches. He walked slowly, with a lady on his arm, and he smiled and nodded as she talked to him. Nonna turned slowly to watch. How different he was now, exercising his charm effortlessly on the woman who gazed adoringly up into his eyes. Sadly, Nonna walked along the pavement, keeping them in sight. The woman leaned on his arm, laughing and flirting constantly, and Nonna noticed how often others who passed them in the busy street doffed their hats or nodded. So, whoever she was, this pretty golden-haired woman in pale blue figured velvet, she was obviously Philip's equal in society. There was little trace of the cold, disdainful man who attended the house in Jacob Street now. At number twenty-nine Bond Street, Philip pushed open the door of Brindley's bookshop and the two went inside.

Curiosity drove Nonna to follow them. The bell of the shop tinkled rather loudly as she went in, watching them as they went to the counter where a bald-headed man with a quill behind his ear bowed and smiled as he attended to them.

Nonna moved closer, picking up an ancient tome as if she was considering purchasing it, but all the while she trying to hear the conversation between Phiclip and the golden-haired woman.

Philip leaned gracefully against the counter, his top hat and cane beside him. The woman inspected the books the assistant brought for her.

'Oh, Philip, this is perfect, absolutely perfect!'

'There are other ways of filling a bookshelf, Harriet, than by purchasing expensive antique volumes.'

'Ah, but that would not be to fill the shelves excellently, would it? I have been promised by Lord B. that he will personally sign a copy of *Childe Harold* for me.'

'And his terms for such a gift?' he asked drily.

'No price,' she said, playfully tapping his arm.

'One wonders – considering the fellow's dastardly reputation.'

'I'm safe from his advances, Philip – I'm not his sister.'

'Ah, that would make a difference, one supposes. But then you are someone else's wife, which makes you desirable again. Forbidden fruits seem to draw friend B.'

'But not friend P.H.?' She glanced provocatively up at him.

'That still remains to be seen, dearest Harriet. But, pray, continue with your purchase.'

'How infuriating you can be at times, Philip.'

'I have a reputation to consider.'

She smiled, glancing at him from beneath lowered lashes. 'A reputation for creating a great deal of feminine interest.'

'Really?'

'A Corinthian, a nonpareil – and devasting with the fair sex. An unusual mixture in the climate of London's present society.'

'You forgot that I am an angel too.'

'That I doubt – indeed, that I pray *not*!'

His lips curved in a slight smile. 'You said the self-same words to Brummell, I'm told.'

'Brummell!' she snorted. 'That dandified scion of Sodom and Gomorrah!'

He laughed. 'A woman scorned?'

'He scorns *all* women – I suspect him to be of the feminine gender himself! I hope he *is* in debt up to his scrubbed, perfumed neck and that he will shortly quit England for good. His reign over half London's gentlemen has gone on by far long enough.'

'The ladies are united, I perceive.'

'About Brummell? Yes. His word is law, and his word is that women are *not* in.'

'More fool the man who follows his word then.'

She smiled. 'Would to God I could win you, Philip Hastings.'

'Anything can happen, Harriet,' he murmured, 'even that.' He tapped the book she was supposed to be inspecting. 'And now, if you please – the purchase.'

Harriet returned her attention to the books a little reluctantly. Obviously the conversation with Philip was of far more interest. Nonna turned the old pages of the book she was holding, glancing up at a mirror which hung on the wall before her. In it she could see the two by the counter quite plainly. Her heart almost stopped as she saw that Philip was watching her.

His dark eyes swept her up and down as he lazed elegantly against the counter, and when she turned, their eyes met for a moment. There was no hint of recognition in his gaze, and as he smiled at her she knew that he had no idea who she was. The smile nearly turned her heart over, and she hastily put the book down and went to the door. He reached it first and opened it for her, inclining his head.

She smiled faintly and went out, her heart thundering, and as she glanced through the dark windows, she saw the flicker of annoyance and jealousy on Harriet's pretty face. In a daze, Nonna walked up Bond Street towards Oxford Street. He had made an impression on her over the weeks at Madame's, but this one chance meeting in Bond Street had proved one thing: if Philip Hastings put himself out towards her, she would find him impossible to resist.

Bewildered by the strength of her feelings for him, she stood by the roadside, waiting for a chaise to appear. When she hailed one eventually, she had mastered her emotions a little, and as she sat back against the dull brown upholstery, on her way back to Hebel Street and Mother Carter for the last time, she looked at the bookshop's windows again, but there was no sign of Philip Hastings

Madame's was crowded as usual that night, and Nonna was called for time and time again before she was due to sing, so that Madame sent her on to the dais far earlier than usual. She was greeted with enthusiastic clapping and whistles, and she looked across at Philip's table to see him glance around, a look of great irritation on his lean face.

She sang and he didn't look around again, not even when the applause became rapturous as she moved to the music. Justin was there, of course, leaning against a column, a glass in his hand. He didn't take his eyes from her once throughout the performance, and there was a brightness in his dark blue eyes.

As she curtsied, a tall, thin gentleman in wine red came forward and thrust a bunch of pink roses into her hands. Their perfume was sweet and warm, and there were so many of them that she knew they had cost a great deal to purchase in the middle of February.

'Thank you, sir,' she smiled.

He kissed her hand. 'A song at my request?'

'I —'

'Please, I beg of you. It is one of Princess Charlotte's very favourites, and as we have today heard when she is to marry her Prince of Orange, I thought to hear her song would be fitting, eh? What do you say?'

She smiled. 'Very well, sir.'

When he told her which song, she nodded at the orchestra and they began to play it. She glanced at Madame and her smile deepened, for if it had not been for Madame's forethought, she would not have known the song well enough to sing it.

She began to sing the pretty melody, and she sang it well for it was one she liked herself. She looked across the room and to her surprise saw Philip put down his hand of cards and get up to come through the crowd by the dais. He stood close, watching her as she sang, and when she finished he applauded with the rest. But that was the extent of his interest, for he immediately returned to his table and picked up his cards again.

Disappointed, even though she knew it was senseless, she stepped down from the dais, to be immediately accosted by Justin.

'Nonna! Never have you sung better.'

'Thank you.'

'This time you must grant me a favour.'

'My lord. . . .'

'Justin. Surely you can call me Justin after all these weeks.'

'Justin, I am only here as a singer, my company cannot be obtained simply because you wish it.'

He caught her arms then, his fingers pinching her flesh. 'Nonna!'

Philip put a hand on his cousin's shoulder. 'Justin, I think the lady has refused you.'

'Damn it, I won't be refused!'

'I'm afraid you have to accept the fact, dear boy. Come

now, a scene will not enhance the family name, eh? A buzz over town that you were in a scrape over a *demi-mondaine* at Madame Siffre's? Think of the rattling chatter.' Philip disengaged Justin's hands from Nonna's arms. 'Mayhap you're in your cups and should take yourself home while you can still stand.'

Justin turned on him, his eyes dark with anger, but Philip held his gaze steadily and there was something in his face which quelled Justin so that without another word he walked away, pushing through the interested crowd of onlookers.

Philip looked at Nonna. 'Madam, if you cannot stand the heat, then pray stay away from the damned fire!'

'Sir, if your cousin cannot behave in public, then – pray – keep him locked up!'

Gathering her skirts she walked away, her head high, but she was glad of the mask which concealed how much her face had flushed at his cold rebuke.

As she reached the door leading into the passage by Madame's rooms, she heard Lord Ryan's loud voice drift after her. 'That's Farnsworth's odds lengthened a mile!' It was followed by raucous male laughter.

She paused around a corner, shaking from head to toe, both from the humiliation of Philip's attitude and from the embarrassment of being haggled over so frivolously. For all the benefits of what she now did, there were so many penalties.

'Nonna, are you all right?'

'Yes, Josie.'

Josie's new pink tunic hissed over the polished floor as she came towards her. 'Justin Farnsworth is becoming more and more of a problem, isn't he? Or wasn't it *his* behaviour which upset you?'

'I don't know what you mean.'

'Liar. But come on, come back with me, for I want you to see someone.'

'Who?'

'William Lamb, of course.'

'He's here at long last?'

'Yes. For backgammon – unfortunately. But I would like you just to take a peep at England's most handsome man.'

Nonna laughed. '*That* statement would stand challenging!'

'No it wouldn't – to me he *is* the most handsome man in the realm.' Josie took her hand and they returned to the door. Josie pointed towards Philip's table. 'At the far end there, the one in black. See?'

Nonna looked at the dark-haired man as he studied the men on the backgammon board. He was about thirty-seven, she judged, and a little older than she had expected, but he was undoubtedly very handsome. He smiled at his companions and leaned forward to move some pieces.

Josie leaned over her shoulder. 'And to think, his wife actually preferred Lord B. to him – if ever a woman is moonstruck, it must be her! See the sadness in his smile? Oh, it breaks my heart each time I see it.'

'Good heavens, Josie, you'll melt in a moment!'

'I've heard a whisper that Lady Caro's writing a book – thinly disguising everyone, but it's really about her affair with Lord B. That'll be another scandal for her husband to endure.'

'He could divorce her. If ever a man had grounds. . . .'

'He won't. I suppose he loves her.'

Nonna glanced at her, grinning slyly. 'I've heard a more likely reason for that look on his face. His wavering from being Whig to nearly being Tory has made him *persona non grata* at Holland House. Now *that* would seem to me to be a more acceptable reason for his glum expression. I listen to the chatter and read the papers too, you know.'

Josie smiled in return. 'I'd rather believe my more romantic explanation, it suits me to. I wonder – I wonder if I could persuade him to give me some of his attention tonight? Shall I try?'

'I don't know – you know him better than I do. But he does look engrossed in the backgammon.'

'He doesn't really like gambling all that much, I think he

only comes for the company. I've noticed he comes with your precious Philip when he does come.'

'He's not my precious Philip.'

'You'd like him to be, though.'

'A cat can look at a king.'

'Ah, so you admit it!' exclaimed Josie triumphantly.

'I admit nothing.'

'You just did. Anyway, I shall make a bid for the Hon. William. I may be lucky enough to find him in a lonely mood, eh? Are you recovered now, Nonna?'

'Yes. Fully.'

'That's my girl.'

Nonna watched her friend thread her way to the far table. William Lamb looked up at her and smiled, and she went to stand behind him, a hand resting lightly on his shoulder. He continued with the backgammon, glancing up at her occasionally to say something. After a while Philip's card game came to an end and he got up, speaking to William, who nodded and then tossed the dice for a last time. William laughed, acknowledging defeat as he got up. He smiled at Josie, taking her face in his hands for a moment to kiss her on the lips, and then he went out with Philip, leaving Josie standing dejectedly by his empty chair.

Poor Josie. Nonna's heart went out to the girl in the rose pink tunic. Josie might laugh and make light of her infatuation, but beneath it all she was deeply and hopelessly in love with William Lamb who regarded her fondly, but no more than that. There was always one who would break your heart, Madame and Josie had both said, and for Josie how true it was. Had she been a society lady his interest would maybe have gone further; Philip's momentary interest in Nonna at the bookshop in Bond Street had proved the same point. But any woman who frequented Madame's was obviously of dubious character and therefore would be treated lightly. Or with contempt. Or both.

5

In April, the scandal concerning Lord Byron and his sister ceased to be a rumour and was suddenly on everyone's lips as he fled the country after attending the opera one night. For a while the chitter-chatter was about only this and not the imminent wedding of Princess Charlotte and Prince Leopold.

It was a fine spring, clear and sunny, and the daffodils in the parks were unharmed by sudden, fierce rain. There was blossom on the trees and a warmth in the air which promised the approach of summer. Everywhere there were preparations for the royal wedding, and from her room in the Black Horse, Nonna watched the to-ing and fro-ing from the fashionable tailors in the street below. Any apartments taken by gentlemen of note were all occupied as the second day of May approached. London was filled to overflowing with people and there was an atmosphere of excitement.

On the day of the wedding, Nonna took a chaise to Jacob Street a little later than usual, for the wedding was at Carlton House in the evening and so anyone who came on to Madame's would be late.

Josie and Nonna sat at one of the empty gaming tables and Josie sighed. 'I wonder what the Princess looks like. They say her gown is to be of silver tinsel. I went past Carlton House this morning, and you never saw so many people, it was almost as bad as when the Monarchs were here two years ago. Such a crush! Oh, I'd love to be there, wouldn't you? Actually an invited guest?'

'I don't really know – I suppose we'd be acceptable where it matters if we warranted an invitation, wouldn't we?' Nonna glanced at her.

Josie smiled. 'We'll never be accepted though, will we? Not where it matters.'

'No.'

Josie leaned back, chinking some backgammon men in her hands. 'I wonder, I really wonder how far you'd get with Justin Farnsworth? I say it purely as an exercise, of course, but it would be interesting to know – he's taken to the point of lunacy over you.'

'Well, it's a mental exercise I don't intend to take into practice, Josie. I cannot say *I'm* taken in the slightest by the future Duke of Aldane, no matter how young, wealthy and handsome he is. He is also a drunkard, an ill-mannered boor, and he reeks of musk!'

'That neatly sums up his lordship,' grinned Josie, 'and speaking of the Devil. . . .'

She got up as the first group of gentlemen came in, and it was immediately obvious that Justin was already the worse for wear. He wove unsteadily towards Nonna and sat in the chair next to her, smiling a little lop-sidedly. 'Ah, Nonna, a fairer vision than anything at Carlton House – even if you do hide behind that damned mask.'

Josie went to him. 'Have you been to the wedding, my lord?'

'Yes, I went to the mummery. The champagne was all right, I suppose, but the food – as always – was appalling.'

'What did the Princess wear?'

He looked at her for a moment. 'Something silver – *I* don't know what it was! She looked like a damned chandelier.'

'And to go to Oatlands in?'

He smiled slightly. 'How you keep abreast of what goes on, eh, Josie? You're as blasted particular as one of the Almack's dragons. To go away in? A white satin pelisse, I believe, trimmed with ermine. And a foolish bonnet covered in white feather. Like a chicken to be plucked –

which I suppose she will be tonight, eh? If Slender Billy has the energy – he looks as if he'll be letting *her* do the work! Well, Nonna, shall you be kind to me this evening? You haven't my ever-present damned cousin to step between us this time, eh?' He reached out to take her hand. 'He's dining with William Lamb at Long's – pleasantly far away from me. Will you at least share a bottle of champagne with me? That you surely cannot refuse me, for to do so would be tantamount to a grievous insult on this royal day.'

'I would like to share some champagne with you, my lord.'

'I said before that my name is Justin. *Justin*.'

He snapped his fingers, turning to catch a footman's eye, and as he turned, his face changed. 'God above, it's the guardian bloody angel again! Good evening, Philip. William too boring for you tonight?'

'He cried off,' said Philip, sitting down.

'Caro's literary masterpiece, eh? I'd cry off too if she was mine. Always thought she was unhinged, and now I'm positive', said Justin, snapping his fingers angrily as the footman didn't see him.

Philip smiled, toying with the spill of lace at his cuff. He was dressed in rich black velvet, and his waistcoat was white and unbuttoned to reveal the frills of his shirt and the fullness of his cravat. His tight black pantaloons clung to his legs as he crossed them lazily before him.

Justin gestured for the champagne at last and, as it was put down on the table before them, he looked at his cousin. 'Why come *here* tonight? I would have thought the attractions of the New Opera House more becoming than this bawdy-house-cum-gaming-hall.'

'I do my pursuing in *my* time, dear boy, and tonight it pleases me to come here.'

'The fair Catrine proving more difficult to wean away than you thought, eh?' said Justin, grinning unpleasantly.

'All in good time. God above, Justin, you smell like something from Covent Garden, not the best Delcroix can brew up!'

'Compliments fly around me like bloody flies when you're around, Philip.'

'They do rather, don't they? Well, what's your hell tonight? Backgammon? Or something more suited to your tiny mind – *vingt-et-un*?

'My tiny mind isn't suited to anything at the moment except peace and quiet from your presence, cousin mine.'

Philip smiled faintly, his dark brown eyes flickering to Nonna's still face for a moment and then back to Justin. He got up then. 'See to it, *cousin*, that there is no kerfuffle here tonight of your causing – I'm not in a humour to be patient, subtle or painstaking tonight! An evening at Carlton House put an end to any human characteristics I may have possessed this morning.' He inclined his head and went away to join some other gentlemen by the roulette table.

Justin scowled after him. 'He'll never forgive the fact that he's the son of the daughter, when I'm the son of the son! A quirk of nature gives me the title and leaves the world of Whig politics to him. They should have stuck him on a blasted pole at Waterloo and let Boney use him for target practice!'

Josie smiled at him. 'He'd have caught the bullets in his teeth!'

Justin laughed then, his mood changing in his usual mercurial way. He smiled at her. 'Sweet Josie, you can lighten my heart so swiftly, eh? And you'd take me to your soft, warm bed and love me so sweetly, wouldn't you?' His gaze swung to Nonna. 'Would that the same could be said of you, my dearest Nonna. God help the man who falls in love with that rarest of all blooms – a pure woman in a brothel. Ah, me. Yet another quirk of nature to batten on to my wretched hide!'

'I'm sorry, Justin —' she began.

He smiled and it was quite a gentle smile. 'Sorry that my heart lies in pieces at your feet? You should be flattered I'm so broken.'

'Madame's trying to beckon to me,' said Nonna with relief, 'I'd better go now. Thank you for the champagne.'

'Then you thank me for nothing,' he said, without looking up at her, 'but I'm not admitting defeat yet, Nonna – not by a very long chalk.'

She glanced at Josie and left the table, and as she passed a group of gentlemen, one of them caught her arm. It was Sir Piers Alvney, resplendent in grey satin. 'Ah, Nonna of the Mask. Is there a clear winner of these great lists of hopefuls at your feet? Pray tell us, put us out of our misery? Is it Charter? Or Ryan? Webster maybe? Or Hastings who swoops to your aid so frequently – guarding his interests is he? Come on, admit to us that this maidenhead is fictitious!'

She pulled her arm away. 'As fictitious as the fact that you are a gentleman? You tell me, sirrah, you tell me!' She swept on past, pleased at the mocking laughter directed at the unpleasant, dandified Sir Piers.

Madame waited impatiently. 'Your progress from one side of the room to the other took long enough, missy. The orchestra is waiting and so are a considerable number of those who come here merely to see you.' She indicated the crowd gathering around the dais where the orchestra was tuning up.

'I'm sorry, Madame.'

'I want tonight to go particularly well; I want them to remember it as a truly grand ending to a perfect day.'

'Yes, Madame.'

'And when you have finished, I want you to go directly to change and leave, no mixing with the clients afterwards this evening.'

'Madame?'

'Sir Philip Hastings has informed me that he thinks his cousin in a strange mood tonight and that that mood centres on you, Nonna. He must have no chance of causing a rumpus here.'

'Yes, Madame.'

Nonna's arrival on the dais was greeted with enthusiasm, and she went straight into her first song, a rousing chorus which always went well with them, for she danced and showed a good deal of white stocking, especially from the audience's vantage point below.

She went through her entire repertoire of Princess Charlotte's favourite songs, interspersed with other popular songs for which the Masked Lady was becoming so well known. Time and time again she glanced at Philip, but he was engrossed only in his card game, his back towards her. Justin took his usual place by the column, a glass of champagne in his hand, and his lips curved in a faint smile as he watched her.

After a number of encores, Nonna saw Madame's nod, which was the signal for her to bring her performance to an end, and she curtsied, shaking her head as they asked her to remain and sing some more. She went down the steps between the overhanging fronds of potted palms, making her way quickly from the gaming room towards her small dressing-room. She closed the door thankfully – tonight somehow she had no desire to be pleasing and charming.

The door opened suddenly and she turned with a gasp, but Justin put his hand over her mouth and held her tightly.

'Not one struggle, not one squeak, Nonna,' he whispered, leaning back to close the door. His voice was thick and slurred and his eyes glazed.

She stared up into his face, terrified, and he smiled. 'Now we'll see exactly how beautiful you are behind this mask, my dearest Nonna.' He bent his head and kissed her. His breath tasted of cigar, and he used such force that he hurt her; she began to struggle, beating her fists against his shoulders. He laughed then, tearing her mask away and flinging it aside.

'Nonna, you are as beautiful and spirited as I had imagined,' he murmured, reaching up to the turban. He tugged it away and her bright red hair tumbled down from its few pins. He jerked suddenly as the door opened again and Philip was there, catching his cousin roughly by the shoulders and thrusting him roughly to the wall, which he struck with a sickening force. He had consumed too much alcohol during the day to withstand Philip's fist, which struck him once on the jaw. Insensible, he slumped to the floor just as Madame and her bodyguards arrived on the scene.

Madame looked at the unconscious man and then nodded at the guards. 'Take him out to his carriage and tell his man to convey his master home.'

They picked Justin up and carried him out, and Madame hesitated in the small room, but Philip turned to her suddenly. 'If you please, Madame, I would like a word with Nonna alone.'

Madame glanced at Nonna, who nodded her agreement, and the older woman went out, closing the door behind her. Philip looked at Nonna, reaching out suddenly to take a curl of her hair between his fingers. 'Tell me, Nonna, could it possibly be that you are related to Melisande Lambert?'

She stared at him in amazement. 'Melisande . . . ?'

'Yes. I can see from your eyes that you know of whom I speak.'

She nodded slowly. 'I admit to being her sister, sir, but I beg of you to keep my secret. That a daughter of James Lambert should be reduced to working in an establishment such as this. . . .'

'Rest assured, I shall say nothing.'

'Thank you.'

He smiled faintly. 'The elegant lady in Brindley's, eh?'

She looked away.

Going to the dressing-table, he picked up a necklace which lay there, inspecting it briefly. 'The double standards employed by the *monde* disgust you, do they not?'

'Yes.'

'As they disgust me, even though I employ them myself. Tell me, Nonna Lambert, why is it that you are forced to work here when your undoubted talents should make you acceptable at the Opera House? Now that I know who you are, your skill in dancing becomes more clear to me – your father taught you, didn't he?'

'Yes.'

'Then why?'

'He died when I was only fourteen, sir, and I was sent to my aunt in Essex. And besides, my father's career lay in ruins after Melisande's death, and he no longer had the influence he had once enjoyed. Now I am penniless, not completely trained, and forced to earn my living as I can.'

'How incomplete is your training?' he asked suddenly, turning to look at her.

'I have not been trained properly since I was fourteen – I've practiced as much as I can, but my training has fallen by the wayside. Sir Philip, why are you so interested in me?'

His dark eyes continued to study her face. 'You're very like your sister, aren't you? More beautiful perhaps – or is it maybe more innocent? I confess, I was doubtful about your claim to such purity – in a place like this – but now that I look at you again I see that perhaps you *are* an innocent after all. Yes. . . .' He took her face in his hands for a moment. 'So very like Melisande. Tell me, Nonna, have you no secret ambition to be as your father always wanted you to be? A second star at the Opera House? Another flame to brighten London's seasons? I know that was his desire because he once told me so.'

'You knew him?'

'I was acquainted. No more. Have *you* that ambition too, Nonna?'

'Yes.'

'And if I were to tell you that I could most probably help you realise that ambition?'

'How?'

He smiled a little. 'Trust me.'

She stared up into his face, wanting more than anything to trust this one man. His very touch burned her skin, and she felt weak at being so close to him. The emotions he wrought in her she had never experienced before. Trust him? She *loved* him, how could she not place her trust in him when her heart ached so?

'Trust me, Nonna,' he said again softly, 'and you will

dance at the Opera House, that I swear to you.'

'I want more than anything in the world to dance at the Opera House, Sir Philip, but my father's name is ruined now because of Lord Justin. He saw me and soon he too will know who I am. I can't face the world after this.'

'Justin was hardly in a condition to know his left hand from his right. And besides, I shall say nothing of where I found you. No one here knows you – *I* didn't recognise you until now. Your secret is safe with me.'

'Sir Philip, forgive me being ungrateful and suspicious, but why would you – who obviously have a little more than contempt for me – put yourself out to help me?'

He smiled again. 'My reasons are purely selfish – as you would no doubt expect. Helping you in this would aid me in something, and be of undoubted use to you. As to having contempt for you. . . .'

'Please honour my intelligence enough not to deny it, Sir Philip, for your behaviour towards me until now has been ample proof of the way you feel. Don't attempt to flatter me now.'

'I was not about to. Well, Nonna? How strong is your desire to follow in Melisande's footsteps?'

She looked at him for a moment. 'But Madame will not. . . .'

'Hang Madame! She took you on to further her own interests, not yours. In this life, Nonna, you look after number one, and only number one.'

'Is that what you do?'

'Yes.' He saw the hesitation in her face and spoke again quickly. 'You can walk out of here now, with me, leave your hotel or wherever it is you live now, and no one would be any the wiser about your whereabouts.'

Leave? With him? There was nothing on God's earth she wanted more than to be with him, whatever the reason. As she nodded, he smiled slowly. 'Look after number one, Nonna Lambert, always look after number one.' He picked up her clothes and draped them over his arm.

'But I must change. . . .'

'By all means, if you wish to delay. Madame is not going to leave me alone in here with her prime attraction indefinitely.'

'I'll come now then.'

He opened the door and looked into the deserted passageway, then he took her arm and hurried her along the carpeted way towards the grand staircase. She was conscious of the two negro pages watching them, and for a moment she felt a sudden panic. Why was she doing this? It was foolishness, nothing but headstrong foolishness. Then they were outside in the chilly May night, where the warmth of the spring day had given way to an almost winter cold. She could smell the blossom on the trees in the nearby gardens as she almost ran along beside him to where his landau was waiting. The footmen jumped down to thrust open the doors and Philip handed her into the cool, dark interior where the upholstery smelled of costmary. He slammed the door behind them and the landau lurched away, the team's hooves scraping as the horses strained with the heavy drag.

Nonna leaned back, shivering, for she had not put on her pelisse, and Philip pushed it into her hands and tucked a travelling rug around her knees. He sat opposite her, looking out at the lights in the passing streets. Her heart was rushing uncontrollably now and she didn't hear his question until he repeated it.

'I asked where your lodgings are.'

'The Black Horse in Bond Street.'

He smiled then. 'Hence the visit to Brindley's?'

She flushed, and was glad that the darkness hid the fact. She watched as he stretched forward to the small grille on the front of the carriage, telling the coachman to drive to the Black Horse.

As the carriage drew up at last in the busy courtyard of the tavern, she stood to put the pelisse on properly over the flimsy green gown, tucking her unruly mass of hair into a knot and putting her bonnet on. He stepped down first and went into the tavern with her, following her up the stairs to the floor where her room overlooked the fashionable street.

She took her few clothes down from the wardrobe and laid them on the bed, and he glanced around the lamplit room. 'Definitely not furnished by Gillow,' he remarked softly, holding the curtains aside to look down into the street, 'and the pavement walked by bucks and *beaux* in the daytime is walked by whores at night.'

She folded her clothes slowly, looking at him. 'If my room is distasteful to you, sir, perhaps you should wait in your perfumed landau until I am ready.'

His eyes went to her face immediately. 'Distasteful? Quaint is more the word for a room furnished with an Elizabethan chest, a bed of doubtful period, and a wardrobe which masquerades as genuine French eighteenth century. As I said – definitely not Gillow.'

'The room suits me well enough.'

'But is surely not to your taste – not to the taste of James Lambert's daughter.'

'No, it isn't my taste, but then neither is this harlot's gown I've worn nightly for the past few months.'

'Harlot's gown? My dear Nonna, I've seen worse at court, I do assure you. There are society ladies whose morals would definitely not bear up to to any slight inspection.'

'But they are society ladies, and therefore above reproach.'

'In my eyes?'

'Yes.'

'An hour in my company and you can claim to know how I feel about such a thing?'

She looked away, putting the folded gowns into the single suitcase she possessed. 'This gown I'm wearing – I can't take it with me for it belongs to Madame.'

'I'd give a gold sovereign to see Madame squeeze herself into it. However, if you leave it here, packed and ready, we can have it delivered to Madame.'

She nodded and then looked at him. 'Will you please wait outside then, sir? I have never disrobed in front of a gentleman and I do not intend to begin now.'

He inclined his head and went out. She tried to unhook the gown, but knew immediately she couldn't, and so was forced to go to the door and open it a little. 'Sir Philip?' she asked in a small, embarrassed voice, 'will you unhook me please?'

He said nothing, coming back in and deftly unhooking the tiny fastenings in a way which spoke volumes for the amount of practice he'd had in such things.

Alone again, she slipped out of the gown and selected another, which had a drawstring fastening at the front of the bodice. She stepped into it and hastily finished dressing, folding Madame's gown and casting around for a piece of wrapping paper in which she'd brought a new shawl.

He came in when she called and he glanced at the demure gold merino gown. 'How vastly concealing and uninteresting.'

'And how proper.'

'Spare me from proper behaviour. Are you ready?'

'Yes, I've packed Madame's gown and addressed it.' She retied her bonnet and put on her pellise again, following him out as a waiting boy carried the suitcase down to the courtyard. She paid the innkeeper and then went out into the darkness again.

Philip was waiting in the landau, and he said nothing as the carriage moved out of the inn's busy yard and into Bond Street. Nonna watched the shop fronts slip past as the landau sped towards Grafton Street and the corner where Nonna and Josie had gone into the drapers on the day she first had met the other girl. She gazed at the shop as the landau turned towards Mayfair. She lost track of the streets and squares, taking notice only when the carriage began to go slower. She looked up and saw a name on the side of a fashionable, white-stuccoed house: Padenham Square.

'Is this where you live, Sir Philip?
'In Town, yes.'
'And in the country?'
'Five Ways, in Dorset.' He tapped his top hat on more firmly as the carriage halted, swaying as the footmen jumped down to lower the iron steps and open the carriage door. The cold air swept inside as Philip climbed down, turning to hold out his hand to her.

She stood on the damp pavement, looking up at the front of the house. Number six, Padenham Square was at least four storeys high, its lighted windows throwing a glare over the plane trees lining the edge of the square. The doorway had a round-headed porch and was approached by a flight of three shallow steps. She glanced up at the stone balustrades guarding the first floor windows, and at the iron railings at the windows on the floors above. The white walls were bright and clean, and through the lower windows she could see the glitter of chandeliers and the richness of crimson velvet drapes drawn back to show the luxurious interior of the drawing room.

He took her arm and they went up the steps. The doors were flung open by a butler in white wig and black livery. He bowed low, and she glanced nervously at his stony face. The hallway was square, tiled in black and white, the walls painted pale blue. There were golden marble columns guarding the two staircases leading to the floor above, and white statues in niches around the walls. Paintings hung on the walls, and somewhere a clock was chiming three in the morning.

The butler closed the doors and took Philip's hat, coat and gloves. 'And did Carlton House go well, Sir Philip?'

'Yes, Blythe – as well as it could, I suppose. Will you have Mrs Williams prepare the grey room as quickly as possible? We have a guest for a night or so.'

'Yes, Sir Philip.'

The butler bowed and slid away, his soft soled shoes making not the slightest sound. Philip glanced at her. 'We can wait in the drawing room until he returns.'

She said nothing, following him up to the floor above. The drawing room was crimson and gold, and a crackling fire glowed in the Adam fireplace. The perfume of lemon seemed to be in the air, although she could not have said where it came from.

She went to the fire and held her hands out to the warmth.

'Some cognac, Nonna?'

'No.'

'You say that so quickly – do you perhaps wonder if after all I am about to proposition you?'

'You've made it clear that that is not your intention.'

'Oh, believe me, the thought had crossed my mind. You are, after all, very beautiful – and that air of innocence is surely a challenge to any red-blooded man. But I assure you that this is purely – well, business shall we say? A matter of gain to us both.' He poured two glasses of cognac and came towards her, pushing one into her hand.

She sipped it after swirling it for a moment, gazing into the leaping flames. Had he chosen to proposition her she would have had no pride, not where this one man was concerned. It was a subduing thought, to know that all will was drained by being close to him. She must not look into his eyes now, she must not show him the truth of how she felt. He had no real interest in her, and he'd laugh if he read the love in her face.

The doors opened and the butler appeared. 'Mrs Williams says the grey room is already aired, Sir Philip – it was aired in case Her Ladyship had come after all for the wedding.'

'Oh, yes, I'd forgotten that. My mother's eternal flittings to and fro leave me breathless. Very well, Blythe. Oh, and Blythe. . . .'

'Yes, Sir Philip?'

'If anyone should call here and ask for Miss Park, will you say that there is no such person staying here? In fact there is no one staying here at all?'

The butler's face remained expressionless. 'Yes, Sir Philip.'

'And now, please show Miss Lambert to her room.'

The butler inclined his head and stood aside. Nonna put down her glass. 'Good night, Sir Philip.'

'Good night, Nonna.'

6

'Miss Nonna? Miss Nonna, it's morning.'

Nonna stirred, her eyes still closed. The sheets smelled of lavender, and were smooth and warm against her skin. She heard the maid drawing the curtains and as she opened her eyes she saw the sunlight flooding into the grey and gold bedroom. Sleepily she stared across the dancing sunbeams to the small boudoir with its elegant Chippendale furniture. Elegant. That was the only word to describe rooms so beautiful. Slowly she sat up, running her fingers through her hair.

The maid smiled and bobbed a curtsey. 'Annabelle, Miss Nonna.'

'Good morning, Annabelle.'

'Sir Philip said he'll take breakfast with you at half past nine, Miss Nonna.'

'Did he indeed? At *precisely* the dot of half past, no doubt.'

'Yes, Miss Nonna.' The maid went into the boudoir and looked in the wardrobe. 'I hung out your things last night, Miss Nonna – which dress shall you wear this morning?'

'The white muslin.'

Annabelle lifted it down. She was a plain girl, large boned and freckled, but her smile was evidence of a cheerful and pleasant nature. Her hair was pale gold, cut fashionably short in the same style Josie favoured, and her seersucker skirts were pale blue and spotless, her apron crisply starched so that it cracked occasionally as she moved. Busily she set out stockings, slippers, underskirt and gown, humming all the while.

Nonna looked at her. 'Do you attend Sir Philip's mother when she comes here, Annabelle?'

'Me attend Her Ladyship? Oh, no, she has her own maids, Miss Nonna. I attend – well . . . ' The maid blushed suddenly and fell silent.

'You attend any – er, lady, shall we say – Sir Philip may bring here from time to time?'

'Yes, Miss Nonna.'

Nonna smiled. 'Well, Annabelle, I am definitely *not* such a lady.'

'No, Miss Nonna.' The maid's blush deepened with embarrassment.

Nonna slipped from the bed and went to the window. Her room was at the back of the house, looking over the narrow walled garden which swept back to the mews lane. Beyond the stables she could see the rear of the houses in the next square, so ugly from the back when their front facades were all beauty and symmetry. Peacocks strutted on the spring lawns, their long tails brushing through the tulips and polyanthus. A gardener was selecting new bedding plants from racks on a wheelbarrow, handing them to a small boy who planted each one and watered it from a watering can he could hardly lift. The gardener cuffed him for bruising the leaves of a nearby japonica when he put it down, and Nonna winced at the clear sound of the blow. The gardens were beautiful, already a blaze of colour, and she could see the fresh young leaves on the rose bushes and ramblers against the mellow brick walls. More colour and perfume to come to grace the walks and paths of Sir Philip Hastings' town house.

Annabelle helped her to dress and pinned her hair up, expertly tweaking it into long dark red ringlets to fall down the back.

She followed the maid along the blue carpeted passage to the staircase. There was a vague smell of gas in the air from the ugly iron gas-stands in the vestibule on the ground floor, but in the breakfast room there was a smell of crisp bacon and hot-house carnations.

Philip lounged in a dark brown brocade dressing-gown, his long legs stretched out towards the fire as he read the *Morning Chronicle*. He glanced up as Nonna came in, but did not pay her the compliment of standing to greet her.

She helped herself to some bacon and sat opposite him at the table. He stirred his black coffee, reading on for a while, and then he tossed the paper down on the table and leaned back in his chair, watching her. 'How exceedingly *pure* you look, Nonna. Nonna the Nun.'

She smiled 'I perceive you are in the mood to be cynical again, Sir Philip.'

'Cynicism is not a mood, Nonna, it's a condition. Without it one cannot survive in London society. And talking of London society, tomorrow evening you will see it at its gaudiest.'

'Tomorrow?'

'There is a gala at the New Opera House, in honour of our royal bride and groom. I have a box and intend going there – with you.'

She stared at him. 'Me? In a box at such an occasion?'

'Yes – but it occurs to me that you have no suitable togs.'

'There's my green silk.'

'Hardly *gala*.'

'It's a very pretty gown,' she protested.

'But it don't suit me, madam.' He glanced at his fob-watch. 'I've an appointment with my damned attorney at eleven. I shall take luncheon back here and then afterwards you can drive with me to Mrs Clarke's in Henrietta Street.'

'*The* Mrs Clarke? The dressmaker?'

'The very same. The lady professes to have garments of every hue for every occasion – and so we will discover the veracity of her claims.'

'At your expense, I trust.'

He smiled. 'Unless you would deem that to put you in my debt.'

'No – you have selfish reasons for this, as you went out of your way to tell me, I recall. I shall not deem myself in your debt in any way whatsoever.'

He paused in the constant stirring of the coffee. 'Ah, the first stirrings of cynicism. You see how infectious the condition is?'

'It is impossible to conduct a conversation with you *without* being cynical, is it?'

The doors opened suddenly and the butler came in, looking uncomfortable. 'Sir Philip, there is a *person* at the door – the *front* door – and she refuses to go away. I am reluctant to have her ejected as she threatens to make the very end in scenes, sir. She said that her name is' – he coughed – 'Madame Siffre.'

Philip glanced at Nonna. 'Show the lady up.'

'*Here*?' asked the butler faintly.

'Yes, Blythe – here. Nonna? If you look behind you you will see a door; beyond that door is another room.'

Without a word she got up and went to the door. It was a small store room, with shelves of costly porcelain and silver-domed dishes. There was a smell of paraffin in the dark closeness of the tiny space, and she leaned against the wall, her heart beginning to rush as she heard the door open in the breakfast room.

'Sir Philip?' asked Madame.

'I sit here before you, Madame. What, may I ask, brings you here at this hour?'

'Nonna – where is she?'

'The Masked Lady?'

'You know perfectly well who I mean!'

'Do I? You seem to have intimate information about my thoughts, Madame.'

'I left her with you yesterday and she hasn't been seen since. I want her back.'

'No doubt. A veritable gold mine, wasn't she?'

'Yes. *My* gold mine.'

'Did you have a contract?'

Madame hesitated. 'No.'

'Then she is hardly to be termed *yours*, is she? Now, pray, leave me to my breakfast.'

'Where is she, Sir Philip?'

'Do not adopt that tone with me, Madame, for I am not one of your minions. I know nothing of Nonna Park, nothing whatsoever.' Through a crack in the door Nonna could see his steady gaze as he faced Madame's disbelieving fury.

'You lie, sir! This table is set for two!'

'Madame, hysterics at the breakfast table are so very vulgar. Now, if you please – get out.'

'If ever I find out. . . .'

'You'll what? Blackmail me? I've played your damned crooked tables, but I fancy my reputation can stand the disgrace of the fact being made public. I am bored at your lack of entertaining conversation this morning, Madame, and shall shortly be virtually suicidal if your presence here continues.'

There was a silence and then Madame went to the door. 'I promise that if ever I find Nonna Park, she'll pay dearly for running out on me like this. After all I've done for her, this is how she repays me! the kid gloves are *off*, Sir Philip, and you can warn her of the fact. Am I clear?' she said coldly.

'Perfectly. *If* I see her. Good day, Madame.' He picked up his newspaper and began to read, and Madame Siffre slammed the door as she stalked out.

Nonna felt weak at the menace in that last threat, and she came slowly out of the store room and went back to her place at the breakfast table, staring at the congealed, cold bacon on her plate.

'Please eat something else if the bacon displeases you so,' he said.

'I'm not hungry.'

'That sour old harridan has surely not frightened you?'

'Yes, she has. I shouldn't have walked out like that, Sir

Philip, she has every right to be angry with me.'

'She has *no* rights, Nonna. No one has any *rights* over anyone else.'

'Number one again?'

'Yes. Always.' He got up and went to the sideboard, selecting some more bacon from the steaming hot-dish. He put it before her. 'Eat, Nonna, and to Old Nick with Madame and her threatening noises.'

She smiled then, looking up at him. 'Would that I had your resilience, Sir Philip.'

'It comes with the cynicism.' He returned her smile. 'You are beginning well, Nonna, I salute you.' He inclined his head and returned to his seat. 'You show promise, and no doubt would make an exquisite addition to any fashionable drawing room.'

'That sounds a little insulting somehow.'

'I have little time for the blossoms wilting around the salons of London, not even for my beautiful young cousin Gillian.'

'Gillian?'

'Lady Gillian Farnsworth – Justin's sister. The Duchess of Aldane, her mama, thrusts me into Gillian's arms at every opportunity – to the point of *ennui*, in fact. I have no intention of marrying Gillian, even though she is accomplished, beautiful, of excellent lineage and flatteringly adoring.'

'I trust she's sitting at her breakfast table saying exactly the same of you, Sir Philip.'

'Is my big-headedness offensive?'

'Yes.'

'I only speak the truth.' He smiled. 'But thank you for complimenting me on my accomplishment, beauty, excellent blood etc. etc.'

'Well, I suppose I must credit you with those three assets. You *are* very beautiful.'

'It's an art, takes me valet hours to achieve such fashionable dishevelment.'

She smiled. 'But then I must also say that you are

arrogant, disagreeable, rude and pompous.'

'Ah, cruel spite lurks in your innocent, pure little heart!'

She finished the crisp bacon and buttered some toast. 'Sir Philip, why are you taking me to the royal gala tomorrow?'

'All will be revealed. Do not doubt, Thomas, do not doubt.'

The landau lurched along Piccadilly, the Haymarket and into the Strand. As it passed Ackermann's, Nonna could not resist poking her tongue out, praying that several more of their horrible old vases had been dropped.

Philip raised an eyebrow. 'What a very common gesture, to be sure.'

'Yes, but it expressed my feelings precisely. I worked there, you see, and because of that dreadful, pompous manager I was thrown out without a reference. That's why I worked at Madame Siffre's.'

'Out of the repository of art and into the repository of vice? How quaint.'

The landau moved on towards Henrietta Street, and Nonna looked out at the busy streets where people crowded the pavements and carriages cluttered the way. The noise of the city was everywhere, shouting, laughing, murmuring, droning. Combined with the clatter of hooves, crunching of wheels, squeaking of ungreased wheels, the sudden fluttering of the pigeons and pealing of bells, it was an atmosphere which Nonna soaked up willingly. Essex had been so quiet, so very quiet – this was the place she craved to be all the time. London was the only place on earth where she could live.

Philip glanced at her shining eyes. 'Such enthusiasm for a dirty, over-populated gathering of bricks, mortar and filth, Nonna?'

'Yes.'

'Not the fresh, clean beauty of the countryside?'

'Dorset?'

'*Is* there anywhere else?'

'Yes, there's London.'

He raised a withering eyebrow. 'Give me an empty hillside, a good horse and my best Iceland falcon and I'm a happy man.'

'You are privileged to possess the wealth with which to indulge your happy pursuits, Sir Philip – even to the empty hillside.'

The landau came to a standstill before the bow-windowed front of Mrs Clarke's exclusive premises. A single model stood in one window, a cream silk wedding gown. In the other was a high-crowned pink satin bonnet with huge white flowers beneath its brim. Nonna climbed down, looking at the bonnet. It caught her imagination somehow, being so beautiful and elegant, and yet frivolous at the same time with its bouncy ribbons and those wonderful white flowers.

Philip drew her hand through his arm and his cane tapped against his leg as he surveyed the bonnet. 'More enthusiasm, Nonna?'

He kept his hand over hers for a moment and immediately the spell she had held at bay throughout the day so far returned to enmesh her. The brave repartee she adopted when speaking to him was a front to hide the painful hurt of loving him. He smiled faintly, and for a horrified moment she thought he was fully aware of the effect he had on her, but he led her towards the door.

'Let us proceed with the mummery then, Nonna.'

Inside the shop it was dark and poky, and the young men assisting behind the counter where the accessories were displayed were hard-pressed by the ladies who clamoured for attention. Philip walked through the busy shop and drew the red velvet curtains at the end aside. Beyond the curtains was a large and gracious room, carpeted in dull sage green and with Chinese silk on the walls. Through the tall windows at one side she could see a small walled garden where a fountain played and ferns grew. A tall woman in black crepe rustled towards them, smiling at Philip.

'Ah, Sir Philip, it seems a lifetime since last we saw you here – with Her Ladyship was it not? Her new riding habit?'

'One of Mother's interminable purchases, Mrs Clarke – she has more riding habits than I've eaten hot dinners, I'm sure. And how is this nest of milliners?'

'Delightfully busy, Sir Philip. I have Spanish milliners now, they are *so* clever with producing new and exclusive designs. To be honest, I find them more enterprising than the Germans and even the French – though 'tis almost heresy to say such a thing, is it not?'

'Many would burn you at the stake for such words, Mrs Clarke. Allow me to introduce Miss Lambert, Miss Nonna Lambert.'

Nonna inclined her head, surprised at the easy camaraderie between Mrs Clarke and Philip.

'Miss Lambert,' said the dressmaker, 'and how may I assist you?'

Nonna glanced at Philip, who spoke immediately. 'A gown for tomorrow's gala. A bright yellow silk gown trimmed with black lace.'

Mrs Clarke smiled. 'So precise a gown?'

'Yes – I trust that you have just one such?'

'Well, yellow silk I have – but not trimmed with black lace.' She clapped her hands and a tiny, bustling woman with her hair in a severe bun on the top of her head appeared. 'Letty? Bring the yellow silk, the one with the white Brussels.'

'Yes, Mrs Clarke.'

Mrs Clarke showed Philip and Nonna to two green brocade chairs. 'Ah, Sir Philip, I stock riding habits, fancy ball gowns, wedding dresses, family mourning togs, day dresses and even court gowns – and you have to demand a gown which I do *not* possess! Why, if I had had but a little time I could have had just the exact gown stitched for Miss Lambert.'

Nonna looked across at Philip, her face still. A yellow silk gown trimmed with black lace . . . The years folded back suddenly and she could see her sister Melisande again, setting off with her father to dance at Carlton House itself. Melisande Lambert had always worn yellow; it was her favourite shade for she knew how well it went with her red hair. And now Philip Hastings wanted Melisande's sister to wear a gown like that. It was her resemblance to Melisande which had caught his interest, and it was that which lay behind whatever it was he was planning.

Mrs Clarke clasped her hands before her. 'So, Sir Philip, you are going to see the great Vania dance tomorrow. How I envy you. Never has there been a more brilliant dancer, never in living memory. They say too that Catrine is as talented as ever Melisande L – ' She broke off as the significance of the surname hit her. 'Lambert,' she finished lamely.

Philip smiled. 'Catrine will never touch Melisande, Mrs Clarke – not in artistry. Or in beauty.'

Nonna lowered her eyes to study the squares of the patterned carpet. *Catrine*. She had heard that name only the evening before, and Justin had used it. What had he said? *The fair Catrine proving more difficult to wean away than you thought, eh*?

Mrs Clarke glanced uneasily at Nonna, for now that she looked again she saw the obvious resemblance to the ballerina who had once purchased her clothes at this very house.

Letty returned at last with the yellow gown, draping it gracefully over the back of a chair. Philip studied it for a moment, and then looked at Mrs Clarke. 'Remove the Brussels and replace it with black lace, and the gown will look very well.'

'*Remove* it?'

'Surely not a Herculean task?'

'No. . . .'

'And not one which cannot be achieved by this time tomorrow?'

'No.'

'Then I shall expect to see it sent around to Padenham Square tomorrow afternoon at the latest.'

'Yes, but. . . .'

'But?'

'Sir Philip, I believe it will fit Miss Lambert, but I cannot be sure unless she tries it on.'

He nodded. 'Very well.'

Without a word Nonna followed the dressmaker behind still more curtains, slipping out of the white muslin and stepping into the rich yellow silk. The dressmaker did up the many little hooks at the back and then fluffed the gown out, standing back to look. 'Sweet lordy,' she whispered, You're so like. . . .'

'My sister?'

'She was your sister?'

'Yes, Mrs Clarke.'

'It's like looking at her all over again. Just like looking at the great Melisande Lambert alive again.'

Nonna felt more uneasy now, the dressmaker's words made her less and less happy about the course she was taking. What *was* Sir Philip Hastings up to? Why was her resemblance to her dead sister of such interest to him? She looked at the dressmaker suddenly.

'Mrs Clarke, was Sir Philip my sister's lover?'

The dressmaker blinked, taken aback at the suddenness and directness of the question. 'I – I beg your pardon, Miss Lambert?'

'Was Sir Philip Melisande's lover, Mrs Clarke?'

'Sir Philip? Why no, not as far as I am aware. No, certainly not, Miss Lambert. Everyone knows she was in love with Vania, with Armand Vania, the man you will see dance tomorrow night.'

7

The following evening Nonna sat unhappily on the edge of the bed watching Annabelle drawing the curtains and lighting the oil lamps. The maid smiled. 'The gas lamps *are* better, Miss Nonna, truly they are.'

'They make me look green, and I don't trust them one little bit.'

'They're ever so good, miss.'

'I'm just happier with old-fashioned oil.' Nonna lapsed into miserable silence. It was time to dress for the Opera House and all day she'd been waiting with mounting anxiety. The doubts she'd felt from the outset, and which had been magnified the day before at Mrs Clarke's, were weighing heavily on her now that the moment was finally here. She stared across into the boudoir where the yellow gown hung on a hook. The new black lace was thick and full, standing out dramatically against the soft yellow silk. It was a beautiful gown, the most beautiful she had ever worn – and yet she hated it suddenly.

'Shall I dress you now, Miss Nonna?' asked Annabelle.

'Yes, I suppose so,' said Nonna reluctantly, going to sit before the dressing table. 'My hair – can you put it *à la Rome*?' As the maid nodded, Nonna looked at her reflection in the polished looking-glass. *À la Rome* was how Melisande had always worn her hair. Always.

A quarter of an hour later she was ready. That she bore a strong resemblance to her sister she had always known, but now, standing there in the middle of the room, she realised exactly how startling the likeness was. It could have been

Melisande herself standing there looking back at her from the cheval-mirror.

Annabelle turned suddenly as the door opened and Philip came in unannounced. He wore formal court dress, a black coat with long tails and ruffles at the cuffs, and a complicated cravat which blossomed from the high starched collar of his shirt. The frilled front of the shirt was revealed by the open buttons of his beige waistcoat and his legs were encased in tight-fitting, knee-length breeches. His calves were shown off by white stockings and his shoes were buckled, and a dress sword swung at his hip as he crossed the room to toss his cocked hat on to the dressing table before turning at last to look at her. 'Good God above,' he murmured.

'Am – am I sufficiently like my sister, Sir Philip?' she asked, an edge to her voice.

He nodded, dismissing Annabelle, and when the door had closed behind the maid, he looked at Nonna again. 'You are like her, even to the hair.' He studied her for a moment, noting the way her tongue passed nervously over her lips. As if he sensed she was about to express her doubts, he diverted her attention by striking a pose. 'And how do you like my natty togs?'

'You look very grand, Sir Philip.'

'I look like a footman at Carlton House! Unfortunately it is *de rigueur* for a gentleman to turn out like this at the Opera House royal galas.'

'Is the sword to hack your way through the *monde* to get to your box?'

Her voice shook a little in spite of the light, bantering words, and he crossed the room to her, taking her hands. 'Nervous, Nonna?'

'Yes. Sir Philip, I really don't think I can go on with this. I'm decked out like the reincarnation of my dead sister, and it's – it's. . . .'

'Distasteful?'

'Yes.' She met his eyes. 'Yes, that's precisely what it is.'

'I assure you, Nonna, that there is nothing bad in what I

intend – and certainly nothing harmful for you. Would you like a drink? Something to steady your nerves?'

'Steadying my nerves will have little to do with the way I feel about this, Sir Philip. I should have said something earlier, I know, but. . . .'

His thumbs smoothed her palms. 'Don't you trust me, Nonna?' he asked softly, smiling at her.

His spell folded gently around her again. Foolish or not, she would have trusted him with her life. 'I trust you,' she whispered.

'Then relax – enjoy your royal evening.'

If he had succeeded in allaying some of her fears for the moment, there were others which came to the surface now. What if someone should recognise her after all? Someone who had visited Madame's – Justin Farnsworth, for instance. 'Sir Philip, will your cousin be there tonight too?'

'Justin? No. Nonna, he doesn't remember anything about that night, you know. His mind is its usual vacuum.'

'How can you be sure of that, Sir Philip? Think of what could happen if he did remember at some time? I can well imagine the scene he would create, the embarrassment and humilation I would suffer – my father's name would suffer. The whore from Madame Siffre's setting herself up as a respectable lady, walking on Sir Philip Hastings' arm, sitting in a box at the Opera House no less!'

He still held her hands. 'Nonna, Justin *doesn't* remember your face, I know because I know him so very, very well. Relax now.'

'I wish I could, but I am not as assured as you are, nor even half as brave. I'm *gauche*, inexperienced and suddenly terrified.' She took her hands away, going to the window.

'*Gauche*? You? How can you possibly believe that? You've got more poise and beauty than a good many blue-blooded ladies of my acquaintance, I promise you that.'

'Poise? Well maybe I have that because I play-act, Sir Philip. The actress in me carries the day, but the real Nonna Lambert is very different.'

He caught her hand again and made her turn towards him. 'Then let the actress run riot tonight, Nonna. Every woman there will be jealous because you are so lovely, and every man will envy me for being with you. And if all goes well tonight, you will have your chance to carry out your father's ambitions. Seize that chance when it presents itself, and you can only succeed.'

The words were carefully chosen, almost guaranteed to make her go to the theatre in spite of her fears. He drew her close then, kissing her on the lips. 'Trust me, Nonna,' he whispered again, releasing her.

The kiss had been a gesture, no more than that, a way of persuading her once and for all. It meant nothing to him, but to her it meant a very great deal. She felt an urge to blurt out how she felt about him, but immediately she discarded such a notion as the height in foolishness. It suited him for the moment to woo her slightly, because above all things he wanted her to go to the Opera House. Whatever his reason, he was prepared to make himself pleasant to her – and besides, he probably knew anyway how she felt about him. A man of his experience could tell at a glance. He would use her affection, play upon it – *anything*, to get his own way.

He draped her evening cloak lightly around her shoulders. 'To battle then?' he murmured, drawing her hand through his arm.

The closer the landau came to the New Opera House in the Haymarket, the more congested the thoroughfare became. The carriages could hardly move the crush was so great. The Opera House was a fine building, its arcades lit by countless wrought-iron lamps which by night made it a glittering palace. Nonna stared out at it. She had come here once before, as a child with her parents to watch Melisande's first performance as a member of the chorus. Even then the atmosphere of the place had caught her imagination, lingering through the years so that each time she practised at the bar she had pretended she was dancing solo at the Opera House.

But inside it was not as she remembered, for the cold blue and silver had been replaced by warming red and gold, and there were so many chandeliers it was like stepping into a gigantic diamond tiara. The heat from the candles was stifling as she waited for a footman to take her cloak. He was an older man and as he smiled and nodded at her, his face changed. 'Miss – Miss Lambert?' he whispered, staring.

Philip took her hand again and they walked up the wide curving steps, knowing that the footman was still standing, watching them.

The box was opposite the royal box itself, and Nonna stood for a moment, looking down into the vast auditorium. She was seeking the seat she had occupied all those years before, and the tears filled her eyes suddenly. She could almost see her mother and father, and the excited young girl between them – so excited she could not sit still and had been admonished by her usually mild mother. Four of the Lambert family had been there that night, and now only she remained. Only Nonna. She took a long breath and blinked away the tears, looking across at the royal box. There was no one there yet, but it looked so rich and fine with its red drapes and garlands of flowers, golden tassels and wine velvet chairs. In a moment she would see Princess Charlotte and her new husband. She would actually sit opposite them throughout the concert. She leaned forward to look down into the pits, at the Fop's Alley, where the young gentlemen sat on elegant display. The hum of conversation filled the auditorium; sometimes there would be a little laughter, and then coughs, and always the shuffling of shoes and the snapping of fans.

Philip waiting patiently for a moment and then leaned towards her. 'Nonna, for as long as you remain standing, then so must I.'

'Oh, I'm sorry, I just wanted to see everything.'

'Then maybe you are *gauche* after all – to reveal yourself as a newcomer so obviously.'

She flushed. It was as though he had rapped her knuckles with a ruler.

As she sat down he glanced at Fop's Alley again. 'Already you've caused a stir among the Melisande Lambert *aficionados*, I see.' He looked at her. 'It's the fashion to be fanatically devoted to her memory and to denigrate any newcomer, no matter how excellent she may be.'

'Is that why you spoke up in my sister's defence yesterday, Sir Philip? Merely because it's the latest rage so to do?'

'No, I spoke up for her because she *was* more beautiful and talented than Catrine. But she had not Catrine's *gamine* charm, nor her delightful figure.'

'So,' she said, forcing herself to smile, 'Lord Justin was right, Sir Philip – you *are* pursuing Catrine.'

'I do not pursue, Nonna – I trap. The quarry comes to me, madam, not I to it.'

'Trapping is still pursuing, no matter what you may say to the contrary, Sir Philip.'

He said nothing to that and she sat back, satisfied that somehow she had won the point. But she was curious to see Catrine now – curious, and jealous. The jealousy sprang immediately into her heart, and she bit her lip. How very silly to be jealous, how stupid and nonsensical to feel *anything* as far as he was concerned. The hopelessness of her love seemed almost oppressive for a moment, but then was forgotten as the royal couple arrived to loud cheers from the waiting audience.

Princess Charlotte was larger than Nonna had expected, a bright-eyed, fair-haired girl with an apparently boundless enthusiasm which her more staid young bridegroom was obviously at constant pains to curb. She wore a white satin gown and carried an exotically coloured Indian Kashmere shawl which she threw casually over the front of the box. A wreath of roses decorated her hair and she waved and smiled at those in the audience whom she knew. She was striking, but not beautiful by any means, and there was something in her face which reminded Nonna immediately of those portraits of her German ancestors which were constantly being published in journals. It was her very enthusiasm, however, which drew Nonna to the Princess, for she was natural and unaffected, adopting no airs and graces. Perhaps there was more of her outrageous mother, Princess Caroline, in her than there was of her father, the Prince Regent.

Nonna only tore her eyes away from the royal box when the performance began. Madame Fodor, the operatic star of the season, sang – her huge voice echoing around the auditorium. She was rewarded with ecstatic applause, which Nonna thought went too far for the quality of the performance. Madame Fodor could not, in her opinion, sing as well as Maria Lambert had done in her heyday.

Everyone was waiting for the highlight of the concert, the dancing of Armand Vania and the French ballerina, Catrine.

The moment came at last, after the long interval which she thought would never end. The two dancers came on to the stage to applause which went on for several minutes, during which they bowed and smiled, blowing kisses to the admiring crowd.

At first, Nonna found herself paying little attention to Vania, for she wanted to see Catrine. The French girl was small and delicate, her face elfin and dark-eyed. Her figure was full, however, although she danced exquisitely and seemed lighter than air. The dancing was magnificent artistry and Nonna watched spellbound. But it was not Catrine who was truly brilliant, it was Armand Vania. The man's genius was evident in each graceful movement, his skill was what made Catrine seem so excellent.

He was tall and handsome, his pale golden hair somehow just right for the role of Hamlet in the new short ballet composed just for this one night. Nonna watched him now as he danced. This was the man her sister had committed suicide over, the man who'd been her lover. Remembering her sister's brilliance when she danced, Nonna could only imagine what a spectacle it must have been when they danced together – the two most talented and gifted dancers in the realm.

As she watched, Vania suddenly looked towards the box and to her horror his steps faltered. Only some clever improvising on Catrine's part saved the ballet from disaster. Nonna was aware of Vania's constant glances after that, and aware too that she was causing more and more interest among the audience. Even Princess Charlotte leaned towards her dark, solemn husband to whisper something behind her fan, pointing at Nonna.

Nonna turned to Philip and saw that there was a look of smug satisfaction on his face. Everything was going as he planned. She looked at the stage, applauding as Vania and Catrine took their bows; and Vania looked into her eyes again, holding her gaze for a long while. That was why Philip had wanted her here: it was Armand Vania he wanted her to attract. The thought was instant, and she knew she was right when the ballet dancer inclined his head coolly at Philip a moment later.

Princess Charlotte's enthusiasm bubbled over and she clapped her fan on the front of the royal box, much to her dour husband's disapproval, but even he smiled in the end as she chided him for being straight-faced.

The applause died down at last and the opening chords of the national anthem sounded as young Madame Lucy Vestris stepped on to the stage to sing. Her voice was clear and sweet, but not startling, and Nonna paid scant attention to the beauty who had taken London by storm the year before.

She glanced around as the door of the box was opened and a footman came in, handing a folded note to Philip, who nodded without opening it.

'Aren't you going to read it?' whispered Nonna, leaning close to him.

'Why bother when I know what it contains.'

'What?'

'An invitation from Vania to go backstage the moment the concert is ended,' he said, pushing the unopened note into her hand.

She read, and it was exactly as he had said.

'So, Nonna Lambert, here is your chance. Vania loved your sister, only he did not realise it until she had killed herself because of his callous behaviour. Let his conscience work for you, let him persuade you to dance again. Take the opportunity as it presents itself, and never look back.'

She stared at him. 'The advantage to me I can see, Sir Philip – but not what yours is.'

He smiled faintly. 'Do not concern yourself about me, I will be content enough. From this moment on our paths will diverge, sweet Nonna.'

She said nothing, staring at the stage where Lucy Vestris was curtseying at the end of the second extra stanza of the national anthem, composed especially to honour the royal couple. From this moment on their paths would diverge? Her mind was racing, and confusion seemed set on making her hesitate. Philip Hastings thought nothing of her, so why be fool enough to dwell on the impossible? Maybe he was right, maybe Armand Vania *would* offer her the way to the future her father had planned for her. But had she the nerve to seize the bull by the horns?

Backstage the atmosphere was close and still filled with the excitement of the occasion, and Nonna looked around at the ropes, scenery and people in costume, listening to the foreign accents and the bustle of the last of the chorus girls as they hurried through to their dressing room, their pumps tapping on the dusty wooden floor. 'Relax, relax,' shouted someone, 'no one's coming backstage tonight – word's been sent around!' Immediately there was an almost audible sigh from everyone, and the pace slowed.

Philip paused. 'So, no Princess Charlotte for them all back here tonight, eh? There'll be a few dents in various fat prides, no doubt.' He looked beyond Nonna, and when she turned she saw Catrine coming towards them.

'Sir Philip?' She halted, her pretty, elfin face dark and unfriendly.

'Catrine.'

'This is deliberate, yes?' The girl waved her hand at Nonna, 'Nothing matters to you but. . . .'

'My dear Catrine, admit defeat.'

Her head was raised. 'I am Vania's, monsieur!'

'Ah, but is Vania still yours, mm?' Philip's dark eyes were warm as he smiled at the dancer. 'Now then, before he can drop you, you must drop him, eh?'

'For you?'

'Why not?' The easy charm was there.

Nonna watched it working on Catrine. She was undecided, wanting to refuse Philip, and yet unable to do so for some reason. 'Very well, Sir Philip,' she said, her French accent heavy, 'very well, I change.'

'I shall wait here for you.'

Catrine nodded, her eyes meeting Nonna's again for a moment. There was no mistaking the enmity Nonna saw there. So, that was what it had all been about, a trick to separate Catrine and Vania; Catrine was the advantage Philip sought.

He turned to her. 'Come then, let us beard the French lion in his den,' he said abruptly.

'You must love her a great deal to go to such lengths to win her.'

He smiled faintly. 'Dear God, Nonna, and what would you know of it, eh? Besides which, it no longer concerns you in any way, for the moment I take you into that dressing room with that one-man mass of self-conceit, then it is entirely up to you how you go on. You will have nothing more to do with me, nor I with you. *Finis. Fertig. Ende.* Which will suit me and no doubt will more than suit you.'

She said nothing, following him miserably to the door of Armand Vania's dressing room. She had known all along that Philip was not interested in her for herself, but his abrupt manner and cold attitude now hurt her deeply.

Armand Vania was taller than she had expected, and infinitely more handsome now that the exaggerated make-up had been removed from his face. His eyes were incredibly large and blue, and his fair hair shone under the oil lamp where he sat by the cluttered dressing table. He got up immediately, acknowledging Philip's presence with the curtest of nods, and holding his hands out to Nonna.

'Nonna?'

'How. . . .?'

'It has to be; no one else but her little sister could look so like her.' The French accent was clear in his low, modulated voice.

He came across the room to her, taking her hands warmly and looking down into her face. 'Do you dance, Nonna? Did James Lambert teach you too?'

'Yes.'

'Then we shall dance together, you and I.'

She stared. 'I need more practice, I haven't danced for so long.

'We dance, Nonna,' he murmured, raising her hands to his lips and kissing each slowly. 'Here at the New Opera House, you and I will dance.'

'But. . . .'

He shook his head. 'I insist.'

When she glanced around, she saw that Philip had gone. She was alone.

8

Vania smiled at her. 'Do not look so frightened, I do not bite.'

'I'm nervous, how could I not be? To dance with you is the greatest honour for any ballerina – and yet you will dance with me, a novice whose training has known great gaps.'

'If you are Melisande's sister, then I know in my heart that you can dance as exquisitely as she. I see it in your eyes, Nonna Lambert. Tell me, what is Sir Philip Hastings to you?'

'Nothing.'

The piercing blue eyes studied her face for a long time. 'I have little liking for him, Nonna.'

'He is nothing to me.'

He smiled. 'I care not about his reasons for bringing you, merely that you are here. You are Melisande's sister, and so you may always look to me, Nonna – for whatever you wish. I loved your sister.' He put his hand to her face again, gazing at her with a strange, faraway look in his eyes. 'You are so beautiful, Nonna, merely to be seen on the stage with you will delight me. Now, did Melisande tell you of Milly Desmond?'

'Her dresser?'

He nodded. 'Milly will take you to find a suitable dancing dress and some pumps, and I shall await you on the stage. Don't be afraid, Nonna, you will dance well – you are with me and I will take care of you.' He went to the door, and Nonna saw immediately that an intersted little crowd of on-lookers had already gathered there. 'Bring Milly to me,' he said to the nearest girl, and she hurried away.

A moment or so later there was a small tap at the door and a tiny woman came in. She was wrinkled and bright-eyed, like a chimpanzee Nonna had seen once in the zoological gardens. Her grey hair was drawn back and pushed under an enormous white mob-cap which bounced as she walked, and each tiny step she took made her heavy, old-fashioned satin skirts rustle. She said nothing, merely staring at Nonna as if she saw a ghost.

Vania smiled. 'No, it is not your Melisande, Milly, but her sister, Nonna.'

'Nonna,' breathed Milly, clasping her hands tightly, her eyes shining with easy tears, 'little Nonna? She spoke of you, she said you would be a finer ballerina than she was, did you know that?'

'I can never be better than Melisande,' said Nonna, glancing at Vania again, 'and I still do not know that I can acquit myself well tonight, Monsieur.'

'No matter,' he said, not looking at her, 'I can tell in a moment if you are truly a Lambert. Go with Milly now. See she has a suitable dress, Milly.'

'Yes, Monsieur.'

Nonna went with the dresser, pushing through the crowd, and she heard the whispers rippling through the theatre as Milly said briefly who she was. She heard her sister's name echoing around the overhanging scenery and curtains as she went with the dresser into a small room at the end of a passageway.

The walls were whitewashed bricks and there were cobwebs everywhere. Dust clung to the dressing table and lay over the pots of make-up littering the stained wooden surface. On the wall hung various posters, each announcing a performance by Melisande, and above the mirror on the opposite wall she saw a painting of her sister.

'This was her room,' said Milly, her voice thick with emotion, 'and no one has used it since her death. It has become a superstition almost that until someone has a first night as your sister did, then the room must not be given to anyone – to do so would be to bring ill luck. I – I thought you would like to see it.'

Nonna nodded, unable to say anything. She could almost feel her sister's presence in the tiny room, and as when she had taken her seat in the box earlier, so now again the past swept agonisingly through her, reviving memories, feelings and nuances to turn the years back. Milly smiled at her. 'Come, you must change in Monique's room.'

'Monique?'

'Another dancer here – she came from France with Vania, but has been eclipsed – first by Melisande, and now by Catrine. Catrine is jealous of the friendship which exists between Monique and Vania, so jealous that she will not share a room with Monique and another room had to be found. It's like a little box, with scarce enough room to swing a cat, but nothing would suit but that Monique was banished from Catrine's royal presence! Since she became Vania's mistress, Catrine has been a bitch to quarrel with everyone.' Milly pursued her lips thoughtfully. 'No, maybe Catrine's bitchiness goes back further than Monique. But now, come to Monique's room and I will find you a dress.'

Monique was changing. She was about thirty years old, a tall, thin woman with long straight brown hair and grey eyes. Her wide mouth broke into a pleasant smile as Milly came in, and that smile faded immediately when Nonna followed.

Milly closed the door, shaking her head. 'No, Monique, it is not Melisande, it is her sister – Nonna. She is to dance with Vania, he *demands* it.'

'Now? Tonight?'

'Of course – when Vania decides anything, it must be done yesterday!'

'I know,' smiled Monique, holding out her hand to Nonna. 'Hello.'

'Hello, Monique.'

'Another Lambert to dazzle us all?'

'I doubt it, I haven't been trained properly since I was fourteen – that's too long.'

'If you are a Lambert and you can dance with Vania, you *will* dazzle,' said Monique emphatically.

Milly took a blue gauze dress from a hook. 'This will do excellently: no frills and bits to distract you, eh?'

Nonna sat down suddenly. The events of the evening were moving so swiftly – too swiftly. She felt Philip's desertion keenly, and now that she was faced with the ultimate test, her brave words of wanting to follow in her sister's footsteps, of realising her father's ambitions, seemed vain bravado and little more. She felt weak and sick. And frightened.

Monique smiled kindly, 'Let me help you change. You're very like your sister, aren't you? Even to the hair.'

Even to the hair. Nonna looked at herself in the dusty, grimy mirror where the oil-lamp's fumes left dull stains over the glass.

Milly was searching for some pumps. 'She was with Sir Philip Hastings, Monique – I need look no further for the reason for her appearance.'

'Ah, the handsome, dashing Sir Philip, would that he was taken with a passion for me instead of Catrine.' Monique paused. 'I do not know why he likes her though; she does not seem the sort to attract a man like that.'

Milly found the pumps. 'A passion for her? Don't be foolish – as you say, a man like that wouldn't want a whore like Catrine, for whore she is and no mistake. She loves Vania, but she will sleep with whatever man she takes a fancy to whether it be Sir Philip or the man in the moon. He doesn't *love* her in the slightest, there's far more to it than that.'

Monique turned to look at the little dresser. 'What do you know, Milly?'

'I know that I was going to the stage door one night and I overheard Sir Philip and another man talking. The second man wagered ten thousand guineas that Sir Philip could not take Catrine away from Vania, and Sir Philip accepted the wager.'

Nonna stared. He had done it all for a *wager*?

Monique shrugged. 'Well, at least my judgement is not at fault then, eh? I couldn't think why he was pursuing Catrine – now I know. *I* would have cost him a lot less than ten thousand guineas, he's so handsome and his eyes say so very much when he looks at you.'

Milly looked cross. 'Such talk from a lady – from Catrine, yes, but not from you, Monique.'

Nonna said nothing, standing for Milly to help her change. Somehow, knowing that Philip's actions had been purely mercenary made things worse, not better. If he had truly loved Catrine, then she could have accepted his callous behaviour, but not now. Was there *any* real warmth and feeling in him? Or was he truly as cold, calculating and ruthless as now he seemed? To break up an affair between Vania and Catrine simply for a bet was so lacking in sensitivity. But then, as Madame had said and as she herself now knew, the *beau monde* would gamble on the outcome of anything under the sun, from whether an egg would have a double yolk, to whether the turn of a card would mean the loss of an entire estate and fortune.

She looked at Milly and Monique suddenly. 'You must both think very badly of me.'

'Of you?'

'For coming here like this with Sir Philip.'

Milly patted her hand. 'My dear, we think nothing, nothing at all. How could be be at odds with someone as sweet as you? And here, Vania is God, all-powerful and all-important. If he wants to dance with you, then we rush to obey his will. There is no one to match him, and we know how he blamed himself for Melisande's death. For months he could not dance. He will do all he can for you, Nonna, and if you are truly a daughter of James Lambert, you will learn everything he can teach you – everything. His genius knows no bounds when it comes to artistry and skill.'

Nonna looked at her for a long moment and then nodded. 'I'm ready, I suppose,' she said nervously, smoothing the drapes of blue gauze with cold, damp hands. Monique hugged her suddenly.

'Do your best, Nonna.'

Nonna went with Milly up towards the stage, where just about everyone in the Opera House had gathered in the wings as news of her identity spread through the dressing rooms. Even the stage doorman had locked the door and come to watch.

Vania awaited her in the centre of the stage, a pool of light from one of the immense chandeliers falling over him. He smiled, holding out his hand. 'You know the *pas de deux* from *The Moonbeam*? It was a favourite of your father's.'

'I know it.'

With some relief she heard him tell the conductor of the small orchestra that they would dance that particular piece, for it was one which she knew particularly well and one she was least likely to make dreadful mistakes in. Her heart was rushing almost unbearably as the first notes rippled over the stage, and she heard conversation dying away among the watching crowd.

Vania began to dance, and she felt the magnetism of the man as he moved. He had feline grace, matched by a strength which was so subtle that it deceived the onlooker into thinking it was effortless. His presence and power affected her, lifting her beyond her lack of practice, communicating with her until she knew she was moving as one with him. She forgot everything but the joy of it, nothing else mattered but turning to meet him, curving and twisting to the sweet, light music, and when the last notes died away she felt as if she had held her breath throughout.

Everyone clapped their approval, and Vania smiled at her, drawing her close and holding her for a moment. 'Ah, my Nonna, you are a true Lambert, a true Lambert,' he whispered, and as he held her she could feel his heart beating against hers.

Tears were in her eyes as she looked out at the darkened auditorium and the empty rows of seats. She had danced at the New Opera House, with Vania. He kept his arm around her waist as he led her from the stage, pausing only as he saw a large man in a black velvet coat and too tight pantaloons.

'So, Richard Langley,' said Vania, 'we have a new Melisande, eh?'

She looked at Richard Langley, for she knew that he was the manager of the Opera House. He was a heavy-jowled man with dark, beetling eyebrows and a ruddy complexion, and his full lips were curved into a smile which did not reach his small eyes. He nodded at Vania. 'She has ability.'

'Ability? *Mon dieu*! She has genius – genius! I want her to join us here, in fact I demand that she does, nothing else will suit me!'

She looked up into the dancer's face, her heart almost

stopping. Join the company at the Opera House!

Langley looked angry. 'She needs practice, Vania, even I can see that.'

'Very well, she will practise – but she comes here. I want her here.'

'What of Catrine?'

'Catrine is a camel – a very pretty camel, but a camel nonetheless. This one is a gazelle.'

Langley sighed. 'Yesterday Catrine was a feather, more graceful than a swallow!'

'That was then – now I have changed my mind. Langley, unless you do as I ask then I will no longer dance here. Wyndham of the Pegasus will always offer well for my services!'

It was a threat the Opera House could not afford to risk, and Langley nodded. 'A compromise then. Let her join us, practise constantly, and then next season . . . I cannot put her on this season, not when she's green.'

Vania took a long breath and then nodded abruptly. 'That I accept.' His arm still around Nonna's waist, he walked down the rickety steps towards the dressing rooms, and outside his own door he halted, turning her to face him.

His eyes were so very blue and clear as he looked at her. 'You will be a great dancer, Nonna; believe it when Vania tells you so. In the next weeks you will practise until you feel your legs are made of lead, not flesh and blood. I will help you, I will do everything I can for you.' He cupped her face in his hands then and bent his head to kiss her on the lips.

Emotion seemed to fill him suddenly, for he turned blindly away and went into his room, closing the door on her.

'Nonna?'

She looked around and saw Milly and Monique coming towards her.

Monique clasped her hands immediately. 'Oh, Nonna, you were very good.'

'Considering?' smiled Nonna. 'I only danced so well

because of Vania, I know that.'

'He is the master,' said Milly, '*le Dieu de la Danse*. Make the most of your chance, Nonna, for he is fickle, as changeable as he is brilliant. While he watches over you you will be the most important person here after him. When he turns his attention to someone else, you will either sink or swim on your own ability.'

Nonna glanced at the closed door again and nodded.

Monique handed her a note suddenly. 'Sir Philip left this at the stage door for you when he left with Catrine.'

Nonna unfolded it and read: *Nonna. I will have your things sent to the Opera House directly. Philip Hastings.* Angrily she folded it, feeling suddenly more used by him than ever. A sharp note, no more words than he was forced to use! But it was the anger of deep hurt which filled her, for each thing he did now was a pinprick to give her pain.

As she screwed the piece of paper up tightly and furiously threw it to the floor, a new and dreadful thought struck her. She had nowhere to go tonight. 'Damn him!' she said, but it was herself she was angry with.

'Damn *all* men,' said Milly drily, 'I'll drink to that.'

Monique linked her arm in Nonna's and they returned to the little dressing room. 'Don't let a piece of paper upset you so, Nonna,' she said gently, helping her out of the blue gauze dress.

'I can't help it.'

Monique smiled. 'You love him, eh?'

Nonna said nothing.

'Silence speaks loudly sometimes,' went on Monique.

Milly looked at the red-headed girl suddenly. 'Have you somewhere to go tonight? If you came with him – forgive me, but I do not know your relationship with Sir Philip. . . .'

'There is no relationship, there never has been, but my belongings *are* at his house in Padenham Square and I did sleep there for two nights.' Nonna sat down miserably. 'I left my lodgings at the Black Horse in Bond Street and went with him because I'm a fool whose head has been more than turned by him.' Why was she admitting all this to two people she hardly knew? But she felt somehow as if she always known them.

Monique put a hand on her shoulder. 'I have room at my house, Nonna. You can live with me. Please say yes, Nonna.'

Nonna looked up into the girl's kind, concerned face, and suddenly it all became too much and, unable to help herself, she burst into tears. She had everything suddenly, the chance of a lifetime to realise her ambitions, and yet she had lost everything too. Philip Hastings was everything – *everything*.

Monique's house was in unfashionable Southwark, and Nonna sat back, watching the late lights on the Thames as the post-chaise travelled slowly south.

Monique looked at the masts of the ships and then up at the clear, star-lit May sky where a half-moon hung in the velvet darkness. 'So fine a night, eh, Nonna? A good night for you, in spite of your unhappiness over Sir Philip.'

'Monique, you won't tell anyone about that, will you? I should never have been so obvious.'

'Of course I won't say, and neither will Milly – what *do* you think we are? But you mustn't look back, you know – for you there is only a future now. Turn your attention to Vania, Nonna, for he is there for the winning. Melisande he treated with frivolity – truly he did. It wasn't until she – died – that he thought himself desperately in love with her.'

'Thought himself?'

Monique smiled. 'Vania is Vania; I do not know if he would recognise a genuine and deep feeling if it jumped up and bit him. He cannot help it, that is the way of genius – don't you think?'

'I don't know. He does seem very affected by the fact that I am who I am, though.'

'He is. He will cry tonight because of his memories, because of you, because of the world, if you like. He's made like that.' There was a softness in her voice and

Nonna looked at her quickly.

Monique smiled. 'No, I don't love him, not now. But a deep and cherished fondness there still is, I suppose. He's a child really, and I am fond of him as I would be of a child. Many of his ways are endearing. He can be so sweet and attentive, so eager to please. . . . And then, in a moment, the other Vania is there, cold and hard, ambitious, hurtful, proud, cutting, fierce, unbelievably cruel. Do not look at me like that, for I say nothing that isn't true. Armand Vania is an enigma – is that not the word?'

'Yes, I suppose it must be if that is how he is.'

'Did not Melisande talk of him? She lived for him, lived through him, she could not exist without him. Forgive me, I did not mean to say anything to bring back painful memories.'

'You haven't. Monique, I was fourteen when Melisande died, and she was twenty-five. Eleven years is a long time, and she was almost a different generation. She spent her time away from our home, and I hardly ever saw her. I heard whispers, conversations which ended if I went into the room and began again the moment I left it. I knew my father was upset at something she was doing, and I knew too that she was unhappy – but never once did anyone speak directly to me about anything. I was "the child", and therefore to be protected from anything unsavoury. No one even truly explained to me when Melisande killed herself, and ever after that my father kept me from the world Melisande had known. He became hard and unfeeling almost, making me practise hours which no one could endure. So, you see, I know nothing really of what went on between my sister and Vania.'

'He toyed with her, as he toys with everyone – as he toyed with me. He left me for Melisande.'

'I'm sorry.'

'Oh, I can talk of it now, for it is past, and my feelings for him have mellowed into fond toleration. He comes to me, you know, to confide, to ask advice, to smile and talk a while, and I do all I can for him because he is Vania. Who can control or expect to control a free spirit like his?' Monique's eyes went up to the heights of Southwark Cathedral, but she did not seem to be really seeing it. 'Vania is everything and nothing, if you understand me. A hollow soul, but a great soul. You will know what I mean in the end. For the moment, you will experience the greatness in him; you will respond to it, admire it, be struck dumb almost by it – and then the disillusionment will come as the other side of him reveals itself. The pattern is the same, always it's the same. When he smiles at you, you will be drawn like a pin to a magnet, like a moth to a flame, for when he chooses he can be irresistible.'

'No. No one is irresistible,' said Nonna, determined that from this night onwards that would be the way of it for her.

Monique laughed. 'Oh, Nonna, Nonna, the folly of even thinking that.'

'I will not give in again, Monique, not to anyone.'

'Especially not Sir Philip Hastings?'

Nonna looked at the girl's shadowy face across the dark interior of the old carriage. 'Especially not him.'

'If it were not in bad taste, I would lay odds on my being right,' smiled the French girl.

Nonna was forced to smile herself. 'Well, it will not arise, will it? It will never arise. Is this your house?'

'Yes, a nice little backwater far away from the Opera House and all that that entails.'

Nonna climbed down and looked up at the narrow front of the old house. It stretched up for three storeys, but had only one window on each storey. In the darkness it was impossible to say anything more about it, but from the taverns nearby there came the sound of drunken singing, and two men were staggering along the pavement towards the carriage.

Monique hurriedly paid the postboy, who kicked his horses away swiftly before the men approached, and Monique and Nonna hurried up the steps to the door and into the safety of the house.

A black and white cat rubbed around their skirts, purring

with pleasure. 'Hello, Minette, did you miss me?' said Monique, bending to scoop the delighted cat into her arms. 'And how are your kittens, eh? Fat and round?'

The cat purred more loudly and Nonna smiled. It was a homely scene and, as Monique had said, a quiet backwater. For the moment, just for the moment, Nonna wanted to get away from the day, from everything about it.

9

The fact that the New Opera House had acquired James Lambert's second daughter caused quite a buzz over London, the *monde* and the newspapers speculating as to whether Nonna could possibly be another Melisande. The general consensus of opinion was that she could not. As Philip had said, it was the fashion to worship Melisande's memory, and no one else was to be considered worthy of taking her place. The interest in Nonna moved inevitably on more than one plane. First that she was James Lambert's daughter, trained and instructed by him; second that she was Melisande's sister and therefore to be judged on that fact. But the third, more gossip-worthy reason for the interest was that she was working with Vania, Melisande's lover. Would Nonna, like her dead sister, become the dancer's mistress? London waited for news of when Nonna would make her debut on the stage, biding its time and its final judgement, and Vania added fuel to the interest by paying constant and flattering attention.

One person resented all this instantly and audibly: Catrine. Her malice was everywhere for Nonna – from the ballet pumps which were always missing, to the grease on the floor where she had to practise and the unrest caused by the unpleasant things Nonna was supposed to have said about the other members of the company.

It was very hard for Nonna to weather all these pressures. Every moment of her long hours of practice was scrutinised closely; eyes seemed to be on her all the time, assessing, comparing, wondering – she was not alone for a minute. She had the friendship of Milly and Monique, but the others hovered on the edge of resenting her presence. Who was *she* to come among them, enjoying Vania's personal tuition and attention when others who had been there longer had never been noticed by him for one hour let alone the many he spent with her? It was like being on trial all the time, her long days like walking a tightrope as she tried not to offend anyone, deliberately holding back and not thrusting herself into prominence. She would *earn* her place! The strain began to tell after a few weeks, though. Hour after hour of standing at the bar, going over and over the set patterns and routines, and enduring the other tensions too, made her feel that she had been stretched until she was about to snap.

And behind it all, refusing to be pushed to the back of her thoughts, was the hopeless love she had for Philip Hastings. No amount of hard work could make her forget him – if she paused for the smallest moment, she found that she was thinking about him. At nights his face filled her dreams – he was everything she should loathe – arrogant, domineering, selfish, superior, and callous – but she loved him.

There was one other thing weighing on Nonna during those weeks – Josie. Nonna felt guilty about leaving her without a word, and she missed the girl's light, easy humour and company. She had Monique and Milly, but she badly missed Josie. And so she worked, never stopping, forcing herself to greater efforts all the time, trying to escape from everything by reaching towards perfection in her dancing.

It was Catrine who unintentionally caused the tide to turn in Nonna's favour – unintentionally indeed, for she had meant the very opposite to happen. The *Morning*

Chronicle had shown great interest in Nonna, most of it unkind, and the reason for the unkindness was an expert on ballet named Jean-Pierre Coty. Monsieur Coty had once been publicly rebuffed and ridiculed by Melisande, and he was now the enemy of any Lambert. Nonna was no exception. He had asked Richard Langley if he could come to see Nonna, and had been refused – and so Catrine went to see Coty at his home. Her dressing-room window opened on to a small alley behind the Opera House, she said, she could leave that window open and smuggle him into the Opera House and he could see for himself what Nonna's skill amounted to – if he wished, of course. Coty accepted her suggestion, and late one morning when it was dull and rainy, he climbed into Catrine's dressing-room and she led him secretly to the room where Nonna was practising.

It was dark, the clouds making everything shadowy, and Nonna stood at the bar, her eyes closed as she went over some steps time and time again. Her whole body ached from head to toe, and she felt that she could indeed have done everything in her sleep. She didn't hear the door open behind her or see the two figures creep in to hide behind a wicker screen which served to shield the room from draughts. She knew nothing of their presence, but the coolness of the air from the passageway swept over her, and she paused, shivering as it touched her warm, damp skin. How long had she been standing here? Two hours? Three? She didn't know anything except that she was unbearably tired. She took a deep breath. She was James Lambert's daughter, she wouldn't give up!

The door opened suddenly. 'Nonna?' It was Vania.

She turned, and at that moment he saw the two behind the screen, Coty busy making notes. '*Qui êtes-vous*?' demanded Vania suspiciously. 'Why hide like a felon, eh? *Allez-vous en maintenant*!'

Coty closed his notebook, stepping from his hiding place, and Vania recognised him. 'Coty! The *Morning Chronicle's* little *chasseur*.' Vania's large blue eyes moved coldly to Catrine. '*Chienne*!'

'Armand,' she began.

'*Taisez-vous*! Get out, both of you!' As Coty tried to slip past, Vania reached out swiftly and snatched the notebook away. 'You will print nothing bad about her, *chasseur*!'

'My memory will serve me well, Vania!' snapped the other angrily.

'So will mine, Coty, so will mine. One word, *one* word and I will remember certain things in your past – like the time you tried to creep into Melisande's bedroom uninvited and had to be thrown out bodily into the street! You take your spite out on Nonna and I will scream about you in all the other papers, do you hear me, *chasseur*?'

Coty hesitated, his thin face and sharp eyes caught in the light from the passageway. 'I hear you,' he said after a moment.

'So, not one word, eh? *D'accord*?'

'*D'accord.*' Shaking his arm free of Vania's hand the man went out into the passage.

Vania looked at Catrine then, and she stepped back, but not swiftly enough. He slapped her cheek once, the sound cracking through the room.

'*Je n'ai rien fait*!' she whimpered, tears springing to her dark eyes.

'You've done nothing? You bitch! You brought him here to do more damage to Nonna!' cried Vania. 'If I hear one more thing that you've done, Catrine, I will have nothing more to do with you. *Nothing*!'

She stared miserably at him. 'Armand. . . .'

'I mean it. One more thing, Catrine. You knew exactly what Coty would write about her; he is more the bitch than you.' Vania nodded at the door. 'Go – and do not cross me again!'

Her large eyes searched his angry face for a moment and then she went out, and he kicked the door closed behind her.

Nonna stood by the bar. She was shaking, and when he crossed the room to her, his hand held out, she took it immediately. She tried not to cry, but after everything else in the past weeks, this last thing was too much. His finger-tips touched her cheek gently, and then he pulled her into his arms. 'Oh, my Nonna,' he murmured. '*Ma petite.*'

'I'm sorry, I shouldn't cry.'

'I have been a bear to you, making you work so hard, eh?' He put his hand to her cheek and made her look up. 'It has been difficult for you, hasn't it? So much work, so much bad feelings?'

'I should have expected it.'

His thumb caressed her very softly. 'And I should have looked after you,' he whispered, bending his head to kiss her.

She moved away. 'No – no, don't. . . .'

'But why? You are. . . .'

'I am Melisande's sister.' She looked at him. 'But I am not her, Monsieur.'

'I know. I know – but you are so like her that I cannot help myself but want you, my Nonna.'

She stared at him. 'I came here to dance, Monsieur, and I will reach for whatever I can on my own merits – not because I am like my sister, and not because you have a conscience.'

He leaned back against the bar, his arms folded across his chest. He wore a white shirt which was unbuttoned almost to his waist, and his skin was pale and smooth. He smiled. 'Vania has a conscience? Mm?'

'Haven't you?' She lowered her eyes. 'Forgive me, I shouldn't have said anything like that.'

He reached out and caught her hand, pulling her close again. 'You are right, my Nonna, I have a conscience. I must put right everything in the past.'

'Your conscience should be clear then,' she said quickly, 'for you have given me my chance to dance here. I ask no more of you, Monsieur.'

He laughed, and she knew that he was intrigued by her resistance. 'No more? My Nonna, you must know how much more I can do for you than this, you are no fool. I *want* to do more for you, I *want* to help you – I want *you*.'

But I don't want you. As a dancer he was superb, gifted and unequalled – but as a man she did not want him. He could be charming, he could make her smile and he could even wring her heart sometimes with his expressive eyes, but she knew him for what he was: a spoilt genius. Had he not been a dancer, he would have been the world's finest actor.

He pulled her close, pressing her against his body. 'My Nonna, it could be so good, you and me.'

'No, Monsieur.'

'Please say Armand. Nonna, is it because you blame me for what happened? Please tell me that that is not so.' The blue eyes were anxious, and he ran his finger lightly over her red hair.

'I don't blame you. How can I when I know nothing about it anyway?'

'I did not understand how she felt, my Nonna,' he whispered, 'I did not understand. I would not have hurt her had I realised. Please believe me.'

She looked up. 'I believe you. Yes, I *do* believe you – Armand.'

His lips were warm as he kissed her, and the kiss became more urgent. He held her so tightly that she could hardly breathe, but she didn't want him – she didn't want him. She pushed away then, breathless. 'Please, please don't. I admire you, as the greatest dancer the world has seen, but I don't. . . .'

He laughed incredulously. 'You don't want me? You don't want *Vania*?'

'No. I don't.' She met his gaze.

He scratched his forehead, grinning disbelievingly. 'This is my – what is that word I have heard to describe it? My *comeuppance*? No, I will not accept my defeat, Nonna, I will *win* you then, I shall lay siege to your cold heart.' He waved his hand expressively, still smiling. 'And why not begin now, eh? I came here to ask you to drive with me in Hyde Park – you will come?'

'I should practise some more yet.'

'Practise too much and you will be as bad as if you had not practised at all. Come, agree to go with me. Your English fair-play must at least give me a *chance* to win you.'

'All right. Yes, I would like to drive with you.'

'*Eh bien*, I shall await you in an hour's time.'

'Yes, in an hour's time.'

He took her face in his hands. 'And do not worry about Catrine; she will not dare to harm you again, eh? I *shall* win you in the end, my Nonna. No one, *no one* turns Vania down, especially not you, *ma petite*. You meant one thing to me when first you came, I admit it, but now that is changed and you mean so much more. I shall take you to my bed, to my heart, and I shall never let you go. Never!'

The door closed softly behind him, and she stood in the empty room for a moment before going to the chair where she had left her shawl.

Milly smiled. 'So, Catrine went too far at last.'

'It was awful, Milly.'

The little dresser nodded. 'But at least there is one thing good in it, everyone here is on your side now. They don't like her, you see – she's so overbearing and unkind, and she was always so sure of Vania which made her formidable to cross. Now she doesn't have him any more, she will have to tread more carefully. It was a bad mistake of hers, bringing that little ferret here like that. She was a fool. Vania is already irritated by her because she tries constantly to win him back, she's like a little fly buzzing round him all the time. He'll swat her, you mark my words.' Milly made an expressive crushing noise and stamped the imaginary fly into the floor.

Nonna laughed. 'After the last few weeks enduring her spite I almost wish he would. Still, if she'll just stay away from me from now on, that's all I want.'

Milly paused. 'Yes, that is all you want isn't it? You *don't* want Vania, do you?'

'No.'

'That will be a new experience for him. Usually he crooks

his little finger and they all come running to his bed. I look forward to the chase, Nonna, I most *certainly* look forward to it.'

'Oh, stop it, Milly, you make it sound like a circus.'

'It will be just that. Vania does nothing by halves, Nonna – he exists by the grand gesture, the dramatic, the exquisitely poetic touch. I think he could out-Byron Byron, eh? Yes, Vania will make a good meal of pursuing you, Nonna Lambert, you mark my words.'

'He won't win.'

'Barrymore's is where the *monde* go to lay their wagers, Nonna, but we here have somewhere less exalted. Hanmill's Tea Rooms.' Milly grinned. 'And the odds will favour Vania.'

Wagers. Always wagers, even here. Was it to be her lot in life to have people laying bets upon her virginity? Nonna went on dressing as Milly went out. Suddenly she was looking at another face reflected in Monique's mirror: Catrine.

The ballerina closed the door and stood looking at Nonna, her dark red costume glowing in the light of the oil-lamp which lit the dark little room.

'Catrine?' Nonna turned slowly.

'I have been warned to stay away from you, and so I will. After this.'

'Catrine, I don't want any trouble with you, *please*.'

'You think you are so clever, eh? First you destroy me – and then Armand. Oh, don't look so innocent, you have practised that innocence until it is almost believable. Armand believes it, but I do not! I know why you have come here – it is to take revenge for Melisande. Already you have made Armand hate me; he hates me so much that he will have me sent from the Opera House!'

'I don't know anything about that, Catrine, and I haven't come here for anything except dancing!'

'You don't know anything! Little Nonna, *sweet* little Nonna. You have crawled in here, curling like the snake you are. If it was not for revenge, why did you come in that yellow dress on the night of the gala, eh?' Catrine studied Nonna carefully, and when there was no reply, she laughed triumphantly. 'See? You cannot answer, for there *is* no answer but the truth. You want to punish me and punish Armand Vania for Melisande's death! And that Sir Philip will help you because he has no liking, no respect for Vania!'

Nonna took a long breath. 'Catrine, you are wrong about me, I do not want revenge. And as to Sir Philip's reason for bringing me here, it was to entice you into his bed and thereby win a wager of ten thousand guineas! *That* was his reason – monetary gain.'

Catrine stared at her. 'I – I do not believe you,' she whispered.

'Don't then – no doubt you would refuse to believe anything I said or did because you hate me so much. Now, if you please, do as Vania says and stay away from me. Get out!' Nonna turned back to the mirror, picking up her bonnet and tying the ribbons with studied care. She saw Catrine go out and the door closed.

She sat down, feeling weak at the force of Catrine's hatred. But what had she meant? Punish them *both* for Melisande's death? Vania she could understand, but why Catrine too?

At that moment Monique came in for her afternoon rehearsal, and she was chattering about the weather. The rain and clouds had gone and it was a bright sunny day outside now.

'Monique? You came from France with Vania, and you were here when Melisande was here, weren't you? I mean, you said you lost him to Melisande, and then *she* lost him to Catrine?'

'Yes.' Monique put her reticule and gloves down slowly. 'Why?'

'So, you must know exactly what happened?'

'Not *exactly*, Nonna. I know as much as anyone who was there at the time.'

'What had Catrine to do with it all?'

Monique sat down. 'Ah, Catrine. So she has been in here?'

'Yes. *Did* she have something to do with my sister's death?'

'Yes and no. Please, Nonna, do not think Catrine *murdered* her or anything like that, it wasn't so at all. I will tell you; I see that I must or your imagination will take you spinning away foolishly. The moment Catrine came to the Opera House she fell in love with Vania. He was already tiring of Melisande – forgive me, Nonna, but it is how it happens always with him, we all know the signs. He was tiring of her, but not quickly enough to suit Catrine. She wanted him desperately, both as a lover and as her partner in the ballet. She was here to take Melisande's place if Melisande was ill, and one day she saw to it that Melisande's morning coffee was a drink to make her very sick so that she would not be able to dance. Melisande *was* taken ill, but she still came to dance that night; and Catrine had been flattering Vania all that day, teasing him, adoring him, making much of him in the way he loves so very much. When Melisande appeared, Vania was miffed. He was persuaded now that Catrine was the ballerina he wanted to dance with that night and – and so he was cruel to Melisande. He can be so cruel, my poor Vania.

'Melisande went away – she had no choice. But no one realised how much she loved him, not even I knew it, or Milly. No one knew until the next morning, when news of her death was brought. Catrine had spent the night with Vania, and it was the only night she spent with him for a very, very long time. She was distraught with guilt, thinking at first that her dosing of the coffee had killed Melisande – but it was laudanum, we discovered. So much laudenum. Vania was guilty too; I have never seen him so upset about anything before, and I've been with him for longer than anyone. He couldn't dance for months. He turned to me – not for loving, but for understanding, he always comes back to me for that.' Monique smiled wryly. 'He *was* upset, Nonna. I think it was the first time he saw the results of his selfish ways – he *knew* he had much to answer for. But he *did* suffer, Nonna, believe me. They both did. It was three years before Catrine won him back. She worked hard to gain his love again and she's held it until now. Until you. It is – poetic justice, eh? That she should lose him to Melisande's sister?'

Nonna looked away. 'Maybe, except that I don't love him, Monique. Anyone must know that.'

'She's jealous and jealousy blinds. She thinks you are playing a very clever game to win him.'

'No, she doesn't, Monique, she thinks I'm here to be avenged for what happened to Melisande. She thinks I am beavering to have her thrown out of the Opera House and that I then intend breaking his heart.'

Monique stared. 'Such foolishness! It is her *guilt* making her think that! As to her being thrown out – well, yes, there is something in that, but it is nothing to do with you. It's Vania. She makes scenes and unpleasantnesses for him. Nonna, *never* be awkward to him, it's the one thing he cannot abide. He rids himself of awkwardness, and I know he's been trying to think of something. The signs are there, always the signs are there with him. I can read him like a book. But now' – Monique held out her hands and drew Nonna to her feet – 'now I hear you are to drive with Vania in Hyde Park. Forget Catrine, she's just trying to get him back again, and it's a part she knows very well by now.'

'I don't even want him.'

'I know, you want that Sir Philip Hastings. You English are mad.'

'I'm half-Italian.'

'That's even worse!' laughed Monique, tying Nonna's ribbons again. 'There, off with you now, and don't worry. And Nonna – ?'

'Yes?'

'Do not think badly of Vania. He is doing what he can for you because of Melisande – you know that, don't you?' Monique's grey eyes were anxious. 'I said that I no longer love him, but I do. I can't ever have him again, but that makes no difference. He is still Armand, still the young dancer I loved in Paris.'

Nonna went to her, hugging her. 'I know, Monique,' she whispered.

Vania's purple landau was as well known in the streets of London as the Prince Regent's phaeton once had been. It had bright yellow wheels and was drawn by a team of six white horses, each one bang up to the mark in every way. The footmen and coachman had purple livery, and the whole equipage made a splendid sight as it turned into Hyde Park to join the daily parade. It was a sunny summer afternoon, with blue skies and brilliant sunshine dappling and flashing through the trees.

Every gentleman doffed his hat to the conspicuous landau, and the ladies smiled. A crowd of noisy little boys ran behind shouting the dancer's name. Vania basked in his popularity, and his enjoyment of all the attention was so infectious that Nonna found herself getting almost as much pleasure from the drive as he was.

The landau swayed to a standstill as the traffic grew too great for the track. As it moved on, Vania looked at her suddenly. 'Catrine has to go.'

'Oh? But surely. . . .'

'She is dancing poorly, and she irritates me.' He smiled at her. 'I will not dance with her any more, I have decided.'

Nonna looked from the window quickly. It was like hearing an echo as he said what Catrine and Monique had predicted. There was no point in trying to talk him out of it – he had made up his mind and didn't want to be talked out of it.

Suddenly, through the window she saw a face that she recognised. Josie! Nonna twisted forward to look at the bench where Josie sat, a dainty figure in cream dimity and an enormous hat laden with crimson ostrich feathers. But Josie didn't look up at the purple carriage as it passed, one of the very few who paid it no heed.

Vania's eyebrow rose as he saw her looking stubbornly

the other way. Nonna knew Josie was doing it to annoy the vain dancer; she sensed it immediately, for that was just what Josie *would* do.

'Nonna, you – you *know* that person?' he asked curiously.

She sat back, sensing his immediate displeasure. 'No!' she said quickly, 'no, she just looked like someone I know, that's all.' Even as she spoke she was ashamed of herself. Josie was her friend, her good friend, and the guilty conscience over leaving her was bad enough already without denying her altogether.

'I trust you would *not* know a Cyprian like that, my Nonna, for that would not be the thing, eh? No, not at all.'

'No. It wouldn't.'

They drove on through the park, and she knew that she could not carry on without making some attempt at putting things right with Josie. She glanced at her fob-watch – maybe Josie always walked in the park at this time now. *Maybe if I sat on that bench again.* Yes, she decided, that was what she would do, she would wait on that bench and hope that Josie would come.

She looked out at the other carriages. Already she had recognised several of the gentlemen from Madame's – Lord Ryan for one. He sat in his beige barouche with his ugly hook-nosed wife. He fawned over her too, making much of her – what a double life he led. At Madame's he had attempted to purchase the favours of the Masked Lady, but when he was out with his wealthy wife he would have cut dead anyone from Madame's. Double lives and double standards, nothing was honest and above-board. Nonna bit her lip, for was not she herself employing those double standards now by denying Josie?

Vania caught her attention suddenly. '*There* is a face to remember, my Nonna,' he said, indicating a black chaise moving along an adjacent track. 'Robert Wyndham, the manager of the Pegasus Theatre. Mark him well, for he is the rival, the *only* rival of note. The Pegasus sets itself up to challenge the Opera House, and sometimes it comes close.

It would come closer if Wyndham were given his head, but they restrict him – thank the Lord, eh? He is better than Langley, but Langley is ours, Wyndham is the enemy.'

'The rival and the enemy – and *your* secret weapon, Armand?' she said, smiling, as she watched the fat man in the other carriage.

Vania laughed. 'But of course, I must keep Langley on his toes. No one should take Vania for granted. But now, you are enjoying the drive, Nonna?'

'Oh, yes.'

'You would enjoy every moment if you came to my side.'

She flushed. 'Maybe.'

'You love someone else?'

'No!'

'You deny it too swiftly, my Nonna. Who is he, this man who keeps you from me?'

'There is no one.'

He smiled, indicating the passing carriages. 'A Hyde Park display of fashionable feathers, eh?' he said, changing the subject.

'Yes.'

'A grand sight, a continuous mating season, everyone preening and showing off their finery. I see the look in your eye, my Nonna – is that not what Vania is doing too, you are thinking?'

She was forced to smile then, for it was exactly what she had been thinking.

He grinned. 'But Vania *is* fine and worth showing off, eh? A more beautiful creature there never was.'

How much he was joking and how much he really believed it could only be guessed. But then his smile faded. 'Maybe I am not so perfect, though.' He took some papers from his pocket and thrust them into her hands. 'See? Vania has one fatal flaw – he gambles his fortune away at the hazard tables.'

She stared at the sums involved. 'But. . . .'

'Even I cannot afford this? You are right, of course. But I cannot help it – it is a compulsion which will not be denied.'

'Refuse it, then.'

'Refuse compulsion? Impossible. You have obviously never experienced anything like it. One night of glory was my ruin, for it has been followed by endless weeks of ignominy. Soon I will be dancing to pay off my debts – now *there* is dishonour for you.'

'Will you be forced to flee to Europe too then? Like Brummell?'

'Ah, my friend Beau. Poor George, he too was perfect and with a disastrous flaw which was his undoing, eh?'

'I wish I had just seen him once.'

'If he thought you'd noticed him, he'd have died of shame that he stood out so. He told me that if a gentleman was noticed, it was because he dressed in poor taste. Real taste passes unnoticed because it is perfection. Ah, will London ever see his like again, eh?'

'Was he – was he *odd*?'

Vania smiled at her. 'Very. He could live without women, and to me that is not merely odd, it is eccentric in the extreme. Oh, George Brummell was very odd – but how far he took the oddness I do not know. Is that what you mean? Did he have lovers of his own sex?'

She felt uncomfortable. It had been what she meant, but she knew that it was considered unladylike ever to mention such things.

Vania looked out of the window. 'Maybe he was, I do not know – he never made a pass at Vania, eh?' He laughed. 'Maybe it was because he did not like fair hair! Brummell and Byron, both leaders of fashion in London society, and as you say – both *odd*. Vania is not odd though, which one day will be proved to you. Ah, how you blush, my sweet Nonna, but I will win you, that I promise you. And I care nothing for this other man you love so secretly. No one holds a candle to Vania.'

She said nothing, conscious of the warmth in his gaze as he looked at her. He sat forward suddenly and took her hands, but she removed them quickly. He smiled. 'One thing you will have to learn about Vania, Nonna – he never knows when the battle is lost.'

'I like you, Monsieur, but I do not want. . . .'

'Entanglement? Well, maybe you are right to be so firm. Dancing must be free of inhibition, eh? And your dancing is so beautiful, is it not? You will be better than Melisande, I see it already in your movements, in the grace and skill, in the ability you have to *act* what you dance. It is not every dancer who can do that. You will be queen of London, my Nonna. And of Vania's heart too.'

She was glad that the moment was broken by the noisy shouts of some young bucks crowded dangerously on to one curricle. They waved their hats at Vania's carriage and the dancer could not resist leaning out to wave back. Nonna watched him. What had Philip called him? A one-man mass of self-conceit. Cruel, but true maybe. And if it was true of Vania, so also in its way was it true of Sir Philip Hastings!

10

Langley tapped the paper on his baize-topped desk. 'Your contract, Miss Lambert.'

Her hand was shaking as she picked it up. A contract at the Opera House! 'But – but I haven't danced yet, Mr Langley – how do you know how good I am?'

'Vania says you are and that is sufficient.'

She smiled. 'He also says Catrine is bad.'

Langley nodded wearily. 'I know, I know. But Vania is necessary to the Opera House, Miss Lambert. His wants are the Opera House's wants – *ergo* you have your contract.'

She flushed at the obvious implication he put in his

words. He thought this was her reward for sleeping with Vania. She dipped the pen in the ink and wrote her name at the foot of the contract.

He sanded it. 'You dance tonight, Miss Lambert.'

'Tonight? But. . . .'

'Tonight.'

'Yes, Mr Langley.'

'Vania insists that you dance *The Moonbeam* with him. Nothing else will do, so you had better make sure you are step-perfect, hadn't you?'

'I am step-perfect, Mr Langley,' she said coldly, disliking him.

He grunted. 'How much influence have you with Vania, Miss Lambert?'

'None.'

'Come now.'

'I said none and that is what I meant.' She met his gaze squarely.

'So, this chitter-chatter about you holding out on him is true then? God above, he must wonder what's hit him!' Langley smiled suddenly, taking a decanter from a cupboard and pouring himself a liberal glass of whisky. 'So you cannot try to persuade him against all this gambling?'

'No.'

'Pity. His blasted creditors have taken to leaning on *me* now and it ain't good enough. However, no doubt we'll survive, eh? But I tell you this, Miss Lambert, unless he curbs his gambling, things will soon come to a pretty pass – a *pretty* pass. He'll need one hell of a Benefit next season if he's to take care of these – er – problems.'

'Can I go now?'

'Please do, Miss Lambert, please do.' He drank the whisky in what seemed like one gulp, holding his breath and screwing his face up as the spirit went down his throat. 'By God, some times there are when a man needs to get drunk! Now I have to tell Vania that I can*not* get rid of Catrine for him because she too has a contract! He won't like it, not one little bit.'

Nonna waited in the wings, looking out at the royal box, which was empty tonight. She felt sick and her mouth tasted as she would imagine the bottom of a bird's nest to taste. Monique put her arm around her shivering shoulders.

'First-night nerves?'

'Yes. I'm sure I'm going to be sick!'

'No you aren't!' said Monique firmly.

'Am I good enough to dance yet, Monique? I made such a mess of my practice this afternoon.'

'Vania says you are. He is going to dance with you out there, Nonna. So he *must* be sure there is no risk of you not dancing well enough.'

Nonna adjusted her dainty headdress again, arranging each tiny silver garland. Then she fiddled with the folds of light gauze on her gown, and Monique smiled. 'You'll begin to restitch it soon! There, that's the end of the first part of the concert!'

Applause broke out in the auditorium as the curtain dropped. The chorus hurried off the stage, chattering excitedly together, and then Nonna could hear the audience coughing, clearing throats, murmuring like a huge beehive. She felt cold. And hot. And so very sick.

Langley came towards the wings, stopping in front of Nonna. 'You aren't dancing after all. Vania is in a miff because I cannot oust Catrine, and he refuses to dance *anything* tonight!'

Nonna didn't know whether to laugh or cry. She had screwed herself up to such a pitch of nerves that now the reason for her state had been removed she felt deflated, as if someone had pushed a pin into her.

Langley smiled. '*C'est la vie*, Miss Lambert. *La vie* and Armand Vania. If you feel bad, think then of me – *I* have to go out and tell the audience that there is to be no further performance tonight. Sometimes, sometimes I wonder if life is worth it, Miss Lambert, truly I do.' Sighing wearily, he went back on the stage, and Monique led Nonna back to the dressing room. The audience's displeasure echoed through the theatre – feet stamping; catcalling and whistling.

As they passed Vania's dressing room, the door opened suddenly and Catrine came out in tears, her face red and angry. She glared at Nonna for a moment and then ran down the corridor to her own room. Vania looked out and saw Nonna, and he smiled, taking her hand and drawing her into the room, leaving Monique outside.

'My Nonna, you must forgive me for tonight. You should have danced and I have been a bear to you again, eh?' He touched her headdress gently.

'It doesn't matter, Monsieur.'

'Armand. But it does matter, that I should be a bear to *you* when I love you so. So, I must make amends, *non*? Tonight we shall dine together. No, no, I will not hear a refusal, not tonight when I wish to be in your good books again.'

'But—'

'We dine.'

The dining room of the fashionable Bond Street hotel was candlelit, with only one of the many chandeliers ablaze in the very centre of the large room. There was a humidity in the air, and a smell of food and cigars, and an orchestra played discreetly at the far end as Nonna and Vania were shown to a table in one corner.

She sat down, arranging her gold silk gown carefully. She still found it hard to accept the daring necklines of the latest fashions; it felt almost as if she wore a skirt and nothing else, she thought, especially when Vania's eyes returned time and time again to the décolletage.

He smiled. 'You are so very beautiful, my Nonna, how I should have liked to dance with you tonight. But it was not to be, eh? Catrine has a contract which states that she and I dance at least twice a week together. She was insisting that tonight should be one of those occasions. I will not be forced into anything, so *I* do not dance and that sorts her out, eh? She must go, she is interfering with my dancing and that must not be allowed. I – I offered to buy her contract for a vast sum.'

'You did *what*!'

'I will buy her off, is that not the expression? Somehow or other I will be rid of her, and then we may dance. Her contract is not to be renewed after this season – or at least, she can dance in the chorus, I have no objection to that.'

Nonna fell silent, glad that the head waiter came at that moment to take their order. She stared as Vania ordered a gargantuan feast more suited to a party of six than a mere couple. And three bottles of wine. *Three*? She pulled her Kashmere shawl around her shoulders, sipping the sherry which was placed before her.

Vania ate heartily, talking non-stop. He thought that he had succeeded in defeating Catrine, and was exultant about it. His favourite topic was himself – always himself, she thought, fascinated by him. He smiled and nodded at just about everyone in the room, and everyone without fail returned the salute. Vania, as he so often said, was Vania.

When the veal and mushroom pie arrived, Nonna was already so full she thought she would not need to eat for another week. She had eaten sole, reindeers' tongues and hodge-podge, and this last course was just too much. She pushed it around the plate from time to time, toying with the stem of her wine glass. Vania's appetite was amazing; how could he eat like this and yet still remain lithe and graceful?

When he had finished the pie and then drunk two more glasses of wine, Vania was in a merry mood, beaming now instead of merely smiling. A noisy group of admiring gentlemen descended upon the table, and he was absolutely delighted. He seemed to forget Nonna altogether, and she sat quietly, watching him virtually wallow in the praise and flattery. He couldn't help it, she thought, smiling a little, he was Vania – the very greatest in the world, and *so* charming and delightful to be with when he wished. Knowing all that, though, she was staggered into immobility when he suddenly got up and left the hotel with his admirers, so carried away by the adulation that he forgot her existence altogether. She sat there, stunned and embarrassed. What should she do? She hadn't enough money with her to pay the bill *or* get herself back to Southwark.

'Deserted, Nonna?'

She looked up. Her heart almost stopped, for it was Philip who stood there smiling down at her. After dreaming and longing for him over the weeks, seeing him was like a shock, a current of something painful passing over her. She smiled nervously. 'I – yes, Sir Philip, it would seem that I am.'

'I will attend to the bill, provided you promise to join William and myself for some coffee.'

She glanced across the room at the table he indicated. William Lamb sat there and he raised his liqueur, smiling. They had obviously been there all the time – how had she not seen them? 'Sir Philip, perhaps Mr Lamb has no wish to sit with me?'

'Not sit with the Opera House's latest dazzler? Not sit with the woman the papers have rattled about? How could he not? And if you do not join us, you will run the risk of Marcel's Gallic fury descending upon you when you cannot pay the inevitably stupendous bill.'

She looked at the empty wine bottles and the remains of the meal, her mind racing. Common sense and self-protective defences told her not to join them, but hearing his voice and seeing his face again robbed her of both qualities. 'I would rather not have Marcel berate me in public, that is true.'

'Then join us,' he said softly, smiling at her as if he knew exactly what thoughts had passed transiently through her mind.

Slowly she stood. 'Sir Philip, does Mr Lamb know about me? The truth, I mean?'

'No. He knows only that you are the daughter of James Lambert, that you are the woman whose name has graced the newspapers these past weeks – but that is all. He visited the Opera House earlier tonight, as did half the *monde* to see you dance, and was as disappointed as everyone else not to see you. No, Nonna, *no one* knows any more about you than that, I swear to you.'

'I must trust you again?' she murmured, smiling faintly.

'Why not? Have I proved *un*trustworthy yet?'

She met his eyes. 'No.'

'Then you agree to join us?'

'Yes.'

He took her hand and drew it through his arm. His touch was like a fire running through her, but she didn't show it as she walked across the dining-room with him. He paused to speak to the head waiter, Marcel, then took her on to the table where William Lamb stood waiting.

'Ah, William, I have captured our prize, eh? Allow me to introduce the lady everyone wishes to know, Miss Nonna Lambert. Nonna, William Lamb.'

'Sir.' She curtsied.

'Miss Lambert. I confess that I was in an ill humour at not seeing you dance earlier, but now I am more than recompensed by meeting you.' William took her hand and kissed it. His hand was large and firm, and his smile so gentle and kind that she could only like him instantly.

Close to she could understand only too well why Josie loved this man so much. He was handsome, dark and warm, and there was an air of melancholy about him which would surely catch even the hardest female heart. As Madame had said, William Lamb, with all his well-publicised problems, was devastatingly attractive.

She took her seat and he sat down too. 'So, Miss Lambert, your family name graces the Opera House again?'

'Yes – well, it *will*, I promise you, Mr Lamb.'

'And when it finally does – you will remember me and send me a ticket?' He smiled. 'That is, I will come if I am still in the land of the sane by then.' – Nonna looked puzzled. He laughed bitterly.

'Don't tell me that I am speaking to the one person in the

realm who *hasn't* read my wife's dreadful book?'

'Book, Mr Lamb?'

'It rejoices under the name of *Glenarvon*.'

'No, I haven't read it.'

He smiled again. 'Then I feel I may approach you as one human being to another.'

Philip grinned then. 'Come now, William, Caro's stab in the back isn't fatal.'

'It may as well have been for all the sympathy I've had from society, Philip. I'm accused of having connived at it.'

'No one believes *that* surely?'

'Some do. The painful and embarrassing truth that I didn't know *any* damn thing about the book until it was on the streets doesn't seem to have occurred to many. Forgive me, Miss Lambert, but I am enduring intolerable notoriety at the moment because of my wife's activities.'

'I know. I don't believe for one moment that you had anything to do with it, Mr Lamb,' she replied, sympathising immediately.

'The book, Miss Lambert, lambastes my friends, my associates, and my family, and I have a leading role in it as the destroyer of my wife's innocence. Not for the first time since its publication have I wished that I was dead!'

Nonna smiled at him. 'What a loss that would be to us all, Mr Lamb.'

'You are too kind, Miss Lambert.'

Philip poured her a cup of thick Turkish coffee, glancing at William. 'My friend, stop shovelling the pathos on when you look at her. Your melting eyes look so sad I fancy she'll dissolve of pity in a moment. The situation you now find yourself in is entirely your own fault. If you had heeded my advice and separated from Caro, you'd be free now – instead she'll persecute you forever.'

'You never did like her, did you, Philip?'

'No – hysterical histrionics are not my idea of feminine qualities. Divorce her – for once I am in agreement with your family.'

'God forbid,' smiled William. His smile faded then as a

small party of newcomers arrived at the hotel. 'Sweet lord, that's all I need,' he murmured, 'Caro's damn blasted publisher!'

'Ignore him, William,' said Philip quickly.

'How *can* I! Because of him details of my damned marriage are common knowledge! That cursed book has been translated now – did you know that? The French and Germans can laugh at it over their *Frühstücks*!'

'Relax, my friend,' said Philip gently, but both he and Nonna were aware of the interest created in the room by the presence of both William Lamb and the publisher.

William shook his head and looked at Nonna. 'Forgive me, Miss Lambert, but even for your sweet company I cannot remain in the same room as that moronic fellow. I will leave you in Philip's care, but with great reluctance.' He stood, kissing her hand and nodding at Philip, before making his swift exit. The disappointment his departure caused was audible.

Philip sat back. 'You know poor William's story, I suppose?'

'His wife and Lord Byron? Yes, I know about it.'

'She is something William never ever deserved.'

'I like him.'

'The women always do – it's the large spaniel eyes, I fancy.' He glanced at her. 'What does your friend Josie have to say about him then?'

She sipped her coffee. 'She loves him – which is her misfortune, is it not?'

'Undoubtedly. It's foolish to *love* anyone.'

'How cynical you are.'

'I get what I want when I want it – what more is there to desire?'

'Oh, I *know* you always get your way, Sir Philip,' she said, thinking of Catrine and the ten thousand guineas.

'Do I detect a note of accusation, Nonna?'

'Should there be?'

'Fencing, Nonna?' he murmured softly.

'When I am taught I like to think I learn.'

'I wonder. Tell me, how is Vania treating you? Is to-night's episode standard practice?'

'I don't know, I haven't been out to dine with him before.'

'What *have* you done with him then?'

Her smile faded. 'That, sir, is my business.'

'Let me guess then.' He put his hand to her chin and stared into her eyes for a moment. 'You've done nothing, Nonna, there's still that God-damned virginal look about you.'

'And that is a sin in your eyes?'

'Maybe. You've had your opportunities and you've muffed them. I'm interested though – Vania must be slipping.'

'Might it interest you also to know that *I* am the one who is refusing?'

'You are running true to form. You don't want Vania, so who do you want then, Nonna?'

She flushed, looking away. Had she said his name aloud it could not have been more obvious, she thought, the embarrassed blush deepening.

He watched her for a moment, his eyes veiled. 'Shall I escort you home then?' he asked gently.

'There's no need.'

'I won't leave you to fend for yourself.'

She got up, knowing as she did so that she had given herself away to him completely; she could see it in his dark eyes as he looked at her. She knew too that if he chose now to take the matter any further, she would not resist at all.

They left the hotel, and as they stood waiting for his landau to be brought around, he drew her hand through his arm, turning her towards him. 'Nonna?' he said softly. Just her name, no more than that.

She closed her eyes as he kissed her lightly on the lips, and the air seemed to spin around her for a moment. She should resist, but she did not want to. Possessing him and being possessed by him was all that mattered to her, just this once, this one, short night. . . .

She did not remember much of the journey from Bond Street to Padenham Square; she seemed to float on air as she leaned against him. His clothes smelled of southernwood, and his skin was so warm as he kissed her. She had wondered how it would be to be courted by him, to have him speak lovingly, to kiss and hold him – and now, *now* it was happening! There was no thought in her head of any consequences, no thought of anything but him.

The moonlight flooded into his bedroom and the house was so quiet as she stood there facing him. His hands were gentle as he undid her gown. Every girl dreams of her first love, of giving herself for the first time; her imagination conjures up a handsome lover, a gentle, experienced lover who will give as much pleasure as he takes, who will consider her as much as he considers himself. As she lay naked on the bed and he made love to her, she knew that he was everything she had dreamed of – everything, except that he didn't love her. The joy and desire flowed through her, but he was still a dream which escaped her, a nuance which could not be trapped and held forever. She possessed him and yet she did not – she never would.

When she lay in his arms afterwards in the huge, velvet-hung bed, she knew all this. Her eyes were closed and the soporific drowsiness seeped through her still, drifting over and inside her like a balm. Nothing was altered by the giving, nothing made any difference – she knew she would have gone with him again. The lesson had not been learned.

But the master was set upon teaching. She heard his low laugh. 'Oh, Nonna, never wear your heart on your sleeve, never let anyone know the truth.'

'Why say it like that?'

'To warn you – you're a babe still, aren't you? Green and innocent.'

'Don't.'

He leaned on one elbow over her, looking at her face in the moonlight. 'I took something from you tonight, Nonna, which can *never* be replaced. I had my pleasure, amused myself out of idle curiosity, no more than that.'

She looked away, her fingers moving over his naked back. '*You* are the man who took from me, Philip, and that is all that matters.'

'Then you are a fool.'

'Maybe, but there is no man on this earth who matters to me as you do, you are the only man I want to lie with. You know that, I think you've always known it – as you say, I'm green, I can't hide my feelings as skilfully as you. I don't *want* to hide them from you, not from you.'

'I *used* you tonight, Nonna, where's your logic when you whisper of hiding nothing?'

'There's no logic in love.'

'There should be cold logic in everything!'

She smiled faintly. 'Your friend William would not agree with that.'

'He is a fool too.'

'Why sneer at everything? Why can't you be as trusting as you want others to be with you? Why set out to try and hurt me?'

'Because to be other than I am now is to give power to others, and no one shall have power over me, Nonna. No one. I'm my own master, I take, use, and then discard.'

'As you discarded Catrine? And as you will discard me?'

'Yes.'

The hurt cut through her like a hot knife, but she would not show it. 'Then I'm sorry for you,' she whispered, putting her hand against his cheek, 'for you will lose in the end, you and those like you.'

'And the meek shall inherit the earth?'

'Yes.'

He smiled at her. 'You really believe that, don't you?'

'Yes.'

His lips brushed hers briefly. 'Your innocence has a certain charm, I'll grant you that,' he murmured, flinging the sheet aside and getting out of the bed.

She watched his slender figure in the moonlight. How

pale and fine he was, the silver light making him almost frail. His lean face was in shadow, but the rest of him was so clear. Clear, pale and beautiful. She could not look away from him, for each moment that passed now brought her closer to leaving. Closer to losing. There was no pride in the way she felt, no room for self-respect. She loved this man, absolutely and completely. Oh, how completely now.

He turned suddenly. 'I go to Belvoir tomorrow.'

'Oh.'

'A house party. I don't know when I shall return. I will in all probability call upon you some time.'

'Don't bother,' she whispered, getting out of the bed. The cool detachment with which he spoke dispelled the memories, dispelled the pleasure.

He handed her her gown, fastening the hooks and eyes without a word. Then he smiled faintly. 'Would you still have done it now, Nonna?' he asked softly.

She slipped her arms around his neck and kissed his mouth, holding him tightly for a long moment. 'Yes,' she murmured, 'for God help me, I still love you, Philip Hastings. I trust I proved an entertaining plaything for the few hours it pleased you to toy with me.'

'You will cease to be entertaining if you recriminate with me,' he said abruptly.

She took her arms away slowly. 'Good bye, Philip Hastings,' she whispered.

'Good bye, Nonna.'

He sent her home in his carriage, and she sat alone on the luxurious seat. Her cheeks were wet with her tears, but she made no sound, no sound at all.

11

Josie halted, her pink parasol swinging to and fro as she stared at Nonna on the park bench. 'Well, well, hello stranger!'

'Hello, Josie.'

Josie remained standing. 'Out of work again?' There was a distinct coolness in her voice.

'No – I just wanted to see you again, that's all.'

'Well, you've seen me.'

'Oh, Josie, please don't be like this. I feel so guilty about leaving you without so much as a nod of the head!' cried Nonna, close to tears. After the previous night she had been miserable all day, and now she wanted Josie's friendship, not her enmity.

Josie hesitated. 'I thought you were all right, Nonna Park, but instead you were an ungrateful opportunist.'

'I went because Philip Hastings asked me too – wouldn't you go with William Lamb, Josie?'

For the first time there was a smile on the other's lips, a smile which broadened into a grin. 'Yes, reckon I would too.' Josie sat down, holding out a gloved hand. 'Friends again, eh?'

'Friends.'

'And how is the Untouchable Philip then? Not so untouchable any more?'

Nonna looked away. 'Yes and no to the last. To the first, he seems very well indeed to me.'

'But all's not smooth?'

'I left Madame's to go with him, hoping that he would

want me as I wanted him, but . . . . It's a long story, Josie, and if I tell you everything, will you promise to keep my secrets?'

'What sort of friend do you think I am? I didn't even tell that I knew you lodged at the Black Horse!'

Nonna smiled, leaning back on the bench watching the carriages passing. She began from the moment she had left the house in Jacob Street with Philip, and ended with telling where she had spent the previous night and Vania's distraught apologies that very morning before she had set out for the park.

Josie stared at her and when she finished there was a long, long silence. Josie took a long breath then. 'So that's where you learned to sing and dance – you're James Lambert's daughter. Well, fancy that! And *Vania* is in love with you?'

'I don't know about that, he's in love with Melisande's memory rather than the real Nonna Lambert.'

Josie smiled. 'And I'm furiously jealous to think that last evening you sat and dined with *my* William!'

'I had one cup of coffee in his exalted presence before he took off like a hare on seeing his wife's publisher come in.'

'And are you impressed with my taste?'

'Yes. Yes, Josie, I am.'

'But he's not a patch on Philip Hastings as far as you're concerned?'

'He's better than Philip, but it's Philip I love. Damn him!'

Josie smiled. 'You *still* do? Even after the way he behaved last night?'

'Yes, even after that. But I don't really want to talk about it. I feel foolish now that I think of all the soft things I said to him, professing undying love and so on.' Nonna toyed with her kid gloves, a dull stain colouring her cheeks. Foolish? She felt the world's greatest idiot in the cold light of the London afternoon – but still she loved him!

Josie put a hand over hers. 'My philosophy's the best one, you see. Life's too short to go making yourself miserable over a man. And if Vania is smitten with love for you, well – indulge him and yourself, Nonna Lambert. Forget the anguish of wanting a man like Philip Hastings. I know – easier said than done. But at least have a try, eh? And talking of being smitten, poor Justin moons around at Madame's, frittering away his father's fortune and asking constantly when the Masked Lady is coming back. Honestly, Nonna, I'm sure he is actually in love with you!'

'I don't think much of him, though.'

'He just can't take his drink, that's his problem. He's a two-bottle man trying to be a five-bottler.'

Nonna laughed then. 'Yes, that's just what he is, isn't it? Oh, Josie, I'm so pleased to see you again, truly I am.'

'The life and soul of it, that's me.'

'Rising above the sorrows of life?'

'What sorrows? There aren't any for me, Nonna. Anyway, I'd better go now, I've a gentleman coming early just to see me. A Duke no less – how's that for style?'

'I suppose I'd better go too. I'm going to a gaming house tonight with Vania – he begged me to, he practically got down on his bended knee imploring me to go with him so that he would know he was forgiven for last night.'

'And is he?'

'Oh, I don't know, I never know what to think where he's concerned. I've never met anyone quite like him before.'

'He's good-looking – I saw him dance once. I wouldn't mind a nibble or two there.' Josie laughed. 'Anyway, you'd better take the chance of tonight, for if rumour is right then he's not going to be able to gamble for much longer. The duns are stirring.'

'Yes, I've seen his debts, Josie – they're frightening.'

'It's his own fault, I've no time for those who gamble like that. Anyway, goodbye Nonna. Yes, I've got your friend Monique's address, and no, I won't tell a soul where you are. On condition that I get a ticket for your first performance – preferably in the seat next to William Lamb.'

Nonna smiled. 'I'll see what I can do.' She watched the dainty figure in pink and white chequers hurrying back along the track and vanishing in the crush of carriages.

As Vania's landau swayed along the Mayfair street towards Barrymore's gaming house, Nonna pulled her shawl around her shoulders a little more for the evening was cool. She wore a white satin gown with an over-skirt of pink patent net. It had long, diaphanous net sleeves, gathered in at the wrists and falling richly over her knuckles, and was stitched here and there with pink sequins. Her hair was dressed up at the back of her head and soft white feathers curled down over her right shoulder. The only jewellery she wore were some exceedingly fashionable and expensive ruby pendant earrings which she had purchased that very afternoon after leaving Josie. A sudden impulse had taken her first to Mrs Clarke's for the bonnet she had seen in the window before, and then to Cartier's for the earrings. Having bought both things she felt a great deal better; buying them had been a gesture, a thumbing of her nose somehow, although how she couldn't have said.

Outside Barrymore's, Vania fussed around her, draping her shawl around her shoulders and complimenting her on her appearance. It was as if he could not say or do enough to make up for his appalling behaviour the night before. Nonna smiled and put her hand through his arm as they walked up the wide, scrubbed steps towards the open doors. She could hear the sound of music coming from inside, and beyond that the whispering of the wind in the lime trees in the square. Glancing back, she saw that it was a square very similar to Padenham Square – perhaps it was.

The doors opened into an immense oyster and white vestibule where chandeliers smoked and glittered overhead, and footmen liveried in scarlet and silver stood on each side of every door leading from the hallway. Ahead, the double curving staircase with its black marble steps and wrought-iron bannisters swept around to the half-landing of the floor above. The sound of male laughter and talk was everywhere, interspersed here and there by a woman's voice, and the smell of cigar smoke made the air heavy.

'Ah, Vania!' A loud male voice echoed down the staircase and they looked up to see Lord Ryan descending, smiling. Nonna returned the smile, but knew she was holding her breath. Lord Ryan had spoken to her at Madame's.

'My lord,' she murmured, curtesying.

'Enchanté' he smiled, sketching a bow. 'Your taste, Vania, as ever is exquisite. This, I take it, is the new Miss Lambert the *monde* chatters of?'

'Yes, my lord,' replied Vania.

'And when are we to see you dance, Miss Lambert,' drawled Ryan, taking out a diamond-studded snuff box.

Before she could reply, Vania spoke for her. 'She dances soon, my lord, very soon.'

'And is she as good as her sister?'

'Better, my lord.'

Ryan smiled, raising an eyebrow. 'Then London will have a new queen, eh? Vania, try me snuff, my own recipe, mixed by Fribourg.'

The dancer took a pinch of the fine powder, putting it deftly to his nose. He nodded. 'It is very good, my lord.'

Ryan grinned. 'I'll give you the recipe – it's tantamount to giving away state secrets, eh?'

He escorted them up the staircase and Nonna relaxed a little more then for it was obvious that Ryan had not the slightest idea who she was or that he had seen her before.

The footmen on the first floor flung the white double doors open as they approached, and immediately the noise of talking and music was louder and tobacco smoke drifted out on to the cool landing. The vast gaming room was decorated in wine red and gold, with velvet curtains at the tall windows and around the arched alcoves. The hazard tables were green and the croupiers wore starched white neckcloths. Most of the clientele were gentlemen, standing or sitting at the tables, leaning against pillars and standing in groups talking, but there were ladies: elegant, aristocratic ladies, who glanced immediately at Nonna as she came in, assessing the price and quality of her toggery and wondering if she presented any rivalry for the gentlemen's attention. The orchestra was playing a Mozart minuet, but the whirring of the roulette balls could be heard above all the noise.

Vania took his place at a huge circular table with its two green-shaded oil lamps, nodding at the other dozen or so gentlemen already seated. She stood at his shoulder, one gloved hand resting on the back of his chair, but she soon lost interest in the gambling, looking around instead.

The room was like Madame's, only very much larger. She recognised quite a few faces from Madame's too, but she knew now that no one recognised the masked singer from the disreputable house in Jacob Street. What would they all say if only they knew the truth?

Vania played the table constantly, pausing only to drink cognac at a rate which began to alarm Nonna almost as much as the vast amount of money he was losing. She knew that there was a supper being served in an adjoining room and she tried to draw him away from the table.

He shook his head, accepting a new hand. 'A moment more, my Nonna,' he murmured in a voice which told her he had no intention of leaving just yet.

'It's no use, Miss Lambert,' said a voice beside her. 'Vania will never leave, even on his usual losing streak.'

Slowly she turned to look into Justin Farnsworth's dark blue eyes. 'Sir?' she whispered, feeling dreadfully cold suddenly.

'Vania will not leave the table. Allow me to introduce myself, Justin Farnsworth – your servant.'

'Lord Justin.' She curtsied.

'Miss Lambert – I made so bold as to enquire your name – have we not met somewhere before?'

'No – no, I'm sure we have not, my lord.'

'You seem familiar to me.' He smiled, drawing her hand through his arm, 'Perhaps it's wishful thinking on my part, mm? If Vania will not take supper with you, may I enjoy the honour in his stead?'

'I – '

'I would advise you to accept my offer, Miss Lambert, for in a very short while something has been arranged here which is hardly likely to be pleasant if the two protagonists are their usual selves.'

'What do you mean?'

'I mean that certain unkind souls here have seen to it that Robert Wyndham of the Pegasus arrives shortly, and when friend Vania has been drinking heavily, the sparks always fly. So, a little supper in the peace of another room, eh? To save you the unpleasantness?'

'Vania and I should leave, immediately!' she cried.

'It will do no good to plead with him, Miss Lambert,' said Justin patiently, but she shook the dancer's shoulder.

'Armand, can we leave please?'

'Leave? But why, my Nonna? This may be my winning hand, eh?'

'Please, Armand!'

'Do not frown so much, *chérie*,' he murmured, reaching up to touch her cheek, and there was almost a pout on his fine lips as he smiled reproachfully at her.

'Armand, Wyndham will be here soon and –'

'Oh, *Wyndham*!' Vania tried to snap his fingers disdainfully, but could not manage. He smiled, a little lopsidedly, 'Wyndham is nothing, eh? Now then, wish me luck, my sweet Nonna?' He held up his cards, and with a helpless glance at Justin she bent to blow on the hand.

Vania grinned and then forgot her.

Justin smiled. 'You see? A block of marble might pay you more heed.'

'Did *you* send for Mr Wyndham, my lord?'

'Me? No, I promise on me mother's soul that I did not. And now – that supper?'

But it was too late, for at that very moment the doors opened and a stout man in dark grey stood there, his ivory cane swinging in his hand. The room went very quiet and the only sound was the bouncing roulette ball as the wheel whirred.

Vania's associates at the table put down their cards, and Vania was forced to pay attention to what was going on around him. He sat back. 'So,' he said thickly, 'Monsieur Wyndham, eh?'

'Losing again, Vania?' asked Wyndham drily, tapping his cane on his hand. 'Never learn, you Frenchies, eh? Too many frogs' legs during childhood, I say. Dulls the brain – what brain there is.'

'It would seem I have an excuse for my dim wits, but what is yours, eh? The Pegasus sinks again, I'm told – the result of *your* handling, sir.'

Wyndham smiled, ignoring the barb. 'It's your Benefit next season?'

'Yes.'

'It's doomed, my laddo, doomed. Don't even bother, we're going to trounce you off the face of the earth.'

Nonna moved closer to Vania, slipping her hand on his shoulder as she too faced the unpleasant man in grey.

Wyndham's eyes flickered briefly to her face and then he stared at her. 'God above,' he murmured, 'I heard that Melisande Lambert's sister was like her, but this beats all.'

Vania stood unsteadily. 'Have you something intelligent to say, Monsieur? Because if not – '

'About the Benefit. The Pegasus has an attraction you cannot beat for that self-same night.'

'Nothing can beat what the Opera House will put on then, sir.'

Wyndham's lazy, insolent smile spread. 'No? Not even the woman who danced naked before the Czar and his court?'

There were some subdued whistles and a murmur of interest at this news, and Vania stood for a moment. Nonna slid her hand into his and squeezed his fingers. He had not a clue what his Benefit would be yet, but there was no way he was going to let Wyndham know this.

'Ah, yes,' he murmured, 'the undressed carthorse – a basking whale has more grace, I'm told.'

'Can you match her?'

'*Match*? Who would want to, Monsieur?'

'I take it then that you have no notion of how to counter such an act?'

Vania smiled. 'We can more than counter, sir, we can wipe the very floor with it. Can't we, my Nonna?'

'Yes,' she said bravely, hoping that she sounded convincing.

'We'll see,' muttered Wyndham. 'But I think the Pegasus will reign supreme this next season, Vania. Unless, of course, the delightful Miss Lambert has a similar dance to perform for London – eh?' He grinned around at the onlookers.

Nonna felt her face go hot. But she raised her chin defiantly. 'If I had such a dance to perform, sir, *you* would be the last person to obtain a ticket!'

A ripple of laughter greeted this, and Vania put his arm around her waist. 'Wyndham, why do you not go to Hell now instead of keeping Beelzebub waiting?'

He was leaning against her, swaying very slightly, and she stood as firmly as she could, but he was heavy.

Wyndham was not finished yet. He had come to provoke Vania into an angry exchange and had not yet succeeded. 'I challenge you to tell what your precious Benefit will contain.'

'Hells waits, Monsieur.'

'Fail with your Benefit, and there will be no hope of ever fleeing to the Pegasus, Vania – which I know you fondly imagine to be the case at the moment.'

Vania flushed at that. 'You are the only one who imagines the Benefit will fail, Monsieur. Look to your own future before you question mine!'

'Admit you have no clever notions for the Benefit,' persisted Wyndham.

'I admit nothing!' snapped Vania.

'Because there's nothing to admit!' taunted the other.

'Anything will prove a bigger draw than a half-dressed Russian matron!'

'Matron? She's young, lithe and beautiful, with the

figure of a goddess. So, friend Vania, you can look forward to a low return for your big night.'

'We'll see, we'll see,' cried Vania, glancing at Nonna as she squeezed his arm. His bright blue eyes flashed with fury, and his lips were pressed tightly together as he tried to control his rising temper. 'Only time will tell, Monsieur Wyndham, only time. And now, if you will excuse us, gentlemen, I think it time we took our leave.'

He took Nonna's arm and they began to leave, but Wyndham was not done yet.

'Tell me, Vania, is this the latest bit of muslin then? I must say she'd make a better armful than Catrine!'

Vania halted, turning and swinging his clenched fist suddenly at Wyndham's fleshy face. Nonna screamed, trying to hold him back, but his temper had snapped and he sprang at the other man, who had been temporarily knocked off balance. Even in the heat of the moment she was aware of odds being laid on the outcome of the bout, but Vania was too drunk to carry the fight to any conclusion. He staggered to lean against a column, rubbing the hand with which he had struck his opponent. Wyndham sat on the floor looking slightly ridiculous, his cravat undone and his top hat squashed, for he had trodden on it.

Vania looked at Nonna. 'Ah, my Nonna, forgive me, eh? Forgive me.'

'It's all right,' she whispered: 'Let's go now.'

'He should not have insulted you.'

'It doesn't matter.'

She turned and found Justin close by. 'Will you help me, my lord?'

He nodded, dragging Vania's arm around his shoulder and helping him from the room.

The purple landau was drawn up outside, as if someone had already sent word down that it would be needed shortly, and Justin bundled Vania inside, propping him up in a corner with his head slumped against the glass. Vania didn't move, he was so drunk that he was almost asleep.

Justin turned to Nonna. 'Shall I accompany you?'

'No,' she said quickly, 'no, it's perfectly all right, thank you.'

'If you're sure. . . .'

'I am.'

'I feel so certain that I know you, Miss Lambert – but the only Nonna I have ever known' – he smiled – 'well she is hardly to be likened to you, I fancy. Tell me, are you perhaps acquainted with my cousin, Philip Hastings? I feel as if *he* may be connected somewhere. . . .'

She stared at him for a moment and then smiled nervously. 'I do know Sir Philip, my lord, but I have never met you.' The darkness of the night hid the fear on her face but could not disguise the anxiety in her voice.

He looked curiously at her, helping her into the landau. 'Good night, Miss Lambert.'

'Good night, my lord – and thank you again.'

She sighed with relief as he closed the door and the landau drew away from the kerb, the horses' hooves clattering in the quiet of the night.

Vania spoke quietly. 'You must forgive me yet again, eh, my Nonna. You must think me so bad.'

'Bad? No. Drunk? Yes.'

He smiled, the passing street lamps lighting his face momentarily. 'Stay with me tonight, Nonna.'

'No.'

'But you cannot go and disturb Monique at this hour,' he said, his voice slurred.

'I must.'

'If you will not accept my love, then at least accept my hospitle – hospli – *hos-pit-al-ity*. Be my guest for this one night, my Nonna.'

'I – '

He smiled again, bending across the landau to take her face in his warm hands. 'I will demand nothing of you, sweet Nonna. I am too drunk to do you justice, eh? Let Monique enjoy her sleep undisturbed, and you too will sleep undisturbed, I promise you. Ah, but if it got out that I had had such beauty under my roof and not proved my love, how I would lose face, eh?'

'I accept your hospitality, Armand, but that is all.'

He kissed her gently on the lips, sitting back as the landau lurched around a corner and he almost lost his balance. 'So drunk – so very drunk.'

The footmen opened the doors of the carriage and Nonna stepped down. The night air was cool and clear and a million stars seemed to be glittering in the velvet skies above. Vania stumbled down, catching her arm to steady himself, and he took a deep breath. 'Would that such a night had not ended so foolishly – what a terrible waste. To have struck that slug Wyndham, eh?'

'He provoked you.'

He nodded. 'If only I *did* have something good for my Benefit.'

'You will, I know you will.'

He smiled at her, pulling her close suddenly and kissing her on the lips. He took his time, savouring each second of the embrace, and then he laughed. 'Yes, my Nonna, I'm too drunk to have any skill tonight.'

He staggered a little as he went up the steps of the house in Cadogan Street, and after a moment she followed him, shivering in the coolness – but it was not the chill of the night alone which made her shiver, it was the delayed reaction of meeting Justin Farnsworth again. He knew he had seen her before – what if he should remember exactly where?

12

Nonna was helped to dress the next morning by a silent maid. She stood there for a moment before going down to the breakfast room on the first floor. In broad daylight the evening toggery looked out of place, but she had nothing else to wear. She looked at her pale reflection in the window-panes. It was raining outside, a grey, cloudy day which contrasted so much with the clear, starry night.

Last night and the night before she had come face to face with those who had seen her at Madame's, and no one had recognised her at all. Oh, Justin had a suspicion of knowing her, but that was all. Surely she was safe now? Philip was hardly likely to blurt the truth across London, and she knew her secret was safe with Josie. Yes, she was safe. The watery reflection stared back at her. Was there a new toughness in her face? Had her experiences this one year turned the green girl into a mature woman? Maybe. She was harder now, more capable of surviving in the Prince Regent's bright London. Harder, but still foolish over Philip Hastings. And why? *Why* this senseless passion for a man like that?

She started as the maid cleared her throat. 'Shall you go down now, Miss Lambert?'

'Yes.'

Vania's house was as eccentric as the man himself. The landings and stairs were decorated in white, even the carpets. Huge bowls of hot-house roses stood at every conceivable window and corner – yellow blooms, heavy and sweet-scented – and if she looked out into the narrow garden from the first landing, she could see the green-houses where they were cultivated.

The dancer had a passion for Ancient Egypt too, and there were two ebony pharaohs standing on either side of the breakfast-room doors. Inside, there was a small obelisk standing on a floor specially reinforced to carry the immense weight. Paintings of the Nile, the pyramids and the temple at Karnak hung on the white walls, and they looked strangely stark and dramatic.

Vania sat huddled in his chair at the table, an ice bag pressed to his aching forehead. He waved her to a chair. 'Good morning, my Nonna. Oh, dear God, never again –

never ever again.'

She accepted the plate of bacon a maid set before her, and poured a cup of Pekoe tea from the Sèvres teapot. 'Do you feel very bad?'

'I am dying.'

' I don't think so. Here, drink some tea.'

Meekly he accepted the tea, pulling a face at the taste. 'Laced with cognac it would be more palatable.'

'Eat some breakfast – food makes you feel better.'

'I shall die most certainly if I force myself to eat,' he said dramatically, but he nodded at the maid, who brought him some bacon too. He ate it without saying much, and then put his knife and fork down with a clatter as he finished. 'There, you are right; I *do* feel better. And what of you, my Nonna, do you forgive this miserable fellow who gave you such a bad evening yet again?'

'Of course.' What else could she say? He was truly ashamed, he would always be truly ashamed, and her forgiveness was all that mattered to him for the moment.

The butler came in. 'Excuse me, Monsieur, but Mr Langley is here and wishes to see you most urgently.'

'Langley? *Dieu*, at this early hour?'

'It is eleven o'clock, Monsieur,' said the butler, almost apologetically.

'Very well, very well, show him in here.'

Nonna sat back uncomfortably in her chair. She knew how her presence at Vania's breakfast table would appear to the manager of the Opera House.

Langley glanced at her as he came in, but seemed to have something far more important on his mind than Nonna Lambert. 'Vania,' he said, throwing his hat, gloves and cane down on a chair, 'last night I had the somewhat dubious privilege of meeting your blasted duns face to face at the Opera House! It ain't good enough, you know. First they send me copies of your debts, and now they come making scenes at the theatre!'

Vania sat stony-faced, glaring at the teapot as if it offended him.

Langley grunted. 'Well? Damn it all, Vania, what am *I* supposed to do? You *are* the Opera House, you're damned essential to its success, but this can't go on. You *must* do something about these debts!'

'I will,' said the dancer vaguely.

'When?'

'How do I know when!'

'I have obtained a little time for you, by promising them payment after your Benefit. So, Monsieur, you had better come up with something truly wondrous for that occasion – for *all* our sakes! And now, I bid you good day, Monsieur. Miss Lambert.'

He grabbed his hat, gloves and cane again and strode from the silent room. The fact that he had dared to speak so plainly to the dancer was proof of how worried he was about Vania's mountain of dangerous debts.

Vania remained still, giving the teapot a look of pure hatred. 'So,' he murmured at last, 'so, they come to get Vania, eh? Oh, Nonna, what am I to do, eh?' His blue eyes swung to her face and he held out his hand.

She could not resist the mute appeal of those magnificent, expressive eyes, and she got up to go to him. He pulled her close, his arms around her waist as she stood beside him. 'What am I to do, Nonna?' he said again.

Hesitantly she put a hand on his golden hair, stroking him gently. Monique had said he could be irresistible, and when he was like this even she could not remain cool. His arms tightened. 'My Nonna,' he whispered, 'if you knew only how much I love you, how much I need you.'

He released her suddenly, getting up to pace up and down the sunny breakfast room, his quilted dressing gown swinging as he walked. 'Langley is right, there must be something wondrous for my Benefit – but what? God above, if I ever needed inspiration, it is now, eh? *Le Dieu de la Danse* without a single divine notion in his head.' He smiled.

She stood there helplessly, but her head too seemed devoid of any clever idea. Wyndham had been right, the

Russian dancer *would* be a great draw – and at any other time the rivalry would not have mattered quite so much, but now Vania needed a success so desperately.

'Nonna, I cannot be another Brummell, eh? Fleeing back to France with my tail between my legs like a cur is not Vania's way – but if I am to stay out of gaol, that is all there is left to me.'

She went to where he stood. His problems were all his own fault, but somehow it did not seem right to think it. He was Vania: brilliant, unpredictable, gifted – and unhappy. She slipped her arms around him and held him close. It was so easy and so right to comfort him, and when he held her tightly she closed her eyes. He was not Philip, but he needed her for the moment and she wanted to help him so very much in spite of all that he had been responsible for of recent evenings.

He turned her face towards his, kissing her for a long long time, and then he smiled. 'This morning I have more skill, eh, my Nonna? More skill, but now I am too miserable!'

'We'll think of something, I know we will.'

'We?'

'I'll try too.'

'Ah, my sweet Nonna, I thank you.'

'You've helped me, why shouldn't I want to help you?'

His smile faded. 'I helped you first because I had a conscience, Nonna, but then I have already told you that. I *did* love your sister, but how much I did not know until she had gone from me. That was why I wanted to help you – at first. But now, now I love you so very much.'

He spoke so sincerely, and he meant it. But Vania would fall out of love as swiftly and completely as he fell in.

He sat heavily in a chair by the cold fireplace where a copper bowl of roses stood by the polished fender. 'What am I to do now though?'

She glanced around and her gaze fell upon some old newspapers. She knew that they contained good reviews of his latest performances; maybe that would help to lighten his mood, for at the moment he seemed about to doubt his own capabilities. She sorted through them for the particular copy of *The Times* which contained a really ecstatic review about his performance at the royal gala. 'Here, Armand, see how they praise you,' she said, crouching beside him. 'They cannot say these things unless you really are the very best in the world. Of *course* we'll think of something.'

'Another Franchot de Berry?' he murmured, reading the review again. 'Well, at least *he* had no problems with his Benefit, eh?' His eyes went to her face then, brightening. 'But of course, Franchot de Berry! Do you remember, my Nonna?'

'Remember what?'

'He brought out his new bride at his Benefit, and the occasion was such a success that hundreds were turned away from the theatre! Franchot de Berry!'

He got to his feet, dragging Nonna up too and hugging her, twirling her around swiftly. 'Inspiration at last, eh?'

'But you'll have to get married to do that!' she said, thinking that the only suitable ballerina would be Catrine, whom he now loathed.

'I know that, my Nonna. You shall be Madame Vania.'

She stopped then, moving away from him. '*Me*? But – '

'Why not? Do not say that you have no feeling for me because I know it is not so. And who better than Melisande Lambert's sister, another daughter of the great James Lambert! Oh, Nonna, cannot you see what an attraction it would be? Oh, I thank God for Catrine suddenly!'

'Catrine?' she asked, bewildered and almost overwhelmed by his enthusiasm and excitement.

'Why yes – but for her I would have danced with you, eh? The moment would have passed and not been used to its full potential. Vania and Nonna Lambert! Say yes to me, Nonna, for you must if I am to be saved.'

She stared at him. '*Marry* you?' she whispered.

'Yes – if I must go on my knee before you, then I will,' he said grandly, kneeling immediately and raising his hands in supplication. 'Please, Nonna, say you will be my wife.' He caught her hand. 'If you do not, I shall be ruined, thrown into jail, humiliated so that I shall never recover.'

'That's not fair, Armand.'

'Yes, it is, because it is true. Only you can save me, Nonna – my sweetest, dearest angel – only you.'

She looked down into his eyes, her mind racing. Marry Vania? But she didn't *love* him! She moved away to the window, staring blindly out at the narrow gardens and the greenhouses, but it wasn't a London garden she saw, it was Philip Hastings standing by a window in the moonlight. Oh, dear God, loving him was a pain, an ache which would never be healed. He was as far beyond her reach as the moon itself.

'Nonna?' whispered Vania, coming to stand at her shoulder, his hands on her waist. 'Please, Nonna. Save me.'

She nodded. 'Yes, Armand,' she whispered, 'I will marry you.'

He rested his cheek against her hair. 'I promised you would be queen of London,' he said softly, 'and so you shall be. As Vania's wife you will be the darling of all London, of England, of the world.'

She turned towards him, and he kissed her, pressing her close. She buried her face against his shoulder. What if he should ever discover about Madame's? No, she mustn't think of that, she *mustn't*!

He went to the decanters on the sideboard. 'It is early, eh, but we shall toast our match.' He smiled at her. 'You, my angel, have saved me.'

She returned the smile, but her mind was numb. What had she agreed to? She was mad to let him persuade her, it was bound to fail – the Benefit would fail and with it this foolish, foolish marriage.

He paced up and down, glass and decanter in his hands, 'We must plan this carefully, eh? Everything must be timed to maximum effect. The betrothal announced soon – yes, and the wedding to take place on the very day of the Benefit!' He turned, his eyes shining. 'Yes, that's it! On the very day. We'll put posters up the day before, announcing both events, and the *monde* will flock to both. I'll show that Wyndham he'll never crawl from his stone again, eh, my Nonna?'

'It must be a very big stone, Armand,' she said lightly.

'Eh? Oh, yes – a big stone for a big slug!'

'Armand, this *will* work? I mean, the Benefit will bring in enough for you to pay your debts?'

'Yes, Nonna – a successful Benefit brings in a very great deal of money.' He put down the glass and the decanter and went to her. 'You look so worried, *chérie*,' he whispered, putting his hand to her chin and tilting her face towards his. 'So little and worried, eh? You think we will not do well together, you and I, is that it?'

'I don't know, Armand.'

'Then I shall prove to you,' he murmured, 'that the ecstasy of dancing with Vania can be more than matched by the ecstasy of love with him.' He kissed her.

She didn't move away as his hand brushed her breasts. She was confused and uncertain, and suddenly she wanted him to make love to her, she wanted the reassurance of being close to him. Doubts crowded her mind, so many doubts. . . .

She lay in the huge bed, her arms twined around him and her head against his chest. Her hair was tousled and caught on the lace edging of the pillow. She could feel his heart-beats against her breasts, just as she had felt Philip's, but there was no lingering warmth, no sweet, sweet pleasure. She closed her eyes, hiding her face to conceal the tears.

Vania held her close. 'You see,' he murmured. 'With Vania there is only ecstasy, eh?'

Monique came into the tiny dressing room and stared at Nonna. 'Is it really true, Nonna? You and Vania?'

'Yes.'

'Langley's been telling the company, but I didn't think it could possibly be right – I thought maybe Vania was behind it all, trying to force your hand.'

'No, I am to marry him, and dance with him on his Benefit night.'

'But Nonna' – Monique went to her and took her cold hands – 'Nonna, you don't love him.'

Nonna looked away. 'If I don't marry him, the duns will get him, and I'm far too fond of him to let that happen without helping in some way.'

'Help him, yes – but to *marry* him?'

'Oh, please, Monique, leave it alone, please leave it alone!'

'Already it's made you unhappy, hasn't it?'

'Unhappy?' cried Nonna. 'Vania isn't the reason for my unhappiness. Oh, damn it, I can't even get used to calling him Armand! No, he isn't the cause of my unhappiness – you know that, Monique.'

Monique nodded. 'Philip Hastings, yes?'

'No, no he isn't either.'

'I know a lie when I hear it, especially from you, Nonna. You love Philip Hastings, but you are going to marry Vania. It's wrong, Nonna.'

Nonna sighed then, gazing down at her aching feet in their pink ballet pumps. Since arriving at the Opera House at luncheon time she had been rehearsing and rehearsing in the dark little room. She and Armand Vania were to dance *The Moonbeam*, but an especially choreographed version, extended and altered so that it was virtually a new ballet. For four hours she had stood at the bar and her feet ached so that she felt she would not be able to stand up on them ever again. She drew her hand across her damp forehead. 'Is it wrong to do this to help him, Monique? *Is* it? I don't think so.'

'Marriage is such a big step, though.'

'Philip Hastings would never marry me; he's made his opinion of me perfectly plain.'

'But you still love him, that's the point, Nonna. You love Philip Hastings!'

Something made them both turn towards the door at that

very moment, and they stared into Catrine's triumphant eyes. Without a word the ballerina turned on her heel and hurried away along the passageway.

Nonna closed her eyes wearily. After everything else, that was all the day had lacked, she supposed – some of Catrine's mean activities.

13

Nonna was walking with Monique towards the stage door when they encountered Catrine. The French ballerina stepped aside, avoiding their eyes, but Monique halted.

'Well, Catrine? Wouldn't he believe you then?'

'Believe me?'

'Yes. The whole company heard you arguing with him, so there is no point in denying it. You told him what you overheard, didn't you?'

'Yes.' Catrine's dark eyes moved to Nonna's face. 'Yes, I told him that his precious Nonna loves Philip Hastings!'

Monique smiled. 'And he refused to believe you. You should know him by now, Catrine, you of all people should know him! He doesn't *want* to believe bad of her because he needs her – he needs her to pay his debts at the Benefit! You can't do that for him, and neither can I – but Nonna can! Her name is all he needs to make that Benefit a success! He loves her now, that's true enough, just as he once loved me, and Melisande and you. When he loves, he loves truly. You can do nothing to stop this marriage now, Catrine – learn your lesson once and for all, eh? *Combien de temps faut-il pour* . . . How long *does* it take with you, Catrine?'

'Take? It will take forever, Monique. He is mine, *mine*! I will not give him up without struggling, not to her or to anyone!'

'If you had paid more attention to keeping him in the past, spent *less* time on various fleeting lovers, maybe you would have kept him!'

'Kept him? Kept him when Melisande's *ghost* is set before him? I am not a magician!' Catrine looked at Nonna again. 'I love him, I will always be there, fighting to get him back. I warn you of that, Nonna Lambert.'

She hurried away down the passage, her pumps tapping on the cold stone, and her pale blue skirts fluttering lightly behind her.

Monique looked at her and then at Nonna. 'She is as hopeless as you, eh? If she doesn't put up a fight now, then she's not only lost him completely, but her contract will end and out she'll go even though she is an excellent ballet dancer. She will maybe bide her time a little now, but she *will* try something before you finally marry him – Catrine is not one to give up where Armand Vania is concerned.

The late summer and early autumn were taken up, day in day out, with rehearsals, for Vania was determined that Nonna would be at the very peak of her ability for the Benefit night. She must complement him in every way to make the evening the success he desired. She knew the ballet so well, she felt she could even have danced it backwards.

The day the ballet was first danced before the entire company with the orchestra instead of a piano, Nonna knew the Benefit would be a success. She and Vania moved as one, gliding and twisting perfectly. She felt possessed, almost. No one else but Vania could have brought out such a mirrored brilliance in her; his strength and skill were compelling. When the last strains of the music died away through the empty auditorium, she felt quite overcome, bursting into tears suddenly in front of everyone.

Vania caught her close. 'You are better than Melisande

ever was, my Nonna,' he whispered, as the rest of the company clapped delightedly. 'So very much better.'

'Because of you,' she cried, 'only because of you.'

She meant the words, for she knew in her heart of hearts that her dancing was a response to his skill and dedication, with anyone else she would not have reached such a pitch. But had she thought her choice of words out carefully, she could not have chosen any more calculated to please him or flatter his vanity.

From the wings Catrine watched in silence. The dancer in her could admire Nonna, but the woman in her hated more than ever now.

Vania smiled at Nonna. 'The perfection we have got, eh? Now we must keep it.' He snatched at the air as if catching a spirit. 'Wyndham's big stone will crush him for all time. And tonight, after the – the *performance*' he said the last word disdainfully, for he was to be partnered by Catrine – 'tonight, my Nonna, you shall wear Vania's ring, eh? And we celebrate a little. Would you like that?'

She nodded.

And so, on a warm September evening in the theatre still heavy with cigar smoke, a magnum of champagne was broached as Armand Vania slipped an engagement ring on Nonna's finger. The diamonds sparkled and flashed in the light of the chandeliers, and the champagne was ice-cold, dry, and it too sparkled. She laughed and smiled as she accepted everyone's congratulations, but it was the actress in Nonna Lambert which came to the fore on the stage where the auditorium seemed to echo all around. She *was* excited by the events which had overtaken her, and still a little stunned by the swiftness with which everything was happening. But at the back of her mind, she wondered if she was set upon a disastrous course. She watched Vania as he shook the champagne bottle so that the froth streamed everywhere and some dancers squealed as the liquid touched their bare arms.

She didn't love him and she never would. She had let him make love to her and knew that he did not arouse her at all, as Philip had done. And even now, at his betrothal celebration, Vania could not resist flirting with a new little dancer, putting his arm around her waist and turning the full force of his charm upon her. What promise he could express with those eyes, she thought, watching the girl flush, her lips parted slightly as she glanced towards Nonna.

As she stood there, a little apart, Nonna suddenly sensed that someone was watching her carefully. Her eyes searched the sea of faces and then she saw Catrine. The French girl was smiling slightly, and then she raised her glass and poured it all over the floor before leaving the stage to the accompaniment of several murmurs of disapproval from those who had seen.

Then Vania remembered Nonna and returned to her. She held out her glass, smiling, and he blew her a kiss before refilling it for her.

Nonna was alone at Monique's house several nights later, enjoying a rare evening of solitude, when someone knocked at the front door. A post-boy stood there, his yellow jacket bright in the shaft of lamp light from the hallway as he doffed his beaver hat to her.

'Miss Lambert?'

'Yes.'

'Moosoor Vanya sends his compliments, and would you go to join him at Barrymore's?'

She glanced past him at the waiting post-chaise. 'Now?'

'Yes, Miss Lambert. If it pleases you.'

What had happened? Had he lost another fortune? Or was he on his way to being too drunk to stand again? Maybe she was being unkind, perhaps he just wanted her company.

'I won't be a moment if you'll wait,' she said, turning to hurry upstairs to change.

Several carriages were drawn up outside Barrymore's as the old chaise rattled up to the kerb, and she looked out around the square at others which waited patiently for their owners to return. There was no sign of Vania's purple equipage at all. The chaise halted and the boy jumped down from the horse, opening the door.

She pushed some coins into his hands and he touched his hat again, slamming the door and quickly remounting to search for another fare before midnight.

She pulled her colourful Indian shawl around her shoulders and hurried up the steps into the warmth and light of the oyster and white vestibule.

The footmen bowed, recognising her. 'Good evening, madam.'

'Good evening. Monsieur Vania, where may I find him? He is expecting me.'

'Monsieur Vania? But he isn't here, madam – at least, he isn't here yet,' answered one of the footmen.

That was why the landau was not outside. 'Is there somewhere where I can wait for him then?'

'I'll show you to the drawing room, madam. If you'll follow me.'

She followed him up past the first landing and on to the second floor. He flung open some double doors and stood aside for her to go in.

She went a few steps and then halted, for she found herself looking at the only two other occupants of the room – Justin Farnsworth and Philip Hastngs.

Justin was seated on a crimson sofa, and he stood immediately. 'Upon my soul, what good fortune brings you to us, Miss Lambert?'

'Good evening, my lord. Sir Philip.'

Justin crossed the room to her immediately, taking her hand and leading her to the sofa. 'Now then, Philip, as we are on reasonably civil terms for once, will *you* tell me where I have met this vision of loveliness before?'

Philip's dark brown eyes moved to her face, and he leaned one elbow against the white carved marble of the mantelpiece. 'Have you met my miserable cousin before, Miss Lambert?'

'Once. Here.'

Justin shook his head. 'Damn it, I *know* we've met before – but how can I have forgotten someone as lovely as you, Miss Lambert?'

'You've not forgotten,' she said, flushing, 'you just have not met me before. And how was Belvoir, Sir Philip?'

'A nest of Tories, would you believe? And me a stubborn Whig. William is threatening to table a motion chastising my appalling taste.' He smiled at her.

Justin grunted. 'William Lamb has more appalling taste than anyone else I know – in women anyway. He's not separating from her after all, did you know? His family worked damned hard on him this time, but she followed him to his lair at Brocket, slept on the mat by his bedroom door all night like a faithful dog, and wheedled her way back into his favour come the morning! The man's mad, completely mad!'

Philip shrugged. 'He loves her, and never was there a bigger fool than a man in love.'

Justin leaned back, surveying him for a moment. 'Are you ever going to make an honest woman of my sister?'

'Having you as a cousin is tantamount to persecution; the thought of you as my brother-in-law as well screws me to a pitch of horror, Justin.'

'Gillian's in love with you – and look at it this way, if I snuff it, you'd get the old dukedom. There's no irritating distaff clauses, eh? Doesn't that tempt you?'

'The dukedom? Yes. All cessation of life in you? Yes. Gillian? No.' Philip glanced at Nonna, changing the subject very obviously. 'And what brings you to Barrymore's all alone, Miss Lambert?'

'I am to meet someone here.'

'No *gentleman* should let you travel alone. And speaking of no gentleman, rumour hath it that you are engaged to marry the frantic genius of the dance.'

'Yes, I'm to marry Vania.'

Justin stared. 'You and that – that – ' He glanced up at Philip, who shook his head slightly, and he fell silent.

Philip turned to look at the clock on the mantelpiece. 'Have you not booked the wheel for this time, Justin?'

'Eh? Oh, yes. Shall you join me?'

'Gamble with you? Spare me. I will remain to be entertained by Miss Lambert. But mind now, Justin, you have been sober – and therefore human and pleasant – for a week now. Please keep it that way, eh?'

'I'm doing my best, but life gets tedious without a certain glow around the edges,' said Justin with a smile. 'I will go then. Good bye, Miss Lambert. I trust we meet again soon.' He kissed her hand, nodded at Philip, and then was gone.

The ticking of the clock seemed loud suddenly in the silent room.

She looked up at Philip. 'How different his behaviour is with a dancer from the Opera House.'

'But of course, you are now respectable. More double standards, don't you know.' He smiled faintly. 'Besides which, I have been prevailed upon by my family to keep him under stricter control. I am become his keeper. What he does when I am *not* around is anyone's guess – indeed, I think I would prefer not to know! Well now, finding myself face to face with you again I note that there is a change in you, Nonna. A loss of innocence maybe, mm?'

'Well, you would know, wouldn't you?'

'Yes, I suppose I would.' He smiled. 'Not an unpleasant experience by any measure, I promise you. Far from it.'

She flushed again. 'Perhaps I should wait for Vania downstairs.'

'You'll have a long wait, then, for he is dining at Long's tonight and is then going on elsewhere. I know it for a fact as I know who he is with.'

'But – but I had a message to come and meet him here! At least . . . Catrine!'

'Why think of her suddenly?'

'Vania did not send me the message, Catrine did, because – ' She looked at him. 'Have you seen her recently, Sir Philip?'

'I think under the circumstances we can drop the "Sir", don't you? Yes, I have seen her – downstairs a little earlier, as a matter of fact. She was with a rather large, fat fellow who was slobbering over her – why?'

Nonna said nothing. Catrine knew she loved Philip and she knew where Philip was tonight; *she* had sent the chaise and the message. It was another attempt to break Nonna and Vania up, by sending Nonna into the company of the man she loved. Nonna's hands twisted in her lap. It could have been a clever plan on Catrine's part, it *could* have been – but for Philip's disinterest in Nonna Lambert! She smiled then. 'Oh, well, a wasted journey on my part.'

'It need not be.'

She looked up at him then. 'Have you nothing better to do tonight then, Philip?' she asked softly.

He smiled. 'How am I to take that question?' He looked down into the fire. 'I have many things I could do tonight, Nonna, but I would *like* to spend the evening in your company.'

'Thank you,' she said suddenly. 'I should like that too.'

Bravely, she met his amused gaze, *Oh no, Philip Hastings, you'll not use me again like that! Not this time*!

'Where would you like to go?' he asked. 'Not the theatre, I would imagine.'

'Wherever *you* choose, Philip.'

'Very well, I'll see that my carriage is brought round.'

'I'll wait here.'

He paused by the sofa, leaning one hand on the arm beside her. 'Do you love Vania?'

'Why does that concern you?'

'Do you love him?' he repeated.

She looked up at him and he bent his head, kissing her for a long moment, his lips teasing her into an unwilling response. She reached up to hold him tightly, almost frightened by the intensity of her love and need for him.

His eyes were dark as he took her face in his hands. 'Nothing's changed, has it? You don't love that French buffoon.'

'I shall still marry him.'

'Don't.'

She said nothing, and he straightened, walked to the door and went out. Her eyes closed for a moment. She loved him, and yet tonight she was determined to snub him – it would be the hardest thing she had ever done in her life. She got up and went quickly to the window, slipping behind the heavy folds of brown velvet. Pressing back against the misty, cold glass, she waited.

He returned a minute or so later. 'Nonna?'

Silence.

He laughed then, a low chuckle. 'Well, I'll be damned! I didn't think she had it in her!' Then he was gone again.

She remained where she was. Snubbing him was the very last thing she really wanted to do, but he deserved it! For once Philip Hastings had been discarded! She felt she had got her own back – just a little – and her pride was restored by a very great deal.

After waiting for a while, she crept out into the warmth of the firelit room again. At the door she listened, but it was quiet. Slipping out on to the landing, she hurried to the back stairs, which led down to the kitchens, startling the cooks and maids there as she ran through and out into the narrow courtyard behind the house. In a nearby street she saw a post-chaise which immediately stopped for her, and soon she was on her way back to Southwark.

14

Monique adjusted the heavy folds of white satin. 'Oh, Nonna, it is such a beautiful wedding gown, such a beautiful one!'

'It should be, it cost the earth at Mrs Clarke's.'

The gown had tiny puffed sleeves and a very high waistline, and the thick, rich satin was stitched in a pattern of pearled leaves which glowed softly. She turned from one side to the other, inspecting herself in the long mirror in Monique's bedroom. The dainty fringe at the hem shivered with each movement, and the wreath of diamonds in her red hair flashed in the lamp light.

'I shall need a great deal of rouge to make me look glowing with health,' she said, pinching her pale cheeks.

'You've been working too hard. Vania has driven you far too much.'

'We must be more than perfect.'

'He thinks only of himself.'

Nonna smiled. 'Vania expects from others what he expects of himself.'

'But he is more than human!' protested Monique, 'and a man can do more than a woman! He is a monster to you!'

'I'll survive. Anyway, after tomorrow, maybe he will relax a little.'

'Tomorrow is quite a day, eh?' said Monique. 'You marry in the morning, and dance the Benefit in the evening.'

'Don't remind me.' Nonna looked at the reflection again. 'Are you sure it all looks well?'

'Of course it does. You look very beautiful, Nonna. Stop worrying. But then, it's not about how you look that you're worrying, is it?'

Nonna said nothing, and in the ensuing silence they distinctly heard someone at the door. Monique looked at the little fob-watch dangling from her belt. 'Midnight! Who on earth would call here at this hour?'

'You'd better see – I can't go down dressed like this.'

They heard Monique's maid answer the door, and a man's voice asking for Nonna. Nonna gasped. 'It's Philip!'

The maid came up the stairs, but before she could say anything, he came into the room behind her.

'Nonna?' he said abruptly, flinging his hat and gloves on

the bed, 'I must speak with you – alone.'

Monique glanced at Nonna, and then nodded at the maid and they both went out, closing the door behind them.

He took off his grey greatcoat and tossed it on the bed too. 'Sweet God, are you going to stand in that damned dress all night until the great moment tomorrow then?'

'And if I am!' she snapped. 'I fail to see what business it is of yours!'

He smiled suddenly. 'My, my, we do learn our lessons, don't we? I was hoping that you had paid heed to my warning last time we met, but after being away a month or so I return to Town to find those blasted posters up everywhere announcing tomorrow's antics in church and theatre.'

She flushed. 'And why should I pay any heed to your warnings, sir? What reason would I have to take your word for anything?'

'I've never lied to you. Many a fault I may have, but lying to you is not one of them. You've never been in any doubt whatsoever about me, have you?'

'No.'

'You mustn't marry him, Nonna. Marry anyone else, but not Armand Vania.'

She looked away. 'Why? Give me a suitable reason.'

He came closer, touching her sleeve gently with his fingertips. 'You don't love him, for one.'

'Are *you* proposing, Philip?' she murmured with a wry smile, looking at him. She moved away then. 'No? Then pray stay out of my affairs. I think you've come here tonight simply for the exercise, haven't you? Just to see what sort of a solomongrundy you can stir up.'

'That isn't so.'

'Then why wait until the very eve of the wedding before coming? Your timing would seem to be nicely calculated!'

'I've told you already, I've been out of Town.'

'Where?'

'Gretna Green – not being spliced in indecent haste, I assure you. On the sixth of October Jack Carter and Tom

Oliver battled it out at Gretna. I stayed with friends in Carlisle and went to see the bout. Aye, and quite a scrap it was too, very much the Fancy. I also purchased a jack-merlin, and a handsome lanner, and then hired the services of an austringer for my short-wings down at Five Ways. There, is that a full enough account of my activities?'

She remained silent.

His fingers drummed on the surface of the little dressing table, and she watched him as he looked around the small bedroom. 'I know,' she said softly, 'definitely not Gillow, eh?'

He smiled. 'Not, definitely not. Oh, come on, Nonna, you *know* you don't want to marry Vania!'

'Oh, but I do.'

He crossed the room and put a hand to her chin, looking into her eyes. 'You'll be miserable with him,' he whispered, kissing her gently.

For a moment she closed her eyes, but then common sense seized her again. 'Oh, Philip,' she murmured, 'how much rests on your success this time, eh? Ten thousand? Or am I worth less than Catrine? Maybe only five for weaning Nonna Lambert away from Vania.'

His hand dropped away immediately. 'Is nothing sacred that even a man's private wagers become common knowledge? I admit to the ten thousand for the Catrine affair, but believe it or not, human concern motivates me this time – not material gain! Has Vania laid a finger on you yet? And believe me, sweet Nonna, I do not refer to a seduction! More a black eye! That is my reason for wanting you to stop this before it goes any further, and I *know* what I'm talking about for I've seen the results of friend Vania's activities at first hand! If a man can beat a helpless woman once, he is quite capable of doing it again. A leopard does not change his spots, especially a strutting leopard like Armand Vania. When I took you to him I thought he'd further your career for you, aye and that maybe you'd grace his bed – but *that* would have been up to you. *How* you used your opportunities was entirely your affair, but this is different, Nonna. Marrying him binds you to him, makes you his property, his chattel! And if you had not unceremoniously ditched me at Barrymore's that night I would have said all this then!'

'I trust being discarded was a novel experience for you!'

He smiled faintly. 'It was.'

'You may have intended saying this then, but that wasn't all you intended, was it?'

'No, it wasn't. Your seduction was on my mind too, very much so. But my lascivious appetites and lusts have nothing to do with this now, have they?'

'I am still marrying him tomorrow,' she said steadily.

'Why? For the glory of being Madame Vania? Is that it? Pure self-concern and self-glorification? Has the dreaded cynicism settled over you at last?'

'You wouldn't understand my reasons for marrying him even if I told you, Philip.'

'There you are most probably right.' He caught her hands. 'Nonna, it's my fault you ever met the fellow, and I don't want you to make this mistake.'

'Consider your good deed done then, for you've done all in your power to stop me. Almost all. You know how I love you, for I have been fool enough to reveal the fact to you on each occasion we met – but you don't want me. Serious entanglements are not for Philip Hastings, love is for idiots, *et cetera*. So leave me to muddle along in my own way, will you? Just leave me alone, Philip. Please.'

He stared at her, his lips parting as if he wanted to say something more. His hands tightened around hers and he pulled her into his arms, kissing her, his fingers twining in her hair. 'Goodbye, Nonna,' he whispered, releasing her. He picked up his coat, gloves and hat, and left the room.

She heard his steps on the stairs, and then the door closed. She bit her lip, blinking back the tears, but as she caught sight of her pale reflection in the mirror, the wedding gown so rich and beautiful, the tears came, and Monique found her weeping on the bed a moment later.

Outside by the landau, Philip hesitated, glancing up at

the window where the lamplight glowed softly. In that last moment he had known she meant more to him than was good for his peace of mind. An idle interest had become more. He pulled on his gloves. She was right: he didn't want any serious entanglements, that wouldn't suit his plans in the slightest. Yes, best forget Nonna Lambert, put her out of his mind completely.

The landau moved away slowly and he sat back on the velvet upholstery, gazing out of the misted window at the shadowy streets. God above, what wouldn't he give to be down in Dorset now? On a damn good horse, with a hawk, and that whole blasted hillside to ride over! Anything to get London out of his hair again for a while! *London*? No, Nonna Lambert!

Nonna and Vania came out of the church into the brilliant sunshine, and the bells pealed loudly over the city as they walked the rice-strewn path to the waiting carriages. It seemed that the whole of London's fashionable society had come to see their favourite marrying. Everyone waved and cheered, and Nonna moved in a daze. She was his wife, Vania's wife. She could hear people shouting greetings and congratulations, yelling that they would be at the Benefit, and the rice pattered everywhere around her as she stood by the purple landau, her gown dazzling in the autumn sunshine. A slight breeze blew the crisp autumn leaves along the pavements, a blur of crimson, gold and brown rustling like live things over the cobbles. And everywhere the bells, pealing and pealing.

Vania smiled at her. 'Ah, my Nonna,' he murmured, his voice almost drowned by the cacophany of noise, 'my sweet Nonna. You are mine, eh?' He kissed her, and the excited, delighted crowd roared its approval.

No one else had reached the Opera House when the landau arrived, and Vania handed Nonna down at the stage door, smiling. 'So,' he murmured, 'we have slipped away from them, eh? Soon we must rehearse yet again, but for the moment we have some time to ourslves, *non*?'

She slipped her hand into his and they went inside, their footsteps echoing through the theatre's narrow little passages, and outside his dressing room they halted. He put his arms around her waist, smiling again. 'You are a beautiful bride, my love. I am proud that you are my wife, do you know that?'

'We gave London a show, didn't we?'

'It means more to me than that, my Nonna,' he said softly. 'I love you. I want you to love me.' He kissed her tenderly, a gentle caress, at once protective and full of desire. As she held him in the darkness of the dusty corridor, she thought fleetingly of Philip's words. But it couldn't be true, not of the man who held her so lovingly now, whispering words of love in her ear as he pushed the door of the dressing room open.

'Well, well, good morning to you, Frenchman!'

They froze at the thick, trenchant voice from the room beyond. Nonna turned quickly as Robert Wyndham got up from the stool by the dressing-table, exhaling a great deal of cigar smoke.

He smiled coolly. '*Monsieur – et – Madame, n'est ce pas*?' he said in an atrocious accent, bowing. 'Congratulations, dear things. May you have a long and happy life together.' Again he exhaled, and the gesture was derisive.

Vania stepped aside. '*Adieu, Monsieur! Vite! Vite!*'

'God above, man, if I run I'll kill myself!' Wyndham sat down again, his hands on his ebony cane as he twisted the cigar from one side of his mouth to the other. 'So, tonight's the night, eh? In more ways than one. A clever notion, this marriage lark, but it won't wash come tonight's grand opening of the doors, Vania. No, indeed. You've tied yourself to this wench for damn all. Oh, she's pretty, I grant you – but is that enough when you're both penniless and the Opera House's doors are closed to pay off your fool debts.'

'Get out, Wyndham!' snapped Vania, indicating the corridor again.

'Don't be rude, dear boy, I've only come for a chat.'

Nonna smiled, crossing the room to remove her gloves. 'No, you haven't, Mr Wyndham – you've come to try to frighten us away because you're worried! The Pegasus can't compete with what we've got to offer, and you know it.'

He blew cigar smoke over her, smiling thickly. 'Is that so? And if I say that the Regent himself is coming to our little do and not yours?'

'I'd say good luck to you, sir,' she said lightly. 'I just don't admire your clientele very much! And now, if you've done with whatever it is you came for?'

He smiled again, tapping his tall hat on his balding head. 'Well, well, Vania, you've found yourself a damned tiger, eh? I salute you, Madame. You have my admiration – oh, and my pity of course. Such a waste of obvious talents. Good day to you both.'

His heavy steps faded away along the passage, and somewhere a door closed dully. She turned to look at Vania and he crossed the room to her, catching her hands.

'You were magnificent,' he said, smiling. 'You sent him with a flea in his mouth.'

'Ear. A flea in his ear.'

He laughed, putting his fingers to her cheek in a way which reminded her instantly of Philip, and she drew away abruptly. He looked at her. 'You're worried about tonight? Is that what it is?'

'If I don't dance well. . . .'

'You will, *chérie* – you cannot dance badly. Hey now, don't look so sad or I will be – miffed – with you. You are Madame Vania now; you should be triumphant, not sad!' He caught her close again. 'Ah, Nonna, the day Philip Hastings brought you to me is the best day of my life, eh?'

'Why – why do you and he dislike each other so?'

He smiled. 'Because I took a woman from him once, that is all! He is a bad loser, Sir Philip. And now, Nonna, we are alone, *non*? And that sofa looks inviting.' He tilted her face towards his. 'Let me love you now, my Nonna. Now is the right time.'

'Someone might come.'

'Here, when Vania is alone with his new bride? I think not.' He laughed, locking the door, 'But we can make sure.'

He kissed her then, holding her close, and as he picked her up and carried her to the sofa she thought fleetingly of what Philip had said. It wasn't true, it couldn't be true, not of this man who was making love so sweetly to her. His mouth was warm, and his breath tasted faintly of cloves. As she held him she came close to loving him, but there wasn't any ecstasy. When he touched her breasts her flesh didn't tingle as when Philip touched her. She felt nothing for this man who was now her husband. His love-making was pleasant and experienced – but there was no ecstasy.

15

'Did you ever see such a crush of carriages?' whispered Monique, standing at Nonna's elbow. 'The world and his wife must be outside trying to get into Vania's Benefit, eh?'

Nonna dropped the lace curtain. 'Oh, Monique, if I do something wrong. . . .'

'You won't. Vania would not let you. With him you are safe, Nonna.'

'I pray so.'

Monique smiled, squeezing her cold hands. 'They're calling for you now.'

Nonna closed her eyes faintly. The moment was here, and she was terrified! 'Philip's box? Is he here, Monique?'

'Yes. And he's not alone – he has a woman with him. A pretty woman in pale green velvet who gazes adoringly at him all the time.'

'Oh.'

Monique shook her hands. 'Nonna, you are Madame Vania now. The deed is done, *non*? There is no room for regrets.'

No room for regrets? Nonna smiled vaguely and went from the room, her pumps tapping on the wooden boards as she made her way up to the stage. The hum of the audience was dull and echoing as she stood by Vania's side in the wings. The *monde* had indeed flocked to his Benefit; every seat was taken and the aisles were full too, with people pressing closer and closer to the stage in expectation. There were coughs and shuffles, and the buzz of whispers as the conductor tapped his score, raising his baton.

The music began, and Vania put his arm around her waist. 'A kiss, my Nonna – for luck?'

'Isn't that *bad* luck?'

'Bad luck to kiss you?' He smiled, putting his lips over hers for a moment.

And then they were walking on to the stage, where the light of the chandeliers made it hot and stuffy, and the faces of the audience were a maze of featureless blobs. His hands were firm and steady as they struck the first pose. She wouldn't look at Philip's box, she *wouldn't* . . . Vania smiled into her eyes, his lips so close, and she concentrated on him. They began to dance, and the ballet flowed through her, just as all those years before it had flowed through her sister. James Lambert's careful, brilliant teaching and coaxing blossomed forth on the stage of the Opera House again as she moved around Vania. He lifted her so lightly, twisting her low and then high, his strength effortless and his skill almost possessed. As before, when they had danced in the empty theatre, she felt as if she was one with him, and it was his genius which held sway over her.

There wasn't a sound from the immense audience. No one dared to clear their throats as they watched the two dancing on the stage. Nonna's yellow gown drifted lightly around her lithe body, her legs pale and graceful as she danced. Once, only once, did she look towards Philip's box – he sat there, lounging in his chair, his dark face expressionless.

The music died away at last, with Nonna leaning back in Vania's arms, her head so low her hair brushed the boards. For only a tiny moment there was silence, and then the applause began. Feet stamped, hands clapped, people whistled and cheered, and flowers showered on to the stage – carnations, roses, orchids.

Vania beamed as he bowed. Had he ordered his Benefit night, he could not have done better. His debts were taken care of, and his admirers were wildly delighted with what they had seen. Beside him, Nonna curtsied too, ignoring Philip's box quite deliberately. When Vania took her hand and led her forward, the cheers were redoubled. *Madame Vania, Madame Vania*. They were chanting her name. Vania graciously and dashingly collected the flowers and presented them to her.

The Moonbeam was the climax of the evening, and they were called back time and time again for curtain calls, but at last the applause died away.

As the curtain dropped for the last time, Nonna closed her eyes with relief. As she opened them again she saw one face in the wings, tear-stained and unhappy. Catrine met her glance for the briefest of moments and then was gone, her full winter cloak billowing behind her as she ran towards the stage door.

Vania frowned. 'She is forbidden here!'

'Oh, leave her, Armand. She loves you, so don't be so unkind to her – especially not tonight.'

'Already you nag me?' he smiled. 'Oh, but tonight we *danced*, did we not?'

She nodded.

'Everything will be all right now, no debtors' gaol for Vania,' he laughed.

He put his arm around her as they walked from the stage, smiling at the rest of the company, who clapped and cheered them again. This was the sort of moment she had always dreamed of, being another Melisande . . . . But this was even better, even more dazzling than anything Melisande had known.

A crowd of wealthy well-wishers waited in the dressing room and the corridors outside, and Nonna knew instinctively that Philip and his companion would be there. And the first person she noticed was the pretty girl in pale green velvet who had sat next to him in the box. She was laughing, hanging on to his arm as she chattered non-stop to those close by, but her conversation broke off in a moment as Nonna and Vania arrived in the doorway.

'Vania, oh, Monsieur!' she cried, hurrying towards him, her hands held out.

Nonna's eyes met Philip's for a quick moment, and then she was looking at the girl as Vania caught her hands. 'Ah, Lady Gillian! It has been so long since last you came to see me!' he cried.

Lady Gillian Farnsworth, thought Nonna instantly, seeing that the girl's dark blue eyes were so like Justin's, although her hair was brown.

'What about going on to Barrymore's?' cried someone from the back of the crush, and in a moment there were murmurs of agreement. Lady Gillian Farnsworth smiled at Nonna and then at Vania again. 'Come with us! Oh, I do so want you to come too, and I'm *determined* that you shall! Philip here had to be prodded into even coming backstage! He can be so awkward, don't you know?'

Vania's eyes slid to Philip's still face, but neither of them smiled. The dancer patted Gillian's gloved hands. 'I think, Lady Gillian, that it is most kind of you to ask us, but tonight I wish to spend alone with my new bride.'

Gillian flushed quickly and there were suggestive laughs from the gathering. Nonna's face reddened too and she avoided Philip's gaze.

'You go, Lady Gillian,' went on Vania. 'Make your solemn friend here enjoy life a little, eh?'

Philip inclined his head, taking Gillian's hand from the

dancer and leading her from the room, still protesting.

When the room was empty at last, Vania turned to Nonna. 'So, tonight we are alone, mm? You do not mind?'

'I shall like it very much, Armand.'

'We dine together, and then' – he raised her hand to his lips – 'and then we make love, eh? Sweet, sweet love. All night long if we wish.' He laughed softly. 'And then again in the morning.'

The sheets were warm and smelled of rose petals as Nonna lay back against the numerous pillows, looking around the room. The walls were hung with white satin, draped and folded intricately, and the white looked pink in the candle-light. Everywhere there were his favourite yellow roses, their stems so straight and long, and their colour so ghostly.

'So,' he said suddenly, 'by tomorrow breakfast you will know that you are as I promised, the queen of London. The papers will praise you for your beauty and your dancing.'

'And for my choice of husband?'

'Ah, but of course. And did you hear what Langley said of the Pegasus? No one who was important went there tonight – it was only half full for the capering Russian cow.'

'That's not very gallant, Armand. I'm told she's very good.'

'Not good enough though, and there is the difference, eh?' He bent to pick up the champagne bottle from the ice-bucket standing on the white carpet. 'It will be the end of Wyndham, and good riddance! The managers there won't keep him after this trouncing, he has too many enemies where it matters.' He poured two more glasses of the champagne.

'Was – was that Lady Gillian Farnsworth tonight?'

'Yes. Why?'

'I've met her brother.'

'Ah yes, of course – on my night of ignominy at Barry-more's.' He smiled. 'She is pretty, eh? And rich – oh, how rich! If her foolish brother gets himself killed she'll be the most desirable heiress in England. Friend Hastings does well for himself there. She's been making sheep-eyes at him for a long time, drooping over him in the box, gazing soulfully into his eyes. Bah, how any woman can like him I cannot begin to guess. So cold, so superior – so distant! *I* would do her more justice, eh, Nonna?'

She smiled at him. 'Of course.'

Someone tapped at the door at that moment, and his smile faded into quick irritation. '*Oui*?'

'A message, Monsieur.' The butler came in, carrying a small white envelope on a silver tray. 'It was delivered a moment ago and I thought you would want to read it immediately, Monsieur.'

Nonna lowered her glass nervously. What could be important enough to be delivered on Vania's wedding night? Not more debts, please let it not be that . . . . Vania took the envelope and waved the butler out again, breaking the envelope's seal and reading. Nonna caught a glimpse of a crest at the top of the sheet of paper.

'What is it?' she asked anxiously, leaning closer, her hair tumbling over her bare shoulders.

He laughed delightedly, tossing his empty glass across the room so that it smashed against the opposite wall. 'Oh, my Nonna! Princess Charlotte has heard already about our dancing tonight, and she commands – she *commands* – that we dance again tomorrow before her! A royal command, Nonna! A royal command!'

The landau bowled along the Surrey lane towards Claremont House, and Vania smiled at Nonna's pale, nervous face. 'Relax, Nonna, relax.'

'If it's possible, I'm even more nervous today than I was yesterday.'

'Be brave now, royal patronage is always important to us.'

'But you already have royal patronage, Armand!'

'It does no harm to keep such a pot boiling, eh?' He glanced out at the sloping land as the landau drove up towards the great house where the princess lived with her new husband. Claremont House was peaceful; a large building in a vast park where there was a lake with a wooded island. Fountains played in the gardens and deer wandered between the trees, and as the landau drew to a standstill by the flagged portico and the doors were opened, Nonna could hear the fountains playing. Footmen hurried down from the house, and Nonna took a long breath as she held her hand out to Vania.

In the oval black and white hallway they stood waiting. Footsteps echoed from the floor above and Nonna thought that whoever it was must be able to hear her heartbeats even from that distance. A sedate young man with a stern face came down the wide staircase towards them, bowing slightly.

'Monsieur. Madame. I am Baron Hardenbroeck, equerry to Prince Leopold. If you will please follow me.'

Nonna glanced at Vania and he smiled, taking her hand. She wore a heavy winter cloak, but beneath it she wore her yellow *Moonbeam* costume, and she felt as if the eyes of every liveried footman they passed could pierce the cloak and see how flimsily she was dressed. They followed the equerry along a gallery with a huge Indian carpet, and then they were by some large double doors.

The royal party waited in the yellow drawing room beyond those doors. Charlotte was dressed in red and white striped muslin, her fluffy fair hair adorned by an ostrich plume. She stood awkwardly, with her hands clasped behind her back, towering over Nonna as she sank in a curtsey. Charlotte nodded, smiling, and beside her her dark-faced, staid young husband stood without expression.

Suddenly Charlotte laughed. 'Madame Vania, is not Hardenbroeck insufferably formal?'

'I – '

Leopold's eyes closed faintly. 'Charlotte – '

'I know, I know. *Doucement, ma chère, doucement*!' The Princess laughed, poking him with her fan, but then she cleared her throat, looking at Vania again. 'We have heard about your Benefit, Monsieur, and it would please us greatly if you would dance it for us again.'

Vania bowed, and the Princess nodded busily, but already her enforced moment of formality had passed. 'Hardenbroeck! Why are the orchestra still waiting in the other room? *Vite! Vite!* I wish to see the ballet before midnight!'

The long-suffering equerry bowed, crossed the room and clapped his hands at a footman. A group of ladies of the bedchamber stood nearby, their fans wafting to and fro as they surveyed Nonna. She felt uncomfortable under such obvious scrutiny – curiosity about the interesting Madame Vania must extend to the Court itself. She glanced around at the elegant room with its yellow silk walls. The furniture was covered in yellow cloth too, and everything about the room was beautiful. Footmen hurried to push the chairs and sofas to the far side of the room to make way for the ballet, and chairs scraped and bumped – and all the while Charlotte chattered to her silent young husband, who either didn't want to reply or had not the opportunity – Nonna couldn't decide which.

A footman came to take the dancers' cloaks. Nonna felt almost naked in the flimsy yellow gauze dress and she shivered in spite of the warmth in the room. At the Opera House she had danced before an immense audience, but it had been impersonal. Here, before such a select, small audience, it was the opposite: personal and close. Uncomfortably, she watched the orchestra settle down, and the princess and her husband take their places. Vania went to stand by the sunny window for the beginning of the ballet. He didn't seem in the least self-conscious as he stood there in the tight-fitting yellow costume, and with his fair hair he looked golden, almost ethereal, as he held out his hand to Nonna. He gently squeezed her cold little fingers, smiling as she came into his arms for the first movements. His strength closed around her again, taking away her nervousness so that there was only the desire to be part of his brilliance, part of him. The music began and they moved into the first steps.

As had happened the previous night, she danced well for him, and when the last notes dwindled away, the Princess was on her feet immediately, clapping enthusiastically. 'Oh, *bravo! bravo!*' she cried, hurrying across the room towards them. 'What do you say, Leopold my dearest, was that not wonderful?'

'Yes, *ma chère*, yes indeed,' he murmured following her, putting out a restraining hand. 'But *doucement*, please, *doucement*!'

'Oh, I think I shall call you that,' the Princess laughed good-naturedly, 'Prince *Doucement*! But now, I shall whisk Madame Vania away to my sofa and claim her entirely. Come, Madame, we have no wish to talk to gentlemen, eh?'

Vania's face was still as he watched Nonna following the Princess to a sofa, where Charlotte insisted she sat next to her. Leopold made no move to converse with him, standing with a disapproving expression on his thin face as his wife chattered conspiratorially with Nonna.

'Tell me, Madame, do you know what a buzz you've caused with the *monde*?'

'Buzz, Your Highness?'

'Why yes! So romantic a background, eh? And now to have snapped up *Le Dieu de la Danse*! Well, how much better could it be? So interesting. I saw you at the Opera House before, didn't I? With that wickedly handsome Sir Philip Hastings.'

'Yes, Your Highness.'

'*Wickedly* handsome. But not a divine genius like Vania, eh?'

'No, not a divine genius.'

'I couldn't believe my eyes when I saw you, you're *so* like . . . . Well, perhaps it's not the thing to chatter of that, is it?' Charlotte smiled, tapping Nonna's wrist with her fan.

Suddenly Leopold was standing by them, and Nonna didn't know whether to get up or remain where Charlotte had indicated. Her face was crimson, and Charlotte smiled. 'I am to be ordered to go in to dine now, Madame, and so I must bid you farewell. But I shall want to see you again. I will attend the first night of your next ballet.'

The Princess stood, holding out her hand, and Nonna sank into as graceful a curtsey as she could manage. 'Thank you, Your Highness.' She glanced at Leopold, who inclined his head very slightly and then offered his arm to his wife.

Nonna remained in her curtsey until the Prince and Princess had passed the group of ladies and the whole party was on its chattering way from the drawing room. She rose then, sighing with relief. Vania stood by a sofa, his face stony.

'Come,' he said, indicating her cloak.

She saw the look in his eyes. He was angry at being shut out of the little *tête-à-tête* and at being ignored as if the only artiste of any consequence was his new bride. 'Armand – ' she began anxiously.

'Come,' he repeated, nodding at the equerry Hardenbroeck, who was still waiting to escort them to the landau. No one moved to help Nonna with the heavy cloak, and she was still tying it at her throat as she almost ran after the two men.

Miserably she sat in the landau as it moved down the driveway, glancing from time to time at Vania's angry face. 'Oh, Armand,' she said at last, 'it was not my fault.'

'Nor, Nonna, was it mine.'

'She – she didn't want to talk about the dancing anyway. She was more interested in how like my sister I am.' She saw the slight mollification clearing his eyes, and so pressed further, embroidering slightly. 'She called you *Le Dieu de la Danse* – I think she admires you very much, Armand. And she wants to come and see the next ballet.'

He smiled then. 'It was not your fault, eh, my Nonna? She – she *swamped* you!' He held out his hands and she slipped across to sit beside him, glad the moment of unpleasantness had passed.

But as the landau moved on its way back towards London, she knew that she had learned a salutary lesson.

Vania must always be first, not his wife, and if peace was to be maintained, then she must see to it that that was how it stayed.

16

The Christmas season approached and invitations began to arrive at the house in Cadogan Street. Vania was on many fashionable lists, sometimes invited as a guest, and sometimes to dance, but there were so many invitations it was impossible to accept them all. Nonna was always included, and if Vania accepted an invitation to dance, he sometimes decided to dance something from *The Moonbeam* so that she could dance with him, but mostly he danced alone. Nonna received one invitation, however, which was simply addressed to Madame Vania, asking her to dance before the Grand Duchess Theodora, a Russian lady who was a guest at Holland House for the season. Nonna thought back to the awkwardness at Claremont House and, without telling Vania about the invitation, she wrote back declining, pleading a prior engagement.

She had not danced at the Opera House again, for *The Moonbeam* was the only ballet in her repertoire and she had to learn more ballets before she could dance again. With Catrine banished, Monique took the leading roles. She was competent, but no more – her only true ability lay in a flair for conveying every mood to the watching audience. Nonna returned to rehearsing in the dark room, but she didn't mind. Princess Charlotte's interest meant that Madame Vania had arrived; she had achieved her father's ambition and her own, and she was content.

Vania was content too. His debts had been settled and life was easy once more. Nonna watched him closely, however, for if he began to visit gaming houses alone again, she knew that there would be little security, in spite of their fame. He teased her good-naturedly, threatening to gamble the night away, but he refrained from going out without her, and he let her draw him away from the hazard tables. Whenever they were out, she was careful to avoid attention focussing on her; she did not need flattery, but Vania did. He adored her, paying constant court. She was his darling, his Nonna, and suitably in second place with the *monde*; and each night in the white bed he gave proof of how much he loved her.

A month after their wedding, he gave her a present, taking her to a coach-builder's and grandly waving his arm to encompass the row of splendid drags awaiting purchase. 'Choose, my Nonna. Which one would you like?'

'A carriage of my own?'

'Vania's wife must have a carriage, eh?' He took her face in his hands and kissed her on the lips. 'Whichever one you wish shall be yours, my darling,' he whispered. 'Nothing is too much for you.'

She looked at them excitedly. Some were gaudy, some dull, but there was one – the one at the very end. It was handsome, painted dark green with black, glossy japanned lamps. 'I like that one, Armand.'

'*That* one? But it is so dull!'

'I like it.'

'Not the red one?'

'No.' She slipped her arms around his waist. 'In the green one I can creep around London without anyone knowing who I am.'

'That would not suit me,' he smiled.

'When I want to be recognised, I will drive out with you, Armand.'

He kissed her again, lingering, not caring that they were being watched. 'Very well, my Nonna, the dull green thing is yours, but *I* shall not drive in it!'

*

Josie stood in amazement as the carriage halted by the bench. 'Nonna?'

'Quick, get inside before anyone sees. Do you like my drag?'

Josie sat back as the carriage moved away. '*Your* carriage, eh?'

'A gift from Armand.'

'You've got him twisted round your little finger, haven't you?'

'If I take care, yes.'

Josie smiled. 'I wouldn't mind twisting him myself. He's very good-looking, and such a *body*!'

'Are you lusting after my husband, Josie Woods?' smiled Nonna.

'In a word – yes.' Josie looked around the carriage again. 'Oh, I *envy* you, Nonna, everything's gone so well for you, hasn't it?'

'Too well, almost.' Nonna looked from the window. 'This time last year I was grateful for the pittance I got from Ackermann's Repository of Fine Arts, and now look at me. I've got beautiful clothes, I'm famous, I've a husband who adores me. It's *too* good, isn't it? I wake up at nights sometimes and I lie there worrying.'

'*Worrying*? Whatever for?'

'What if the truth about me should come out? I'm Vania's wife, I've been presented to Princess Charlotte, I'm accepting invitations to all the best houses – and I once worked at Madame Siffre's! Oh, Josie, I pace up and down in the darkness, looking at Armand as he sleeps, and I'm terrified sometimes, truly I am!'

'You're silly then – and anyway, things are always fifty times worse in the night, *I* know that. And who's going to tell on you anyway? Me? Justin? *I* wouldn't and *he* doesn't remember. The only other person is Philip Hastings, and I don't think he's about to say anything, is he? Talking of the Great Untouchable, how is he?'

'I don't know, I haven't seen him – I don't want to.'

'Liar, Nonna, liar!'

'It's true, Josie, I *don't* want to see him. I asked him to leave me alone and he's done just that. I think he's at Five Ways in Dorset anyway, pleasantly far away from me.'

'They're brave words and I doff my helmet, but I don't believe you.' Josie smiled. 'You've got *Le Dieu de la Danse* but you want Falcon Philip!'

'And you still want William Lamb. We're a pair, aren't we?'

Josie nodded. 'Yes, I still want the Lamb. It's not fair, you know, *you* could embark on an affair with him now and it would be quite acceptable because you're on the right side of respectability. *I* never will be.' She smiled slyly. 'So, you don't want Philip Hastings, eh? You're *glad* he's in Dorset?'

'Yes.'

'He's not in Dorset, he's been back in Town for several days now.'

Nonna's eyes went swiftly to her face, brightening in spite of her efforts at hiding the fact.

Josie laughed, pointing. 'You see? You can't fool me, Nonna, not me!'

'He's back? At Padenham Square?'

'I suppose so. He's back for the Christmas festivities. Justin told me. *He's* grizzling about it – I don't think he likes being kept in hand by his cousin very much. Philip going to Dorset meant that dear Justin had been living life to the full again, he'd been at Madame's every night, getting drunk and being his usual charming self. He really is awful when he's in his cups, and yet he *can* be so nice sometimes. There's a very nasty side to him though, he's black and white if you know what I mean, and sometimes that black bit gets the upper hand all right.'

Nonna nodded. 'Vania and I are going to the Duke of Aldane's ball tonight,' she said quietly.

'Justin's father?' Josie sat back, grinning. 'Well now, and what if Falcon Philip is there then? Eh?'

'He may not be.'

'But on the *other* hand. . . .'

'I know.'

'Justin told me something else, Nonna. Philip is expected to become engaged to Lady Gillian this Christmas.'

'Oh.'

'Yes – *oh*!'

'Well, it doesn't concern me, does it?' said Nonna, looking out of the window. *It doesn't concern me at all.*

Vania was in the drawing room when Nonna returned, and his temper was foul. He said nothing to her as she came in from her first drive in the carriage, and he didn't even look at her as she stood by the fire warming her hands. His fingers drummed the white velvet arm of his chair, and then he poured himself a large brandy from the decanter he held.

'Armand? Is something wrong?' The charming loving husband of only hours earlier had vanished as if he had never been.

'Monique has chosen to sprain her ankle!' he snapped.

'Oh, no.'

'Oh, *yes*! And *you*, Nonna, cannot dance this ballet can you? You do not know it well enough! And so *I* must put up with Catrine's return!' He drained the brandy. 'Vania and that – that *camel*!'

She stared into the fire, wondering how it was that all this had been turned into *her* fault.

'Well?' he asked, sitting forward. 'Have you nothing to say?'

'But, Armand, what can I say? I don't know the ballet, not well enough to dance with you.'

'And *I* must suffer!'

She gazed up at the Christmas greenery hung around the room, wondering what to say to him. 'Armand, Catrine is very good, really she is, and for you she'd do anything, you know that she would.' She went to kneel by his chair, taking the brandy glass from him and putting his hand against her cheek. For her to gaze adoringly up into his eyes was something which always pleased him. His fingers closed over hers immediately.

'I should dance with her, my Nonna?'

'Yes.'

'What if I should like her too much, eh?' he teased gently, sitting forward. 'What if I should wish to make love to her again?'

'Then I shall be jealous,' she whispered.

He pulled her closer, lifting her on to his lap, his hand on her breast. 'Maybe – maybe if you exhaust me first with the sweetness of your loving, then my eyes will not wander, mm?'

'If I exhaust you, then you won't be able to dance either.'

'Always I can dance.' He kissed her, caressing her softly. 'And always I can make love to you, my Nonna. Forgive me that I was a bear with you.'

'I forgive you.' She slipped her arms around his neck, returning the kiss.

'I think – I think maybe I will take you to the bedroom, my Nonna.'

'Yes.'

He stood, his arms around her still as he held her against him. 'You can lighten my moods, take away the gloom, eh? I love you so, Nonna, but never have you said that you love me.'

'Do I need to say it?'

'Yes, for *I* need to hear you say it.'

'I love you, Armand.' She held him tightly. She loved him, how could she *not* love him when he was like this? He could be so dependent, so lost and uncertain. She could play her role, teasing him into smiling, rousing him with a glance, making sure that she said and did nothing to harm the spell, but it was not a role which satisfied her. And it was not the role which she would have chosen. It was the strength of a man like Philip Hastings that she wanted and needed, not the mercurial moods of the man she had married. And yet – and yet she *did* love Armand Vania, but it was a pale shadow of the love she had for Philip.

'Come,' he murmured, tilting her face to his to kiss her again. 'Come, my Nonna, I must make sweet, sweet love to you.'

Later that evening, Monique sat in the chair in Nonna's boudoir, watching her preparing for the Duke of Aldane's ball. 'It is very kind of you to put up with me like this, Nonna.'

'I owe it to you for taking me in when you did, and anyway, you can't stay on your own with that sprained ankle – you'd never get up and down those steep steps in your house. There's plenty of room here and Armand doesn't mind.'

'You are happy with him, Nonna?'

'Yes.'

'You can work wonders with him, I'll grant you that. Earlier today when I did this to my ankle and he realised he would maybe have to have Catrine again, he was a demon – there is no other word for it! He was *furious*; it was my fault, Langley's fault, God's fault and then *your* fault. We were *all* against him! He left in a tantrum, a real Vania tantrum! He came back here and in the blink of an eye you have him all smiles and charm again. He returned to the Opera House, kissed me and told me you wanted me to stay with you, went to Langley and agreed very nicely to having Catrine sent for, and stayed to help teach the new dancers from France some complicated steps. He was all patience, all benign and adorable.' Monique smiled. 'Yes, for a while he was the Armand I first knew, before all the fame and flattery. But being married to him is difficult, isn't it?'

Nonna said nothing.

'Oh, Nonna, I didn't mean – '

'I don't mind what you say, Monique, truly I don't. It *is* difficult.'

'We have not seen the bad side of him for a while, his debts have been paid, he is the centre of attention again, he adores you and life has been treating him well. But today, the other Vania was there.'

'I know.'

'But you don't regret marrying him?'

'No.' There was a hesitation.

'You love him, Nonna?'

'Yes.'

Monique reached out to touch her hand. 'It is still Sir Philip?'

'Hush, you mustn't say that in this house, Monique! Please!' Nonna glanced through to the bedroom where her maid was setting out her accessories for the ball. 'Someone might hear!'

'I only whispered it,' protested Monique. 'Nonna, be careful at this ball tonight, for if Philip Hastings is there . . . . Don't let Vania suspect anything, whatever you do don't let him suspect.'

The maid came into the boudoir. 'Madame? Shall I dress you now?'

'Yes, Geraldine, thank you.'

The maid brought the gown which Nonna had ordered specially for the ball. Monique stared at it as the maid did up the countless little hooks. 'Oh, Nonna, it's beautfiful! So light and yet so wintery, white satin trimmed with fur. For a cloak, yes, but so unusual and clever for an evening dress.'

'It's not too unusual, is it?' asked Nonna, wondering if Monique was discreetly pointing out the gown's fault.

'No, not *too* unusual!' laughed Monique.

'I saw an old print of a medieval lady and she was all satin and fur, and I thought how nice it would be to dress like that again. You *never* see fur on gowns now, do you, and yet once it was always used. Maybe I'll start a new rage, eh? It will soon be *de rigueur* to dress *à la Vania*!'

'It could be that that *will* happen, you know. I've noticed that red hair is in at the moment – a coincidence? I think not. And Princess Charlotte has paid you the compliment of dressing her hair *à la Rome* since seeing you dance at Claremont House. You're the rage, Nonna.'

The door opened and Vania came in. He was splendid in a tight black coat and black pantaloons which outlined his lean, muscular figure very well. He wore a blue waistcoat and frilled white shirt, and a white silk cravat which twisted and frothed at his throat and yet contrived to look excellent. He smiled at Monique, putting his finger to her nose playfully.

'No ball for little Glass Slipper, eh?' he said.

'A fine waltz I would dance, wouldn't I? A grand advertisement for the Opera House.'

He turned to Nonna, his eyes moving admiringly over her. '*C'est épatant*, the gown. And you, my Nonna, are the most beautiful woman in London, eh? Come, we set the Duke of Aldane's guests in a tizzy, mm?' He smiled, offering her his arm.

The Duke of Aldane's Mayfair mansion was brightly lit, and there were Chinese lanterns in the trees in the square outside. Rose petals were strewn on the marble steps, and servants with smoking flambeaux escorted each carriage as it arrived. There was a noise of laughter and music drifting from the large ballroom on the first floor, for the windows on to the garland-hung balcony were open. The air was fresh and cold and there was a hint of snow in the yellow-grey clouds above. Maybe there would be snow for Christmas, she thought, as she slipped her arm through Vania's to go up into the house.

The ballroom was smoky, smelling of wax from the hundreds of chandeliers and candles lighting it, and there was a momentary silence as the steward banged the floor with his staff to announce *Monsieur et Madame Vania*. At the foot of the shallow steps the Duke and his sister waited to receive their guests. The Duke was a tall, angular man with a broken nose and an old-fashioned wig tied with a black velvet ribbon. He was of the generation of eighteenth century gentlemen who adored bright colours, and his coat was of peacock blue brocade, tight-waisted and full-skirted.

'Ah, Vania, Vania, dear fellow, I'm delighted you could come! Delighted!' He held out his hand to the dancer, beaming. 'You've met me sister, eh? Jenny? You know Vania, don't you?'

The woman beside him smiled, nodded. 'Yes, indeed, but Madame Vania, we haven't met, have we?'

Nonna shook her head. 'No, my lady.'

The Duke kissed her hand. 'Madame Vania, allow me to introduce meself. Hal, Duke of Aldane. And this is me sister, Lady Jenny Hastings.'

'Your Grace,' Nonna curtsied to them. 'My lady.'

Philip's mother beamed 'Quite charming,' she murmured, 'and every bit as lovely as rumour had it. You're a lucky man, Vania, to have a wife so beautiful and talented. But then you're beautiful and talented yourself, eh?' Her fan clacked against his arm as she smiled at him.

She was a plump woman, her grey hair dressed high in a wreath of white roses, and she wore a gown of mauve satin which went well with her pink and white complexion. Her eyes were pale blue and she bore not the slightest resemblance to her dark-haired, dark-eyed son. She linked her arm through Vania's. 'I demand your first dance, Monsieur. It's not often that an old biddy like me can tread a measure with the world's most illustrious dancer, eh?'

The Duke smiled at Nonna. 'So, your new husband whisked from beneath your pretty nose, eh? Ah, Philip, Philip, come and rescue Madame Vania, who has been deserted by her husband because of your mother's wiles.'

She turned slowly, and Philip bowed over her hand. 'Madame.'

'Sir Philip.'

He led her on to the floor, where the orchestra was playing a waltz, and his hand was warm against her waist as he held her. 'We meet again then, Nonna.'

'How were the hawks?'

'Satisfyingly unable to cause me trouble.'

'How pleasing for you.'

'You're looking very well, Nonna – as beautiful as ever.'

She looked up at him.

He smiled. 'Does Vania treat you well?'

'Yes.'

'Good.' His fingers tightened over hers. 'I pray I am proved wrong about him, Nonna.'

'So, sir, do I.'

'Oh, you're determined to keep me at my distance this time, aren't you?'

'Yes.'

'I don't like the feeling.'

'Good.'

'La Vania is beyond the reach of anyone as dissolute and undesirable as me, eh?' He laughed.

They danced in silence for a moment and then Nonna caught a glimpse of Gillian Farnsworth dancing close by, her eyes wandering constantly towards Philip. 'I hear, Philip, that you are about to become engaged to Lady Gillian.'

'Oh? And where did you hear that quaint untruth?'

'Josie.'

He looked at her in surprise. 'You still see a demirep like that?'

'Yes – not that anyone else knows.'

'I'm flattered to be so much in your confidence.'

'There hardly seems any point in pretending anything with you, does there? Why aren't you marrying Lady Gillian?'

'Can't stand her, she's so prettily empty of any wit or intelligence. Shall I go on?'

'No, I think you've made your point. You're very unkind about her.'

'*I* see no point in pretending with *you*,' he murmured, smiling.

She returned the smile, her heart almost turning over with love for him. Why, oh why could it not have been different? He nodded at Vania suddenly. 'Have a care of him tonight, sweetheart, he's consumed two glasses of cognac since we've been dancing. And the glasses were rather large.'

The music ended then, and he still held her, glancing up.

'I have engineered the dance so that we stand here at the end. If nothing else, I shall at least have the kudos for being the first man to kiss the delectable Madame Vania in public.' He pulled her close, kissing her on the lips in front of everyone. Then he bowed, smiling, walking away through the watching guests.

Her face was crimson, and something made her glance up. They had been standing underneath a large, ribbon-strewn bunch of mistletoe.

The butler caught Vania's arm quickly as he lurched into the hallway. Dawn was lightening the skies outside and tendrils of morning mist swirled around the door as Nonna closed it. She stood there, sighing inwardly. Vania leaned against the butler, looking at her.

'I will talk to you, Madame,' he said thickly. 'Go upstairs!'

'Armand, perhaps in the morning – '

'Now!'

Without another word she walked past him and up the stairs towards the drawing room. She could hear him shouting at the butler downstairs, and his voice carried into the drawing room even after she had closed the door. He was more drunk than she had ever seen him, his voice almost unintelligible at times, and a foul temper had settled over him, all of it directed at her. She waited in the white drawing room, knowing that he would come to carry on his campaign, begun first as they were dining at the Duke of Aldane's house. He disliked the attention she got, the incident caused by Philip kissing her, the gown she wore, the way he claimed she stole the admiration of *his* audience by cutting him from any conversations. He had accused her of every conceivable thing on the way home, even to saying that she had tricked him into marrying her. His drunken haze took away all sense of reason, and as she heard him stumbling up the staircase she was frightened.

He threw the doors open and stood there unsteadily for a moment, before slamming the doors behind him. '*Eh, bien,*

Madame, you explain, eh?'

'Explain? Armand, I've done nothing!'

'*Non*? This harlot's gown you wear, that was not to draw attention to yourself? And the little scene of tenderness with my enemy, Philip Hastings. That was not calculated to insult and humiliate me?'

'No, Armand, I wouldn't do anything like that to you, you know I wouldn't.'

'I know no such thing!' He staggered closer, his fists clenched. His eyes were glazed and he was breathing heavily; it was like seeing some monstrous stranger standing there, not Armand Vania, her husband.

'So, my little Nonna, you would put horns on Vania, eh? Cuckold me with your Philip? Catrine told me the truth, didn't she?'

'No!' she cried. 'No, Armand, I've been a faithful wife to you, I swear that I have!' She hurried towards the door, thinking only that she had to get away from him. But in spite of his drunken state, he turned swiftly, snatching at her arm, his strong fingers digging into her flesh.

She screamed as he flung her to the floor, and he held her still, hitting her across the face with his other hand. 'No one laughs at Vania!' he cried, beyond all reason now, and his fist struck her jaw again. She struggled, terrified by the pain and by the blind fury with which he attacked her. He was strong, and his grip did not diminish as he continued to strike her, the blows raining over her body and face.

At last, at last he seemed content – or maybe his strength was spent. He fell to the floor beside her, breathing in heavy gasps. She lay whimpering beside him, her body hot and full of pain, and then slowly, she dragged herself up, looking down at him. His eyes were dazed, disbelieving, as if by beating her he had vanquished the grip of the alcohol. He stared, reaching up suddenly, '*Mon dieu*, Nonna – Nonna. . . .'

'Don't touch me,' she cried, 'don't touch me!' She staggered to her feet, holding her torn gown.

'Please, Nonna, forgive – '

But she had gone, running to the door and out on to the cold landing. A sob caught in her throat as she ran up the stairs and into Monique's room.

Monique sat up in bed, startled, and by the light from the landing she saw the cuts and bruises on Nonna's face and the rips in her gown.

'Oh, dear God,' she whispered. 'Oh my dear, dear God!'

17

Josie stared at Nonna as she sat back in the carriage. 'A veil? Is this another new fashion for the *monde's* wife to take from *La Vania*?'

Nonna glanced out at the stark winter scene, the snow-covered grass of Hyde Park slipping past the window. She drew the veil back from her face. 'I think not, Josie.'

'God above!' cried Josie, sitting forward, 'Who. . . .?'

'The great Vania.'

'But – '

'He was drunk and turned on me. This is the result.'

'Oh, Nonna, what shall you do?'

'What can I do? I'm his wife; there's no law which says a man may not keep his wife in order, is there?'

'But those bruises! It must have been dreadful.'

'It was. This is the first time I've come out since before Christmas. Oh, *he's* been to all the balls and masquerades, but he tells everyone that I'm indisposed.'

'Had – had you done anything?'

'I wish now that I *had*. In fact, I was being so careful, trying not to upset him in any way. The artistic tempera-ment, don't you know, can't put up with losing the centre of the stage for one tiny moment!'

'Aren't you supposed to dance with him tonight? The New Year ballet or something?'

'Yes. Either I plaster my face with thick powder and paint, or Catrine takes my place. He wants me to dance – the audience want Vania *and* his wife!'

Josie leaned forward, putting her hand over Nonna's. 'Oh, my poor love. There you are, all respectable and famous, and black and blue – and here's me, a disreputable harlot and never a bruise in all the years. My poor Nonna.'

'Don't sympathise too much, I just might burst into tears.' Nonna twisted her handkerchief in her hands. 'Princess Charlotte may attend tonight, and Vania's all sweetness and light towards me – *anything* to get me to dance. But what if she comes backstage to see us afterwards? She's done it before, I'm told. Oh, Josie, she'd see in a moment the state I'm in; no amount of make-up can hide it close to.'

'What does everyone else say at the Opera House? They must wonder – '

'I haven't been there – this is the first time I've come outside since it happened.'

'Is he . . . ? I mean, how does he treat you now?'

'At first he was horror-struck, and he pleaded with me to forgive him – oh, the usual heartbroken implorings. I've heard them before for one reason or another. This time he was frightened I'd scream to the world that Vania beat his wife. I struck a bargain with him: I'd say nothing of what he did, but he had to stay away from me. I couldn't bear him to touch me, not now.'

'I know the feeling. Revulsion, eh?'

'I'm frightened of him, Josie. You've never seen . . . . It wasn't him, it was some dreadful creature from a nightmare.'

'Oh, I know, I've seen them change like that, and it isn't always drink that does it. So, the *monde's* favourites are not happy any more.'

'No, they aren't. And do you know the irony of it? Philip

warned me about him. He tried to dissuade me from marrying him – and I was mulish and stubborn and refused to listen to him. I even accused him of having another ten thousand resting on the outcome. Most unfair, eh?' Tears hung on Nonna's lashes.

Josie slid across to sit beside her, an arm around her shoulder. 'Never mind, Nonna, never mind – it won't hurt Mr Fancy Hastings to have someone tell him where to get off once in a while. He's devious so often, no wonder you didn't believe him.'

'Yes, but this time he was trying to help me.'

'It still wasn't your fault. Anyway, what are you going to do now? I know you're Vania's wife, but you could leave him.'

'I may be the popular Madame Vania, but the *monde* doesn't like wives who desert their husbands. I wouldn't survive, would I?' Nonna looked out at the snowy scene again. 'I suppose I've got to stay with him, or go back to being destitute like before.'

'I don't know what to say, Nonna.'

'There's nothing *to* say. I think I must try to dance tonight. I must make as much of a name for myself as a ballerina as I possibly can, then perhaps if the worst comes to the worst my reputation for dancing may carry me through.' She pulled a wry face. 'I can't even take myself to the opposition now, Wyndham's been dismissed from the Pegasus, and until they sort themslves out there, the theatre's closed. The Opera House is unchallenged.'

'I – I had heard whispers that all was not well between you and Vania, Nonna – he's been seen out driving with Catrine. Justin told me.'

'Oh, yes, she's his darling again. She simpers and clings, and he loves the spaniel eyes and delicate blossom act. She's learned her lesson this time and she intends getting him back. She can have him. I refused him very definitely, Josie, and he won't come near me for that again – he doesn't know how to cope with being turned away quite so decisively. I lock myself in at night, but I don't think he's even tried the door, thank goodness. Anyway, enough of all my problems, how are you? Did you have a good Christmas?'

Josie smiled then, nodded. 'Better than you could possibly imagine.'

Nonna studied her bright eyes for a moment. 'Let me guess. You've actually seduced the Hon. William Lamb! I can tell that's what it is!'

'Yes. For two whole days he was all mine, Nonna. All mine. And, *oh*, did I love him! It was all his fool wife's fault. He's forgiven her, taken her back, refused to divorce her, defended her for that awful book, and she repays him by tirades, hysterics, more affairs, and being too drunk even to stand sometimes. He was just ripe for the plucking one night, Nonna, and I did not miss my chance!' Josie's smile deepened. 'I know one thing, he was happier and more relaxed with me than he's been for a long time.'

'And you're sunk once and for all.'

'Well, I was before, wasn't I? He's the only one for me, always will be.'

Nonna glanced at her fob-watch. 'If I'm to dance tonight, I'd better get myself to the Opera House and do a few hours at the bar. Wish me luck, Josie.'

'Good luck.'

'Josie – '

'What?'

'Word always gets around to Madame's, doesn't it? I mean, if my husband has done this before. . . .'

'If he has I don't know about it. Not *everything* gets to us, Nonna.'

'I just wondered what it was that Philip heard about, why he felt he should warn me about Armand.'

'Ask Philip.'

Nonna smiled. '*If* I see him.' She sighed, 'I hope Milly can concoct a heavy enough make-up to hide these bruises.'

'You'll be all right,' said Josie, smiling gently, 'and I'll see to it that things look up for you.'

Nonna looked quickly at her, but Josie reached up to tap

the grille of the carriage and it came to a standstill. 'Goodbye then, Nonna.'

'Goodbye, Josie.'

The hum of the audience was quite audible as Milly closed the dressing-room door. 'Here, this greasy paint should do the trick, eh? Oh, lord, lord, your poor little face. That he had a temper everyone knew, but not that he could do this – especially not to you, Nonna.'

'He's never done it before?' asked Nonna, wincing as the dresser patted the make-up over a bruise on her forehead. Surely Milly would know.

'Done anything like this? Oh, Nonna, would I have stood by and let you marry him without warning you, *would* I? But no one must know, Nonna – you understand that, don't you? No one must hear of this beyond the walls of the Opera House – no one untrustworthy, that is. Vania is a god here, and he is respected in society.'

'It won't get out. *I* know which one of us would be blamed, Milly, and it wouldn't be him, would it?'

'No, it wouldn't.' Milly smiled gently. 'Sometimes life is cruel, eh?'

'Yes.' Nonna looked at her reflection. 'Oh, Milly, they can still be seen!'

'Close to, yes – but the audience won't see. Relax now, the Princess *is* here tonight, but she isn't coming backstage. And if she doesn't, then no one else will either. By tomorrow the bruises will be less. The Princess isn't coming backstage because she is unwell – *enceinte* they say.'

The door opened suddenly and Vania was there. He nodded curtly at Milly, who raised her chin accusingly at him before leaving him alone with Nonna.

'What do you want, Armand?' asked Nonna, keeping her face averted.

'Tomorrow we are to dance a special performance of the Benefit again. Langley has had so many requests for it that he's decided to end this season with *The Moonbeam*.'

'Very well,' she said stiffly, still not looking at him.

'There will be posters put up tonight so that they can be seen first thing tomorrow – so you and I will drive together in Hyde Park.'

'Very well.'

Her attitude goaded him suddenly. 'Tonight Catrine accompanies me to Barrymore's; you, Madame, can find your own way home!'

'Very well.' She turned, knowing that he hated to see the bruises he had put there. He stared at her, his eyes very blue and large, and then he went out, slamming the door behind him.

She closed her eyes for a moment. In so short a time everything had changed. When they had set out for the Duke of Aldane's Christmas ball they had been happy and loving; now they loathed the sight of each other. How could they dance as they had done before? How could there be any rapport? Wouldn't they be like wooden figures, stiff instead of flowing?

Her silver gauze dress shimmered in the pale light from the single chandelier suspended above the stage, and silver spangles winked and flashed at the back of the stage. The dim light was intended to pick out those sparkles and the two lonely figures on the stage. It was dramatic and unusual, Vania's idea, and it looked beautiful and unearthly.

Vania took Nonna's hand, holding her close for the first pose. His hands were warm and steady, and their eyes met for a moment before the light music began and she twisted her body, arching against him as he lifted her into the air. She knew then that in spite of everything they would dance as well as ever. The ballet meant more than their feelings – maybe their feelings even added to the way they danced. Her dislike did not deter her from wanting to come up to his standards again, and her appreciation of his brilliance was not impaired by their bitterness.

At the end of the dance, the audience was on its feet, and when Nonna looked up towards the royal box she saw Princess Charlotte standing too. The Princess nodded, smiling, raising her hand once to the two on the stage. Flowers were tossed by their feet, and Vania picked them up, handing them to Nonna.

He smiled faintly. 'You hate me, my Nonna, but your spirit answers me still, eh? Only with me will you dance like that.'

'I know.'

He inclined his head coolly, and as the curtain dropped he turned and walked away to where Catrine waited for him in the wings. The French girl tossed a triumphant glance back at Nonna as they walked away together, but Nonna felt nothing. Catrine could have him; Nonna felt only a strange loathing for him now – a loathing touched with that reluctant admiration which he knew was there still. He was right, there was no one else she would ever dance with as beautifully: he was the greatest in the world.

Monique hesitated. 'Come with me, Nonna. I must go to Southwark first to collect something, but – '

'No, Monique, I'll go back to Cadogan Street, but I'll wait until everyone has gone and slip out quietly. The bruises are going gradually but they're still a little too plain. The Princess liked us tonight, didn't she?'

'It was magnificent to watch, Nonna,' said Monique, smiling. 'And the *monde* adored its favourites, eh?'

'Was he ever – in the past, in Paris, was he violent then?'

'No. Never. He gets angry, he slapped me once – but then that is not like this, eh?'

Nonna sat there alone after Monique had gone. What had Philip known about Vania? It was something only Philip could answer, as Josie had said.

Half an hour later, with her veil over her face again, she walked through the silent theatre. The small crowd of admirers at the stage door had long since gone, but with luck she would find a post-chaise to take her back to Cadogan Street.

Her face tingled from removing the greasy paint, and the doorman smiled, touching his hat and glancing at the veil.

Everyone in the company knew what had happened, but they said nothing about it. There was a mutual and instant understanding that Vania's reputation and therefore the reputation of the Opera House had to be protected at all costs.

There was quite a heavy mist outside, and the air was so cold she could immediately see her breath. She adjusted the veil and then ran quickly from the stage door and out into the cobbled lane behind the Opera House.

'Nonna?'

She hesitated, turning in the direction of the voice. A carriage was drawn up by a street lamp, its team stamping and shorting, and as she watched the door opened and a man got out, his evening cloak swinging heavily as he walked towards her. 'Nonna?'

'Philip?'

He took off his top hat. 'I had begun to think I had missed you.'

'I – I stayed to practise alone.'

'Fibs, Nonna? I know why you stayed behind until everyone had gone – Josie told me about it.'

'She shouldn't have.'

'Yes, she should. Come on, I'll take you wherever it is you want to go.' He took her hand and drew it through his arm. 'I saw your loving husband leave with Catrine.'

'Yes, she's back in favour now and I am most definitely *out*.'

'Where were you going just now?'

'Home.' She smiled wryly at the inappropriate word.

They halted by the carriage, and he looked up at the coachman. 'Just drive for a while, until I give you further orders, Sims.'

'Yes, Sir Philip.'

There was a faint smell of cigar smoke in the carriage. Nonna's face was still hidden by the veil as the team moved away, their hooves clattering and echoing around the silent buildings.

'Am I to talk to that veil then?' asked Philip lightly.

'I think it better, don't you?'

'No, I don't.' He leaned forward suddenly and lifted the veil back from her face.

She took the bonnet off then, dropping it on the seat beside her. There was no shadow now to conceal the bruises, and as the carriage turned a corner, the street lamps threw a pale light across her face. She looked miserably at him. 'Now you see them,' she whispered.

'Dear God above,' he murmured. 'That French *bastard*!'

'Aren't you going to say *I told you so*? You warned me and I paid no heed.'

'Oh, Nonna, do you really think I'd gloat at being proved right?'

'I don't know – I never know anything where you're concerned.'

'Right now I'm thinking of breaking Vania's foul little neck.'

She searched his angry face for a moment. 'Philip, how did you know about him? What happened?'

'I saw the results of his violence – on a face as sweet and pretty as yours,' he said softly, 'but she was more terrified of her husband finding out of her affair with Vania than anything else.'

'Who was she?'

'Her name was Kitty and I would have married her once, but I was deemed a poor match compared with the Earl of Glynne, who also wanted to marry her. Her mother insisted that Kitty became the Countess of Glynne. Her husband was very jealous and the marriage was unhappy. I saw her from time to time – we moved in the same circles, attended the same balls *et cetera*. She met Vania and fell for his extraordinary charm – his spell I suppose you could call it. But she too fell foul of him. I was awakened one night by her arrival at Padenham Square. She was hysterical, terrified, her clothes torn and her face battered. She was supposed to be in Town on a shopping spree, an annual fortnight when her husband took off her leash and allowed her out. She spent the entire fortnight hidden at my house waiting for the bruises to go. I sent my maids out to purchase items to prove she had indeed been shopping. She swore me to secrecy about it – she lived in terror of her husband finding out she had been unfaithful to him. She begged me to say nothing, when I wanted more than anything to run a sword through Vania. I promised her in the end; I couldn't bear to see her so miserable and frightened. But I *did* let Vania know his activities had come to my notice. That is why he and I have such a dislike for each other.'

'And Kitty?'

'She died in childbed a year later. Five years ago.' He smiled. 'Vania was Melisande's lover too at the time – a very versatile and energetic fellow, mm? Kitty was so unhappy in her marriage, she had loved me all along. She had kept to the straight and narrow though, not straying to my bed or anyone else's, until Vania set her at sixes and sevens. One night she spent with him, that was all – her one little fall from grace. And he beat her.' Philip's hands clenched. 'Poor Kitty – she had so much and yet had nothing at all. And now I find myself looking at you, Nonna, and I see the same look in your eyes that I saw in hers. Say nothing, *do* nothing! The truth mustn't get out.'

'That's right, Philip. And it's different this time – I'm his wife. No one can hope to challenge a man's right to chastise his wife. There isn't a male soul in the realm from the Regent down who would back such sentiments. And the *monde* adores Vania. *Le Dieu de la Danse* can do no wrong; they don't *want* to find out anything like that about their adored genius. So, my bruises – like Kitty's – will be covered up, I will dance with him, and life will go on. Q.E.D.'

'The cynical condition fitting *you* like a glove, Nonna? I can't believe that.'

'Well, your philosophy about life is being proved right all around me all the time. I can't ignore that – or miss how successful your way seems to be. If you can't beat it, then become part of it.'

'Being cynical – or trying to be anyway – won't protect you from his violence, Nonna,' he said gently. 'What if he loses control again? And then again? What if he breaks your arm – or your leg? What price your cynicism then – or your damned dancing?'

'What would you have me do? Leave him? Make a scandal by claiming he is brutal? I'll lose, not him. I've been destitute before, terrified of how I'm going to exist. I can't face that again. So, I'll stay, and I'll say nothing and I'll beg *you* to say nothing. Armand won't do it again. He frightened himself as much as he frightened me – he's afraid of his violence, Philip. He stays away from me except for the dancing, and Catrine is his mistress again. I am content to leave it at that. Content because I must be, I have little choice in this man's world, have I?'

He said nothing, for she was right – the glittering society which adored her now would turn its back not on the culprit, Vania, but on his victim. A man had the right to be a monster in his own home.

She smiled a little. 'You must have other things to do tonight but listen to my problems.'

'Nothing of any importance,' he said, putting his hand gently to her cheek.

'Don't,' she whispered, closing her eyes as she felt tears pricking her lids. But she couldn't hold them back, and he pulled her across into his arms, holding her close as she wept. His cheek rested against her hair, and he stared out at the misty streets as the landau moved slowly through the city.

'Don't leave me alone tonight, Philip, please don't leave me alone.'

'I won't.'

'I love you.'

'I know,' he murmured, kissing her. He could taste the salt of her tears on her lips.

She lay awake in the bed, watching the dawn lighten the curtains. A thin pencil of brightness crept through into the room, lying palely across the carpet and falling over a porcelain Buddha standing on a small table. She turned to look at Philip as he slept beside her, his dark hair ruffled by sleep. Why had he come to the Opera House like that? Pity, after what Josie had told him? A suspicion that she would be a pushover for the night? Conscience? Because she was an echo of his beloved Kitty? Why didn't he stay away; did he need constant reassurance that his power over her was still as strong as ever? Did his vanity need that reassurance? Maybe he had had nothing else worthwhile to do and the notion of toying with her appealed to him. It could have been any of those reasons, anything but the fact that he loved and treasured her. She touched his hair gently. But even knowing that, nothing changed her love for him. Lying in the darkness, her body close to his; nothing could compare with or diminish that.

Quietly she got out of the bed to dress. As she buttoned her pelisse, she paused by the bed again to look down at him. Resisting the temptation of waking him, she left, hurrying down the stairs and out into the misty dawn in Padenham Square.

She crossed the wide, grassy square, her steps visible in the dew. Seagulls cried overhead as the morning tide came up the Thames, and she walked slowly beneath the trees. A dog was barking somewhere, and the church bell sounded hollow as it chimed in the next street, picked up then by other bells, at different pitches, different seconds. She knew nothing of the man Philip had sent to follow her, to see that she reached home safely.

Philip stood by the window, looking at the faint trail of her steps in the grass. He ran his ringers through his dark hair. 'Oh, Nonna,' he breathed, 'what did I do the night I found you? What in the hell did I do?'

18

Monique handed Nonna the green turban. 'Vania does not like to be kept waiting, Nonna, and you're already a quarter of an hour late.'

'Let him wait.'

'Where *were* you all last night? I was so afraid he'd come back first and know you'd been out.'

Nonna smiled, twisting her hair into a knot and fitting the turban carefully over it. 'Ask no questions, Monique. . . .'

'I know, and get told no lies. So, you weren't just practising at the bar, eh?'

'My gloves! Where've I put the horrible things?'

'Here.'

'How do I look?'

Monique surveyed the elegant figure in green dimity. 'You look perfect.'

Vania's impatient voice echoed up the stairs, an unintelligible but definitely irritated sound. Nonna took a deep breath. 'Hyde Park, here I come,' she murmured, snatching up her reticule and leaving the bedroom.

Monique pulled herself up from the edge of the bed, limping to the window to look down at the purple carriage waiting at the kerbside. Vania came out, with Nonna on his arm, and there was no hint of the terrible rift between them as he handed her into the carriage and climbed in behind her, waving at the small group of people gathered outside. The posters advertising the repeat of the Benefit had been put up overnight, and the inevitable interest immediately aroused.

Nonna sat silently, waving from time to time as the well-known carriage bowled along towards Hyde Park. Opposite her, Vania did the same, but his smiles did not reach his eyes.

'And where were you last night, Madame?' he enquired suddenly, nodding and beaming from the window.

'What do you mean?'

'Do not play the innocent! Where were you?'

'Practising,' she said drily.

His piercing blue eyes searched her face suspiciously. 'You expect me to believe that?'

'You want me to be perfect for the Benefit tonight, don't you?'

He looked away then. 'You have too much paint on your face, Madame; you look like a harlot.'

'The paint is to hide your handiwork, Monsieur – paint or bruise, which would you prefer the *monde* to see?'

He flushed. 'I made a fool of myself by marrying you, eh, *my* Nonna?

'You married me for a specific reason – the settlement of your debts.'

'You cannot claim that you did badly from the arrangement!'

'*I* haven't claimed that, *you* have. Armand, I see no point in arguing like this. You've made it obvious to me that you no longer particularly like me – very well, I accept that. I will behave perfectly in public, and I will say nothing to your private activities provided they do not touch upon me. But please, please, let us at least speak cordially together. Armand? Is there no friendship left at all?'

'No, Madame, there is not. You are a viper in my bosom, using me to further yourself – you've made *that* perfectly clear. I will tolerate you, and no more!'

She fell silent again, smiling out at a gentleman and lady in a barouche. And so the drive went on. Outwardly Vania and his wife were so happy and complete, but inwardly everything was so disastrous.

The crush of carriages was worse than ever today, for so

many expected Vania to drive out and therefore came to see. Nonna leaned her head back against the upholstery, watching without really seeing. Only hours before – only hours – she had been in Philip's arms, and now where was she? What lay ahead for her? As Madame Vania, she was assured of fame – but what of happiness? Where was the happiness? The joy?

She stared out, and suddenly, unexpectedly, her breath caught. The landau travelled alongside another carriage towards the exit, and she was looking at the Farnsworth equipage. Justin sat with his lovely sister, and he had chosen that very moment to look out too. He began to smile at her and then the smile froze, his eyes widening in disbelief.

She stared back, her heart almost stopping within her. He had recognised her, he suddenly knew where he had seen Nonna Lambert before! Stunned by the suddenness of it, she turned away, glad that a break in the jam ahead meant that the landau could pull away and leave the park. Her heart was thundering then, and her mouth dry. Justin knew who she was! He *knew*! Because of the damned, damned turban! He had seen his Masked Lady again.

She knew very little of the rest of the drive. She waved automatically, smiling and nodding, but inside she was terrified. The past, so very recent, was suddenly all around her again. She looked across the carriage at Vania and the dislike gazed back at her. What possible help could she expect from him, or understanding, or support? *None*.

Dazed, she got down from the landau outside the Opera House. What would Justin do? How long would she have to wait to find out that her name was buzzing all over Town, the delighted scandalmongers spreading it thickly, their lips smacking?

'Madame? Must I stand here all day waiting for you to go inside?' Vania's cold voice interrupted the train of thought. Inclining her head, she went inside to begin the rehearsals for the night's performance.

*

The Farnsworth carriage was outside when she left again that afternoon, and she paused for only a moment as the door swung open. Justin was inside, but he said nothing. She glanced around and then got in.

He smiled, leaning to close the door. 'Drive on.'

'Yes, my lord.'

She clasped her hands nervously in her lap. 'Where are we going?'

'For the moment – a drive. But later? That is up to you, isn't it?'

'I don't understand.'

'Come now, Nonna. We are under no illusions, are we? Madame Siffre's is hardly the same without your sweet presence.' His dark blue eyes were warm. 'What would the *monde* say, eh?'

'What do you want of me, my lord?'

'What I've always wanted of you.'

She flushed. 'No.'

'Then I – er, spill the beans, as they say.'

'Why? What have I done to you?'

'Nothing. But then I'm mean and small-hearted, I fear – and consumed with a gnawing lust for you. I've wanted you since first setting eyes on you – I even wanted you when I met you in your second guise. I didn't know you were one and the same, but now that I do – well, I am not above using whatever weapons come to hand to force you into my bed, Nonna. I'll bleat over Town about you, and I'll embroider – you won't be merely the Masked Untouchable, you'll be the Masked Available. Madame Vania, anyone's for the right price.'

She stared at him. 'The veneer of breeding and culture is remarkably thin on you, isn't it?'

'I cannot argue. I'm a spoilt brat not used to being turned down, don't you know. I want you, Nonna, and I intend having you. Many times over.'

'How delightful a thought.'

'Don't be acid with me, Nonna. *I'm* holding the cards, not you. Society will make mincemat of you if the truth gets out; it will chew you up into the tiniest of pieces and then spit the remains into the gutter.'

'Unless I come into your *loving* arms?'

'Correct.'

'I can hardly imagine that our coming together is going to be a matter of joy and wonder, is it?' she remarked drily, her mind racing.

'It'll do.' He smiled, flexing his long fingers in his pigskin gloves. The sunlight shone on his golden hair and his face was boyishly good-looking as he leaned across to take her hand. 'Oh, come on, admit that the notion is not that displeasing to you.'

She stared back, hiding the loathing she felt. What could she do? How could she endure the scandal if he carried out his threat? The answer was there, immediate and uncompromising. She *couldn't* endure, not at all. She felt as if she were in a corner, and that the walls were pressing in on her, crushing, stifling, robbing her of everything.

He squeezed her fingers encouragingly. 'Let me love you, Nonna. Come now, forget my threats, forget everything but that I love you.'

Love? What did he know of love! Nothing! But she smiled a little. 'And the terms?'

'Terms? Who speaks of terms when love is concerned?'

'Am I to leave my husband for you? Or receive you in an hotel room? How is this *affaire* to be conducted?'

He sat back. 'You're playing with me, aren't you?'

'No. I just wanted to understand *exactly* what you want, that's all.'

'Very well. Leave your husband? Hardly, my dear Nonna. I don't want ridicule, just your body. I have a house; we can meet there. I take it then that you accept?'

'I don't know. I need time.'

'No time, Nonna. I want a decision.'

She looked miserably at him. 'Until tonight, just give me until then. There is a party of sorts before the Benefit, if you would come then I will tell you my decision.' It was so short a time to decide, so very short a time, but what choice had she? In the end she would have to give in to him; the alternative was too dreadful to consider. Too dreadful. . . .

She looked at him. 'Stop the carriage, my lord. I would prefer to walk from here.'

'My lord?' He smiled as he tapped the grille with his cane. 'Surely after all this time you can call me Justin?'

She didn't reply, picking up her reticule, and getting out as the footman opened the door. Justin followed her, catching her hand and making her look at him. 'I mean every word, Nonna,' he said quietly. 'I'll break you if you refuse me.'

'And you speak of love?'

'I do love you – in my way. But I'm very selfish.' He raised her gloved hand to his lips. 'Until tonight then, Nonna.'

He could not mistake the dislike in her eyes as she inclined her head, and he stood beside the carriage, his cane tapping thoughtfully against his boot. He watched her until she passed from sight around a corner, and then he glanced up at the patient coachman. 'Jacob Street, if you please,' he said suddenly, climbing back inside.

The coachman tooled the six horses around in the cobbled street, and set off back in the direction of the notorious house in Jacob Street.

Monique stared at Nonna. '*You* were a masked singer at Madame Siffre's?'

'Yes.' Nonna drank a glass of wine, taking the bottle again. 'Oh, *yes*! So, there you have it, Monique, the truth about Nonna Lambert.'

'But –'

'I'm sorry, Monique, you've always been so kind to me.'

'Sorry? Don't be silly, Nonna. You don't think I believe you were a *demi-mondaine*, do you? I believe every word you've said to me – including what you've told me about Lord Justin Farnsworth. An English toad.'

'The description fits him to perfection.'

'What are you going to do?'

'I don't know.'

'If you drink much more of that wine you won't be able to *walk* straight let alone think straight!'

Nonna smiled, putting the bottle back in the ice-bucket. 'I don't know what to do. Having a glass or two of this has helped though.'

'Be his mistress – and when he tires of you what has he to lose by telling the truth anyway? My guess would be that sooner – or later – Justin Farnsworth will split on you, Nonna.'

'I'm done for, aren't I?' Nonna looked at her friend, her smile fading as she realised the truth of what Monique said. Justin *would* do that, for there was no honour in him at all.

'Yes, Nonna, I think so. So why give him his pleasure? Tell him to go to the devil.'

'Make my downfall sooner and not later? If it is later maybe I would be able to survive the scandal – I could be established enough to weather it. . . .'

'Oh, Nonna, be sensible. The *monde* will not countenance a woman who has apparently done what you've done – you even went to Claremont House and danced for Princess Charlotte. You set yourself up as respectable, when your life has been anything but. Oh, *I* know you're innocent of anything, but *they* won't! There's an expression – further than the bucket, yes?'

Nonna smiled. 'Beyond the pale.'

'Yes. The pail. That's where you will be, Nonna, sooner or later.'

'So, I turn him down. What then? Oh, Vania will dance a jig on me, won't he? A month ago he adored me; now he loathes the very sight of me.'

'You stole his thunder. Vania is not a man to understand or cope with that. But the decision is yours, my poor friend. Put off the misery if you wish.'

'You'd loathe Justin to have his pleasure of me, eh?'

'Yes. But that is a personal view. It does not concern me, does it? If *I* was in your place though, who knows what I would do? Probably, as you now consider, I'd put it off by going with him.' Monique got up, wincing as her sprained ankle gave a twinge again. She went to Nonna, putting her arms around her. 'You can come back to my house. There will always be a home for you there, you know that.'

'Thank you, Monique. You're a good friend.'

'True friends find true friends, *n'est ce pas*? But now, I'm afraid, I must point to the clock and say that it is time to leave for the Opera House.'

'Come with me, Monique. Please.'

'I come. We brave it out together at the party, eh?' The French girl smiled.

19

That evening Nonna dressed in her *Moonbeam* costume in the little dressing room she once again shared with Monique.

'Nonna?' It was Catrine.

She turned slowly. 'Catrine?' she murmured suspiciously. She was enduring all the miseries of the world, and now Catrine was here to prod and prick a little more.

Unexpectedly Catrine smiled, her elfin face friendly. 'I think maybe we are quits, *non*?'

'Quits?'

'Do not misunderstand, I am not here to fight with you – I am not your enemy now.'

'Because you have my husband?'

'Yes. No – because *you* do not have him. I intend always to keep him, you know that?'

'Yes.'

'I have done and said many things to you, and at the time I meant them – *all* of them. You took him from me, *n'est ce pas*?'

'*He* did the taking, not me.'

'Well, it does not matter now, for it is over for you and Armand, yes?'

'Yes, there seems little point in denying that.'

'Then, Nonna, I no longer wish to be your enemy. As a dancer I can admire your skill; you have great talent. But that is because of Armand, isn't it? *He* is the ballet dancer in you. You are wasted at the Opera House.'

Nonna took a long breath. 'I'm out of his bed, Catrine – are you now intent on having me out of the Opera House too?'

Catrine shook her head. 'No, that is not how I meant it. I am not the bitch now. You have skill, talent, genius – call it what you will – but it is not Opera House genius. You are an actress, Nonna. No one can bring out a part as you do. Except Armand.' The French girl smiled. 'But then he is the emperor, eh? Nonna, I wish a truce between us. Please.'

Nonna nodded wearily. She had too much on her mind tonight, too many worries and fears. 'Yes, Catrine. A truce then.'

Catrine looked curiously at her. 'You are so pale, Nonna, are you all right?'

'Yes. Just tired.'

When Catrine had gone, Nonna finished putting the makeup on the remains of the bruises. They were fainter each day now, easier to hide. She stood there then, looking at herself. Would this be her last night at the Opera House? She lifted her chin then, turning to go up to the stage for the small celebration Langley had arranged for this last night of the season.

Her yellow gauze dress was not warm enough – or was it that she trembled with fear? She accepted a glass of champagne from Vania, holding it up to toast the success of the night. She stood with Vania, but he did not address a word to her, and everyone pretended that nothing was wrong, even Langley – especially Langley. High above, the auditorium ceiling was in darkness, the chandeliers not yet lit for the evening's performance, and the laughter from the stage echoed around the huge space, carrying to the gods and beyond. The champagne was dry and very cold, and its taste lingered. She listened to the speeches without really hearing; she felt numb inside. This was all a charade now, an empty mime. Those who were laughing and joking with her, toasting and admiring her, would soon be disdainful, shocked and cold. As cold as the champagne.

She watched Vania as he talked with Langley. He was so golden, so fine to look at, and in that costume he reminded her of the day at Claremont House when he had stood by the sunny window. It was all gone now – his love, her place at the Opera House, her good name. Everything was slipping away.

She knew the moment that Justin stepped on to the stage, although she could not see him. She turned and he was there. He wore the formal court dress which all the gentlemen wore for the Opera House, the cocked hat under his arm and the sword hanging low at his hip. He looked so gallant and handsome, so graceful and fair as he smiled, bowing over her cold hand.

'Good evening, Nonna.'

'Good evening.'

His dark blue eyes were steady. 'I await your decision then.'

'My answer is no, my lord,' she said lightly, as if she commented on the weather, 'I will not succumb to your blackmail.'

His eyes flashed then. 'That is a harsh word to employ!'

'It is the *correct* word for what you are doing to me.'

'Think of the consequences of this.'

'I have, and I have decided that you are louse enough to betray me in the end anyway. So do your worst, my lord – you'll have no pleasure of me!'

'Do you imagine my threats were empty?' he asked quietly, his voice low and angry.

'No – you are despicable enough to do everything you can to hurt me. Quite the noble scion of the House of Aldane, aren't you?' Now that the moment was on her, she was oddly brave and defiant; she would fly in the face of anything and anyone now! Catrine had said she was an actress, and so she was. Justin could not see in her eyes how miserably frightened she really was, how Nonna Lambert wanted to curl up somewhere and just die.

He caught her wrist, releasing her quickly when some curious glances were turned on them. 'Do not think I haven't come prepared for this, Nonna!'

'Shall I call everyone's attention now? You can have the floor to make your little speech. You can entrance my husband and the whole company with your sordid little tale.'

'Oh, no. No, I have something more subtle than that in mind for you. You will regret this, Nonna – I promise you that.'

'Regret turning your bed down? Even when my name is in the dirt, my lord, I shall hold up a banner proclaiming my innocence of that particular misdemeanour!'

He nodded slowly. 'I knew – I knew this would be your answer. I could almost doff my hat to you. If your answer hadn't mattered so much to me, that is what I would have done. But possessing you does matter, Nonna – it matters one hell of a lot, and I won't be defied and then let you go free to laugh at me. I said I have come prepared and so I have. Don't under-estimate me; this is your last moment of London's adoration. Before the end of tonight's performance you will be the laughing-stock and the object of dislike for everyone who has loved you until now.' He inclined his head and turned to leave the stage.

Monique came to stand at her side. 'It is done?'

'Oh, yes. It is done.'

'And he didn't do anything?'

'Not yet. Before tonight is out though, the English toad

will spring his little surprise during the performance itself and there's nothing I can do about it.'

Nonna was in the dressing room, waiting for the call to go on stage. Her body was cold and felt clammy. Dread filled her, and yet she knew she would go on and dance as well as she could. Giving in to fear and pleading illness would do no good; she was James Lambert's daughter, and she would do justice to her name on this last night. . . .

Someone knocked quickly on the door, and at the same moment she heard the boy calling her name. 'I'm coming,' she said, getting up.

The door opened, and she stared into Josie's anxious face. 'Oh, Nonna, I must talk to you –'

'I have to go on now. They're calling me, Josie.'

'But – '

'Afterwards.'

'It's important, very important, that you don't go on stage.'

'I must.'

Nonna walked past her and up to the wings, where Vania waited impatiently for her. The curtain rose, and as she looked towards the boxes, revealed in the arc of light from the stage, she saw that Philip was in his box and that Justin was with him. And then the music increased slightly in volume and Vania was leading her to the centre of the stage.

She danced as if sleep-walking, following Vania perfectly, complementing his every move, being everything to his brilliance. She knew, too, that incongruously and almost ridiculously, she had never danced better – and probably never would again. She curved and swayed; she was light and pliable, possessed by the spirit of everything which was precious to ballet – and on this one final night, she knew that Vania finally appreciated her. He had praised and flattered her, but now in truth she was better than Melisande – she was everything James Lambert could have desired – just for this one – last – night.

There was a hush in the auditorium, a mesmerised silence. The light music tinkled out into the quiet so that the steps of the two dancers could be heard clearly. But then – gradually and insidiously – Nonna became aware of another sound. There was a stirring in he audience, a light whispering which filtered through everything, dissipating the spell of the dancing.

As they turned and twisted, she saw Vania's eyes glance nervously out at the audience, for the whispering had become a hum. Her steps faltered, and she glanced at the boxes as chairs scraped. Some of the important members of the aristocracy were leaving – before the end of the ballet. Someone laughed aloud then, and the music faltered momentarily. With that the hum of conversation became a loud and instant chatter, and the music drifted away entirely as the conductor and the orchestra became upset by what was going on behind them.

Without music, Vania and Nonna ceased the dance, and Nonna stood beside him, looking out at the auditorium. Sheets of paper were being passed from hand to hand along the rows, and it was these sheets of paper which were causing the unrest.

Vania glanced at her. 'What is this?'

'I don't know.'

She looked swiftly towards Philip's box. This must be Justin's work . . . . Philip was sitting forward, looking down at the rest of the audience, and he turned to Justin to say something. Justin grinned, nodding. But Nonna saw no more, for at that moment Langley came on to the stage, gesturing for the curtain to be dropped. But the ropes were entangled and it remained up.

He had one of the papers and his face was flushed with anger. 'Well, Madame? What have you to say?'

Vania looked at her. 'Nonna? It is to do with you?'

She took the paper and read.

Madame Vania, the delectable Miss Nonna Lambert, is better known to half of England's gentlemen as the

Masked Lady of Madame Siffre's whore-house. She sells her favours to those who pay the highest price, and oh how she pleases. The wench who has been presented to Princess Charlotte, and who now dances before you all, is a common harlot, her body is for sale. She is the darling of one of London's most notorious bawdy houses, and the darling also of rather too many gentlemen. Those who wish to test the veracity of the claims of this sheet should toss a suitable coin upon the stage and let the bidding commence.

As she finished reading a solitary coin tinkled on to the stage at her feet. It was quickly followed by others, and Nonna looked miserably up at Philip's box, but only Justin remained, lounging back in his seat smiling at her.

Then a loud, brash, female voice from the back of the auditorium sounded above all the other laughs and sniggers. 'Call my house a whore-market, would you? I'll teach you!' It was Madame Siffre herself, accompanied by quite a number of her girls. She was brandishing her parasol furiously at Justin. 'I came here in good faith, my lord, and you make a fool of me!' Delighted laughter greeted all this, and Justin got up, bowing first to Nonna and then to the furious Madame. As the infuriated woman swept towards the box, he turned and left. At that moment the curtain fell at last on all the confusion.

Langley looked faint, mopping his brow as he shook the paper under Nonna's nose. 'Well? Is it true? I demand an explanation!'

'And I do,' said Vania. '*I* wish to know if I have married a common whore!'

'I am not a whore, Monsieur,' she whispered. It seemed like a nightmare. Beyond the curtain, the audience was shouting and cat-calling, and the curtain shook from time to time as missiles of various kinds were thrown at it.

Vania's new loathing for her spilled over into vitriolic hatred. 'You do not deny working there though!'

'No, I don't deny that I was the Masked Lady.'

'*Sans blague*!' He bowed coldly. 'It slipped your memory

perhaps when you set yourself up here?'

She said nothing.

He caught her arms, shaking her roughly. 'You would make a fool of Vania? Put horns on me? A miserable prostitute and you bear *my* name!'

Langley put a restraining hand on him. 'Take it easy, Vania, that won't help.'

'The only thing to *help* would be for her to go. *Tout de suite*!'

'She has a damned blasted contract – ' began the harassed manager.

'Destroy it!' screamed Vania, beside himself with humiliation and fury. 'She must go! Get rid of her!'

Oh, how many times had Langley heard *that*. The manager looked at Nonna. 'Perhaps it would be best, for the moment. . . .'

'I'll go, Mr Langley.'

'And the contract?'

'I suppose under the circumstances I have little choice but to agree to tear it up.'

He nodded thankfully. Vania shoved her arm furiously. 'Get out!' he shouted hysterically, pushing her so that she stumbled. Langley caught her.

'Vania, if you want the world to know what a bastard you can be, then pray carry on in this vein!'

The dancer's mouth dropped in amazement; Langley had never spoken to him like that before. But the rebuke had the desired effect, for he said and did nothing more.

Beyond the curtain, the Opera House was in uproar, and one word was chanted over and over again. *Whore, whore, whore* . . . Josie and Monique led Nonna from the stage to the dressing room. The sounds and voices were whirling around her dazed head in a giddy way: she had expected something from Justin, but not this, not anything quite as dreadful as this. Monique eased her into a chair and pushed a glass of something into her hand.

'Drink, Nonna, drink up.'

Nonna felt too numb to weep. 'Philip left,' she whispered,

closing her eyes. 'He left at the very beginning of it all.' She felt more betrayed than she had dreamed possible.

Josie looked at Monique. 'Damn all bloody men,' she said softly.

'Josie, you tried to warn me. One day I'll begin to listen to advice when it's given.'

'I was at Madame's when Justin Farnsworth came. Oh, he was careful not to inform her of the exact contents of the broadsheet. If he had, she'd have maimed him for life on the spot.'

Nonna smiled, looking at them both. 'Have you introduced each other?'

Monique nodded. 'Yes, Nonna.'

'What can I do now? Listen to the crowd.'

The whole theatre echoed with the shouting anger of the people who only minutes earlier had adored Madame Vania. Those who appeared at the Opera House were expected to behave properly, and therefore be fit to be presented to royalty. Madame Vania had slipped through the careful net – a low harlot had dared to kiss the royal hand! Nonna looked helplessly at her two friends. 'What am I to do?'

Josie sighed. 'I'm in the same boat – Madame knows I came to warn you, so that's me out on my ear.'

Monique shrugged. 'Well, you can both come to me, of course – but that is the first place they'll think of looking for you, Nonna.'

'Looking for me?'

'They'll hound you, Nonna.' Monique put a gentle hand on Nonna's shoulder. 'They want revenge for your impertinence.'

'Oh, dear God!'

Josie stared at Monique. 'Revenge? What'll they do, for God's sake? Stone her? There's not one of them fit to throw the first stone anyway!'

'No, I've seen before, something similar. In France. Goose-grease and feathers they used then – I was only little but I remember. They're angry, listen to them – they won't let her escape without doing *something*!'

The door opened behind them and Catrine came in.

'Have you come to gloat?' demanded Monique immediately.

'No, I've come to help'.

'Help? *You*?'

Catrine smiled. 'I told Nonna I was not her enemy now, and so I come to prove it by helping. Here.' She dropped some keys into Nonna's lap. 'My house. You can go there – they'll never think of that. You know where it is, Monique.'

'And you?' asked Monique suspiciously. 'Where will you be?'

'With Vania, of course. I will see to it that all Nonna's things are sent to my house. Use it for as long as you wish; I shall not be requiring it.' Catrine held out her hand to Nonna then. 'I *am* your friend now, yes?'

Nonna hesitated, but then took the proffered hand. 'Yes, Catrine. Thank you.' She smiled wryly.

But Catrine saw nothing of the oddnesss of the situation. 'Vania and I will manage – I will manage him, *non*?'

'And the best of luck!' said Josie, not smiling. 'You deserve each other from all accounts.'

Catrine turned and went out, and Josie leaned back against the dressing-table. 'Well, if that doesn't beat all! As calm as you like – I'm taking over your home and your husband!'

'Oh, believe me, Josie,' said Nonna, 'she's welcome to both – more than welcome! I loathe that house, all white and stark, and I begin to more than just loathe my famous husband. I was a fool, such a fool – nothing is worth all this. Not even . . . .' Philip Hastings' name hung unspoken in the air.

Monique was brisk suddenly. 'Well, we've got to get out of here past the crowd at the stage-door. There is a side door, into a tiny yard, and some steps in the wall take you up on to a flat roof and then down again into Harrington Alley. They won't know of that way; we keep it secret for just such occasions at this. Get changed, Nonna, and I will take you and Josie to Catrine's house.'

'Here,' said Josie, 'are you sure about that Catrine? I wouldn't trust her further than I could throw her!'

Monique nodded. 'She won't double-cross – she has Vania and that's all that ever matters to her. Her sting is removed. She will be as she says, Nonna's friend.

Nonna finished the glass of malmsey and began to unhook her gauze ballet dress. A short while later, her hair hidden beneath the hood of her cloak, she went with Josie and Monique to the little yard and up on to the flat-roofed building alongside the Opera House. The shouting anger of the crowd was clearly heard in the night, and Nonna felt almost faint as she paused to listen. Monique caught her arm. 'Come on, we go down here.'

Harrington Alley was deserted, with only a black cat to watch their escape. Several streets away they hailed a chaise, and were soon several miles from the Opera House. Nonna sat staring out at the buildings and thoroughfares of the city she loved so much but which would turn against her now. This morning it had lain at her feet; now it was kicking her. But nothing, nothing mattered quite so much as Philip's desertion. The betrayal was complete.

20

'Oh, Nonna, come away from that window, there's no one there.'

Nonna turned to look at Josie. 'I keep thinking they'll find out where I am.'

'I think they've passed the stage when they want to grease and feather you,' said Josie, smiling. 'Come on, have some of Catrine's fancy coffee.'

Nonna left the window and crossed to the sofa by the fire. Catrine's house was luxurious, and everything about it was French, from the furniture to the colours – dark red and gold, rosewood, dainty ferns, Sèvres porcelain, and Louis Quatorze chairs.

'Lives well, doesn't she? Maybe I was in the wrong trade after all,' said Josie, pouring the thick black coffee into the dainty blue and white cups.

'She's the best.'

'Second best.'

'Best now. He's dancing with her again, and anyway that supposes that I could ever claim to be the best.'

'You were – Monique says so.'

'Only because of Vania – he was why I danced so well. With any other partner I doubt that I could have reached such a pitch.'

Josie stared. 'You can say that even after the way he's behaved? If I was you I'd be remembering his faults, not his brilliance!'

'As a dancer Vania had no imperfections. As a man – well, that's another story.'

Josie stirred some dark brown sugar into her coffee. 'He's goodlooking, but what a dreadful person he was, the way he behaved toward you on that stage – I've never seen anything like it! He all but stamped his pretty foot. And now, all these things he's said in the newspapers about you – I hope he falls and breaks his neck, I do, so help me!'

'He's bound to say them, Josie – he has to protect himself. Any sign of lenience on his part and he'll be assumed to have known the truth about me and therefore to have condoned it. He can't afford that.' Nonna smiled. 'He's no William Lamb, flying in the face of public opinion and careless of surviving.'

'William?'

'Yes. Taking his wife back even after the publication of that book. There were a great number of people thinly disguised in its pages, Josie, and many of them wrote to William saying that unless he set her aside once and for all, they would presume that he had been party to the book's writing and publication.' She smiled again. 'Philip told me, that's how I know. But William took Caro back in spite of it all, because he loved her, because he understood her maybe – I don't know. But Armand Vania is a world away from William. He'll wash his hands of me – and wash my dirty linen in public in an attempt to show how innocent he is of anything. He'll say things about me which he knows aren't true, but he'll say them all the same. It says here in the *Morning Post* that he went on stage after the performance two nights ago and made a speech to the audience denying me, calling me a temptress, a liar, a witch – he virtually asked for some faggots and a torch to burn me! Oh, he'll have played the part of the injured, misused husband with such eloquence, and every man and woman there will have been on his side. I'm England's most notorious woman, and for what? For nothing. I didn't do a thing at Madame's, but no one will believe that – they'd prefer the juicier version.'

'Someone's been out and about nailing titillating posters up about you, did you know?' asked Josie after a moment.

Nonna shook her head. 'No, but it doesn't surprise me. Vania – or Justin, I wonder? Maybe both – separately of course, but two minds with but one thought! What do the posters say?'

'Oh, you know – wild tales of your activities. How many gentlemen you entertained at once. How you spent nights of debauchery with Lord B.'

'Byron? I've never even *met* him, let alone spent a night of debauchery with him! And did *I* sleep with his sister too?' Nonna put her cup and saucer down with an agitated clatter. 'It's a witch-hunt, that's what it is!'

'Calm down, Nonna. I only told you because I thought it only right you should know. Anyway, it doesn't really matter much what else they say now, does it? The damage is done and there's no going back. The question is – where do *we* go from here?'

'I know, that's what I've been thinking. Monique can still

work at the Opera House. No one has a grouse against her. But for you and me it's a little different, eh?'

'Well, the oldest profession ain't so bad! And you'd not lack customers, would you?'

'Turn to prostitution? Never! I'd die, rather. Forgive me, Josie, but that's how I feel. And let's face it, this time round you wouldn't be in luxury at Madame's, would you? And I noticed that when my things were sent here, my jewels weren't among them; Vania wouldn't permit me to have them. So, you have your clothes, and I have mine. We live in Catrine's house until she wants it back – then what? There must be something!'

'Go and foist yourself on Philip Hastings – it's all *his* fault anyway!'

'No, I'll not go near him again,' said Nonna quietly. 'Never.'

'The hurt's showing, sweetheart,' said Josie, leaning across to squeeze her hand.

'He just left the theatre, Josie, and I can't forgive him for that. Maybe – maybe he even knew what Justin was doing.'

'Knew about the broadsheets? Oh, come on, Nonna, I doubt that very much!'

'Why? Why believe the best of him any more – he's shown once too often that he hasn't got a best side. He came to the theatre after you told him Vania had beaten me. I'll grant that he did that. But why? His real reason can only be hazarded.

'He *was* concerned when I told him. He threatened to run Vania through.'

'Well, he didn't – he bedded Vania's wife instead!'

'There's no answer to that, is there?' Josie got up and went to the window. 'God above, you've got me doing it now, twitching the lace aside and peering suspiciously out like a blasted felon. Hullo, Monique's brought someone back from the Opera House with her.'

'Who?'

'I don't know – a fat man. Not my cup of tea anyway.'

Nonna joined her, looking out at the chaise by the

kerbside. The winter wind snatched at Monique's skirts as she turned, holding her bonnet on as its ribbons flapped around her face. As she turned, Nonna saw her companion properly. 'Wyndham! Robert Wyndham! Oh, what on earth has she brought *him* here for!'

'Wyndham? The chap who was chucked out of the Pegasus?'

'Yes, the one and only.'

'They're coming in – better make the best of it, Nonna.'

When Monique and Robert Wyndham came into the drawing room, Nonna and Josie were sitting by the fire with their coffee again.

'Nonna?' said Monique after a moment's hesitation, 'Nonna, I've brought Mr Wyndham to speak with you. I – well, I thought you would be interested maybe in what he has to say.'

Nonna looked at Wyndham. 'And how would *I* be interested in anything *you* say, Mr Wyndham?'

'I'll tell you if you pay me the courtesy of inviting me to sit, missy. I ain't young any more and sneaking round London in so secretive and furtive a manner does little for me dignity.'

'Please sit down, Mr Wyndham.'

He took a seat beside her on the sofa, and she felt herself rise slightly in the air as his weight descended upon the delicate springs. He sniffed, leaning forward with his fat hands clasped on the handle of his ebony cane. 'Well now, my little chicken – plucked, trussed and ready to be roast, are you?'

'That is one way of describing my present state.'

'Or maybe the thought of donning those pretty feathers again would appeal to you?'

'I hardly think that is very likely, Mr Wyndham.'

'But it could be, it could be. D'you mind if I take some snuff, Madame?'

'Please do.'

He flicked a gold snuff box open, sniffed loudly up each nostril, and then closed it again with a snap. 'Now then, I have a proposition. You see, I'm not a vindictive man, Madame – far from it. You were responsible for my departure from the Pegasus; but I do not look back, I look forward. The theatre in one form or another is in my blood, I can't live without it, and so I left the Pegasus and looked around immediately for a replacement. And I found it – the Dove in Pentland Lane.'

'The *Dove*?' laughed Josie. 'It's the end in dumps, that's what that place is!'

'Maybe so, Miss – '

'Woods, Josie Woods.'

'Miss Woods. But it is under new management now – my management. So, I have a theatre and I have enough backing to put on a show. All I need is a magnet to draw the crowds.'

Nonna stared at him. 'Me? Is that what you're saying?'

'Yes. Don't labour under a misapprehension, Madame. The Dove ain't about to become another Opera House, or Pegasus. No, by God, I'm in this now to put on *burlesque*, shall we call it? Saucy shows, Madame Vania, shows just on the right side of polite but almost tipping over. If you were the Masked Lady, then I know what you're capable of – you can dance, act and sing. And by all the Saints, you've a reputation second to none at the moment. That's my proposition; accept and I'll put you back where you belong – at the top of the proverbial glittering ladder.'

'But on the naughty side of the rungs,' she said drily.

'Why not? You've done it before.'

'I was incognito then,' she reminded.

'Then you had something to lose; now you do not. You can only gain from this, Madame. Your good name is non-existent. You're the natural choice, and I pray you will accept.'

'I do not know whether to be pleased or insulted.'

'To be insulted would be a little like shutting the stable door by now, would it not? Please do not look so offended and outraged, Madame, for I am not set upon insulting you for the sake of it, I merely wish to point out to you that you have nothing to lose and every single thing to gain by hearing me out.' He smiled faintly. 'Indeed, you had my reluctant but sincere admiration on the two occasions when we met before. Yes, I regard you as a woman of great strength of character and great insight – hence my belief that you will view my offer with favour.'

Nonna looked down at her hands, which were clasped demurely in her lap. Had she anything to lose? What was left anyway? Her father's name was already dragged through the mud because of Justin's pamphlets and Vania's vehement speeches and denials. Wouldn't James Lambert have wanted her to salvage what she could? Wouldn't he? Her green eyes went from one face to another in the little drawing room. What should she do? She wasn't alone – Josie was destitute too. Wasn't there an obligation to take what was offered and seek something to help Josie too?

Josie smiled at her. 'Don't let him push you into anything you don't want, Nonna. It's not worth it if you're miserable.'

'Monique?' Nonna looked up at her other friend.

'I thought you would want to hear him. I can say no more than that.'

'You think I could do it?'

Monique nodded. 'Oh, yes, Nonna, you could do it. Vania himself said that you had the ability to act what you danced – I *know* you'd do well with Monsieur Wyndham.'

Nonna looked at Wyndham. 'I presume that I am to be billed as Madame Vania?'

'Naturally. Any other name would be pointless in the present climate. I make no secret of it, Madame. It's your notoriety which gives this the piquancy and appeal, is it not? I am in the business to be successful, to have a nose for what will catch the public's imagination. You, Madame Vania, are It. I tell you what, this afternoon I shall be at the Dove. If you wish, I will meet you there and we can look the theatre over together, view the prospective scripts and so on.' Wyndham toyed with the handle of his cane for a moment. 'I can imagine that your circumstances at the moment are hardly what one might call *comfortable*, that financially you are in dire straits? That, of course, can be rectified. I have patrons well prepared to back a project such as this – especially with *you* involved. The theatre cannot be ready for a first night before November at the earliest, so there is time and money enough to make certain that this is a success, Madame.'

She nodded. 'I am almost convinced, I promise you, but first of all I would like to see the Dove, Mr Wyndham.' She stood. 'This afternoon?'

'I'm there all day from now on. Until later then, Madame Vania.' He rose slowly, tapping his hat on, and then he bowed and went out to where the chaise still waited for him.

The room behind him was silent, and then Nonna chuckled. 'Oh, Vania is going to *love* this!'

'I hope he chokes when he hears,' said Josie, grinning.

But Monique put a newspaper into Nonna's hands. 'I do not know a gentle way of breaking news like this, Nonna, perhaps you had better read.'

'Philip?' The word slipped out immediately in sudden fear.

Monique smiled. 'He's all right, Nonna, just read.'

Nonna read the little article where Monique pointed. 'A duel? With Justin? But – '

'Justin was left for dead and Philip Hastings was forced to flee the country. Duelling is a serious crime, Nonna. It seems that it may have been over Lady Gillian. There are whispers that Philip dishonoured her and then refused to marry her, and she had to be hastily married to a poor northern gentleman who was prepared to take her as his wife for a sum of money.' Monique glanced at Nonna unhappily. 'I'm sorry, but I had to tell you.'

Josie spoke lightly. 'He only left Justin for dead? A pity he didn't finish the little dungheap off completely while he was at it!'

Pentland Lane was narrow and busy, with a daily market

taking place noisily before the closed doors of the Dove theatre. Nonna adjusted the veil which hid her face, and then climbed down from the chaise, paying the post-boy. She glanced at Josie who climbed down behind her.

'This is it?'

'That's the Dove all right – I've been here before. Oh, a while back, when I was a kid. It hasn't had a lick of paint since then by the look of it. And what a neighbourhood – more harlots and footpads per yard than anywhere else in London.'

Nonna looked up at the old building. Plaster was crumbling from the facade and, as Josie had pointed out, it badly needed new paint. There was an air of desolation and past glory about the old place, but even as they stood there on the pavement among the discarded old vegetables and fruit from the market, the doors of the theatre opened and two workmen came out carrying a ladder. Pails of paint swung from the ladder, and the men whistled cheerfully.

'Mind out, luvs, that's the job!' they called in warning.

Nonna and Josie stepped quickly aside as the men pushed through.

Josie shrugged. 'Nothing to lose, Wyndham said, so let's get on with it, eh?'

Nonna smiled. 'After you.'

The theatre was dark and noisy, hung with oil lamps which spluttered and hissed smokily. The seats were half old and half new – the new at the back, their green velvet clean and tidy; the old at the front, moth-eaten, dull and tawdry with poor gilt paintwork on the arms. Everywhere there was the smell of paint, sawdust and candlewax, and the place was so noisy with hammering, shouting and laughing workmen that Nonna could hardly hear herself think. She gazed around in amazement at the transformation which was taking place gradually before her eyes. The old Dove was being reborn, the ancient, decaying red and gold decorations being changed into crisp green and cream. Men were working close to the ceiling, painting fresh gilt on the moulded plasterwork.

Robert Wyndham's wheezy voice spoke behind them suddenly, and they turned. He smiled. 'A reformation, eh, Madame Vania?'

Josie nodded. 'It certainly is.'

'Ah, but of course, you are acquainted with the old place, aren't you?' He tipped his hat back from his forehead, swivelling his cigar from one side of his mouth to the other. 'I've great plans for a veritable metamorphosis. The inside is being done secretly – very few know what's going on. And then, lastly, the exterior will blossom out and London will have its eyes opened! The Opera House will retire to lick its wounds when we've finished! Yes, by *God* they will! We'll see to it, won't we?' He grinned slyly at Nonna.

'We? *We* might not be doing anything, Mr Wyndham.'

'We will. I have a feeling that we will, Madame. I've one particular script I would like you to cast your eyes over – a young writer's first effort. He's a shy fellow, but his writing's clever and witty. It flows from one situation to the next like honey.' He glanced around the theatre with a satisfied look on his heavy face. 'There's to be a room behind the stage, Madame – a *reception* room – for want of a better description. I thought it a natty idea, eh? The adoring public can come there and meet La Vania, fall at her feet, profess their love, *et cetera*.'

'A reception room?' she asked slowly, glancing at Josie.

He intercepted the look and laughed. 'For talking in, dear lady, no more than *talking* in! You must be a little accessible, eh – but not too accessible. Anyway, that's for the future – for the moment you must meet young Bannister, my captive author.' He stepped over some planks and pots of paint, helping them both over after him. They followed him backstage, passing through the beginnings of the reception room of which he'd spoken. A large package had been delivered, and they paused a while as it was opened and Wyndham grinned delightedly as the men began to unfold the new drop curtain of bright green velvet trimmed with golden braid.

Wyndham's cluttered office was dusty and littered with papers, scripts, piles of books and still more pots of paint. A thin, pale young man was sitting at a piano at the far end of the room, and he stood shyly as they came in. He had ginger hair and freckles, and his light brown eyes had pale, curling lashes. The hand he held out to take Nonna's was long and white. 'Madame Vania.'

'You know me?'

'I've seen you dance.'

Wyndham skipped through introducing Josie, and ushered everyone to sit down, which was achieved after a few moments when a fourth chair was brought from a store room.

'Now, Madame,' wheezed Wyndham. 'Young Peter Bannister here has written a musical play concerning the activities of Don Giovanni. The Don dies and is, naturally, despatched down to Hell – but alas for Old Nick, the Don is too hot for Hell and has to be got rid of with as much haste as possible. But where is he to go? That's the problem. Old Nick comes up with the only possible answer, for in the whole universe only one place is even hotter than the wicked Don. England. Hence the play's title, *Don Giovanni in England*. Peter's seen to it that everything is in it: saucy songs, cheeky lines, a woman dressed as a man – everything to titillate the interest, d'you see.'

'A woman dressed as a man?' asked Nonna suspiciously.

'You, of course, my dear Madame.'

'*Me*? Dressed as a man?' Nonna stared at him for a moment and then stood. 'I think sir, that you are under something of an illusion about me!'

'Sit down, dear lady, please sit down,' he waved her gently back to the seat. 'Don't take umbrage. Nonna – forgive the intimacy – you are perfect for such a role. They'll pay a fortune to come and see you as Don Giovanni, and by God, you've got the figure to set them into raptures when they get a peek at your legs! Legs revealed in the ballet are not to be revealed in tight hose or trousers? It don't seem much different as far as I can see.'

Double standards? She sat down again. 'Very well, I'm still listening.'

Peter Bannister sat forward. 'Madame, the possibilities of this play are legion.'

'I can imagine,' she replied. 'The notorious, headline-hogging, tongue-clattering La Vania, swaggering around the stage swinging her hips suggestively from side to side and singing bawdy songs! As you say – legion.'

Josie touched her wrist suddenly. 'He's right you know, Nonna. It could be absolutely *marvellous*!'

'You'd do it, I suppose!'

Josie grinned. 'Yes, I would – except that I can't sing, dance or act. You'd sail through it, Nonna, honestly you would. I can just see it now. . . .'

'So can I.'

'Oh, come on, admit that it's a good idea,' pressed Josie excitedly, glancing at Peter Bannister. 'I can *tell* that Mr Bannister's play is going to be a success!'

'Oh? How?' Nonna sat back. 'You haven't even glanced at the title page of the horrible thing!'

'I can tell, believe me.' Josie blushed slightly, looking at the young writer again. 'Oh, *please* Nonna, please say you'll do it! There'd even be something I *can* do – I can sew anything you care to mention, it's my only real talent apart from – well, I can sew, put it like that.'

Wyndham lit a new cigar, blowing wreaths of smoke across the room. 'Well, there's always room for seamstresses in a theatre, especially good ones. So, Madame, we are all waiting for you to agree.'

'I don't know.' Nonna stood, going to the tiny, grimy window and looking out into a narrow alley where damp dripped down the walls. What should she do? This was so different now, everyone would know exactly who she was.

Peter Bannister came to stand beside her, reaching out and drawing a silly laughing face on the dirty window with his finger. 'Madame, my play is cheeky, I grant you, but it is also clever and witty. The audience will laugh, lick its lips – and appreciate the humour at the same time. And they'll leave the Dove in good spirits, looking forward to coming again.'

She looked at him. He was slightly-built and not much taller than she was. 'You're proud of it, aren't you, Mr Bannister?'

'Yes, I am. This whole thing is my opportunity of becoming a well-known writer, much in demand and assured of a comfortable life. It is also Mr Wyndham's opportunity of showing that he's still the best manager in the land. And for you, it's an opportunity too. We all need the success of *Don Giovanni* for one reason or another, Madame. Please consider your answer most carefully.'

She studied his face for a long while, and he met her gaze without looking away. 'Very well,' she said, 'very well, Mr Bannister, I'll be your Don Giovanni.'

Josie beamed and Wyndham clapped his hands. '*Hallelujah*! We're in business, *mes enfants*!'

He bent down and took a bottle of champagne from a bucket by the side of an old desk, and she smiled – he'd been sure of her all along. He popped the cork and poured the frothing liquid into waiting glasses. 'And we've the rest of the winter, all the damned summer and so on to prepare, rehearse and gradually let the *monde* know what's going on. By God, we'll have them in a frenzy come November and the first night, eh? My dear Nonna, I shall make of you the greatest attraction London's known. You'll be everybody's sweetheart – and by that I mean *everyone*! Not just society nobs, but lesser beings too.'

She smiled. 'And shall I carry a tricolour and yell for liberty while the orchestra plays the Marseillaise too?'

Josie shivered as the chaise rattled along the wide thoroughfare, and she tucked the rug around her knees again. 'All that champagne and I'm still cold!'

'Yes – it's fright, I think. It is for me anyway. Have I done the right thing, Josie?'

'You're going to *thump* London around the ears this time, Nonna.'

'Yes, but will it thump me back?'
'Peter's right.'
'Oh, it's *Peter* is it?'
'I like him.' Josie looked away. 'I believed him anyway, about the play.'
'Yes, so did I. That's what decided me. Let's pray our trust is well-placed.' Nonna stared down at her lilac pelisse and cream skirts beneath. 'Armand's going to have a fit of the vapours to end all fits of the vapours when he hears about it.'
'Serves him right, the nasty little frog.' Josie smiled. 'He may look like the Archangel Gabriel, but he's Old Nick in disguise! Let him froth at the mouth for all you should care after the way he's behaved towards you. You didn't do anything wrong – '
'I did, I committed adultery with Philip.'
'He doesn't know that! He's accusing you left, right and centre without any proof at all. Anyway, he's committed adultery too.'
'That's acceptable; he's a man and therefore he'll be regarded as a fine buck for his activities. *I* am branded a whore.'
'I'm not just branded, I *am* a whore.' Josie grinned. 'I liked Peter Bannister, Nonna, and do you know why? Because when I was talking to him and he asked me about myself, I was perfectly honest – and it made not the slightest difference to him. He's like you – all right.'
'Exit the Lamb?'
'Oh, I wouldn't go *that* far. I can't stand ginger hair and freckles.'
Nonna looked out of the window, her glance moving up the sweep of a church tower. 'I know one thing: if I can make *Don Giovanni* a success, then I will. I've decided, and I'll make the most of whatever I can.'
'You'll do, Nonna, you'll do. Wyndham's right, there won't be anyone to touch La Vania in the whole of England. And I'll stitch you costumes more exotic and wonderful than anything yet seen on the stage, I promise you.'

'Yes, that's what I'm doubtful of – your notion of what's exotic and wonderful.'

Josie laughed. 'After all this, you're still a prude, Nonna Lambert!'

The chaise slowed at a corner and they both saw the newspaper placard at the same moment. *Hastings flees England*. Nonna looked away quickly.

'Forget him, Nonna, he's not worth a moment's worrying.'

'I know. But it's easier said than done, isn't it? He's been a rat, every time he's been a rat, but still there's something – '

'Forget him,' said Josie again. 'We've got better things to think about now. The Dove is all that matters, making the play a success. I'll be there, prodding you with a pin if you start dithering.'

'We'll have to find somewhere to live. We can hardly stay at Catrine's for long.'

'A bit longer, eh? Until the hue and cry over you has died down a little. Then we'll see. Let Wyndham find you somewhere – if he wants a bright new attraction then he'd better find her a little bit of heaven to hang her hat in, hadn't he?'

21

Six months later, when the summer sun was warm and bright, and flowers made everything colourful again after the grey cold of winter, a black barouche turned slowly into the driveway of a large detached house in a quiet side-street. The team of dark bays snorted a little, their harness jingling as the coachman tooled them around the curving drive towards the house with its array of windows, its cupolas and portico. Nonna draped her Indian shawl around her shoulders and sat forward to look at the house. Beside her, Robert Wyndham swivelled his cigar thoughtfully. 'Well, it's fancy enough, anyway.'

'And expensive,' she said.

'Appearances must be kept up; the Dove's premier attraction don't live in hotel rooms.'

'I'm quite happy at the Black Horse.'

'That's not the point. You are to live *grandly*. Anyway, let's take a look around and then decide, eh?'

After inspecting the whole house with its galleries, fourteen bedrooms, bathhouse, immense kitchens, drawing room, dining room and ballroom, Nonna felt almost struck dumb at the size of it. She stood in the drawing room, looking around at the dust-covered furniture. Through the tall windows she could look out over the roof of the ballroom and into the formal Dutch gardens with their regular lily pools and carved trees.

'You like it?' Wyndham jingled his keys.

'It's so *large*!'

'*Ergo*, it's suitable.'

She smiled. 'I suppose so. I'm glad Josie will be with me – I'd hate it on my own. I'd be talking to my shadow in a week.'

'You won't be alone much after *Don Giovanni* rocks the realm, that I promise you. The reharsals are going better than even I hoped. You're very good, Nonna, *very* good.'

She linked her arm through his. 'I hope so. If *I* fail then everyone goes down to the sewers with me.'

'Nobody's about to go down any damned sewer, I assure you. Don't worry all the time!'

She'd become fond of Robert Wyndham during the months she'd been at the Dove. His interest and kindliness were fatherly and sincere; like Nonna, the real Robert Wyndham was quite unlike his public image.

'It's the waiting,' she said. 'I seem to have been going

over parts of *Don Giovanni* for ever!'

'I know. Time with leaden feet and all that. I'll warrant Princess Charlotte is saying that too, now, eh? She and you both due *out* in November!'

'I hope we are both pleased with the outcome of our labours.' She smiled. 'I wonder what the Princess thought when Madame Vania's terrible past became public knowledge?'

'From what I've heard of her, I would imagine she fell about laughing at the joke of it, and then was rebuked by that sour young husband she adores so much.'

'*Doucement, doucement*,' murmured Nonna, remembering.

'I hear your every sallying forth is greeted with interest still.'

'Yes. The snubs continue in public – and the *billets-doux* continue in private. La Vania is still notorious.'

'Keep it up.'

'I haven't got to try – I just have to show my face. Barrymore's won't admit me, and neither will half of the other so-called respectable clubs and hotels. And all because I worked as the Masked Lady – that's *all* it's about! And when I think of the activities *they* get up to in private, I fail to understand why they can be so aghast at that!'

'Brave it out, my dear. They'll be licking your feet again soon.'

'If they put their noses by my feet I shall find it hard not to kick them!'

'While you're in a fighting mood, perhaps we should have it out about my Yellow Room.' He folded his arms the cigar working busily.

'A reception room for La Vania to meet her admirers in has too obvious a connotation for my liking.'

'There is not a *bed* in it!' he said wearily, for it was an argument which had been going on for some time. He was determined to have the Yellow Room, and she was equally determined that she would not agree to it.

'It's just the way it will be seen.'

'Ah, but it's such an elegant room, so superior and tasteful. And, damn it all, you won't be left alone with half of London's *beaux*!'

An elegant room. Yes, it was – furnished by Gillow. By Gillow. She turned to look out of the window again, and she could almost hear Philip's voice. 'Yes, definitely Gillow,' she said, smiling faintly.

'Yes? Did you say yes? That's it then, the Yellow Room stays.'

'All right, I give in, I give in. Have the Yellow Room. But hear me out now – La Vania may become everyone's darling, but she'll be no one's bedfellow. I mean it; there'll be no one able to point a finger at me ever again.'

'That is entirely your concern, but I admire your decision. Besides, as the resourceful and crafty Madame Siffre knew so well – your *un*availability will be the magnet. Every man-jack of them will think he will be the one to succeed.'

She nodded slowly. 'You know, for all the chitter-chatter about me, there's only one man in the whole world who could truly and honestly point a finger and accuse me of anything. And that man is not Armand Vania, who knows nothing of what I have or haven't done but accuses me left, right and centre of every cardinal sin from eating the ancient apple onwards!'

'The more noise he makes about you, the better for us, my dear. Let him rant and rave until the cows come home and after. This divorce rumour – it's true?'

'I've had a preliminary visit from a lawyer, that's all. Oh, Armand is going to toss in every single nasty little thing he possibly can.'

'Hysterical *parlez-vous*. We should have sent the lot of them to St Helena.'

She smiled. 'If he goes on the way he is at present, I shall end up with a reputation like Boadicea, Eve, Delilah, Jezebel and Messalina all rolled into one neat, poisonous package.'

'What a stirring notion.'

'It's true though, and if you were me I doubt if the notion would please your finer feelings any more than it pleases mine.'

'If *I* were *you*, my dearest Nonna, I'd be set upon making capital out of all this. There's the difference between us, eh? I ain't *got* any finer feelings!'

'Yes you have, Robert Wyndham – you can't bear the thought that you are considered less than the best. That's *your* Achilles heel.'

'Oh, God above, Greek mythology now. I think you should do what any damn feller does occasionally – drink yourself under the proverbial table!'

'That *would* do the Dove the world of good, wouldn't it?' she smiled.

'If Vania starts creating mayhem about getting his divorce, you contest it,' he said suddenly, chewing the cigar.

'Contest it? How can I – my guilt is plan and obvious!'

'Argue then. Say he beat you – which I for one know he did. Sling a little unpleasant mud around – anything to keep interest at fever pitch for November.'

'I don't think I can,' she said, turning away from him. 'It's not *me*, Robert.'

'It's not *you* we're concerned with, it's La Vania of the Dove. An entirely different kiddle of fish. And if you're too delicate and refined for it, let me step into your shoes. I'll write as dainty and vitriolic a letter to Vania's lawyers as has ever been penned since the days of papyrus.'

'You?'

'You sign the blasted things. My dear, we have to make as much noise and commotion as we can. We want the production of *Don Giovanni* to be the beginning of bigger and better things, so let your unpleasant little husband pay the price of his selfish, self-centred manipulations and blusterings. He is loathsome in the extreme and it would delight me to poke his pretty little French nose.'

'All right, all right, I agree. But there must be no untruths in my accusations. That must be perfectly clear from the outset. I'll accuse him of living with his mistress, of beating me, of neglect, of anything like that, but nothing more. *He* may be able to lie, but I won't.'

'You're too damn nice! Pay him in his own coin, blast it!'

'No. I won't sink to his level.'

He shrugged. 'All right, it's agreed. I'll set his crooked French heart in a tizzy, don't you fret. He'll miss every damn cue at the Opera House after reading my missives.'

She pulled the window catch and opened it, sniffing the perfume of the roses climbing the walls close by. 'It *is* lovely here.'

'Well, it fits you, Nonna. You're the most beautiful and faultless wicked lady I've ever come across in my whole damned life. You've the reputation of the world's greatest whore and yet are a saint!'

'My reputation,' she reminded him, 'is now becoming partly *your* responsibility. You are making certain the pot keeps boiling.'

'Yes, and I warn you, when the posters are out and the identity of the Dove's new attraction becomes common knowledge then I shall be tossing fuel on the fire under that pot. I mean this venture to work, Nonna.'

'I had noticed.' She smiled. 'Do your worst. As has been pointed out, I've nothing to lose any more.'

'Ah, now that brings me to a more delicate and personal point.'

'What?'

'Philip Hastings.'

'There's nothing to be said on that!' she said quickly, 'And Josie had no right to tell you.'

'She had every right. I wanted to know why you moped around by yourself so much, why there wasn't some young buck hogging your evenings and nights. A wench as handsome as you. Anyway, I prevailed upon our adorable seamstress to tell me the truth, and so – eventually – she did. I now know that the man you want is Sir Philip Hastings – late of London's fair parish, ex-Dorset hawker, *et cetera, et cetera*.'

'So, you know the laughable truth.'

'Laughable?'

'Well, someone like me falling in love with someone like him. Anyway, it's over and done with.'

'No it isn't – not when you dream and moon when left alone. You're as in love with him as ever. So, I thought you might like to know. . . .' He removed a dust-cover from a velvet-upholstered chair. 'Sit down, Nonna. Now, your precious Hastings fought a duel with his cousin – yes?'

'Yes.'

'A duel which smelled somewhat at the time for various reasons. The first reason suggested was that he had – er – *soiled* Lady Gillian Farnsworth. The second – murmured about a little more surreptitiously – that he picked the quarrel with Lord Justin because with him out of the way the Dukedom of Aldane comes whistling through the air to friend Hastings. Right?'

'But Philip wouldn't do that!'

'The first or the second?'

She looked away. 'The second.'

'Well, whatever the real reason for the duel, the matter left an almighty odour in high places. Duelling is against the law, and this particular one went so far that Lord Justin was apparently mortally wounded. Exit Hastings – stage east. So, there he is, sitting disconsolately somewhere in Europe, unaware of the fact that all is forgiven and he is free to come home to Mother England.'

'What?' she asked softly. 'All charges against him dropped?'

'They had to. Aldane wasn't about to let his son and heir – who miraculously recovered d'you see – be prosecuted for duelling. Strings had to be pulled, and quickly. And to release one duellist, the other had to be released too. So your Philip is not a wanted man in England any more.'

'He can come home?'

'Ah – there is one small problem – no one knows where he is. Apart from that minor irritation, yes, he's free to return. Maybe you'll cease to mope now that you know, eh?'

'I'll *always* be moping about him, Robert – always. He doesn't want me and it's a fact I must learn to accept.'

'The man's a bloody idiot.'

She smiled, getting up and rearranging the dust cover. 'Let's go now. I've a rehearsal to do soon.'

'And I can set in motion the various bits and pieces to get this house for you?'

'Yes.'

'And the Yellow Room?'

'Yes.'

'Ah – sweet success – I *knew* if I bleated long enough I'd win.'

'You're unbearable when you're triumphant.'

'It's part of my charm.' He tapped his top hat on and offered her his arm.

As the barouche moved away down the drive again, Nonna turned to look back at the house. Eighteen months ago she'd been destitute and living in Mother Carter's; now she was about to live in a magnificent London mansion. Eighteen months ago too she'd been dismayed and shocked at the gown she was expected to wear at Madame Siffre's; now she was prepared to wear tight hose and show her legs to the world.

The summer turned to autumn, and the preparations at the Dove continued on time. The costumes, songs, dances, chorus – everything was perfect. Nonna moved into the house in Bettersleigh Street, much to the annoyance of Sir Piers Alvney, who was one neighbour, and Lord Ryan, who lived on the other side. But after their initial efforts at preventing her from acquiring the property, they left her well and truly alone. She even found, to her amazement, that their servants were not permitted to speak to her servants – even to the extent that when one day she was returning from rehearsals in her carriage and found Lord Ryan's new barouche with a loose wheel, his coachman refused the offer of extra hands which would have meant an instant repair. She had shrugged; very well, let the silly drag remain where it was – in imminent danger of final collapse into a ditch. As she drove on, she heard a crunching sound from behind and looked from the window to see that that was indeed what had happened. She glanced up and caught the eye of her footman in his perch at the back; in a moment they were both laughing, and by the time she reached home she realised that she felt better than she had for a long time! Let them snub her, let them worry in private that she might reveal too much to their wives – let them *stew*!

Josie collapsed with laughter when she heard the tale. 'Serves them all right, stuck-up, snotty-nosed, two-faced prigs!'

Nonna handed her gloves and bonnet to the neat maid in green seersucker.

'Some tea, Madame? asked the maid.

'Yes, Jenny, thank you.'

Josie sat on the sofa by the fire, her pink muslin dress deepened to rose by the flickering light. 'The posters have arrived. I've got one to show you.' She tapped the paper on the little table beside her.

Nonna shook out the skirts of her donkey-brown dress. 'Are they very awful?'

'It depends on your point of view.'

'That means they are.' Nonna picked it up. She read it through once, paused and then read again. 'Oh, Josie, how many of these are up?' she asked in dismay.

'Hundreds. All over Town. Nonna, tomorrow's the big night. Robert wants *everyone* to sit up and take notice.'

'They'll do *that* all right once they read this! '*Madame Vania, formerly of the New Opera House and now of The Dove Theatre, the Libertine reclaimed – Don Giovanni in England! With Curious and Amusing Scenes! Interesting and Singular*!' It's dreadful!'

'It's eye-catching – especially the verse at the end.' Josie grinned, 'I helped to compose it.'

Nonna glared at her and then struck a pose to recite the verse.

'Surprise or joy alike to yield,
Thy various pleasing form is made;
To deck the Warrior for the field,
Or bless the Lover in the shade.
Oh, please us long till midnight hour,
Either in petticoat or breeches,
For none like La Vania has the power
In everything to "run through stitches"!'

Josie looked satisfied. 'I think it's good.'

'You would.' Nonna dropped the poster on the table again. 'Oh, dear, I think this is all getting a little out of hand.'

'Nonsense, there'll be a stampede to get tickets.'

'Yes, there will – and a riot when they're disappointed afterwards.'

'They won't be. Anyway, Peter says it's good.'

'You and he always agree with each other – it's sickening.' Nonna sat down and smiled then. 'It *will* cause a kerfuffle, won't it? Armand's going to burst a blood vessel.'

'We made sure the very first poster went up on the wall of the Opera House too!' Josie drew her knees up and sat on the sofa hugging them. 'We couldn't resist the gesture.'

'Did you nail that particular one up personally?'

'Yes, all by my little self. With Peter.'

'Spare me. Well, who'd have thought a skinny, ginger-headed writer would oust the wondrous William Lamb in your affections?'

'Don't tease me about it,' said Josie suddenly, lowering her eyes.

'You're in love with him, aren't you?' asked Nonna gently.

'Yes.'

'And he with you?'

'I – I think so.'

'Well, he certainly spends enough time and trouble over you. I heard you both yesterday – you sang my songs very well, you know.'

'It was only messing around.' Josie went as pink as her dress. 'And I was only copying you.'

'You were good, better than my understudy, I thought. I told Robert to come and listen and he agreed.'

'You *what*?' Josie's eyes were huge. 'Was the rest of the company listening too? I didn't know anyone else even *knew* about it!'

'Singing does carry past a closed door, you know. Anyway, I came back to tell you – Robert and I've decided you ought to be my official understudy.'

'What about Miss What's-her-name? Jenkins.'

'She was awful, Josie – she could dance a little, but as to the singing. . . .'

'Yes, and I might be able to sing a little – but as to the dancing . . .' Josie got up, looking agitated. 'I can't do anything like that, Nonna, and you *know* I can't.'

Nonna took a card from her reticule. 'Monsieur Charles Lefebre of Grattan Street, Dancing Master. He's good and he'll get you into the sort of shape for this. It's not ballet, you know – you don't need years and years of training for the sort of struttings we do at the Dove. Anyway, it's up to you, but you'd be a fool to say no.'

Josie took the card, glancing at it and then back at Nonna. 'Do – do you think I can do it, Nonna? Really?'

'Yes. And you've got the right sort of nerve. Oh, when *I* think of tomorrow I could *die* without any bother.'

'Cheer up, tonight's Guy Fawkes' Night and we're going to see the fireworks in Hyde Park.'

'Are we?'

'Yes. Peter's taking us both.'

'With me in the role of gooseberry? No, thank you. No, honestly, Josie, I would much rather stay home here by myself.'

'Oh, but – '

'No.'

'All right. But they say the fireworks are going to be better than ever this year.'

'If I stand in my bedroom window I'll just about be able

to see them from here. Why bother to go out in the cold to see them?' Nonna smiled. 'Go and hold hands with him without me hovering there beside you all the time like three left legs in one stocking.'

The maid came in with a tray of tea which she set on the little table. 'Excuse me, Madame, but there's a gentleman to see you.'

'Gentleman?'

The maid looked uncomfortable. 'Moosoor Vania, Madame.'

Nonna glanced uneasily at Josie. 'Show him in, Jenny.'

'Shall I go or stay, Nonna?' asked Josie.

'Stay. Please.'

Vania strode into the room. 'So, Madame – ' he began, stopping when he saw Josie. 'We need witnesses, eh?'

'Yes. I have little desire to risk being alone with you, Armand.'

His blue eyes hardened at the oblique reminder. 'Very well. Are these posters true? Are you to perform for Wyndham at the Dove?'

'Yes.'

'I forbid it!'

'Indeed? And how do you intend doing that?'

'I am your husband!'

'You chose to forget that fact, Armand, not me.'

He came closer, his eyes angry and his fists clenched. 'You have already made enough trouble for me, Madame, lying and scheming your way into my bed and so on. Now you would ridicule my name further by this – this – '

'I shall go on that stage tomorrow whether you like it or not, Armand, and there's nothing you can do to stop me. You are the one who's been doing all the lying and scheming. I've not done any of the things of which I've been accused by you, and you know it in your heart. You are divorcing me, claiming all manner of insult and so on at my hands. Maybe I should fight you all the way by divorcing *you*, for *you* are the guilty party really, Armand, not me. You beat me and you took a mistress – within months of marrying me. How grand that will look when the newspapers print it. So, don't come here threatening me!'

He stared at her. 'Quite the bitch now, eh, my Nonna?'

'In you I had an excellent teacher. And now, leave me alone. Divorce me, by all means, but tone down your extravagant claims or I promise you, I *will* make your name a dirty word.'

He glanced at Josie. 'Perhaps it is as well you *are* here, Mademoiselle, for in truth I would have exercised a man's right to correct his wife had you not been! And if ever a man was justified, I am!' He turned to Nonna again. 'I'll stop you, Madame Chienne. Somehow or other I'll stop you from carrying on with this. Be warned!'

'Goodbye, Armand.'

The incredible blue eyes rested on her face a moment more, and then he turned and went out. Nonna exhaled slowly. 'Oh, Josie!'

'I wonder what's in his mind,' murmured Josie thoughtfully, getting up and twitching the curtains aside to watch the purple landau drive away into the gathering gloom of the November afternoon. 'I don't trust him.'

'What can he do? There's no law which says I can't go on at the Dove, and no law which says I can't try to divorce him.'

'He's really upset by it all, Nonna, and when a man like that gets a bee in his bonnet . . . I just don't like it, that's all.'

Robert Wyndham sat down, pushing Josie's copy of the poster aside and looking across at Nonna. 'There'll be no show tonight.'

'No show? But why?' she gasped.

'Two reasons. The first one – well, you've no doubt wondered at the tolling of the church bells this morning.'

'Yes, but no one here knows what's happened. I've sent a boy to find out – '

'Princess Charlotte died in childbed last night. The baby, a boy, was stillborn, to add to the tragedy.'

Nonna stared. Charlotte? Dead? But she had been so hearty and full of life, so carefree and happy . . . *Doucement, ma chère, doucement.* 'I can't believe it,' she whispered.

'It's true, not a wild rumour. Deep mourning at Carlton House and so on. Every theatre in London is closed until after the funeral, whenever that is. The main guess is the eighteenth of the month at Windsor, but no one knows that much as yet. Anyway, we wouldn't have been able to put *Don Giovanni* on tonight even if – '

'Even if what?'

'Even if someone had *not* tried to burn the Dove down last night.'

'*Burn* it?' She stood. 'But who . . .?' Vania. The name came into her head almost immediately. That was what he had meant by stopping her.

'I see from your expression that you have thought of the same culprits as I have. The Opera House – Vania in particular.'

'Yes. But it's a guess, no more than that. He did come here, threatening and demanding and leaving with veiled warnings about stopping me one way or another.'

Wyndham sighed. 'He'll try again.'

'Was there much damage?'

'Part of the stage and *all* the damned curtain spoiled, and some of the props. Luckily the watchman heard something suspicious and got help before the fire went far. But friend Vania will have to be stopped.'

'If it's him.'

'It's him all right! He's the only one with good reason to stop us, isn't he? So, *we'll* have to lean on *him*.'

'How?'

'My dear Nonna, I don't think you really want to know, do you?'

'Yes.'

He smiled. 'Well, I think a little threatening of our own might do the trick. A threat that maybe, if anything else suspicious happens at the Dove, he'd better make sure he's never alone. A broken-legged ballet dancer is hardly likely to be up to much, eh?'

'You wouldn't!'

'I won't have to, my dear, the threat itself will stop *le Dieu de la Danse* in his tracks.' He got up. 'I'll toddle off to visit him this very minute, no time like the present, eh? Oh, by the way, did you tell Josie about our decision?'

'Yes.'

'And?'

'She's accepted, in fact she's gone to Monsieur Lefebre this morning to begin lessons.'

He nodded. 'She'll come up to scratch – she's plucky.' He put his hand to Nonna's cheek, 'And she's got better nerve than you, eh?'

'Yes.'

'I – er – I was at the hazard tables with the Duke of Aldane last night.'

'Oh?'

'I asked him about Philip Hastings. They haven't found him yet, not a trace. Indeed, well, they begin to think maybe he's. . . .'

'Dead?' she whispered, 'Oh, no!'

'No news is good news, sweetheart. Look on the bright side, eh?' He chucked her under the chin lightly. 'La Vania of the Dove don't look miserable – ever! Anyway, we rehearse on our merry way until the day after the funeral. Then – *then* we let you loose on London, eh?'

22

Nonna adjusted the sash of her costume, and her fingers were shaking and cold in spite of the fire crackling in the dressing room. She looked at herself in the mirror. The scarlet coat was tightly-fitted over her breasts and waist, with a short, full skirt. It was richly embroidered in gold and white, matching the large and ridiculous feathered hat which Josie held out to her.

'Are my hose wrinkled?' asked Nonna, turning around for her to see.

'Not a wrinkle to be seen.'

'It's at times like this I miss having Milly to fuss around me. She was always so efficient, never missed a thing.'

'I don't miss a thing either. There's nothing wrong with your costume. Everything's perfect.'

'I know I shall walk out, strike a pose and forget the very first line.'

'No, you won't.'

'Is there as big a crowd as we hoped?'

'Bigger. They're standing in the aisles, bulging out of the boxes almost, and in very high spirits. All gentlemen, of course – not a woman to brighten the rows of black coats, white shirts and cravats!'

'*Ladies* would hardly come to a play like *Don Giovanni in England*.'

'They'd like to though, I'll wager. Anyway, that audience out there is waiting to have a good night out – all the gloom of yesterday needs blowing away now.'

Nonna sat on the stool by the rosewood dressing table. 'I

still can't believe it, you know. Princess Charlotte was so – exuberant, I suppose. That she's dead. . . .'

'That's the way of it, eh? The Lord giveth and the Lord taketh away and all that.'

'Was the funeral very splendid?'

'Yes.'

'Tell me about it – or were you too busy mooning into Peter's eyes to pay attention?'

'We didn't go all the way to Windsor *not* to see it!' protested Josie, laughing. 'Well, it was midnight and brilliant moonlight when the procession appeared. There were footmen first, four abreast carrying torches, and behind them eight black horses drawing the hearse. The horses had black housings and huge black plumes on their heads, and each one had a groom walking beside it. The – the coffin had a pall of blue velvet. I couldn't speak. The crowd was so quiet, except for some people crying. You could hear the hooves so clearly. I thought back, you know – to the day she got married. We couldn't wait for the gentlemen to come to Madame's to find out what her gown had been like. It's so sad, Nonna.'

'Yes. It's funny, I thought about that day too. Oh Lord, they're calling me, Josie!'

'Good luck!' Josie hugged her as she got up, picking up her cane.

In the wings, Robert and Peter were waiting. Robert pecked her cheek reassuringly. 'It's a good audience, Nonna, a grand mixture – plenty of nobs and plenty of lesser beings, eh? More nobs than I expected though.

Nonna smiled, but inside she was terrified. It was just as it had been at the Opera House, only this time there was no Armand Vania to carry her through the ordeal. This time she was alone.

Peter hugged her tightly. 'Go out and enchant them all, Nonna,' he murmured, kissing her.

'I'll try not to let you down.'

'You won't. There's your cue.'

She took a deep breath to steady herself as best she

could, but then the curtain was rising and she could hear the jaunty notes of her first song. She put her hands on her hips and strode out into the bright light of the chandeliers, and a huge roar of approval went up from the eager audience. Her voice was drowned for the whole of the first verse, but gradually the noise died away and her clear, sweet voice carried clearly to everyone.

She strode around, jeering at the Devil, mocking and swaggering – and all the while so very feminine and beautiful. There was something about the elegant figure in male clothes, something which caught the audience from the very first moment and held it until the notes of the last chorus faded away and the curtain fell an hour later. For ten minutes the applause rang out, and Nonna was called back time and time again to bow. They chanted her name over and over again. *La Vania, la Vania, la Vania. . . .*

Robert rubbed his hands together like Shylock, grinning as she left the stage for the last time. 'Nonna, we've struck gold! *Gold*!'

She stared at him, confused and overcome. Tears sparkled in her eyes as he swung her into his arms and twirled her round, laughing delightedly. 'You darling!' he cried. 'You darling angel!'

'I – I don't remember anything,' she cried. 'I just don't remember anything from the first note!'

Peter grinned. 'You were marvellous, Nonna, absolutely marvellous!'

Robert released her then. 'Now, the Yellow Room, eh?'

She nodded. 'Yes, the Yellow Room.'

Peter pushed open the door that led from the interior of the theatre into the reception room, and immediately the buzz of male voices came out. The rest of the cast were already there, still in their costumes, but when Nonna appeared shouts went up and she was whisked from Robert and Peter and besieged by her new admirers.

Quizzing-glasses were raised by the dandies as they ogled her; praise floated around her; assignations were begged. But she began as she meant to go on, turning down all invitations without exception. La Vania was to be seen, but that was all. She was sweet and charming, smiling and teasing – but unavailable. She was a challenge therefore, just as she had been at Madame's, and she knew that there would soon be wagers on the identity of her conqueror, that she was set, once again, to become the rage of London. She talked and flirted with them for an hour and then left them, immune to their pleas. That was how it would be, she thought firmly – one hour and then a graceful and determined exit!

In the quiet of the dressing room she sat with Josie, Robert and Peter. Robert had a bottle of champagne and he grinned as he poured the glasses. 'Well, if they can't have La Vania, they are making all the headway they can with the rest of the girls, eh? *C'est la vie*!'

Peter nodded. 'There were some names there tonight – two lords, an earl no less, and four viscounts! Those were the ones I recognised; who knows who else was there! By tomorrow word will have spread a little – a week after that the songs will be hummed and whistled in the streets.' He raised his glass to Nonna. 'I toast you, Nonna. You've made us all tonight!'

She smiled happily. This first important night had gone so much better than she had ever dreamed.

Robert smiled fondly at her. 'I knew we had found ourselves a winner in all this, and so I have a small present for you, Nonna. Well, it's not *that* small – I had to leave it outside the stage door.'

'Outside? Whatever is it?'

'When you leave you'll find out,' he said mysteriously. 'But before then, I made it my business to send someone nosing around the Opera House. Half the seats were empty for Vania's new ballet. Only old fogeys there, and dowagers. And the ladies of course, eyeing their favourite. The real audience came here, to the Dove. To watch a bawdy show like this! Tut, tut! But God bless 'em, eh?'

Josie grinned. 'One thing though, the Dove will *never* get royal patronage!'

'We'd have to be polite and well-behaved for that, and the joy of us is that we ain't!' said Robert. 'Well, a celebration dinner is in order, I think. The four of us somewhere pleasant – the Chinese House?'

'Will they let me in there?' asked Nonna. 'It's a bit – well. . . .'

'It's a bit part-owned by yours truly, my dear. They'll let you in, and gladly. Come, you've a present to accept.'

When she had changed, she put on her fur-lined cloak to leave the Dove with Josie. Peter and Robert waited at the stage door. 'Listen,' said Peter, 'there's a crowd out there still waiting to see you leave, Nonna.'

'But they must be frozen!'

'Adoring admirers can't feel the cold,' he said drily, opening the door.

The ice-cold November night air swept over them, a slight mist swirling in the light of the oil lamps by the doorway. There were cheers and shouts of encouragement from the small waiting crowd – not, she noticed, a crowd of fashionable gentlemen, but the other half of the audience. She smiled and waved, and then her face changed as she saw the waiting carriage.

It was white, its brasswork gleaming and polished, and it was drawn by six white horses. It was like something from a fairy-tale, and she turned to look at Robert. He nodded. 'For you, Nonna – a carriage more distinctive than the Frenchman's, eh? And see the door panels? A beautiful dove on each one!'

'But, it's lovely!' she cried, her eyes shining.

'It's an advertisement wherever it goes too.'

'Don't spoil it,' she said, smiling. 'It's supposed to be a thoughtful gift, not a business investment.'

'It's both.'

A footman in red livery opened the door for them, and when the carriage drew away from the stage door, the shouts of the crowd followed it down the narrow lane.

La Vania, la Vania, la Vania. . . .

23

The success of that first night continued. *La Vania of the Dove*. Her name was on every tongue, her songs whistled in markets, inns and clubs alike. Peter Bannister was in demand to write new plays and new songs, and he did. In that first year of the Dove he wrote shows for Nonna and shows for other theatres. Robert Wyndham became the acknowledged king of London's theatres, and Nonna – well, Nonna was the queen. Her startling white carriage was seen everywhere. She was as adored as Vania himself had ever been – but she was not acceptable in fashionable places. Clubs, gaming houses, hotels and dancing places of note all closed their doors to someone of La Vania's reputation. She performed at nights to crowded audiences, recognising many of them as gentlemen who frequented the clubs she was forbidden. And in the Yellow Room afterwards she was fêted, flattered, invited, enticed, propositioned – by the men who saw to it that she was banned from so many places. Double standards – always double standards to rule what was acceptable in public or private. And she took great delight in refusing them all. Occasionally she would dine with them, but never, ever anything more. Those who frequented the Yellow Room could find solace with the girls of the chorus, but never with La Vania herself. Heavy wagers did indeed rest on who would cause her downfall, but no one could collect. Her mysterious and interesting reserve increased her appeal; it was as Robert and Madame Siffre had said – every man secretly believed that *he* would succeed where everyone else had failed.

Now that there were no secrets to be hidden, no dark past to be pushed into the shadows, Nonna was herself. She danced and sang, captivating each audience. Her training and inherent skills blossomed on the stage of the Dove. She was wicked, suggestive, exciting, dramatic, endearing, sad and happy – she was everything. And with her success and popularity, came Vania's jealous spite. He had been intimidated by Robert Wyndham's threats, but with regard to his divorce, nothing held him back. He publicly accused her of every sin, making so much noise about it that Robert Wyndham rubbed his hands with glee. The more noise, the more publicity, the more money rolled into the Dove's expanding coffers.

Don Giovanni in England was replaced by *The Virgin's Regret*, and then *The Private Life of a Courtesan* and *A Sultan and his Slave*. Each successive play guaranteed to be as naughty as its predecessor. Nonna could do no wrong; but nice society still shunned her in public. She had stepped beyond the bounds of propriety, and that was not allowed.

The hearing of the scandalous Vania divorce came closer, and public interest was at fever pitch on the first night of *A Sultan and his Slave*. Nonna put on her flimsy, transparent costume, glancing at Josie.

'A capacity audience again?'

'Of course. Vania made another speech from the stage at the Opera House last night, so of course they've poured in here tonight. He's doing wonders for your popularity, you know.'

'Poor Armand.'

'*Poor* Armand? The man's odious; he thinks only of himself. How can you stand there and sympathise with him?'

'He can't help the way he is. He's a genius, Josie – coping with the unpleasantnesses of everyday life doesn't come easily to someone like that.'

'He doesn't cope with them, he creates them.'

'Talking of creating – how is your dancing coming on? You're very secretive about it, Josie.'

'When I'm ready I'll dazzle you all. Until then I shall remain secretive.'

'Doesn't even Peter know?'

'Ah, well he's different.'

'He's London's most popular writer of songs, a young man of means now – will he make an honest woman of you?'

Josie blushed. 'I don't know what you mean.'

'Yes, you do, Josie Woods, yes you do. There have been nights when the only person sleeping alone at my house in Bettersleigh Street is La Vania!'

'You don't have to sleep alone,' said Josie. 'You could accept an invitation from Sir Toby Charles. He's so faithful and adoring, I don't know how you can refuse him.'

'La Vania must always be above reproach.'

'You accept expensive gifts, and you dine out with admirers.'

'That's still above reproach.'

'Sir Toby Charles is a gentleman, a *real* gentleman.'

Nonna smiled, putting on the yashmak which hid nothing of her face. 'I know.'

'Then why? Surely not because of Philip Hastings, not after all this time!'

'Josie, Philip Hastings has nothing to do with it. I will *not* give anyone any hold over me, ever again. Not even Toby. Oh, I like him, he's more honest than most of them – he'd take me anywhere, acknowledge me anywhere – but I don't like him that way.'

'Philip Hastings you do though.'

'Yes.'

'Oh, Nonna, life's too short – '

'*My* life's my own business, Josie. This is the way I want to conduct it.'

'I suppose you've seen Justin Farnsworth out in the audience sometimes?'

'Yes.'

'He never comes to the Yellow Room though.'

'No.'

'I wonder why?'

'Oh, Josie, does it matter? I *detest* Justin and he must know it. What he did to me was despicable.'

'Yes, but I would have thought he'd have come to talk to you at least once. La Vania is The Thing now, the absolute rage of rages, and yet the fashionable, rich, handsome young Lord Justin Farnsworth doesn't come to the Yellow Room. Why come to the Dove at all if he won't come backstage with the rest of the *monde*?'

'I don't know – and I don't care.'

'He's out there tonight.'

'Really.'

'He asked me to give you this.' Josie held out a note.

Nonna stared at her. 'Josie!'

'I only said I'd give it to you, and anyway, he asked very nicely.'

'I'll warrant he did! I wonder how much of a wager rests on his success, eh?'

'Read it. I'm dying to know what it says.'

Nonna read the brief note. 'He only wants to meet me in the Yellow Room tonight, that's all.'

'Will you?'

'No.'

'But – '

'No! He is the very end in lice and I will *not* see him. I don't have to and cannot be forced to.' Nonna smiled then. 'The Yellow Room is La Vania's territory, what *I* say is the law there. *He* may be acceptable everywhere from Almack's to Carlton House, but here *I'm* the lord!'

'What a pity, I was so hoping for a set-to tonight.'

'Listen, they're calling for me now. Wish me luck, Josie!' Nonna patted her hair for a last time and Josie hugged her. It was a ritual they both went through every night, and if it could not be performed they felt ridiculously uneasy.

The chill of autumn seeped through into the passages of the Dove as Nonna hurried up to the stage, and her diaphanous gauze costume gave her little protection.

A great cheer went up as the curtain rose for *The Sultan*

and the Slave, and that cheer rose until it was deafening as Nonna moved on to the stage in her revealing costume. When she dressed as a man she was splendid, but now, as the malleable, beautiful slave, she was adored again. There was no hint of masculine swaggering in this role, and she knew as she danced and sang that this new facet of La Vania was as popular as the last. The whiteness of her thighs flashed in the bright lights and her hair tumbled from its pins, falling in a dark red cloud around her shoulders as she twisted and danced, a dainty, graceful figure in silver gauze. She knelt before the actor who played the sultan, her arms outstretched, and at that very moment, with the music pausing for the beginning of a love song, someone shouted from the back of the auditorium.

'Vania's dead!'

Nonna turned towards the voice, and a buzz swept through the audience. The man with the news pushed forward to the front of the stage. 'Vania's dead, Madame. Your husband's snuffed it!'

She knelt there, frozen with the shock of what he said. Should she answer? Remain silent? What should she do?

Someone else shouted then. 'How did he die?' Murmurs greeted this, for everyone wanted to know.

'His carriage overturned, hit a high kerb and the horses took fright. He was killed. No Vania any more.' The man took off his top hat and ran his fingers through his hair.

There was silence in the Dove then, a breathless hush as all eyes moved to Nonna as she knelt before the startled sultan. What did they expect of her, she wondered in that long, long moment of hesitation? They expected the *un*expected. They wanted to be entertained, shocked, drawn. She got to her feet, curtseying deeply, and then she waved at the conductor of the orchestra. 'Play on, Monsieur,' she said clearly.

There were gasps at this, and then some clapped, and from silence, the Dove was transformed into a bear garden of noise as the orchestra began to play and the audience clapped and cheered over the music. Nonna knelt again, singing the gentle love song, and by the time the first verses were over, the noise had abated and *The Sultan and the Slave* continued as if nothing had happened at all.

The end of the performance was met with ecstatic applause, but Nonna took no curtain calls that night. She turned to Robert Wyndham. 'Robert?'

'It's true, my dear, you're a widow now.'

She leaned against some scenery, feeling strangely sad suddenly. 'We've lost a great dancer, Robert.'

'A dancer maybe, but as a man he's no loss at all. They're waiting in the Yellow Room, Nonna.'

She looked quickly at him. 'I don't think – '

'Your public expects you to be unconventional – be that. Go in as you do every evening. You saw how your decision to carry on was greeted: they *loved* it! Your maxim here has been to start as you mean to carry on, so you go into the Yellow Room as you always do.'

She smiled then. 'You have a plausible reason for everything, don't you?'

'Yes. That's what I'm here for, to poke you into doing the right thing all the time.' He put his plump, warm hand to her face for a moment. 'You're not really upset about Vania are you?'

'I suppose not.'

'Because if you are that's maybe different.'

'No, I'm not upset. I feel nothing for him any more – he saw to that. I'll go to the Yellow Room.'

She weathered the Yellow Room's curiosity and morbid interest in the death of her husband, but she glanced at the ormulu clock occasionally, willing the minutes to tick by more swiftly.

'So you've vanquished the opposition now, Nonna?' asked a voice behind her.

Justin. She turned from talking with two gentlemen. 'I do not wish to speak with you, sir,' she said quietly. 'In fact I wish you to leave. Robert?' But Robert Wyndham was across the room laughing raucously with an elderly gentleman in black satin.

Justin smiled. 'Nonna, I know your dislike for me is justified – *more* than justified – but I only want to speak with you. To apologise.'

'I accept your apology. Now will you leave?' she said coldly.

'I could apologise more sweetly over dinner.'

'The day I accept an invitation from you, sir, will be the day it rains elephants and sawdust!'

'I have a table at Long's – '

'Long's does not admit La Vania. And besides, I already have a dinner appointment with Sir Toby Charles.'

He raised his eyebrows. 'Somewhat stuffy company for you, isn't he?'

'I would sooner spend my time constantly in his company for a year than spend two minutes in yours, sir.'

'Grief would not seem to have taken the edge off your tongue, would it?' he said softly.

Her eyes flashed. 'My conduct is *my* business, Justin, not yours!' She turned then, waving everyone from the room. Usually it amused her to see superior gentlemen of breeding hurrying to obey her whim, but tonight she took no notice. She was too angry with Justin – and with herself for permitting him to needle her.

'Nonna, I seem destined always to rub your fur the wrong way, and I'm sorry. Yes, don't look like that, I *am* sorry. In the past I've behaved abominably towards you, I know that.'

'And I'm to believe in a miraculous change of heart?'

'No – I'd still get you into my bed if I thought I could.' He smiled, leaning back against the wall to look at her. 'I had a notion for you at Madame's and at the Opera House – but now, seeing you in that thing you're just about wearing, I could make sweet, sweet love to you all over again.'

'Never. Now, Justin, please go.'

'At least it's *Justin*. Well, surprisingly enough, I do admit defeat. Having sinned so much, I thought it time I performed a good deed for a change, but if you're in with Toby Charles, maybe you'd no longer be interested in the whereabouts of Philip Hastings.'

She paused, her hand on the door. 'Philip?'

'Ah, a flicker of interest at last. Yes, my dear couz is home again. Safe – and very sound.'

'In London?'

'Dorset. In London he'd have to face me and I think that is the last thing on God's earth he wishes to do.'

'How long has he. . . .?'

'A week or so – I'm not sure.'

She studied his face suspiciously. 'And why, I ask myself, would you be telling me this?'

'Ah, that's a ticklish one.'

'Tell me.'

He sighed. 'Does it matter? He's back and you've been told. What more is there to be concerned about?'

'A great deal. Why tell *me* where he is? Why would it matter to me?'

'Because it does, doesn't it? You're in love with him, aren't you?'

'No.'

'Then I *have* wasted my time – and my – ' He broke off.

'Money? That's what you were going to say, isn't it, Justin Farnsworth! There's money resting on this somehow!'

He smiled. 'All right, all right, I'll tell you the sordid details. The duel which nearly saw the end of my good self was brought about because of Philip's objection to my treatment of you that night at the Opera House. Indeed, he was *very* touchy about you. He called me out and he meant to put an untimely snuff over my little flame. Fortunately – or unfortunately according to your point of view – he didn't make a quite good enough job of it and I survived.'

'The duel was over *me*? Not over your sister?'

'Gillian? No. He never could stand her very much. No, it was coincidence that she hurriedly married when she did – but the gossips *were* right about the reasons for her haste. I am now the uncle of twins, would you believe?The duel was all yours, sweet Nonna, every painful, nerve-jarring moment of it. I've always been wary of Couz Philip; he's not a man to cross. I crossed him once too often that night. I had already drawn my conclusions about your affections, Nonna – I guessed it was Philip. *That* my dear, is the reason for my benevolence tonight. I tell you where he is, you toddle along to comfort him, *I* collect a goodly sum.'

'The huge wagers which have been mounting at Barrymore's!' she cried. '*That's* what you're after, isn't it?'

'Yes,' he said, with disarming frankness.

'Justin Farnsworth!'

'I know – a sinner, eh? It's a family tradition.'

'Well, you won't be collecting *any* goodly sum, do you hear me? I'm not toddling to Five Ways or anywhere else! You've wasted your time and mental energy on this one!'

He stared at her. 'God above,' he murmured. 'It *is* Toby Charles, isn't it?'

'Good night, Justin,' she said wearily.

He bowed, his hair very golden in the light from the elegant chandelier above them. 'Good night, Nonna.'

She stood alone in the room when he had gone. Philip had fought the duel for *her*; it hadn't been anything to do with Gillian Farnsworth. For her! But the moment's exultation was soon gone. He was back, forgiven and free, and he had gone to Five Ways, not the Dove. The conclusions were obvious: whatever his reason at the time for the duel, it was not love of Nonna Lambert.

Taking a deep breath, she left the Yellow Room to go and change for her evening with Toby – but before dining, she would have to go to the Opera House.

As Toby's brown carriage moved along the dark streets towards the Opera House, Nonna gazed out at the lights of the city. Vania was dead. It was so strange, she had come to loathe him and yet – and yet, he had been so very special, so brilliant and gifted. And now he was gone. Ballet had lost someone very precious today.

Toby Charles was twenty-four, ruddy-complexioned and good-natured. He had a ready sense of humour, dressed in the very tippy of the latest fashions, wore his light brown hair in a carefully tousled disarray of curls and was kind and considerate. Of all her admirers, he was the one Nonna liked most, for she felt he was genuine and honest. She knew he would take her anywhere, that he respected her and valued her friendship. The Yellow Room knew few of Toby's mould, and she appreciated his candour. She smiled as she caught his eye. 'I'll be the cause of another stir for carrying on my show tonight. Shall you mind?'

'If I minded I would not chase you so busily.'

'I just feel I must go there, to try to speak to them. Well, tonight it seems only right.'

'Do you grieve for him, Nonna?'

'No, not as a man. As a dancer, yes. It will be a long time before the world sees his equal. He even made me brilliant. No, don't think I'm seeking false praise, for I'm not. I could dance really well only with him. He seemed to draw some inner genius to the fore. Only Vania could do that – *he* made me the dancer I was for that short time at the Opera House. What I do now is nothing compared with that, and I readily admit it.'

'There's not an *aficionado* of the Dove who would agree with you.'

'It's true, for all that.' She glanced out and saw that they were close to the Opera House now, and she put up her white, fur-trimmed hood, smiling at him. 'It wouldn't do for the crowds to recognise La Vania going in, would it?'

'If there *are* crowds at this time of night. In the morning, maybe.'

'They'll be there, Toby – he was *le Dieu de la Danse*. They'll be there.'

She was right. The carriage slowed to a walk at the Opera House, for there were silent crowds by the stage door, watching and waiting. The coachman edged the carriage close to the door and Nonna sat back as Toby got out and went to the door. The doorman looked out suspiciously, his face changing as Toby spoke. He glanced at the carriage and then nodded. Toby handed Nonna down and she was inside the Opera House without anyone knowing who she was.

She pushed the hood back, looking at the doorman's stony face. 'Is Monique here?'

'Everyone's here. Where else would they be on such a night – Madame?'

Her eyes flickered at the insolence in the man's voice, but she caught Toby's hand, sensing his anger. 'It's all right, Toby.'

'Shall I wait here, or would you like me to go with you?'

'Stay here. I think it's best, mm?'

He watched her go, her white satin cloak pale and ghostly in the dim light of the silent building.

She walked slowly. Remembered smells and sounds were everywhere, echoes which she had forgotten – the loom of ropes and pulleys hanging, like those at the Dove and yet so different. She passed several people who recognised her, but no one spoke. She sensed their surprise – and resentment – but she walked on.

Milly came out of a store room, some costumes over her arm. 'Nonna!'

'Hello, Milly.'

'Oh, Nonna!' Milly's little face crumpled and she dropped the costumes.

Nonna went to her, holding the shaking little figure close. 'I still can't really believe he's gone,' wept Milly. It was as if a door would open and Vania would be there, his hair so golden and his eyes so blue . . . 'We don't know what to do without him, we've no one like him, Nonna.'

'I know.'

'Monique's with Catrine. I was just going there.' Milly wiped her eyes and picked up the costumes again, sniffing. 'Did you want to see them?'

'That's why I came.'

Catrine lay on the sofa, her eyes red from weeping, and she twisted a handkerchief in her hands, staring at the cobwebs draped over the grimy ceiling. Monique stood, staring at Nonna. 'Nonna!'

'I came to – to – I don't really know. I just thought I'd come to see you. I'm so sorry.'

Monique nodded sadly. 'It hasn't struck me properly yet. I cannot cry.' Her eyes went to Catrine, who hadn't moved.

Nonna went to crouch beside the sofa. 'Catrine.'

'You carried on with your show, eh, Nonna? You heard and yet went on.'

Nonna met the ballerina's accusing eyes. 'Yes.'

'*Vania* was dead, and you danced on!'

'I did only what Vania himself would have done had the news been reversed. And you know it, Catrine, don't you? Armand wouldn't have gone into mourning for me; the ballet meant everything. *My* shows mean everything to me too.'

'Why come here? For more publicity? Did you come in your fancy white carriage then?'

'No, I'm with a friend, in his carriage. I've come – I suppose to tell you all how sorry I am. I *am* sorry, Catrine. Armand was divorcing me and it was sordid and unpleasant but – '

'But good for business at the Dove.'

'Yes, good for business, I admit it. I still appreciated Armand though. His dancing was possessed of something beyond ordinary ability. I appreciate too how much you loved him. If I hadn't come, what would you have thought of me?'

The dark eyes so full of misery searched her face for a moment, and then Catrine nodded, slipping her hand into Nonna's. 'I know,' she whispered, 'I know.'

Nonna stood. 'Now I'm going out to dine. There will be raised eyebrows, a great deal of disapproval and censure, but I'm going to do it – *my* public expects it of me and I'm like Armand, I do not fail my public. But *you* will understand, won't you?' She looked around at them.

Monique smiled. 'We know you, Nonna. We'll understand, of course we will. Who – who are you dining with?

Sir Philip Hastings?'

'No.'

'I thought maybe – well, he was here tonight, in his box. He saw Vania's last performance.'

'Philip is in London?'

'Yes.'

Nonna smiled faintly. 'Well, I did not even know – that's the extent of his interest in La Vania. But now, I must go.' She put up her hood again. 'Goodbye.'

She turned and hurried out, almost running through the echoing, dark theatre which seemed so empty of anything on this cold, dismal night.

Toby was waiting for her, and she went out into the carriage without anyone knowing that La Vania of the Dove had been there.

24

Nonna's performances at the Dove went on over the next few days. Disapproval mushroomed all around, with comments in the papers, fingers pointed in print at the brazen insensitivity of Madame Vania. Her further notoriety meant that the audiences were at the Dove's limit, and the Yellow Room was crowded with more and more gentlemen intent upon her attention. One visitor she had not expected was Justin, who came to the shows and to the Yellow Room frequently. He was never offensive, being careful not to cross any unseen barriers. But Philip Hastings never came near the Dove. He was in Padenham Square again, attending all the *soirées*, balls, clubs and masques. His return to England had been welcomed; he was eligible, rich and handsome – a great catch for any woman, and according to Justin there was no shortage of willing aspirants. Nonna talked with Justin, anxious to find out all she could about Philip, but she was careful not to reveal the truth to him. She let him believe she was in love with Toby, let them all believe it. No one could hurt her then, especially not Philip Hastings. Not again.

A week after Vania's death was the day of his funeral. The day dawned bright and clear, a crisp late autumn day when the frost was so hard it robbed the trees of the last of their leaves. Toby called at the Dove at the time when he knew Nonna would have finished her rehearsals for the day.

He tossed his top hat on her dressing-table. 'A drive? It's such a fine day.'

'Armand's funeral is today. I think I should stay out of the way, don't you?'

'I thought Hyde Park. The funeral is at St Peter's – miles away. Come on, you don't get many days like this.' He put his hand to her chin and made her look at him. 'You're pale, Nonna – I insist you drive with me. And tonight, after your performance, I've a table booked at Cartwright's.'

'Cartwright's? I doubt if La Vania would be admitted – especially after this last week's goings-on.'

'The table is booked. That is the end of it. And now, that drive?'

'St Peter's *is* a long way from the Park, isn't it? All right, Toby, I'll come – just give me a moment to dress properly.'

He nodded, turning away, but then he turned back. 'Nonna, I – '

She put a finger to his lips, shaking her head. 'Nothing serious, Toby, nothing serious.'

'I want you to marry me,' he said suddenly, and then he smiled. 'Damn, I meant to be more romantic and subtle than that! But it's said now – I *do* love you, Nonna.'

'I know, Toby.' She smiled. 'But no – thank you, no. As a friend I love you dearly, but it's not the love of a wife for a husband. I'm honoured that you should ask someone like me. . . .'

'Well, maybe I hoped too much, but the offer will always be there, Nonna.' He kissed her gently. He looked into her eyes then. 'Who is it, Nonna? There *is* someone, isn't there?'

'Yes, there always has been, Toby.'

'Who?'

'That's not – '

'I want to know, I *need* to know. Please, Nonna, trust me.'

'Sir Philip Hastings.'

He stared at her. '*Hastings*? But I've never seen him anywhere near you and he's been back in England for – ' He broke off. 'Poor Nonna, I didn't realise.'

'Why should you? And now, that drive?' She smiled brightly, reaching up to take his face in her hands. 'Thank you for asking me to be your wife, Toby. I *am* honoured, very honoured.'

When he had gone, she went to the wardrobe she kept permanently in the dressing room. She chose a golden, open-mesh dress with an underskirt of oyster satin, a heavy, fringed shawl of jewel-colours, and a neat gipsy bonnet with golden ribbons and roses.

The frost had gone, leaving an oddly summery warmth in the air as Toby's carriage pulled out of the narrow lane past the busy market, and then turned into a wide thoroughfare, bowling along towards Hyde Park.

The park was as crowded as ever – a clutter of horses, gigs, light drags and elegant carriages. The sunshine and warmth seemed to have attracted everyone to its green and russet openness. Nonna sat back, enjoying the sun on her face. It was such a *good* day – The carriage lurched sideways suddenly, and Toby reached out to catch her as she was thrust from her seat by the force of the jerk. Then the carriage was still, leaning at a precarious angle. They heard some shouts and a woman screamed, and then the doors were opened and the coachman looked in, his face pale. 'You all right, Sir Toby? Madame?'

Toby helped Nonna carefully down from the crippled carriage, and as she stood on the track she saw what had happened. The carriage's wheels had touched those of a curricle travelling in the opposite direction, and a wheel on both had been broken off. The woman who had screamed was being helped from the high perch of the curricle by her male companion. Nonna sighed with relief; no one was hurt and there was only a little damage to the drags. All around them the traffic moved on, no one paying much attention to the accident.

'Are you all right, Nonna?' asked Toby anxiously, taking her hands.

'Yes, yes, I'm all right. It was so sudden, that's all.'

He led her to a nearby bench. 'You wait there and I'll see what can be done about this.'

She sat down, looking around, and it was then that she realised that this was the bench where she had always met Josie, the very same bench. Well, with her past history such common knowledge and, as Josie had always pointed out, with this bench having the reputation it did – there would be more chatter now about La Vania. Looking for customers? Business bad at the Dove? She could almost hear the sly whisperings now. She was aware of glances from the passing carriages, raised fans, lorgnettes and quizzing-glasses. But those who drove along in Hyde Park were those who would not speak to La Vania in the street, those society people whose menfolk came to the Yellow Room so secretively but who would not deign to acknowledge her existence outside its four walls.

She resisted the temptation to put her tongue out at them all, sitting demurely on the bench waiting for Toby to return. She could see him with the coachman, bending over the stricken carriage, shaking his head doubtfully. It was some time before the tolling of the bells caught her attention. All the bells in London, it seemed, were tolling. The funeral – it must be Vania's funeral. There was little traffic passing now, and she looked along the way towards Park

Lane. A solitary landau was coming slowly towards her, but she didn't look at it; her horrified gaze went beyond it to the funeral procession making its slow way through the park. The *cortège* was taking the dead dancer on a last journey through the city which had adored him, and a final farewell to Hyde Park, where his carriage had been so often, was obviously the intention now. She watched the black plumes bobbing on the horses' heads, and the glass-sided hearse with a white-draped coffin inside. Her horror mounted. The procession came this way and she had been seen, sitting on this dreadful bench, dressed in bright gold as if she were thumbing her nose at her dead husband! She got to her feet in dismay. This was awful. 'Toby!'

He was already coming towards her, glancing at the funeral. 'Oh, Nonna! Damn! *Damn*! Forgive me for this.'

'It's not your fault, Toby, but I must get away. I'll cross the grass that way. I can't possibly remain here dressed like this.' Agitated, she looked at the approaching procession again, and it seemed that the tolling of the bells was booming inside her head. 'I've gone out of my way to be notorious,' she said miserably, 'but I'm not as bad as this will make me look.'

The solitary landau stopped suddenly. 'Nonna?'

She turned sharply at the voice. 'Philip!'

'Get inside, for God's sake!' He beckoned, thrusting the door open.

'Toby?'

'Go on, I'll stay with the carriage.' He smiled. 'Go on.'

She hurried across the track and caught Philip's hand. He pulled her swiftly into the landau, and it was on its way even before the door had closed.

She sat back thankfully, looking across at him. He was not alone. The woman called Harriet who had been with him in Brindley's bookshop was there, her face frosty and furious. She turned away, staring out fixedly, her lips a tight line. Nonna glanced at her for a moment and then back at Philip.

'I must thank you, Sir Philip,' she said. 'You've saved me

from much embarrassment and distress.'

'Distress?' said Harriet. 'I'll warrant!'

Philip smiled. 'Now then, Harriet, today we are Good Samaritans.'

There was no reply. Harriet's black military hat with its plumes seemed to bristle almost, as if the fur's hackles were rising at the insult of having to drive out publicly with the harlot from the Dove. Her hands were clasped tightly in her lap, and her body stiff in its grey and white pelisse.

Nonna smiled faintly. 'I would appear to be an unwelcome addition to the entourage, Sir Philip.'

'I do not pass on the other side of the road.'

He was a little thinner, his face lean and tanned by the sun. His hair was as dark and curly as ever, and his clothes as splendidly Bond Street as she remembered. His cravat was complicated and crisp, and his coat unbuttoned to reveal a brown brocade waistcoat and frilled white shirt. He lounged in his seat, his legs stretched out so that they touched the folds of her gown. She wanted to stare at him, to gaze at his face, but she forced herself to look from the window.

The track curved, and across the grassy slope she could see the funeral procession wending its slow way past Toby's carriage.

Philip watched her. 'Toby is left to fend for himself, then.'

'You know him?'

'Yes.'

She looked uncertainly at the ominously silent Harriet. 'How is Mr Lamb, Sir Philip? Well, I trust?'

'William copes, that is all I think may be said of him. Caro is drunk more often than she is sober, and he trails behind picking up the pieces.' He leaned an elbow on the armpad, and he seemed vaguely amused as he watched her.

'Do you still have your hawks?' The polite words limped into the quiet.

'Yes – where would a man be without his feathered friends?'

Harriet's angry silence was heavy.

The landau moved along Oxford Street and Nonna looked out uneasily. She saw a white facade she recognised: it was Cartwright's, where she and Toby were to dine that evening. It looked very fashionable, very austere, and very forbidding – not La Vania territory at all.

'You've dined at Cartwright's?' asked Philip curiously.

'No, I'm to dine there tonight.'

There was a choked sound from Harriet, and her eyes swung furiously towards Nonna. She said nothing, a myriad of expressions passing over her pretty face. The carriage slowed as a waggon blocked the way, and Nonna leaned to open the door.

'I think, Sir Philip, that two is company, three is most definitely a crowd. Thank you for being a Good Samaritan.'

He reached forward to help her, but she dropped lightly down and hurried through the busy street and down an alley, where she paused thankfully. She was by a florist's stall where the chrysanthemums were bright gold, white and rust. She stood there for a long while without moving. No man on earth had such a power over her as Philip Hastings; a glance could melt any determined resistance as if it had never existed. That wry curve of his lips, the light in his dark eyes, the way he lounged so gracefully and yet so untidily at the same time. Every damn thing about him she loved. Every damn thing. . . .

She walked down the alley, hoping to find a post-chaise in a nearby street, and it was then that she realised she could still hear Vania's funeral bells tolling over the city.

After that night's performance at the Dove, she was soon left in no doubt that the incident in Hyde Park was common knowledge. There were references to it in the Yellow Room, some veiled and some forthright. Those who mentioned it to her face praised her – although she had no doubt that in the comfort of their own drawing rooms they censured her as loudly as anyone. She wondered how many more doors would be closed to La Vania now? She had set a foot badly wrong, and quite unintentionally – but there was nothing to be done about it now.

Toby was waiting for her in her dressing room, and she closed the door quickly. 'Toby, I think this outing to Cartwright's is a mistake. We'd best leave it – or go somewhere less exalted.'

'The table's booked – and they *know* you are to accompany me.' He toyed with the heavy frill at his black velvet cuff, smiling. 'Your worries are groundless.'

'They know? You're sure? Toby, I always make certain of where I go. I avoid being publicly insulted and turned away.'

'They know. I made sure of it when I booked the table.'

Reluctantly she nodded then. 'All right, if you're sure. I've made *faux pas* enough for one day. The thought of trouble again tonight makes me feel quite faint. I'll get ready. I won't be long, I promise.'

She opened the wardrobe door and smiled as Josie came in. 'I feel a perverse desire to put on this scarlet creation from Mrs Clarke's, but I think that an unwise notion, eh?'

Josie grinned. 'Yes – I know what you mean though. Perhaps that dark blue silk is better, more sombre and polite anyway.'

Nonna took the dark blue gown down and shook it so that the sequins adorning the bodice and hem sparkled in the light of the oil lamps. Its dainty, silky fringed hem trembled gently and the silk had a magnificent sheen. 'All right, the dark blue silk it is. Will you help me out of my slave garb?'

A short while later Nonna was ready. 'I'm still not sure about this jaunt, Josie. Toby *says* it will be all right, but I've a *feeling*. . . .'

'Oh, it'll be perfectly all right, Nonna, and you look splendid.' She smiled shyly then. 'Nonna, Peter's proposed to me.'

'Josie!' Nonna hugged her. 'Oh, I'm so glad for you!'

'The most popular writer in London and he's proposed to

me! I must be dreaming!' Josie laughed. 'I'm so happy I could cry, honestly I could.'

'Cry then, the sofa's all yours.' Nonna picked up her reticule. 'I'm very happy for you, Josie, truly I am.'

'I only wish you'd love Toby and accept him, Nonna.'

'I don't love him, not in the right way. Anyway, tonight isn't for moping, it's for celebrating. Are you and Peter off somewhere interesting?'

'Yes. The Pegasus of all places. Some of Peter's songs are in the repertoire and he wants to see they're doing them justice – *that's* our celebration! Anyway, off you go to Cartwright's. Drink our health, will you?'

'Of course.'

The footmen threw open the doors of the carriage and Toby handed Nonna down outside Cartwright's. The sound of music drifted out into the ice-cold night where the clear skies had brought a thin mist. Nonna shivered. The unease was still there as she stood looking up at the white walls of the imposing building. The windows were bright; she could see crimson walls and chandeliers, and the smell of French cooking hung in the still air.

Toby offered her his arm and they went up the six white, scrubbed steps to the double doors. The footmen inside turned as Toby tapped the glass, but then they halted as they recognised him, and to Nonna's horror, they turned back again and remained solidly in their places.

'Toby? Let's go,' she said quickly, 'Please don't make a scene about it!'

'Damn it, I won't be insulted like this! Nor will I have *you* insulted!'

'Toby – '

'Trouble, Toby?' asked another voice, and she held her breath, for it was Philip.

Toby turned. 'Philip, they've barred the blasted door on us!'

'Yes, I rather thought they would. That's why I'm here. They won't bar the door on the man who owns half of this pile of bricks and mortar, eh?' He smiled. 'You shall dine at Cartwright's, Nonna. Nothing and no one shall stop you.'

'I'd rather not, Philip, not now.'

'What?' he said, smiling faintly. 'La Vania of the Dove is become faint-hearted? I can't believe it!'

'After this morning. . . .'

'To Hell with this morning! Did you come here to dine or didn't you?'

'Yes, but – '

'No buts then. You shall dine.' Philip glanced at Toby. 'Cartwright's will never be closed to her again, Toby. I shall see to it.' He brushed past Nonna, tapping his cane peremptorily on the glass.

The footmen hurried to open the doors immediately, and he turned, holding out his hand to Nonna. She stared at him for a moment. She was afraid to go in; suddenly and for the first time, La Vania was really afraid to go in and brave the world. He stretched down and caught her hand, drawing her into the warmth of the green and gold vestibule with its white marble statues and tall pots of ferns. A fountain played in the centre of the white tiled floor, its water tinkling and splashing in the ensuing silence. Sounds came from the dining room, music, chatter and laughter, but in the vast hallway of Cartwright's it was very quiet, the footmen looking uncertainly at her and then at Philip.

She stood for a moment and then turned. 'No, Philip, I can't.

'Yes, you can. Can't she, Toby?'

'I – ' Toby was uncertain now, looking miserably at her. 'I'm sorry about this, Nonna. I wouldn't have had it happen for the world. Philip, if she wants to go perhaps I should take her.'

'Are *you* faint-hearted, my dear chap?' asked Philip quietly.

'I don't view the prospect with great joy.'

'Then off you toddle, dear boy. Warm your toes by a friendly fire. I will take *great* care of her, I promise.'

Toby looked at her and then smiled. 'Very well,' he said,

deciding. 'I leave her with you, Philip.' He kissed her cheek, squeezing her fingertips gently, and then he was gone, leaving her alone with Philip – and she knew exactly why he had apparently deserted her.

Philip looked at the footmen as they closed the door. 'Well, I'm damned. I didn't think he'd actually go!'

She smiled, turning as the footman came back to take her cloak. Philip surveyed him coldly. 'By whose orders did you bar that door upon Sir Toby and Madame Vania?'

'Sir Philip?' The man jumped as if scalded.

'I was perfectly clear, man! Who ordered you?'

'Lord Kenningworth, Sir Philip.'

'In future I pray you remember that *I* am the be all and end all at Cartwright's, not Kenningworth!' snapped Philip.

'Yes, Sir Philip.'

'The list of those not permitted into these walls remains the same as it was yesterday and neither Sir Toby's nor Madame Vania's names are upon it! Do not presume again, and if Kenningworth or anyone tries to alter things, then I'm to be told, is that clear?'

'Yes, Sir Philip.'

Philip nodded, turning to offer Nonna his arm. She walked up the staircase with him towards the dining room on the first floor. 'Who is Lord Kenningworth?' she asked. 'Why did he do it?'

'Kenningworth is Harriet's husband. Harriet is the force there, I fancy. She is very miffed with me for this morning. You should not have blurted that you were coming here – you gave her a weapon.'

'I know. Now.'

He smiled. 'Still the innocent in so many ways, eh – even after all your activities at the Dove?'

They paused at the doors and two more footmen waited, glancing at each other and then waiting patiently for Philip to indicate that he wished the doors to be opened.

Philip spoke softly so that only she could hear. 'I shall take great delight in escorting you in there tonight, great delight – *and* in cocking a snook at the lot of them! I intend introducing you to every one I can corner, and I'll *make* them acknowledge you!'

'It sounds as if dining with you promises to be relaxing and peaceful,' she said drily, but inside she was miserably nervous and apprehensive.

'But you'll still come through those doors with me?'

'Yes. I'm still green and trusting, d'you see?'

He smiled. 'That may have been sarcasm, but I suspect it to be painfully true,' he said, turning to nod at the footmen.

The doors were opened immediately and the noise and clatter of the dining room sprang out on to the landing. Philip walked in, nodding at the head waiter, who stared, his mouth open ridiculously before he controlled himself and bowed, leading Philip to a table across the room. A silence fell on the whole gathering, and the orchestra faltered at the change in the atmosphere.

Philip paused by one table, and Nonna saw Harriet sitting there with a grey-haired man in dark brown. 'Ah, Kenningworth,' said Philip in a clear voice, 'I trust you are dining well. Good evening, Harriet.'

She glared at him. 'Good evening,' she said in a choked voice.

Nonna looked at Lord Kenningworth, catching his eye, and he went pale. She had seen him so many times in the Yellow Room, rebuffed him countless times too. He stood suddenly, obviously confused, and then he took her hand. 'Madame Vania,' he said, bowing over it. 'Shall – shall you join us?'

Philip shook his head. 'Thank you, Kenningworth, but no – we have a table.' He inclined his head and offered Nonna his arm again and they walked on. Nonna resisted the urge to glance back. Harriet's *husband*? The old man with the lecherous eyes and lecherous suggestions – small wonder he had been so keen to have La Vania barred from Cartwright's!

She sat down, nodding at the head waiter, who still looked confused and embarrassed. She looked at Philip. 'Kenningworth frequents the Yellow Room.'

'I thought perhaps he did. Double standards again, eh?'

She smiled 'He wants to bed me, she wants to bed you – and they have the nerve to look down their supercilious noses.'

'You committed the first crime of being caught out, and the second one of perpetuating the first on the stage of the Dove every night. Society – *polite* society – don't like that!'

'It's only because I'm a woman that I'm condemned, isn't it? *You* committed a crime too, but now you're free again, welcomed back to England's fashionable bosom and fêted by all the prospective mamas-in-law as if your character were spotless.'

'Is that a stamp of the pretty foot by any chance?' he asked softly, leaning back in his chair.

'Yes, it isn't fair, right, just – whatever word you wish to put to it.'

'*I* don't cavort on a stage in my undress, flicking my legs hither and thither for the *hoi polloi* to ogle.'

Before she could reply, the head waiter approached. Philip inspected the menu and pointed to several places without saying a word. The head waiter bowed and left the table.

She glanced around the still quiet room, although some hum of conversation had broken out again and the clatter of knives and forks joined the slow return of the orchestra's aplomb. 'There are some very red faces in this room, Philip. I'll warrant you're to be cut dead tomorrow wherever you go.'

'I can survive such pinpricks.'

'Why did you do this? Why bother to wait outside for us to arrive?'

'I like you too much to let them snub you and get away with it.' He sipped the sherry a waiter set before them.

'I'm quite overcome at your kindness,' she murmured.

'I expect you are.' His eyes were dark and mischievous then. 'Anyone should be.'

'You are insufferably big-headed at times.'

'That's what makes me so adorable. Hello, and here we have the Hon. William no less, looking as hang-dog as ever.'

'Now we'll see, won't we?' she said softly. 'When *he* cuts you because I'm here.'

She turned towards the entrance to see William Lamb speaking with the head waiter. He glanced across at their table and then, playing with the thick, starched frills peeping below the dark blue cuff of his coat, he crossed the room towards them. 'Madame? Philip? Do I detect an *atmosphere*?'

'You do indeed, William.'

'Can't think why,' said William, smiling at her as he drew a chair from an adjacent table and sat down. 'I'm to join friends here tonight, but they appear to be late.'

'And how has life been treating you?' asked Philip.

'Abominably.'

'All your own fool fault, dear boy.'

'I know – and I *don't* need reminding. Still, she's at Brocket Hall now and about to be confined to one bottle of sherry a day. Maybe that will do the trick.' William glanced at the watching room. 'We *are* causing a stir, aren't we? I'm beginning to think that's my lot in life.'

Nonna put her sherry down. 'Are you fresh in Town today, Mr Lamb?'

'No.' He met her gaze. 'I'm perfectly aware of what all this is about and I don't give a – a cuss, shall we say?' He smiled. 'Scandal has to be endured. I'm beginning to feel immune. Ah, my companions arrive, and by all that's holy they seem the worse for wear already. Good night, Philip. Madame.' He took her hand and kissed it, lingering over the gesture. Then he walked away, nodding at those he knew, and Nonna watched him.

'He's older and greyer,' she said.

'If I lived with Caro, I would be too. She had a man like William and yet fell so heavily for a nothing like Byron.'

'He was hardly a nothing!'

'As a man he was. As a poet – well, superlative. Just as

your freshly-grounded Vania was nothing as a man, but as a dancer . . . .' He flicked his fingers expressively.

She glanced up as a shadow fell across the table, and she found herself looking into Justin's eyes. 'Ah, dear couz, I run you to earth at last,' he said, bowing to Philip.

'Am I to be overcome with emotion?'

'You are supposed to be on your knees thanking God I'm in the land of the living.'

Philip smiled. 'I've long since passed that stage. How are you, Justin?'

'Well, as you see. I also see that you are set to overturn the proverbial applecart here tonight.'

'Correct – so if it bothers you, cousin mine, off with you this instant.'

Justin flicked his lace kerchief over his sleeve. 'It don't worry me. I've made few bones about frequenting the Yellow Room. So, to make up for my execrable past conduct, I shall sit and take sherry with you. How does that do to get back in your good books?' He waited, his hand on the back of the chair William had left.

'Pray do,' said Philip. 'My good books are hardly worth being in anyway – but Madame Vania's are most certainly worth the effort.'

Nonna sighed inwardly as Justin sat down. She could feel the steady stares boring into her back, indeed she could feel the animosity of the whole room. Justin remained a while, and left when the first course was brought. She had little appetite; it was only Philip's presence which kept her in her seat in that dreadful room.

When they had finished eating, he was true to his word. He introduced her to everyone he possibly could, insisting upon being answered politely. And everyone, for one guilty reason or another, smiled and bowed to her. The women hated her, the men feared her – that was what lay behind everything. The Yellow Room had received so many secret visitors, but the wives of those visitors knew nothing of it. Afraid she would say something, the men hastened to be pleasant to her; suspicious and jealous, the wives loathed her with their eyes while their mouths smiled.

Nonna was miserable. She should have been elated, but she wasn't. By the time Philip took her down from the dining room and out to where his landau was waiting she was on the verge of tears, but she hid the fact from him. He had used her again, just as he had always done. Through her he had thumbed his nose at them for his banishment and then for his welcoming back because of the Duke of Aldane's frantic efforts on Justin's part.

They sat in silence in the landau as it pulled away from Cartwright's.

'Where do you live now?' he asked suddenly.

'Bettersleigh Street.'

He leaned forward, speaking through the grille to the coachman. He leaned back, watching her. 'You seem not as delighted as you should be by your triumph tonight.'

'Because I'm not. The only one there tonight who was genuine was William Lamb. Not even you were truly genuine, were you?'

'Why do you think that?'

'Oh, come now, Philip. You got your own back for that business of the duel, that's all. That's why you waited outside Cartwright's tonight, that's why everything!'

'Oh, Nonna – '

'No, Philip, I won't listen to platitudes this time! You fought a duel with Justin because of those posters at the Opera House, didn't you?'

'Yes.'

'Why?'

'I did not like his treatment of you.'

She stared at him. 'And?'

For a long time he was silent. 'And nothing, Nonna. That's it. Marry Toby.'

She felt the tears pricking her eyes and she bit her lip, staring out at the dark night. The minutes of that journey passed so very slowly – would she never reach home so that she could cry in private? It seemed that a lifetime almost must have passed before she recognised the driveway of her house.

As the landau came to a standstill and the footmen jumped down, she looked at him for a last time. 'Goodbye, Philip.'

'Goodbye, Nonna.'

She climbed down without another word, running up the wide, shallow steps and into the house. The tears were wet on her cheeks when she reached her own room at last. She dismissed her startled maid, who hurried out quickly, leaving her alone.

Nonna undressed, crying silently, and then she crept into the warmed bed, curling up in the darkness. What would her admirers have said if they could see their favourite now? Weeping her misery away in the loneliness of her bed? Oh, if only she had left Cartwright's with Toby, then she would have been spared this final unhappiness. . . .

The stone pattered against the window and she awoke, looking immediately at the clock on the mantlepiece. In the moonlight from the badly-drawn curtains she could see that it was four o'clock – she'd been asleep for two hours. There was another chinking sound at the window and she sat up, slipping from the bed and pulling the curtains aside to look out. The moon slid from behind a cloud and she saw the figure of a man standing in the driveway. He waved, doffing his hat, and in the moonlight she could see Justin Farnsworth's fair hair. She pushed the window open slightly, and the cold night air made her shiver.

He bowed low, pointing at the entrance of the house. 'I win, after all, Nonna. Barrymore's falls to me!' he called, and then he turned and hurried away down the drive.

She leaned out, looking down. Philip's landau was drawn up before the house. With a gasp she turned.

He was leaning against the door jamb of her room, his top hat swinging slowly in his gloved hand. 'I decided to come in unannounced and thereby defeat any notion of yours to have me barred from your doors,' he said softly, coming in and closing the door.

She reached for her wrap, holding it against her naked body. 'This is neither right nor fair, Philip,' she whispered. 'You've come here to use me again, to play upon my love, to hurt me – I won't have it! Not ever again! *That's it.* Your words, not mine.'

'And lying little words they were too,' he said, tossing his hat on a table and removing his gloves, teasing each finger very slowly. 'It can never be ended for you and me, can it?'

'Yes. Yes, it can – it's ended now. I asked you to leave me alone once before, and now I'm doing it again. I'm hurt every time – it means nothing to you, but to me it's everything.'

'I know I've hurt you. I knew it as I did it tonight, Nonna. Forgive me.' He reached out, gently taking her hand. 'Forgive me for that, for everything if you like. I can't damn well leave you alone. You refuse to be forgotten; you're there all the time, wherever I am, whatever I do!'

'Smooth, silken words, Philip – and you use them so well. A man of great charm, great experience, and great falsehood. I don't understand anyone who can behave as you've behaved.'

'Can't you? *Can't* you? The great Corinthian, the swell Philip Hastings, falling in love with a little dancer with red hair and green eyes? You had no place in my plans, Nonna, no place at all – but still you were there. I made love to Catrine for ten thousand guineas, but it was you I wished I held, and there was no damned wager there to put *that* notion in my fool head! I set about seducing you then. Bedding you would end the matter once and for all, the good old *status quo* would return and life would go on. But it didn't – I wanted you the more. I felt guilty too – guilty because I'd thrust you into the arms of a monster like Armand Vania.'

'Am I really to believe you, Philip,' she whispered, dragging her hand from his, 'when on the night those broadsheets went around the audience at the Opera House, *you* left the theatre? You didn't even stay to give me the small comfort just your presence would have given me? You betrayed me then, and it hurt me more than you will ever know.'

He nodded. 'Is that what you think I did then? Left you? Betrayed you? Laughed at you and connived with Justin too, no doubt?'

'*Isn't* it what you did?'

He loosened his cravat, smiled faintly. 'No. It isn't. I knew how that audience would react in the end – I'm one of the pack, remember? I know them so well. I had my carriage brought around to the stage door. I meant to get you away from there, but I couldn't get in and *you* didn't come out. I sent my seconds to Justin that night, and fought the duel with him the following morning. I meant to harm him for what he did to you, Nonna, and I'd have loosened a few of Vania's perfect teeth for him too, had I not been forced to flee the country. I couldn't find you, I didn't know where you were and I had no time, Nonna. No time at all if I was to save my life. That's what really happened, not what you think.'

She searched his face in the moonlight. 'Why say what you did tonight then? If all the rest is true, why say it? Why slap my face with your disinterest?'

'I don't know. Yes, yes I *do* know. Because I was refusing to admit it all to myself, I was still clinging to that old *status quo* which I've persuaded myself over the years is the one which matters to me. But it *doesn't* matter, not any more. I've driven around London these past two hours, thinking and deciding. Toby Charles wants to marry you; he's a formidible opponent for me, Nonna – I don't misjudge him, he'd win you in the end if I stood aside yet again. So I'm not standing aside, I'm here, trying to convince you that I've told you only the truth tonight. Look at me, Nonna.' He put his hands on her bare shoulders, turning her to face him. 'I've asked you to trust and believe me before. Don't change that now. I've been guilty of some of the things I'm accused of – I *have* hurt you deliberately and I *have* used you callously. You've a right to spit in my eye if you want, I know that. But I'm going to have you, Nonna. I'm not going to let Toby Charles or anyone else ease their fashionable legs under your table. You're mine.' He cupped her face in his hands and looked into her eyes. 'Yes, you're still mine, aren't you?'

The softness in his voice and the touch of his fingers made her feel weak. 'Damn you, Philip Hastings!' she whispered. 'Damn you to Hell! I wish I'd never set eyes on you! I *should* spit in your eye, I should have you thrown into the street – '

'Maybe you'll do just that when you learn what else I've been responsible for tonight.' He released her. 'I've informed Toby that he has escorted you for the last time, and I then took myself along to the Dove and informed them that they've enjoyed your services for the last time too.'

'You've *what*?' she gasped, staring at him, 'You've done *what*? By what right?'

'No right at all.'

'You must be very sure of yourself – and of me!'

'No, I'm not. Not this time. That's why I'm closing all the doors I can think of. Toby accepted the situation – confining himself to a threat of extinguishing me if I hurt you again. The Dove – well, I left them in some confusion, it's true. I don't know if Wyndham was about to laugh or cry. Josie was chasing around in ever-increasing circles of panic, for she is to take your place tomorrow night. That's your two main doors closed, Nonna – Toby and the Dove. I'm determined that there'll only be me; there won't be even the smallest corner for you to escape into. Just me.'

'Ousting Toby I can understand – yes, that I can understand, Philip. But why the Dove? You know you have no right to do that – it's my concern, not yours!'

He caught her hand, pulling her close and holding her for a moment before picking her up and carrying her to the bed. 'I've come here tonight to have my way, Nonna, my own selfish, arrogant, superior male way – there's to be no competition, no rival in any form.' He looked at her as she lay on the bed, her skin pale in the moonlight from the window, and then he began to undress. 'If I have to make love to you all night and all tomorrow to get the answer I want from you, then I will.'

'What answer do you want, Philip?' she whispered. 'You know you can have me – you have only to look at me, smile at me and I'm yours. I'll be your mistress – '

He smiled, lying on the bed beside her, his arms behind his head. 'Oh, Nonna,' he said, a hint of amusement in his voice. 'Oh, Nonna, I don't want a mistress, I want a *wife*!'

She stared at him. 'Your wife? But a man like you doesn't marry a woman with a reputation like mine! I'm the most notorious demirep in London. I'd ruin you socially. You talk of closed doors, well those doors would be closed against you if you married me!'

'So, let them close, let them be locked, barred and nailed for all I care. Nonna, a man like me does as he pleases.' He reached up and drew his fingertip across her parted lips, smiling. 'And right now it pleases me to make love to you. I want you absolutely and forever – no man can demand that of his mistress, but he can of his wife. I love you – I want you to be the lady of Five Ways, the woman I wake up beside every morning and the woman who is there with me always. These last years since I met you have been damned torment because I didn't have you – by God, am I going to put that fault right! Nothing less than marriage, Nonna. Will you be my wife?'

He pulled her down into his arms, his mouth moving slowly over hers. She closed her eyes. This man, this one man . . . Nothing could compare with loving him, with lying close and warm in his arms, with possessing him – and being possessed by him. Nothing.

He leaned over her, smiling. 'Your answer, Nonna,' he murmured.

'Yes,' she whispered. 'Yes, Sir Philip Hastings, I'll marry you.'

NON-FICTION

GENERAL

☐ **Truly Murderous**	John Dunning	95p
☐ **Shocktrauma**	Jon Franklin & Alan Doelp	£1.25
☐ **The War Machine**	James Avery Joyce	£1.50
☐ **The Fugu Plan**	Tokayer & Swartz	£1.75

BIOGRAPHY/AUTOBIOGRAPHY

☐ **Go-Boy**	Roger Caron	£1.25
☐ **The Queen Mother Herself**	Helen Cathcart	£1.25
☐ **Clues to the Unknown**	Robert Cracknell	£1.50
☐ **George Stephenson**	Hunter Davies	£1.50
☐ **The Borgias**	Harry Edgington	£1.50
☐ **The Admiral's Daughter**	Victoria Fyodorova	£1.50
☐ **Rachman**	Shirley Green	£1.50
☐ **50 Years with Mountbatten**	Charles Smith	£1.25
☐ **Kiss**	John Swenson	95p

HEALTH/SELF-HELP

☐ **The Hamlyn Family First Aid Book**	Dr Robert Andrew	£1.50
☐ **Girl!**	Brandenburger & Curry	£1.25
☐ **The Good Health Guide for Women**	Cooke & Dworkin	£2.95
☐ **The Babysitter Book**	Curry & Cunningham	£1.25
☐ **Pulling Your Own Strings**	Dr Wayne W. Dyer	95p
☐ **The Pick of Woman's Own Diets**	Jo Foley	95p
☐ **Woman X Two**	Mary Kenny	£1.10
☐ **Cystitis: A Complete Self-help Guide**	Angela Kilmartin	£1.00
☐ **Fit for Life**	Donald Norfolk	£1.35
☐ **The Stress Factor**	Donald Norfolk	£1.25
☐ **Fat is a Feminist Issue**	Susie Orbach	95p
☐ **Living With Your New Baby**	Rakowitz & Rubin	£1.50
☐ **Related to Sex**	Claire Rayner	£1.25
☐ **The Working Woman's Body Book**	Rowen with Winkler	95p
☐ **Natural Sex**	Mary Shivanandan	£1.25
☐ **Woman's Own Birth Control**	Dr Michael Smith	£1.25
☐ **Overcoming Depression**	Dr Andrew Stanway	£1.50

POCKET HEALTH GUIDES

☐ **Migraine**	Dr Finlay Campbell	65p
☐ **Pre-menstrual Tension**	June Clark	65p
☐ **Back Pain**	Dr Paul Dudley	65p
☐ **Allergies**	Robert Eagle	65p
☐ **Arthritis & Rheumatism**	Dr Luke Fernandes	65p
☐ **Skin Troubles**	Deanna Wilson	65p

TRAVEL

☐ **Guide to the Channel Islands**	Anderson & Swinglehurst	90p
☐ **The Complete Traveller**	Joan Bakewell	£1.95
☐ **Time Out London Shopping Guide**	Lindsey Bareham	£1.50
☐ **A Walk Around the Lakes**	Hunter Davies	£1.50
☐ **England by Bus**	Elizabeth Gundrey	£1.25
☐ **Britain at Your Feet**	Wickers & Pedersen	£1.75

HUMOUR

☐ **Ireland Strikes Back!**	Seamus B. Gorrah	85p
☐ **Pun Fun**	Paul Jennings	95p
☐ **1001 Logical Laws**	John Peers	95p
☐ **The Devil's Bedside Book**	Leonard Rossiter	85p